ABLE ONE

TOR BOOKS BY BEN BOVA

Able One

The Aftermath

As on a Darkling Plain

The Astral Mirror

Battle Station

The Best of the Nebulas (editor)

Challenges

Colony

Cyberbooks

Escape Plus

The Green Trap

Gremlins Go Home
  (with Gordon R. Dickson)

Jupiter

The Kinsman Saga

Mars Life

Mercury

The Multiple Man

Orion

Orion Among the Stars

Orion and the Conqueror

Orion in the Dying Time

Out of Sun

Peacekeepers

Powersat

The Precipice

Privateers

Prometheans

The Rock Rats

Saturn

The Silent War

Star Peace: Assured Survival

The Starcrossed

Tale of the Grand Tour

Test of Fire

Titan

To Fear the Light (with A. J. Austin)

To Save the Sun (with A. J. Austin)

The Trikon Deception
  (with Bill Pogue)

Triumph

Vengeance of Orion

Venus

Voyagers

Voyagers II: The Alien Within

Voyagers III: Star Brothers

The Return: Book IV of Voyagers

The Winds of Altair

ABLE ONE

BEN BOVA

TOR®

A TOM DOHERTY ASSOCIATES BOOK · NEW YORK

This is a work of fiction. All of the characters, organizations, and events portrayed in this novel are either products of the author's imagination or are used fictitiously.

ABLE ONE

Copyright © 2010 by Ben Bova

A Tor Book
Published by Tom Doherty Associates, LLC
175 Fifth Avenue
New York, NY 10010

www.tor-forge.com

Tor® is a registered trademark of Tom Doherty Associates, LLC.

Library of Congress Cataloging-in-Publication Data

Bova, Ben, 1932–
    Able one / Ben Bova. — 1st ed.
        p. cm.
    "A Tom Doherty Associates book."
    ISBN 978-0-7653-2386-6
    1. Satellites—United States—Fiction.   2. Lasers—Military applications—Fiction.
    3. Nuclear weapons—Korea (North)—Fiction.   4. Korea (North)—Fiction.
    5. United States—Fiction.   I. Title.
    PS3552.O84A25 2010
    813'.54—dc22

                                                                          2009040642

First Edition: February 2010

Printed in the United States of America

0 9 8 7 6 5 4 3 2 1

To the memory of Arthur R. Kantrowitz,
who guided the invention of the first high-power laser

ACKNOWLEDGMENTS

Although this is a work of fiction, the U.S. Missile Defense Agency's Airborne Laser program actually exists. It consists of a megawatt-plus laser mounted in a specially modified Boeing 747-400F four-engined jet aircraft, much as described in this novel. The purpose of the system is to shoot down ballistic missiles soon after they are launched, while their rocket engines are still burning and they are quite vulnerable.

The program's principal contractors include three major aerospace corporations:

Boeing: 747-400F aircraft; active ranging system; battle management system

Northrop Grumman: high-energy chemical oxygen iodine laser (COIL); advanced resonator alignment system; laser fuel supply

Lockheed Martin: laser beam control system; illuminator optical bench; nose-mounted turret

This novel could not have been written without the generous assistance of Colonel M. V. "Coyote" Smith, USAF, Scott Herman,

Judy Reemtsma, and many others who provided invaluable information and insights. The accuracy of this work is in large part due to them; any errors of fact are my fault, not theirs. However, this is a work of fiction, so I have felt free to extrapolate from what is known today, where necessary to the story.

BEN BOVA
Naples, Florida
July 2009

It is the policy of the United States to deploy as soon as is technologically possible an effective National Missile Defense system capable of defending the territory of the United States against limited ballistic missile attack (whether accidental, unauthorized, or deliberate).

NATIONAL MISSILE DEFENSE ACT OF 1999
(PUBLIC LAW 106-38)

FIRST STRIKE

H ank Barstow frowned at the blank screen of his GPS box. Rolling down Interstate 75 at nearly eighty miles per hour, he was looking forward to making a breakfast stop at the Sticky Fingers restaurant a couple of his trucker pals had told him about. Food's not all that much, they'd said, but there's this really stacked blonde waitress. . . .

But he needed the doggone GPS to find his way through the streets of Chattanooga and get to the restaurant. Hank had been through Chattanooga plenty of times on his runs down I-75 to Tampa. But this time he had to get off the highway and find that blonde.

And the GPS was dead. Hank pounded a big fist on the gray box mounted on his cab's dashboard. Didn't do any good. The doggone screen stayed blank.

A sign whizzed by: TRUCK STOP FIVE MILES AHEAD. I'll pull in there and dig the road atlas out of the pile in back, he decided.

To Hank's surprise, the truck stop was filled with tractor-trailer rigs. Unusual for this time of the morning. Drivers were standing around their rigs, a lot of them talking into cell phones. He found a spot out on the grass, parked his rig, and killed the engine.

As he climbed down from the cab he heard a familiar voice yell, "You too, Hank?"

Turning as he stepped onto the grass, he saw one of his old buddies, Phil Camerata, heavy with belly fat, face stubbled, plodding up toward him.

"Me too what, Phil?" Hank asked.

"GPS dead?"

"Yeah? How'd you know?"

Waving at the jam-packed parking area, Camerata said, "Everybody's GPS is down. Whole GPS system is out."

"Everybody's?" Automatically, Hank fished in the pocket of his jeans for his cell phone.

Shaking his grizzled head, Camerata said, "Lotsa luck, buddy. Looks like most of the cell phones are out, too."

IN MANHATTAN THE air was filled with the bleating horns of thousands of taxicabs, trucks, cars, and buses, like a rising chorus of wailing lost souls.

The automated tollbooths in all the city's bridges and tunnels had abruptly shut down, piling cars in long lines behind their unmoving barrier arms. Even in the subway tunnels automated Metro-Card dispensers had gone dead.

Drivers leaned on their horns in maddened frustration. The streets and avenues were choked with honking, steaming vehicles whose sweating, puzzled, cursing drivers stared at the traffic lights, which had all gone blank.

Gridlock, all across Manhattan and rapidly spreading through the other boroughs. The helpless bleat of thousands of taxi, automobile, truck, and bus horns filled the air all across New York's crowded, choked streets.

GORDON HATHAWAY SWIPED his Visa card through the slot in the taxicab's bulletproof window, scribbled his signature on the strip of paper that came stuttering out of the chugging machine, then ducked out of the cab while the driver sat in sullen silence. Some sort of Asian, Hathaway thought: the driver was swathed in a white turban and had a deeply black curly beard.

Lower Broadway was a total bedlam of gridlock, cabs and trucks and city buses sitting unmoving, horns blaring insanely, drivers and radiators fuming. Do better on foot, Hathaway told himself as he headed down toward Wall Street.

Fifteen minutes later he was panting from the unusual exertion, his three-piece suit rumpled, his brand-new shirt soaked with perspiration. When he finally got to the lobby of the building where his brokerage firm was quartered, he saw a crowd of his fellow brokers milling about in dazed confusion.

"You hoofed it out here for nothing," one of his buddies told him as Hathaway tried to push through the throng to the elevators. "The office's closed."

"Closed?"

"Whole damned market's closed. All the computers are down. Nothing's going to happen today, Gordo."

Hathaway's jaw dropped open.

"The New York Stock Exchange is closed? I can't believe it!"

"Believe it," said his buddy sourly.

IN BOSTON'S CHILDREN'S Hospital the head of the surgical team gaped at the suddenly blank display screen, his blue eyes above his surgical mask going so wide you could see white all around the irises.

"What happened?" he whispered harshly.

His chief nurse shook her head. "The screen's gone out."

"I can see that!" Louder, snarling.

One of the assistant surgeons said needlessly, "The patient's open."

The baby on the surgical table was only three weeks old. She was undergoing surgery to correct an aneurysm in her aorta that threatened to kill her before she'd seen one month of life.

"Get the screen back up!" the head of surgery demanded of no one in particular, of everyone in the surgical theater.

The actual surgery was being performed remotely, over an electronic link, by a surgeon in Minneapolis who was recognized around the world as the best and most experienced man for this particular procedure. But the link had abruptly shut down in the middle of the operation.

"Get it back up!" the head of surgery shouted again.

"We're trying," said the computer technician from her console off in a corner of the surgery theater. She was almost in tears.

"The patient . . ." said one of the nurses.

With a growl that was almost feral, the head of surgery said, "I'll have to finish this myself, goddammit to hell."

He was a very good surgeon, but not good enough. The infant died on the table, four days short of her first month of life.

IN THE HEADQUARTERS of Travis Broadcasting Systems, in Atlanta, Herman Scott blinked unbelievingly at the wall full of monitor screens. Seven—no, eight—of the thirty had crapped out. Make it ten. In stunned amazement he watched as, one after another, the remaining twenty screens broke into hissing snowy static and then went dead gray.

The big electronic map that covered one entire wall of the monitoring center froze. Every last one of the pinpoint lights that showed where the satellites were in their orbits winked out.

We can't have all thirty satellites going down at once, Scott said to himself, trying to remain calm. Must be a power failure here in the building.

But the big map was still lit, and a glance at the lights and gauges of his console told him that electrical power was normal, and the backup power system was in the green too.

A couple of the other engineers were getting up from their consoles, confusion and outright fear on their faces.

"What's going on?" one of them asked.

As if I know, Scott said to himself.

"How can all thirty birds go down at once?"

Something very bad is happening here, Scott realized. Something terrible.

His console phone buzzed. Picking it up automatically, his eyes still on the dead screens, Scott heard the angry voice of the news bureau's chief:

"We're off the air! How the fuck can we be off the air in the middle of the sports report?"

IN LONDON, SIR Mallory Hyde-Grosvener was pacing up and down his office, desperately trying to get a phone connection to Singapore. He had pulled off his tweed jacket ten minutes earlier, crumpled it into a ball, and thrown it with main force against the wall where the portrait of his grandfather hung watching him with hard unblinking eyes. Through his office window he could see chaos on the floor of the market, absolute chaos. All the boards were down; where up-to-the-second market numbers should be flashing there was nothing but dead darkness. Every bloody man on the floor had a telephone jammed to his ear, red-faced and screaming.

Sweating, his impeccable gray tie pulled loose from his collar, he bellowed into his own dead phone while his grandfather's image frowned sternly at him.

COLONEL BRADY DESILVA was also sweating heavily as he sat in the command center at NORAD headquarters in Cheyenne Mountain, Colorado.

"They're *all* out?" he asked, his voice already hoarse from yelling at his staff officers.

Captain Nomura nodded. "Almost, sir. Four commsats are still on the air, but they're in and out. Sputtering, kind of."

"Sputtering," DeSilva echoed darkly.

Nomura was normally unflappable. But even his usually deadpan face was sheened with perspiration, his dark eyes blinking nervously.

"The milsats are okay, mostly, sir," the captain said. "But the commercial birds have gone dead, just about all of them."

"Half our communications traffic goes through those commercial satellites," DeSilva muttered.

"The early-warning system is functional," said the captain, trying to sound cheerful. "If anybody tries to attack us while the commercial birds are down, we'll spot them right off."

DeSilva growled at his aide. "And how the hell will we get the warning out? Carrier pigeons?"

GENERAL "BERNIE" BERNARD had been holding the phone to his ear for so long he felt as if it had taken root in his skull. He was pacing behind his desk, too edgy to sit.

To his credit, he and his staff at Space Command headquarters had not panicked when the satellite communications system started to break down. But he was scared; for the first time in his life, this former B-52 pilot who had flown combat missions over Bosnia, Iraq, and Afghanistan was scared.

At last a voice crackled, "The President is coming on the line now."

A click. Oh shit, Bernard thought. It's gone dead again.

But then a crisp voice said, "General Bernard."

Bernard automatically stiffened to attention. "Mr. President."

"What's going on?"

"All the commercial satellites over this hemisphere have gone dark, sir."

"I know that. What about—"

"The birds orbiting over the other side of the planet are degrading rapidly. They're dying, one by one."

"Jesus."

"As you know, sir, yesterday we tracked an unannounced rocket launch from North Korea. We went on alert, but the bird went into a geosynchronous orbit, twenty-two thousand miles up. It was a satellite, not a missile."

"So?" the President demanded.

"Three hours ago there was a nuclear detonation at geosynch

altitude. The electromagnetic pulse from the explosion knocked out almost all the unhardened satellites over our half of the globe."

"The communications satellites?"

"Commsats, yessir. Weather satellites too. Landsats, ocean surveillance — they're all down, sir."

"But your military satellites are protected, aren't they?"

"Yes, sir. Most of them. A few of the older ones have gone dark, but the others seem to be holding up. So far."

"Our military communications, the early-warning satellites, they're all okay, aren't they?"

"For the most part, sir."

A heartbeat's pause. Then, "What do you mean, 'for the most part'?"

General Bernard replied, "Sir, our communications needs have grown a lot faster than our milsats can support. The Department of Defense has been using commercial commsats for almost half its day-to-day traffic."

"And now those commsats are down."

"Yes, sir."

Again a pause. Then the President asked, "What about satellites on the other side of the world? Over Russia, China?"

"They're degrading, sir. It's not just the EMP that kills 'em. The nuke puts out a big cloud of energetic particles, too: high-energy electrons, protons. They bounce around along Earth's magnetic field lines like Ping-Pong balls. Those particles can kill unhardened satellites, too."

"So what you're telling me is that we're back to 1950, as far as telephone communications are concerned."

"Television, too, sir. Computer networks. Anything that uses satellites to relay information or data. All kaput."

For several long moments the President said nothing. Then he asked, "Is this the first strike in a war, General?"

General Bernard hesitated, then answered, "It's a good way to start a war, sir. Pearl Harbor, in orbit."

Harry Hartunian was having the same nightmare again.

He was at the test center out in the desert, standing in the control room as the team powered up the big laser. Through the thick safety glass of the observation window he could see the jumble of tubes and wires, the stainless steel vat that held the iodine, the frosted tank that contained the liquid oxygen, the complex of mirrors and lenses at the output point where more than a million watts of invisible energy would lance across the desert floor to the target, half a mile away.

Five technicians were at their posts, but Pete Quintana was out beside the optical bench on the other side of the observation window, right in the middle of the laser assembly. Pete was worried about the effect of the rig's vibration on the sensitive optical setup. Quintana.

"Iodine pressure on the button," one of the technicians in the control room called out.

Don't pressurize the oxy line, Harry warned. In his nightmare he tried to say the words out loud, but not a sound came out of his mouth. The tech was sitting five feet away from him, but he couldn't make him hear his warning.

"Electrical power ramping up," another technician said.

"Optical bench ready."

"Atmospheric instability nominal."

"Adaptive optics on."

"Iodine flow in ten seconds."

"Oxygen flow in eight seconds."

Don't pressurize the oxy line, Harry tried to scream. But he couldn't speak, couldn't move, couldn't do anything but watch them go through the same disaster again.

"Pressurizing iodine."

"Pressurizing oxy."

"No!" Harry screeched.

The explosion knocked him against the back wall of the control room, shattering his ribs against the gauges mounted on the concrete. Pain roared through Harry as the laser blew up in a spectacular blast that knocked the roof off the test shed. The heat from the oxygen-fed fire poured through the safety glass of the observation window, hot enough to melt the gauges on the back wall.

Pete Quintana was enveloped in the flames, screaming, gibbering, flailing in agony. Harry tried to reach out to him but his own pain was so intense that he blacked out.

"Rise and shine, Harry!"

Hartunian blinked awake. The room was dark, but somebody was flicking a flashlight beam in his eyes.

Harry was drenched with sweat, gasping for breath.

"You were yelling in your sleep, pal."

Monk Delany. Harry recognized his voice and dimly made out the outline of his heavy, bearlike body in the darkness of the strange bedroom. Elmendorf Air Force Base, Harry remembered. *We're in Alaska.*

"C'mon, buddy, we're gonna miss breakfast if you don't get going."

Harry didn't mind the flashlght glaring in his eyes. It was Monk's chipper, cheerful tone that irked him. *Can't be more than* four o'clock in the friggin' morning, Harry thought, and Monk's as jolly as a goddamned Santa Claus.

"Come on, Harry," Delany coaxed, flicking the flashlight beam back and forth across Harry's face again. "Rise and shine."

"Go 'way!"

Delany laughed. "You gotta get up, Harry. Time's a-wasting."

With a groan, Harry sat up, blinking, rubbing his stubbled jaw. Reluctantly he switched on the bedside lamp.

"What time is it?"

"Nearly six."

Squinting at the room's only window, Hartunian said, "Christ, it's still dark."

"Alaska, buddy. We're not in sunny California anymore."

"Tell me about it."

Hartunian swung his legs out of the bed and stood up, shivering slightly in his boxers and undershirt. His back ached dully. He was a short, round-shouldered man with baby-fine thin dark hair that flew into disarray at the slightest puff of breeze. His midsection showed a distinct middle-aged bulge. He hadn't come to Alaska willingly.

You're the program engineer now, Harry, Victor Anson had told him. *Wherever that plane goes, you go. We need you to make that damned laser work, Harry. Forget the accident. Just make it work. The company's ass is on the line. We're all depending on you.*

"Okay," he said to Delany, "I'm up. Go on down to the restaurant—"

"Mess hall," Delany corrected.

"Whatever. I'll meet you down there in ten minutes."

Delany was several inches taller than Hartunian and outweighed him by more than thirty pounds. His hair was dark and thick, but despite his formidable appearance his normal facial expression was a genial, lopsided smile. He was already dressed in his white coveralls with the Anson Aerospace Corporation logo on its chest and back.

"You know how to find the mess hall?"

"I'll find it," Harry said, reaching for his bathrobe.

"Ten minutes." Delany went to the door. He turned back, though, and advised, "Wear the heavy coat. October out here can be pretty damned chilly."

"Where's your coat?"

Delany flashed a grin. "I never feel the cold."

Blubber, Harry thought sourly.

It *was* cold outside, he discovered. Cold and still dark, although the sky was lightening enough in the east to silhouette the rugged snowcapped mountains. Despite his brand-new goose-down-lined parka Harry's back twinged from the cold. Psychosomatic, the doctors had claimed. Your ribs have healed and there's nothing wrong with your spine. Still, ever since the accident, Harry's back ached.

If I'd stayed in California like a sane man, Harry thought, I could've gone to the beach today.

Yeah, a sardonic voice in his head replied. And you'd have Sylvia and her lawyers pounding on your door, trying to get you to sign the damned divorce papers.

With a shake of his head, Harry looked around for the mess hall. He'd arrived at Elmendorf Air Force Base the previous afternoon, and most of the buildings in the sprawling facility looked pretty much alike to him. Last night, though, before going to sleep in the room they'd assigned him and Delany to share in the Bachelor Officers quarters, Harry had checked the route from the BOQ to the mess hall and put it into his cell phone's memory. Now he pulled the phone from his pants pocket to orient himself.

Damn! The phone was dead. No, he saw, it was getting power from the battery. But the screen said NO CONNECTION.

Harry looked up. A young airman was walking along the bricked pathway toward him.

"Hey . . . Sergeant," Harry said, noting the stripes on his jacket sleeve.

"Can I help you, sir?"

Feeling sheepish, Hartunian admitted, "I'm kind of lost."

The sergeant directed him down the street one block and then to the first right. "You can't miss it," he added cheerily.

Harry, who had been raised in the tangled suburbs of Boston, thought of all the "you can't miss it" locations he'd missed. But he went to the corner and turned right.

And there was the mess hall, with dozens of men and women streaming into it. Most of them in uniform.

But what caught his attention was down at the end of the street, where a little Day-Glo orange tractor was towing ABL-1 out of its hangar. Harry gaped. The sight of the big 747, all white, never failed to awe him. It was an immense airplane with that graceful hump up front and the huge raked-back tail towering over the other planes parked in front of the hangars. Somehow she looked dignified to Harry, regal, like royalty as she grandly allowed herself to be slowly rolled out onto the tarmac.

Make it work, Harry, Victor Anson had told him. *The company's ass is on the line.*

Jerry Jarusulski frowned as he sat at the controls of the Airbus A350 XWB. Halfway between Hawaii and California, he grumbled to himself, *and the nav system craps out.*

Through the cockpit's windshield he could see nothing but cloud-dotted ocean, steely gray and rippled with waves. Not a ship in sight. No land for another thousand klicks or more.

"Anything?" he asked his copilot.

"Not a peep, JJ," said Pete Jacobson. "Every damned freak is out. I'm getting some commercial stations, L.A. and 'Frisco. But all the air control frequencies are off."

"What the hell's happened to them?"

"Something weird," the copilot said.

"Well, we'll reach the California coast in another couple of hours. We can go to VFR then."

Jacobson nodded, but he looked doubtful. Jarusulski shared his worries. Flying a big-ass jet airliner on visual wasn't going to be easy, he knew. *Always a helluva lot of traffic at LAX. And the last weather report they got predicted rain. Those guys in the tower better have their systems working if they expect me to bring this bird down. What a time for the navigation satellite system to go kablooey.*

Jacobson started chuckling softly.

"What's so goddamned funny?" Jarusulski growled.

"It's like that old joke, the one about good news and bad news."

"Yeah?"

"You know. The pilot gets on the intercom and tells the passengers, 'I've got good news and bad news. The bad news is that we're lost. I don't know where the hell we are. The good news is we've got a tail wind and we're making good time.'"

Jarusulski didn't laugh. He was thinking about trying to land this jumbo bird in the rain. LAX better have its comm systems working, he said to himself. If they don't, we're toast. Burnt toast.

THE OVAL OFFICE

The Oval Office was crowded.

Hunching forward in the padded chair behind his gleaming broad desk, the President muttered, "From North Korea," his lean face bleak, his voice ominous.

In a shallow semicircle in front of the desk sat the Secretaries of Defense and State, the National Security Advisor, the director of Homeland Security and the director of the Central Intelligence Agency. Off to one side of the room the President's chief of staff sat on one of the striped sofas in front of the empty fireplace, his hands clasped tensely on his knees. Half a dozen aides were back there, too.

"Pyongyang has been on the wire with us for three hours now," said the Secretary of State. Her normally cool demeanor was gone; she looked just as worried—almost frightened—as the rest of the people in the Oval Office.

"They're pissing themselves, they're so scared," the National Security Advisor added, with a grim smile. A former admiral, he still looked as if he were in uniform, despite his light gray hand-tailored three-piece suit. His silver hair was tousled, though; he'd been running his hands through it since this meeting had begun.

Frowning slightly at him, the Secretary of State said, "The North Korean government is begging us to show some restraint—"

"Restraint?" the President snapped. "They've attacked us!"

State raised a brow. "*Someone* has attacked not only us but the whole civilized world. It's not just our satellites that have been wiped out. But Pyongyang says it wasn't them."

"That missile came from North Korea," said the Secretary of Defense in his heavy, rasping voice. "We traced its launch and its orbital track."

"But it wasn't launched from one of their regular launching bases," State insisted. "Pyongyang assures us that the North Korean government did not authorize the launch or the detonation of that bomb in orbit."

"What difference does that make?" the President growled. "It came from their territory. It's knocked out just about every satellite in orbit."

"Except for our hardened birds," Defense pointed out. He was the oldest man in the room, a former longtime senator, bald and jowly. He and the Secretary of State had been senators together and rivals for the nomination that the man behind the desk had won.

State raised a manicured hand. "Wait a minute. Since Kim Jong Il died last year North Korea's been in turmoil, practically civil war."

"Their military took control of the government," the National Security Advisor said.

"Yes," State agreed, "but there are factions within the military. One of the rebel factions must have fired that missile."

"What difference does that make?"

"Pyongyang tells us they're sending troops to the site where the missile was launched. They're asking us to allow them to solve the problem by themselves."

"Won't wash," said the Security Advisor.

"Are you saying we should send in our own troops?" the President asked.

"Or hit that launch site with an air strike?" State added.

The Security Advisor turned slightly toward the oversized television screen mounted on the wall between portraits of Theodore and Franklin Roosevelt. Without asking the President's permission, he half rose from his chair and reached for the remote control unit on the desk.

The wall screen flickered, then showed a satellite image of rugged, mountainous country. Snowpacks covered many of the peaks; from orbit they looked like bony white fingers stretching across the bare brown mountains.

"NRO satellite imagery, two hours old," said the Security Advisor. "That's the area where the missile came from."

The view zoomed in dizzyingly, then steadied to show a leveled area of ground where a dozen brown military trucks were parked in a ragged circle. At the center of the circle two missiles were standing on portable launch pads. A third pad was empty.

"That's where the missile was launched," said the Security Advisor. "As you can see, they have two more ready to go."

The President sagged back in his chair. "They're armed with nukes?"

"We've got to assume that they are."

"Hit them now!" the Secretary of Defense urged. "I can get a submarine within range in a few hours. Wipe them out with one missile."

The President's eyes never left the image on the screen. "In a few hours they could launch both those missiles."

"What's their range?" asked Defense. "Could they hit us?"

The CIA director said, "Our people have identified them as Taepodong-2s. From where they're sited now they could reach Alaska or Hawaii."

"The West Coast?" asked the President.

"No, that's a bit beyond their range."

The President smiled weakly. "Good. I'm scheduled to give a speech in San Francisco tonight."

"But they could hit Japan," said the Security Advisor.

"The Japanese will go apeshit when they see this," Defense rumbled, almost as if he was enjoying the thought.

CIA pointed out, "You remember a couple of years ago North Korea launched a whole series of missiles across the Pacific and we didn't do anything about it."

"Those were just tests," said the President.

"Yes, and now they put a bird into orbit. We've got to assume those other two missiles they've got on their pads won't be tests, either. They could hit Hawaii, the Philippines, even northern Australia."

"Screw Australia," the Defense Secretary snapped. "They could wipe out Honolulu! We've got to take them out!" Banging a fist on the arm of his chair, Defense insisted, "We've *got to!*"

"And start World War III?" the Secretary of State countered. "How do you think the Chinese would react if we hit North Korea?"

"Hell, their satellites have been knocked out, too."

The President asked, "What do the Chinese have to say about this?"

State hesitated a fraction of a moment, then replied, "It's been difficult communicating with them. The satellites are down and we don't have a direct cable link with Beijing."

"They're being inscrutable, I bet," said Defense, allowing himself a tight smile.

"They have a fleet of nuclear missiles with the range to reach every city in the United States," the Secretary of State said firmly.

The CIA director spoke up again. "Do we want to take the risk of starting World War III? A nuclear war?"

"I do not," said the President.

"But those missiles," the Security Advisor said, jabbing an accusing finger at the wall screen. "They're going to fire them. And soon, before Pyongyang's troops can reach the site."

Turning to the Homeland Security director, the President said, "How soon can you get Hawaii and Alaska alerted?"

Homeland Security looked startled. He had formerly been the head of one of the nation's largest construction companies, known to the media as a can-do kind of executive who wasn't afraid to roll up his sleeves and get his hands dirty.

"We're talking about evacuating Honolulu?" he asked.

"And Anchorage, maybe Juneau."

"On a half hour's notice," added Defense.

The former construction executive shook his head. "We'd have to start right now."

"That's going to cause quite a panic," State pointed out.

"But you can't evacuate a city the size of Honolulu in half an hour!" Homeland Security said, almost pleading. "You've got to start right away. Now."

"Wait a minute," the President said. "What about our missile defense system?"

All eyes turned to the Secretary of Defense, who shifted uneasily in his chair. He and the President had cut funding for missile defense every year they'd been in office.

"Um . . . the system's still in a test and evaluation stage." Defense temporized.

"I was told it was operational," said the President.

"It was declared operational . . ." Defense let the implications hang in the air.

"You mean we couldn't shoot down those missiles if the North Koreans launch them?"

"*When* they launch them," the Security Advisor corrected.

"Can we shoot them down or can't we?" the President demanded.

Defense answered with a shrug and said, "We can try. But we certainly couldn't stop a full-scale Chinese attack."

"There's the Russians, too," the CIA director pointed out.

The President raised both hands, silencing them all.

After a moment's thought, he said, "We will activate our missile defense system. And alert our own retaliatory forces: missiles, submarines, and the manned bombers."

"Defense Readiness Condition Three?" asked Defense.

"DefCon One," said the President. "Let's not waste time on this. Full alert, everybody ready to go."

Before anyone could object, the President turned to the Secretary of State. "Let Beijing and Moscow know our moves are strictly defensive. Tell Tokyo what's going on. Maybe they'll want to attack that missile site. That way we could keep our hands clean."

"I wouldn't depend on that," the Security Advisor muttered.

The President went on, "But we will *not* make an attack on North Korea. Not yet. We'll give Pyongyang the opportunity to clean their own house. Our moves will be strictly defensive."

"And when those two nukes are launched?" asked the Security Advisor.

"We'll hope to hell we can shoot them down," the President replied. "And if we can't, if they hit an American city, we'll blow those fuckers off the face of the earth."

Dead silence in the Oval Office.

Then the Secretary of Defense muttered, "Maybe we ought to get the chaplain in here." The President glowered at him.

They rose and left the Oval Office, all except the chief of staff, who got up from the couch by the fireplace and settled in one of the emptied chairs in front of the President's desk.

"It's a mess, Norm, isn't it?" said the President.

"Yeah, but I think you're doing the right thing."

The President shook his head. "I wonder. Why'd they knock out all the satellites?"

"Economic terrorism. Wall Street's shut down. Markets all over the world have closed."

"Damn. I'll have to work this into tonight's speech."

"In San Francisco? You're still going?"

"I won't cancel it," the President said. Then, rubbing at the bridge of his nose, he added, "My wife wanted to go with me, but I told her I'd only be there for a few hours."

"The First Lady will be safer here," the chief of staff agreed. "You would be, too, you know."

"No, I've got to go," the President said. "There's enough panic out there, with all the satellites out. My job is to show the people that everything's under control."

"Even when it isn't?"

The President flashed his famous grin. "Especially when it isn't, Norm. Especially when it isn't."

MISSILE DEFENSE BASICS

The Missile Defense Agency (MDA) has developed a research, development, and test program focusing on a layered defense system based on the three phases of a ballistic missile's trajectory: boost, midcourse, and terminal.

Boost Phase Defense
The boost phase is the part of the missile flight from launch until its rocket engines are exhausted and it stops accelerating under its own power. Typically, the boost phase ends at altitudes of 300 miles or less, and within the first 3 to 5 minutes of flight. During this phase, the rocket is climbing against Earth's gravity.

Intercepting a missile in its boost phase is the ideal solution. We can defend a large area of the globe and prevent midcourse decoys from being deployed by destroying the missile early in its flight. Of the boost phase defenses, the Airborne Laser (ABL) is the most mature.

Midcourse Phase Defense
The midcourse phase of a ballistic missile trajectory allows the longest window of opportunity to intercept an incoming missile: up

to 20 minutes. This is the part of the missile's flight where its engines have stopped thrusting so it follows a more predictable coasting path. The midcourse interceptor and a variety of radars and other sensors have a longer time to track and engage the target compared to boost and terminal interceptors. Also, more than one interceptor can be launched to ensure a successful hit.

A downside to the longer intercept window is that the attacker has an opportunity to deploy countermeasures against a defensive system. The warhead and decoys are detached from the spent rocket stages during the midcourse phase. However, the interceptor and other sensors have more time to observe and discriminate countermeasures from the warhead. The midcourse defense segment has ground- and sea-based elements, including the Ground-based Midcourse Defense (GMD) and the sea-based Aegis Ballistic Missile Defense (Aegis BMD).

Unlike the Airborne Laser, which fires a beam of light energy to destroy the missile, the midcourse and terminal phase systems employ smaller, high-velocity missiles to strike the incoming warhead; this is known as the "kinetic kill" method.

Terminal Phase Defense

A missile enters the terminal phase when the warhead falls back into the atmosphere. This phase generally lasts from 30 seconds to one minute.

The primary elements in the terminal defense segment are:

Terminal High Altitude Area Defense (THAAD), which will destroy a ballistic missile's warhead as it transitions from the midcourse to the terminal phase of its trajectory. THAAD consists of four principle components: truck-mounted launchers; interceptor missiles; radars; and command, control, and battle management (C^2BM). The system has rapid mobility so that it can be airlifted to almost anywhere in the world within hours.

Patriot Advanced Capability (PAC-3), the most mature element of the ballistic missile defense system. Built on previous Patriot air and missile defense infrastructure, PAC-3 missiles were deployed to Southwest Asia as part of Operation Iraqi Freedom in 2003.

Arrow, a joint effort between the United States and Israel, provides Israel with a capability to defend its borders and U.S. troops deployed in the region against short- and medium-range ballistic missiles. The system became operational in 2000.

Medium Extended Air Defense System (MEADS), a co-developmental program with Germany and Italy to develop an air and missile defense system that is mobile and transportable. Using the combat-proven PAC-3 as a platform, MEADS' role in ballistic missile defense is to bridge the gap between manportable systems like the Stinger shoulder-fired missile and the higher levels of the ballistic missile defense system, such as the THAAD system.

Missile Defense Agency
Overview and BMD Basics

T he mess hall was big and crowded, but not as noisy as Harry expected from the size of the place. The rest of his laser team was finishing up their breakfast by the time Harry worked his way down the counter and carried his tray to their table. He could spot them from across the cafeteria by their white Anson Aerospace coveralls, like a cluster of ice floes in a sea of Air Force blue.

"She's hot, I tell you," Wally Rosenberg was saying as Harry dragged a chair from the next table and sat down between him and Taki Nakamura.

"What do you think, boss?" Angie Reyes asked. He was a chemical technician, in charge of the volatile mix of iodine and oxygen that powered the big laser. Reyes was a wiry bantam cock of a guy, short, slim, dark-haired. He had replaced Pete Quintana; Rosenberg kidded that the company's management wanted to keep its quota of Hispanics on the project.

"Think about what?" Harry asked, taking his English muffin and mug of coffee off the tray.

"Our new pilot," Rosenberg answered. A chemical engineer, Rosenberg always had a sly grin on his long, horsey face. "I say she's hot."

Taki Nakamura, the only woman in the team, made a mock scowl at Rosenberg. "You say every woman you see is hot."

"Not you, Tiki-Taki," Rosenberg shot back.

"You'd better not. Unless you want your nose stuffed up your butt."

"Kung fu engineer," Monk Delany cracked. Everybody laughed, even Rosenberg.

"Colonel Christopher?" Harry replied to Rosenberg's question. "I just met her last night, same as you guys. I guess she's good-looking, all right."

"Well, you're an eligible bachelor, aintcha?" Rosenberg said, his grin turning into a smirk.

"I'm still a married man," Harry said. "We're separated; we're not divorced yet."

Delany shook his head. "When are you gonna bite the bullet, Harry? Go through with the divorce, pal. Get on with your life."

Harry said nothing.

Nakamura asked, "Is the colonel married?"

"Nope," Rosenberg answered. "I Googled her. She's in hot water with the Air Force, as a matter of fact. They caught her sleeping with a married guy—some general, no less."

"Your kind of woman," Delany said.

"Yeah. A slut," added Reyes.

Harry decided the banter had gone far enough. "We've got work to do. Let's get moving."

As they carried their trays to the disposal area, Taki asked, "Did any of you see the northern lights out there? They're spectacular!"

Delany said, "So that's what it was! I caught a glimpse just before the sun came up. Then they faded out. I was wondering what those lights were."

"Well, shit, we *are* in Alaska," Rosenberg said.

Nakamura shook her head. "They were awful bright. Must be some big flare on the sun to work them up like that. Or something."

. . .

STANDING IN FRONT of the desk in the cubbyhole of an office that the base commander had given her, Lieutenant Colonel Karen Christopher was not in a happy mood. Bad enough to be exiled to this godforsaken dump in Alaska. Even worse to push the regular pilot of this oversized bus out of his job and into the right-hand seat. He's already pissed off at me. Now they've stuck me with a navigator who's so inexperienced he looks like a skinny high school kid who's snuck into Air Force blues.

Her navigator, Lieutenant Eustis Sharmon, was tall, quite lean, with skin the color of dark chocolate. He was standing at attention before Colonel Christopher, who stood a full head shorter than him. Sharmon looked uncomfortable; Christopher felt grouchy.

But as she looked up at Sharmon's young face and troubled, red-rimmed eyes, Colonel Christopher said to herself, It's not his fault. The brass assigned him to me and he's stuck with the job. Just like I'm stuck with driving this clunker of an airplane.

"Take it easy, Lieutenant," she said, trying to put some warmth into it. She extended her hand. "Welcome on board."

Sharmon loosened up a little. "Thanks, Colonel," he mumbled.

Christopher perched on the edge of the desk and gestured to the chair against the wall. "Have a seat. Relax."

The lieutenant settled into the chair like a carpenter's ruler folding up, big hands on his knees.

"I bet you played basketball," Colonel Christopher said, trying to smile.

"No, ma'am. Track. Ran the distance events."

Her brows rose. "Marathon?"

Sharmon smiled for the first time. It was a good, bright smile. "Did the marathon once. Once was enough."

She laughed. "Well, what we're doing here is easier than a marathon."

"Racetrack, they told me."

Nodding. "That's right. We take the bird out to a designated test area over the ocean, then fly a figure eight while the tech geniuses downstairs get their laser working. Piece of cake."

But in her mind she was thinking of the missions she had flown over Afghanistan: twelve-thousand-kilometer distances, midair refuelings, full stealth mode, pinpoint delivery of smart bombs. Going from flying a B-2 to jockeying a dumbass 747 was more than a demotion, it was a humiliation.

"So there's not much for me to do, then," Lieutenant Sharmon said.

Christopher nodded. "Not as long as the GPS is working."

W hattaya mean there's no satellite pictures?" Heydon Kalheimer demanded indignantly.

He was standing in front of the studio's blue wall, due to be on the air with the weather report in forty seconds. As usual, he had shown up at the last possible moment. The monitor screen that usually showed the National Weather Service satellite imagery was as blank as the wall. Kalheimer felt very put out.

His producer shrugged her heavy shoulders. They made quite a pair: Kalheimer was long and lanky, all arms and legs, even his head was narrow and long-jawed. He always had a slap-happy grin on his face, even when he was furious. The producer was built like a squat teddy bear, short, heavy, given to sighs of long suffering.

She sighed in her long-suffering way, then repeated, "No satellite pictures. Something's screwed up. News reports say that all the satellites are down, malfunctioning."

"How in hell am I supposed to do the weather without satellite graphics? What'm I supposed to do, just stand in front of the camera and look stupid?"

"That wouldn't take much," the producer muttered.

"What?"

Louder, she said, "You'll have the local radar imagery and the National Weather Service's forecast. Just read it off the monitor, like you always do."

"That'll take ten seconds. What do I do with the rest of my two minutes?"

"You'll just have to wing it." She knew that Kalheimer did not like winging it. Behind his façade of overweening self-confidence he was still as insecure as he'd been his first day in front of the cameras.

"Heads are gonna roll over this," Kalheimer growled. "And your head's gonna be the first one!"

"In five!" the floor manager shouted. "Four . . . three . . ."

The overhead lights turned on and Kalheimer turned to camera one, his toothy professional grin spread across his long, bony face.

"Hi there! It's time for your up-to-the-minute weather report."

T he first meeting of this emergency action team is convened"—
General Franklin P. Higgins glanced at his Breitling
wristwatch— "at 11:46 a.m., 23 October."

The situation room was in the basement of the Pentagon, in the
wing that had been rebuilt after being blasted and burned by the ter-
rorist attack of September 11, 2001. It was a small room; it felt
crowded, tense, even with fewer than a dozen men and women sitting around the oblong table. Almost every one of them had opened
a laptop or notebook computer on the table before them.

Three of the room's walls were floor-to-ceiling smart screens,
showing various images from hardened Defense Department satellites. The ceiling was paneled with glareless lights. The seats around
the highly polished table were dark leather, plush, comfortable.
Each place at the table had a built-in phone jack and power plug.

General Higgins was a big, morose-looking man with a flabby-
jowled face and a bulbous nose that had earned him the nickname
Possum when he'd been a cadet at the Air Force Academy. Although he was presently on detached duty with the Defense Intelligence Agency, he still wore his blue uniform.

Zuri Coggins sat at the general's right hand. She was from the

White House, a member of the National Security Advisor's staff, sent to this emergency action team as the West Wing's representative. She was a tiny African-American woman, almost elfin, but very intense. Wearing a stylish short-skirted red jacket dress, she was the only woman in the conference room.

The rear door opened and Michael Jamil stepped in, looking apologetic. All eyes around the oblong conference table turned to him.

"Sorry to be late," he said, his voice soft, contrite. "They held me up at the security checkpoint outside."

Jamil, a civilian analyst from the National Intelligence Council, was in a suede sports jacket and baggy, creaseless chinos. No tie, but a sleeveless V-neck yellow sweater beneath the jacket. He slid into an empty seat at the foot of the conference table, glancing at the displays on the smart screens that lined three of the room's four walls. The images showed a satellite view of the missile launching site in the rugged mountains of North Korea, an electronic map of the North Pacific Ocean with each U.S. Navy surface vessel and submarine highlighted by a pinpoint light, and other satellite pictures of Air Force bases in Alaska, Okinawa, and Japan.

Jamil was of medium height, spare of build, his face fringed with a neatly trimmed light brown beard. His skin was the color of tobacco leaf, although he had never smoked in his life. He brushed at a lock of sandy hair that stubbornly fell across his high forehead and nervously adjusted his tinted eyeglasses. His eyes were caramel brown. He felt very junior to this assemblage of uniformed brass and high-powered civilians, even though he was convinced that he knew more about the situation than most of them did.

"Are we all here now?" General Higgins asked, his tone biting, his fleshy face clearly displeased.

His aide, an Air Force major sitting on his left, replied, "The representative from the Chief of Naval Operations is on his way, sir. And the chief of the Homeland Security office at Honolulu was going to attend via a satellite link, but the link isn't operative this morning."

Higgins grumbled, "Which is why we're here, isn't it?"

Zuri Coggins said, "The President and the National Security Advisor have both instructed me to assure you that any and all resources you may need will be made available." She peered down the table toward Major General Bradley Scheib.

Brad Scheib gave the impression of being a dashing sky warrior in his crisp blue uniform with its chest full of ribbons, and his handsome, chiseled features. In reality he was more of a tech geek than a jet jock. A graduate of Caltech, Scheib had spent more of his career in laboratories than cockpits.

"What about it, Brad?" General Higgins asked. "Is your missile defense system up and running?"

With a curt nod, Scheib answered, "We've activated all our ABM units in Fort Greely, in Alaska, and at Vandenberg Air Force Base. The Navy has alerted all four of its Aegis battle groups in the western Pacific. Two of them are steaming at full speed for the Sea of Japan; the other two are deploying between Japan and Hawaii."

"There's only two missiles to worry about," one of the civilians on the other side of the table said, pointing to the satellite image of the North Korean launch site.

"Two that we know about," Scheib replied.

"How many do the Chinese have?" an Army officer asked.

"And the Russians?"

"They both have missile-launching submarines, too."

Zuri Coggins said, "The President has decided that our moves will be strictly defensive." Poking at the air with one finger to emphasize her words, she added, "We will not do anything that could provoke a Chinese response. Or a Russian one."

"But they've both gone on alert, haven't they?" asked the admiral sitting across the table from her.

"Not yet," Coggins replied, "although the State Department was tasked with informing them that our own nuclear retaliatory forces are being placed on full alert."

"State Department," the admiral muttered distastefully.

General Higgins looked toward one of the civilians sitting down the table from Coggins. "Are our snooper satellites still working?"

"They are," said the civilian. "ELINT birds have picked up coded messages sent along landlines in China and Russia." Glancing at Coggins, he continued. "They are in the process of putting their missile forces on full alert."

Higgins nodded morosely, as if he had expected nothing less.

"Pakistan and India, too," the civilian added.

"Sweet Jesus," said the admiral. "That's all we need, those two pulling the trigger."

"What about the Iranians?" Higgins asked.

"They've only got a half dozen missiles."

"Guess where they'll fire them?" asked Higgins' aide, who was Jewish.

"What if the Chinese or the Russians take advantage of this situation to attack us?" Higgins snapped.

Coggins replied firmly, "That will trigger a full-scale retaliation by our missile forces and both the Chinese and Russians know it. What's more, they know that our systems are on full alert. We could respond with a devastating nuclear counterstrike at a moment's notice."

"Even if the President is dead?" Jamil asked. His voice was soft, tentative, as if he'd surprised himself by speaking up.

Everyone turned to him. Her dark eyes narrowing, Coggins demanded, "What do you mean by that?"

Suddenly the focus of everyone around the table, Jamil blinked his brown eyes nervously and pawed at his unruly hair. At last he said, "Well, the President is scheduled to give a speech in San Francisco tonight."

General Scheib pointed to the wall screen with one hand as he pecked with a single finger at his laptop's keyboard. A schematic drawing of a ballistic missile appeared on the screen, with a list of performance specifications alongside it.

"Those two missiles are Taepodong-2s," Scheib said. "They don't have the range to reach San Francisco. Or the reliability. The last time they fired one it splashed into the Pacific several hundred miles short of Hawaii."

Jamil had to turn in his chair to see the drawing. "According to our information," he said, "the Taepodong-2 has a range of ten thousand kilometers."

"That's Pyongyang propaganda. In the real world, the Taepodong-2 doesn't have the range to reach San Francisco."

"I admit that San Francisco is at the extreme fringe of the missile's capability." Jamil's tone was conciliatory, yet he was clearly contradicting the general.

Scheib glared at the civilian analyst. "Even so, the missile doesn't have the accuracy to hit San Francisco, not at that range."

Jamil nodded slightly but countered, "Yet they launched a bird into geosynchronous orbit. General, I submit that their guidance system has demonstrated a sophisticated degree of accuracy."

"You can submit whatever you want," Scheib retorted with a humorless grin. "They can't reach San Francisco."

General Higgins pointed down the table at Jamil. "Are you saying those two missiles *could* hit San Francisco?"

"It's within the realm of possibility," Jamil replied.

Shaking his head vigorously, General Scheib insisted, "They're Taepodong-2s! They don't have the range. Or the accuracy."

"Then how did they get a nuclear warhead all the way up to geosynch orbit?" Jamil asked. "If you do the math, you can see that they do indeed have the capability."

"For Chrissakes, we can *see* the missiles on their pads," Scheib retorted. "We can count the solid rocket units they've strapped onto their first stages. They don't have the range to reach San Francisco."

"But if you do the math—"

"Screw the math," Scheib snapped. "We've got satellite imagery."

Zuri Coggins looked from Scheib to Jamil. "Do you seriously believe that those missiles could hit San Francisco?"

"It's theoretically possible, if their payloads are light enough."

"How light?" General Higgins asked.

Jamil hesitated. "Well, according to our estimates, they could each carry a two-hundred-and-fifty-kiloton weapon over the distance to San Francisco."

"That's half a megaton between the two of them."

"Twenty-five times more than Hiroshima."

"More like thirty."

"What makes you think that's going to be their target?" Higgins demanded.

Jamil was unaccustomed to being in the spotlight. And unhappy with it. He had done his analysis in the taxi on his way to the Pentagon, using his iPhone's calculator application, plus a lot of figures he'd pulled from his own memory. It was shaky, but it made sense to him.

"Whoever launched the first missile wanted to wipe out our satellites. They must understand that the North Korean army is rushing to their site as fast as they can. Yet they haven't launched the other two missiles they've got on their pads. Why not?"

"Because they're waiting for the President to arrive in San Francisco?" Coggins asked.

Jamil nodded. "That's my conclusion."

"Bullshit!" Scheib scoffed.

But Coggins asked, "Why would they do this? What do they hope to gain?"

"It's the Sarajevo scenario," Jamil replied. "We've run the analysis dozens of times back at Langley."

"Sarajevo?"

"It's how World War I started. Some Austrian archduke got assassinated in Sarajevo, in Serbia. The Austro-Hungarian Empire declared war on Serbia. Russia had a treaty with Serbia, so they declared war on Austria-Hungary. Germany had an alliance with Austria-Hungary so they declared war on Russia. England and France had an alliance with Russia so . . ." Jamil spread his hands. "World War I."

Higgins shook his head ponderously. "I don't see how that connects with what we've got here."

His brows knitting slightly, Jamil explained, "North Korea hurts us. We hit back at North Korea. The Chinese don't like that, so they attack us. We counterattack China. Russia comes in, and once that happens NATO gets involved."

"Full-scale nuclear war," Higgins' civilian aide breathed in an awed voice.

"Armageddon," someone whispered, loudly enough for them all to hear it.

The GPS is off-line?" Lieutenant Sharmon looked shocked.
The iron gray–haired tech sergeant standing behind the counter made a face that was halfway between apologetic and disgusted. He was more than twice the lieutenant's age and had spent most of his time in the Air Force making young shavetails look good.

"The system went off-line a couple hours ago, sir. All the satellite links are down. Must be those damn northern lights." Then he added, "Sir."

From the other side of the flight control center, Colonel Christopher could see the alarm on Sharmon's face. She walked across the worn tile flooring toward him.

"Something wrong, Lieutenant?"

Sharmon shook his head, his brows knit into a tight furrow. "The GPS is down, ma'am."

Christopher almost smiled, but she held herself in check. "Then you'll just have to navigate without it."

"I guess I will, ma'am." Sharmon clearly was not happy with that prospect.

Christopher stepped away from the counter and the listening tech sergeant, motioning Sharmon to follow her.

Lowering her voice, she asked, "Do I call you Eustis? And you don't have to be so formal; you can drop the 'ma'am' business while we're on duty together. Just call me Colonel. Unless there's bigger brass around, of course."

She remembered how some of the wiseasses at the Academy used to call her Chrissie, just to rile her. She had kept her temper under control, hidden, until graduation day. That's when they found their shoes had been glued to the dorm ceiling, all of them. They had to attend the graduation ceremony in bedroom slippers and flip-flops and got reprimanded for being out of uniform. They never tumbled to the possibility that five-foot-four Karen Christopher could reach the ceilings of their rooms while they slept.

Lieutenant Sharmon made an effort to smile. "Thank you, ma . . . uh, thank you, Colonel. My middle name is Jon. Without an aitch. My friends call me Jon."

"All right, Jon. That's what I'll call you. We're not friends yet, but maybe we will be."

He did smile, faintly. "Thank you, Colonel."

"Now, don't sweat this GPS business. It's just a crutch anyway. You're a trained navigator. You can get us to our correct position out over the ocean without it, can't you?"

"Yes . . . uh, Colonel. But I'd feel a lot better with the GPS to back me up."

Christopher said, "You'll do fine, Jon. This is just a milk run anyway. We run a racetrack pattern while the nerds play with their laser. So don't sweat it."

"Thank you, Colonel." Sharmon still looked unconvinced.

Christopher nodded at him once, then turned and headed for the meteorology desk. Poor kid looks scared to death, she said to herself. Then a voice in her head warned, He's not a poor kid and he's not your friend. He's supposed to be a navigator and you're supposed to be his superior officer. Keep it that way.

Her copilot, Major Obadiah Kaufman, was already at the weather desk, looking red-nosed and bleary-eyed. Either he's had a

late night, Christopher thought, or he's got some bug—which he'll
pass on to the rest of us, for sure.

"No metsat data," said Major Kaufman, in lieu of a greeting.

He was a round butterball of a man, not much taller than Christopher herself. She wondered how he passed his physicals, he looked so
out of shape. And miserably unhappy. So would I be, she thought, if I
got bounced out of the pilot's job for some stranger.

"What do you mean, no metsat data, Obie?"

Kaufman's bloodshot eyes flared at her use of his nickname, but
he immediately clamped down on his resentment.

The harried-looking female captain in charge of the meteorology desk confirmed from the other side of the counter, "The weather
satellites went down a couple of hours ago, Colonel. We don't have
anything for you except the local weather forecast, from the base's
met instruments."

"All the metsats are down?" Christopher asked. It was hard to
believe.

"The whole civilian satellite system is down, ma'am," said the
captain. She looked frightened, as if the system failure would be
blamed on her.

"What about our own metsats? Are they down, too?"

"No, ma'am. The milsats are operational. But the comm system's
overloaded. Swamped. Data requests from everybody, all at once.
They're running half an hour late. More."

Christopher studied the captain's face for a moment. The
younger woman looked as if she expected to get reamed out by the
colonel.

"Give me the latest you've got, then," Christopher said mildly,
"and update me as soon as you get more data."

"Yes'm." The captain looked distinctly relieved. Major Kaufman
took out a large red-and-white-checked handkerchief and snuffled
into it. Looks like he swiped it from an Italian restaurant, Christopher
thought.

Kaufman mumbled an excuse and headed for the men's room.

Colonel Christopher decided not to wait for him and left the control center together with Lieutenant Sharmon, he tall and gangly, she petite and graceful. Both in Air Force flight suits, plastic helmets cradled in their arms. As they headed out toward the flight line, Christopher thought, This could be an interesting flight. "Interesting" was a term she reserved, like other fliers, for situations that were either hairy or downright terrifying.

OUT ON THE flight line it was gray and raw; the wet wind gusting in off the water sliced right through Harry's goose-down coat. It made his back ache sullenly. He squinted up at the clouds, low and dark, thick with moisture. A low gray bank of fog blanketed the far side of the airfield; he couldn't even see the end of the runway. Harry wondered if they'd have enough visibility to get the plane off the ground. Nothing seemed to be moving out on the flight line. No planes were taking off; everything was as quiet as a tomb except for the low moan of the wind.

We moved to California to get away from this kind of miserable weather, Harry thought as he trudged out toward the ABL-1 plane. Had enough dark, cold winters in New England. It's dry in California; even when it rains it's never bleak and nasty like this. When we wanted snow we drove up into the mountains.

Harry remembered teaching his two daughters to ski. They loved the snow. Why not? he asked himself. They never had to shovel the stuff off a driveway. Wonder what they're doing now? Probably taking a dip in the pool. Sylvia liked to swim. She spent more time in that damned pool than she did in bed with me. And after the accident . . .

He reached the plane. The huge 747-400F loomed above Harry like a giant aluminum iceberg. He stopped at the foot of the narrow ladder that led to the plane's innards and tried his cell phone again. Victor Anson had made it painfully clear that he wanted to be called each time Harry and his crew flew a mission.

But the damned phone was still on the fritz. Harry scowled at it.

Modern technology at its finest, he grumbled silently. It can perform nineteen dozen different functions and none of them are working.

The flight crew was climbing aboard up front, by the plane's bulbous nose. He saw the new pilot and a tall, lean, black lieutenant with her. They ride first class, Harry thought. We ride coach, in the back of the plane. He shrugged. He'd met the new pilot only briefly the night before, when she'd introduced herself to his team. She was good-looking, that was true. Rosenberg had barely kept his eyes in his head.

Delany and the rest of the Anson team trudged across the tarmac and started climbing the stairs and entering the plane. Wally Rosenberg, last in line, noticed Harry trying to work his phone and cast him a snide grin.

"Calling our new flygirl?"

Fuck you, Harry thought. Aloud, he answered, "Phoning the boss."

"Levy? He's prob'ly heading for coffee break. It's an hour earlier back in sunny California."

"Not Jake. Anson."

Rosenberg's brows rose. "The big boss?"

"The man whose name's on our coveralls. Yeah."

"You talk to Anson?"

Harry nodded wearily. "He wants to know what we're doing. He's got a lot riding on this system."

For once, Rosenberg did not have a flip retort. He merely nodded, then clambered up the shaky aluminum ladder. Harry gave up on the dead phone, stuffed it into the pocket of his bulky coat, and started up the ladder after him. His back twinged with every step.

T hey can't *all* be down!" Tad Travis insisted. "Not ever' last one of 'em!"

Herman Scott pushed his rimless glasses up against the bridge of his nose more firmly. He'd never met Mr. Travis before, except once at an office Christmas party where the corporation's founder, CEO, and self-proclaimed genius was more interested in the younger female staffers than a tech geek with an MIT ring where a wedding band ought to be.

"Every last one of them, I'm afraid," Scott said softly.

Travis glared at him as he paced feverishly between the rows of useless consoles. The great man had come down to the monitoring center, the first appearance he'd ever made below the top floor of the office tower, as far as Scott knew. The wall screens were still dead, the monitors still showing nothing but hissing static.

"For what it's worth," Scott continued, standing in front of his useless console, "every other satellite constellation is down, too. GeoStar, Intelsat, Galaxy, AMC . . . all of them."

"XM, too?" Travis asked. "I got money in XM."

"XM, too. They've all been wiped out."

"Sweet Jesus!"

Scott waited for the outburst. Travis was famous for his volcanic temper.

The great man stopped his pacing and whirled on Scott. "You get the White House on the line! I wanna talk to the President! Pronto!"

Scott wondered how he could break the news to his boss that he'd called Washington an hour ago, trying to reach the corporation's office in the capital, only to find that all the satellite communications links were down and the landlines were jammed with frantic, urgent calls.

Z uri Coggins closed the phone link on her book-sized mini-computer, which she had plugged into the Pentagon's communications network. Cell phone reception was too spotty for this call; besides, the landline was more secure. Looking up at the people sitting tensely around the table, she said, "The Oval Office says the President's already on his way to San Francisco. Air Force One took off twenty minutes ago."

"Then call it back," General Higgins snapped.

Shaking her head annoyedly, Coggins said, "Only the President himself has that authority."

"You've got to get him to turn back," said one of the civilians on the other side of the table.

"I'm trying," Coggins said. "I have a call in to him aboard the plane."

Down near the end of the conference table, Michael Jamil muttered something.

"What was that?" General Higgins demanded.

Looking suddenly embarrassed, Jamil said, "The President has a sort of macho reputation. Maybe the terrorists—or whoever has those missiles—are counting on him going on to San Francisco despite the risk."

Higgins' thick-jowled face darkened. "How do you know they're going to hit San Francisco?"

Jamil shrugged slightly. "It's only an educated guess, General, but San Francisco's the logical target. The place where they can do the most damage to us."

"How do we know they're terrorists?" Higgins demanded. "From what we know about this, they're a faction of the North Korean army."

"A faction that wants to plunge the world into nuclear war," Jamil argued.

"Fanatics?" asked Higgins' aide.

"Muslim jihadists?"

"The Koreans aren't Muslim."

"They're Communists," Higgins said firmly. "Atheists."

Coggins said, "But the fact is that, for whatever reason, they've knocked out just about every unhardened satellite in orbit around the entire world."

"It could be the Chinese behind it all," Jamil suggested. "The North Koreans could be pawns for the Chinese."

"But why would China . . . ?"

Unconsciously going into a lecturer's tone, like a schoolteacher, Jamil said, "The Chinese have been hit by this global recession harder than we have. Their people were starting to expect a rising economic tide. Now they're facing cutbacks, unemployment, economic slowdown."

"Who isn't?" General Higgins retorted.

"There's been a lot of unrest, especially out in the provinces. Riots, even. And Beijing blames us for it. They claim the recession started in America and then spread to China and elsewhere."

"And for this they're willing to go to war?" Coggins asked, clearly unconvinced.

"Their government isn't monolithic. They have factions, just like everywhere else. The hard-liners in Beijing have long maintained that they could survive a nuclear war," Jamil replied. "They've got more than a billion people, and they've built extensive underground shelter complexes deep in the mountains of their western regions."

"Are their government leaders moving to those shelters?" General Scheib asked.

"How would we know?" replied the man from the National Reconnaissance Office. "Both of our recon birds looking down at the region have gone dark."

"Like the civilian satellites?" Higgins asked.

The NRO man shook his head. "No, it's more like their optics have been degraded. Maybe by a laser beam."

Jamil tapped a fingernail on the tabletop. "Maybe that's why they've knocked out the other satellites as well. So we couldn't see them heading for their shelters."

Coggins looked down the table at him. "What did you call that doomsday scenario?"

"Sarajevo," said Jamil.

"Sarajevo," she whispered.

ABOARD AIR FORCE One, the President was frowning at his chief of staff. Norman Foster was accustomed to such scowls from his boss: the President did not take kindly to bad news.

"Turn back?" he asked. "Why?"

The two men were facing each other, sitting in plush chairs in the President's private quarters aboard the massive airplane. Foster was tall and lean, his head shaved totally bald, the expression on his face as hard as the President's.

"They think the gooks might hit San Francisco with a nuclear missile," he said.

"Gooks?" The President frowned with distaste. "You mean the North Koreans, don't you?"

"The Democratic People's Republic of Korea," Foster replied, his voice dripping irony. "Yes."

"Why would they do that?"

Foster shrugged his lean shoulders. "Some analyst from the NIC came up with the idea."

"And I'm supposed to turn tail and run home because some academic has a theory?"

"It's a long shot, maybe, but—"

The President jabbed a forefinger at Foster's ice blue eyes. "Norm, I'm not going to run away from a goddamned theory."

"If they do hit 'Frisco . . ." Foster left the thought dangling.

"And if they don't I'll look like a goddamned coward!" the President snapped. "I'm supposed to be the leader here. Hell, the real reason I'm going to San Francisco is to calm the people down over this satellite business."

"They could deliver half a megaton smack on the Cow Palace," Foster said, his voice as calm as if he were quoting stock market quotations.

"Two missiles. That's all they've got, right? We've got a missile defense system, don't we? God knows I've taken enough flak for cutting the funding on that system. Okay, now's the time for them to show what they can do."

"That's crazy," Foster said flatly. No one else in all of Washington, all of the government, would speak to the President that way. But Foster could. He'd been with The Man since the President had been a very junior congressman. He'd guided him through elections and conventions and nominations and finally into the White House.

The President stared at his old friend and adviser, tight-lipped.

"Now look," Foster went on. "You can't trust your life to that cockamamie missile defense system and you know it. Half its tests have been out-and-out failures."

"They've had three successes in a row."

"It's like trying to hit a bullet with another bullet."

"But they've had three successes in a row," the President insisted. "They're working out the kinks in the system."

"And you're going to put your life on the line based on that?"

For a moment the President did not reply. Then he said slowly, "We have military satellites watching their launch pad, don't we?"

Foster nodded tentatively.

"If and when they launch you can pull me out of San Francisco, okay?"

"The missiles can reach 'Frisco half an hour after they're launched. You couldn't even get to Air Force One in half an hour from the Cow Palace."

"I'm not going to run away based on some analyst's theory," the President insisted. "I'm not going to look like a coward. Or a fool."

"But—"

The President ticked off points on his fingers. "One, the idea that they'll try to hit San Francisco is just a theory cooked up by some academic with a computer scenario, right? Two, from the briefings I've had, the North Korean missiles probably couldn't reach San Francisco." He grinned at his old friend. "Y'see, I do listen to those briefings. And I remember 'em."

Foster shook his head. "They do have the range, according to this analyst."

"Three, we have a defense system that can shoot those missiles down while they're still thousands of miles from San Francisco."

"Maybe."

"Four, I'm not turning tail. That's final."

"Final?"

"Final."

Foster knew when to give up. "Okay. You're the boss."

"Damned right I am."

With a sigh, Foster pushed himself up from the seat and, grinning, gave his President a sloppy military salute. The President grinned back at him and snapped off a crisp salute in return.

But as he left the President's compartment, Foster found himself wishing that he didn't have to be on this plane with his boss. He had the distinct feeling that they were flying to their deaths.

I wish we had some satellite data," muttered Sid Golden. "I feel like a blind man groping through this storm."

Golden was not tall, but very broad in the shoulders, with heavy, well-muscled arms and legs. In his youth he had been a good enough baseball player to get a tryout with the Los Angeles Angels. He'd shown up at the camp filled with hopeful excitement, but badly sprained his left knee on the very first day. He went to college that autumn, eventually got his degree in meteorology. Now, his thinning hair barely covering his pate and his belly rounded from years of doughnuts and pizzas, he leaned back in his creaking desk chair and glowered unhappily at the blank electronic map on the wall above his desk.

Ralph Brancusi shook his head. "No satellite data. We're just gonna hafta figure this one out the old-fashioned way."

Golden stuck a finger in his mouth and then held it high, as if testing the wind. To his surprise he felt a slight draft coming from the vent up near the ceiling of his office.

Brancusi laughed. He was short, lean, wiry. Golden secretly envied him his thick waves of dark hair.

"Come on, Sid. We've gotta get an eleven o'clock forecast out on the wire."

"Rain and cold," Golden growled. "Snow in the higher elevations."

"And tomorrow?"

"Who the hell knows? More of the same. The storm's moving inland. It'll probably develop into a full-scale blizzard once it clears the Rockies."

"We oughtta get a warning out, huh?"

"Yeah, sure," said Golden. "I just wish we had some satellite imagery. This is like being back in the mother-humping Stone Age."

General Higgins didn't like Jamil's looks. Must be an Arab, he thought. Or at least Arab descent. Put a turban on him and he'd be a poster boy for those damned terrorists.

Aloud, though, he asked General Scheib, "If they launch those two remaining missiles, can your people shoot them down?"

Scheib glanced at Zuri Coggins before replying, "We'd have a good chance to do that."

Higgins' jaws clenched visibly. "And just what in hell does that mean, Brad, 'a good chance'?"

Sitting up straighter in his chair, Scheib answered, "The system has been declared operational." He paused, then added, "Sir."

Coggins said, "The White House made that pronouncement during the Bush administration. George W."

"Operational," Higgins echoed.

Scheib said, "We've shot down test missiles out over the Pacific from our Fort Greely site in Alaska. Our record isn't one-hundred-percent perfect, of course, but it's improving with every test we fly."

"You're hitting a target missile with a missile of our own, right?" asked the admiral sitting next to General Higgins' aide.

"That's right," Scheib replied. "It's the kinetic kill mode. Bash the warhead with an interceptor vehicle."

From the end of the conference table, Jamil asked, "What about decoys?"

With a slight grimace, General Scheib admitted, "That could be a problem. If the missile releases decoys when it detaches its warhead, our people have to figure out which object has the warhead in it and which ones are dummies."

"How much time do you have to do that?" Zuri Coggins asked.

"If the missile's in midcourse, coasting after its rocket engines burn out, we could have as much as ten, fifteen minutes."

"They can tell which object is the warhead?"

"Not with one-hundred-percent reliability. It's something we're working on."

"Working on?" asked one of the civilians, looking shocked.

"For what it's worth," Jamil said, "if the North Koreans try to reach San Francisco their missiles probably don't have the throw weight to carry both a warhead and decoys."

"You're certain of that?"

Jamil nodded. "Reasonably certain. Of course, if they strike at Honolulu or another target that's not as far as San Francisco, then they could include a set of decoys to spoof the defense."

"Wonderful news," General Higgins muttered.

Coggins turned to the admiral sitting across the table from her. "What about the Aegis ships? Can they shoot down the missiles?"

"If they're in the right position. It's easiest to spot them when they're in the boost phase, with their rocket engines still burning. Once the engines burn out and the missile goes into its midcourse coasting phase, it gets harder."

Coggins nodded uncertainly.

"That's why we're rushing two battle groups into the Sea of Japan. Closer to the launch site, so we'll have more time to shoot at them."

"They wouldn't release any decoys in boost phase," General

Scheib added. "The warhead would still be attached to the main body of the missile."

Higgins said, "So we have your anti-missiles in Alaska and California, and the Navy's Aegis ships in the Pacific."

"Heading for the Sea of Japan," the admiral added.

"And that's it?" Coggins asked.

General Scheib said, "There is one additional possibility."

"What?"

"The Airborne Laser. ABL-1."

"What's Able One?" Coggins asked.

"It's a megawatt-plus laser carried aboard a 747 jet. The laser can shoot down a missile—"

"A ray gun?" Coggins asked, her face clearly showing disbelief.

"It works," Scheib said. "At least, it's worked in flight tests so far. If they can get close enough to the missile. The laser's range is only a hundred miles or so, a hundred and fifty, max."

"So you'd have to get the plane to North Korea for it to be effective," Higgins said.

"It's in Alaska right now, for testing under bad-weather conditions."

"A ray gun," Coggins repeated.

"It's a laser," Scheib corrected. Hunching forward eagerly in his chair, he went on. "Its beam can reach out a hundred miles or so from the plane and hit the missile while it's in boost phase. Deposit a megawatt or more of energy on a square inch of the missile's skin for a second or so and it burns through the aluminum skin. The missile explodes."

"But the missile isn't standing still for you."

Scheib let a tight smile crease his face. "That laser beam strikes with the speed of light. Nothing in the universe goes faster. In the time it takes the beam to cover a thousand miles, the missile moves maybe one foot."

Coggins blinked down the table at the general, absorbing this information. "And the beam blows up the missile?"

"It burns through the missile's skin and goes through to the propellant tanks," Scheib replied. "Remember what happened to the space shuttle *Challenger?* The way it exploded when its propellant tank burned through? Boom! That's what happens to a missile when that laser beam hits it."

"You said the laser plane is in Alaska?" asked Higgins.

"At Elmendorf Air Force Base, sir. The evaluation program calls for tests in a foul-weather environment."

With a huff, Higgins muttered, "Plenty of foul weather up there, God knows."

"The plane operates above the weather, of course. Forty-thousand-foot altitude or higher."

"Then what's the point of a foul-weather environment?" Coggins asked.

"To make sure the plane can operate under zero-zero conditions. Make certain it can get off the ground and up to its operational altitude no matter what the weather conditions on the ground. ABL-1 has to be able to react to a missile threat regardless of the weather where it's based."

"Can you get the plane to a spot where it could intercept the North Korean missiles?" General Higgins asked.

Scheib pecked briefly at the keyboard of his laptop, checked his wristwatch, then looked up. "According to its schedule, it's just about to take off from Elmendorf for a test flight over the northern Pacific. There's a four-hour time difference between here and Alaska."

General Higgins glanced at Zuri Coggins, who nodded.

"All right," said the general. "It isn't a test flight anymore. Get that bird to a spot where it can shoot down those goddamned missiles."

Scheib blinked once. "We'll have to set up a couple of air-to-air refuelings."

"Do it," said Higgins.

"Yessir," Scheib snapped.

"Without violating North Korean airspace," Coggins added. "Or Chinese airspace."

"I understand."

Coggins gave Scheib an appraising look. "Can your plane do the job?"

The general hesitated for a heartbeat, then replied, "I'll need a direct communications link to the plane."

Higgins nodded. "You'll get the comm link. Can the plane do the job?"

"Yes, sir, I believe it can."

"It better," General Higgins growled.

It was a modest split-level house on the cul-de-sac at the end of a quiet, tree-lined street. The Hartunian family had lived in it for nearly sixteen years, ever since their first daughter had been born. Even with the separation and now the divorce proceedings, Sylvia Hartunian had held on to the house. She had raised her daughters here and she had no intention of moving them away from their school, their friends, and the safety of the only home they'd ever known.

Sylvia was a determined woman. She and Harry had been drifting apart for years. At first she thought it was his job at Anson Aerospace. He spent more hours at that laboratory than he did at home. Usually he left for work before the sun came up and arrived home long after the girls had gone to bed. Sylvia had to raise their daughters by herself, just about.

Then Harry started going out to the Mohave Desert. Test operations, he claimed. Classified work; he couldn't tell her anything about it. He'd be gone for several days at a time. Weekends, sometimes. Sylvia began to get suspicious, but at first she couldn't picture Harry fooling around with another woman. Harry was a nerd, after all. He was more in love with his damned high-tech hardware than any human being, including her.

As the weeks turned into months, though, and stretched into years, she became convinced it was more than his work that was separating them.

It was when Harry was hospitalized after the explosion at the test facility that Sylvia realized she didn't really have any feelings for him anymore. She went to the hospital and it was like she was visiting a stranger. She couldn't even cry about it. She had married an engineer, a man who couldn't or wouldn't show his feelings; maybe he didn't really have any. She'd thought she loved him. She bore him two daughters. But now it was all gone. Turned to ice. He lay there unconscious on his hospital bed, burned and battered, and she felt like she was looking at a stranger.

When he came home to recuperate Sylvia kept her distance from him. She made up the guest room for him and even after he was completely healed and had gone back to work, she refused to let him into her bed. It was over. Even the girls knew it. They knew their father was a cold, unfeeling man.

When he finally admitted that he'd had an affair with one of the women at his laboratory, Sylvia told him to get out. He acted as if he were numb, as if he'd expected them to break up but couldn't take the first step himself. He left without an argument, without raising his voice even once, which angered Sylvia even more.

But that was all in the past. Sylvia settled down to the task of raising her teenaged daughters by herself and found that she enjoyed being on her own, with no one to contradict her. She could sit up in bed and read all night if she wanted to.

She was still reasonably attractive, she thought. At least that's what her friends told her. A little overweight, but men liked *zaftig* women with generous bosoms. Still, she dated very little. It was just too much of a chore, too much of a stupid ritual. She'd been through it all with Harry and found that she didn't really have any interest in going that route again.

Sylvia took a job at their congresswoman's local office. It didn't pay much, but with the child support money that Harry paid every month, they were getting by nicely.

Today she was especially happy. She had a surprise for her daughters. She'd made all the arrangements and everything was set.

At the breakfast table she announced, "No school today."

Her daughters looked up from their cereal bowls in surprise.

"How come?" asked the elder, Vickie. Harry had insisted on naming her after the founder of Anson Aerospace, as if that had made any difference in his career advancement.

"I got permission from your teachers to keep you out of class today."

"What's going on, Mom?" Denise asked.

"We're flying to San Francisco and staying overnight in a hotel," Sylvia told them. Beaming, she explained, "Congresswoman McClintock has given me three tickets to the big rodeo at the Cow Palace."

"Rodeo?" Clear distaste showed on Denise's fourteen-year-old face.

"Horses and all that smell," said Vickie.

Her smile even bigger, Sylvia explained, "You don't understand. The President of the United States is going to officially open the rodeo. He's giving a speech and we're going to be sitting in the front row!"

"The President?" Denise looked truly surprised.

But Vickie moaned, "That phony. He said he was going to start a big green-energy program and he hasn't done a thing."

"Congress hasn't voted on his energy program yet," Sylvia said firmly.

The girls looked at each other. "I guess," Vickie said with a resigned shrug.

Sylvia told them, "You'll be the envy of all your friends when you tell them you were right there with the President."

"I guess," they said in unison, equally unenthusiastic.

Teenagers, thought Sylvia.

Lieutenant Colonel Karen Christopher came through the cockpit hatch without needing to duck and slid easily into the pilot's seat. It was still misty gray outside, but visibility was good enough for takeoff. She remembered one of the older jocks telling her that when the 747 was first introduced to the commercial airlines, the FAA had to raise its ceiling limits for takeoffs because the huge plane's cockpit sat so high above the ground it was sometimes in cloud while the ground was clear enough for smaller planes to take off.

As she pulled the safety harness over her slim shoulders, her copilot, Major Kaufman, squeezed into the cockpit and settled his bulk into the right-hand seat, red-nosed and sniffling.

"That's some cold you've got," said Colonel Christopher.

"Alaska," he said. She thought it sounded sullen. Major Kaufman did not like the fact that Karen had been jammed down his throat by headquarters, forcing him to relinquish command of the plane.

He sneezed wetly. That's right, Colonel Christopher grumbled silently, spread your damned cold to the rest of us.

She pulled her plastic flight helmet over her short-cropped hair and plugged it into the communications console.

"You want me to take her out?" Kaufman asked.

Christopher realized that the major knew she had only a half dozen hours of piloting a 747. "I'll do it," she said tightly. "I can fly anything that has wings on it, Obie."

She saw his eyes flash again. He doesn't like his nickname, she realized. But Kaufman said only, "You're the boss."

She said nothing. Stick to business, she told herself. He'll just have to get used to being in the right-hand seat.

"ABL-1 ready to start engines," she said into the pin mike that nearly brushed her lips. Out of the corner of her eye she watched Kaufman as he pulled up the takeoff checklist on the control panel's central display and started scrolling it down the screen.

"ABL-1, you are clear to start engines," said the flight controller's clipped voice in her earphones.

Turning to Kaufman, she said, "Spool 'em up."

With a bleary nod, the major murmured, "Starting one."

As the first of the plane's four turbojet engines whined to life, the flight controller called, "ABL-1, message incoming for you from Andrews."

Colonel Christopher felt puzzled. "Andrews Air Force Base?"

"Relayed from the Pentagon."

"Better pipe it to me," she said.

A series of clicks. Then a mechanical voice started dictating a formal military order. Computer-synthesized audio, Colonel Christopher realized. The voice droned through the date, routing, and classification level: Top Secret.

Then it said, "From: Major General Bradley B. Scheib, deputy commander, MDA. To: Lieutenant Colonel Karen R. Christopher, command pilot, ABL-1.

"A nuclear device apparently launched from North Korea has been exploded in orbit. All commercial satellites have been either knocked out completely or seriously degraded.

"You will proceed to a site to be designated over the Sea of Japan and orbit until further orders. Navigational information is

being transmitted in a separate order. You will avoid violating territorial airspace of the Democratic People's Republic of Korea and/or
the People's Republic of China. You will attack and destroy any ballistic missiles launched from DPRK. Confirm receipt of this order
immediately."

Christopher looked at Major Kaufman, who sat wide-eyed and
suddenly pale.

Swallowing hard, she said into her mike, "Order received and
understood. Please confirm to General Scheib."

"It's going to take a little time, Colonel," said the flight controller's voice. "The commsats are overloaded with traffic."

"Send the confirmation," Colonel Christopher said in the hard
voice of command she had learned at the Air Force Academy.

"Yes, ma'am."

Major Kaufman seemed frozen in his seat. "Shoot down any
missiles launched from North Korea? Are they crazy?"

"Get on with the engine start," she snapped. "Maybe they are
crazy, but orders are orders."

As Kaufman punched up the second engine, Christopher un-
buckled her safety harness and got to her feet. "I'd better talk to the
chief nerd."

But as she stepped through the hatch and into the area where
the navigator and communications stations were, she wasn't thinking of the chief of the laser crew or of her surly, suddenly frightened
copilot, or even of the possibility that her orders meant a war was
starting. She was thinking of the last time she had seen Major General Bradley B. Scheib.

"YOU'RE OUT OF uniform, Colonel."

She smiled at the general. "So are you, sir."

She was standing nude in the bathroom doorway while he
lay on the thoroughly rumpled king-sized bed. The motel was a
little on the seedy side, but Karen hadn't minded that. Over the
months since she'd fallen in love with Brad Scheib she'd become

accustomed to being furtive. It even added a touch of spice to their relationship. Brad was married; she'd known that from the outset, but she knew how to make him happy and his preppy socialite wife didn't.

The Air Force brass did not like it when an officer had an affair with a married officer. But there was this handsome hunk of a man, so serious, so troubled when she'd first met him. And now he was smiling and contented. At least, most of the time when they were together. But he wasn't smiling at the moment.

She went to the bed and snuggled beside him. He wrapped his arms around her. For long moments neither of them spoke a word.

At last he half-whispered, "I'm up for the deputy director post at the MDA."

Delighted, she asked, "That means a second star, doesn't it?"

He nodded. Only then did she realize how grave his tone was.

"You want the job, don't you?"

"I sure do."

"So you'll be moving to Washington, then. It's okay. I can get there often enough."

"I don't think so, Karen," he said.

She suddenly understood where he was heading, but she didn't want to believe it. "What do you mean?"

"There's going to be an investigation."

"Of you?"

He shook his head. "Of you. My wife . . ." His voice trailed off.

"She ratted you out?" Karen felt anger seething up inside her.

He wouldn't look into her eyes. "No. She ratted *you* out."

"What?"

"She got one of her Georgetown friends to tip off the AG that you're having an affair with a married officer. She didn't say with who. She's too devious for that. She expects you to finger me once the AG investigation starts."

Karen pulled away from him. "The Advocate General's office is coming after me?"

"They'll want to know who you're sleeping with." His voice was misery personified. "If you tell them, I can say good-bye to the MDA job and the second star."

"But if I don't . . ."

"They can't do much to you," he'd said. "A slap on the wrist, that's all."

A slap on the wrist, she thought. They bounced me out of the B-2 squadron and gave me this bus driver's job with a bunch of tech geeks. Some slap on the wrist.

But now this bus she was driving might be heading into a shooting war. Karen almost smiled at the irony of it.

C olonel Christopher saw that Lieutenant Sharmon and the communications officer were staring at her.

"You heard our orders?" she asked.

Sharmon said, "I got the navigation data. Fed it into the flight computer." He looked uneasy, almost scared.

"Good. We'll need a couple of refuelings on the way. Must be a ten-, twelve-hour flight."

Nodding, the navigator said, "Approximately ten hours, Colonel. They're workin' out the refueling rendezvous points at Andrews. They'll send the fixes while we're in flight."

The communications officer, red-haired Captain Brick O'Banion, said grimly, "Looks like we're flying into a war."

Karen felt her insides clutch. "Looks that way," she said. Taking a deep breath, she tried to calm herself. "All right. Call the tech chief up here. This isn't a test flight anymore."

AS THE PLANE'S first engine rumbled to life Delany complained, "Christ, it's colder inside this bucket than outside."

Harry agreed. Cold and damp. Not good for my back, he thought as he followed Delany and the rest of the laser team past

the color-coded pipes and gleaming stainless steel tankage toward
the cramped compartment that was their station during takeoffs
and landings. His nose twitched with the faint iron tang of iodine.
Like dried blood.

A leak? Harry asked himself, alarmed. That's all we need; the
damned stuff is corrosive enough to damage your eyes and lungs.

"Wally!" he called to Rosenberg, three bodies ahead of him.
"You check the tank pressures yet?"

"Last night," Rosenberg called over his shoulder. "Like I do
every night before a mission. We all went over the whole damned
system, remember?"

The night before, Harry and the rest of the team had inspected
every part of the laser system, from the bulbous turret in the plane's
nose to the COIL fuel tanks in the tail. Every pipe. Every electronics console. Every gauge and switch and display screen. Routine.
They'd done it the night before every flight.

"Check 'em again," he said.

"Now?" Rosenberg turned around to face Harry, forcing Taki
Nakamura to sidle past him in the narrow passageway.

Harry thought, If I make him check the pressures now it'll delay
our takeoff by half an hour or more. The new pilot won't like that.
He can check it while we're flying out to the test range.

"Once we're at cruising altitude," he said.

Rosenberg nodded, muttering, "There's nothing wrong with the
friggin' tank pressures."

Yeah, Harry retorted silently. There was nothing wrong with
them when the damned rig blew up in the desert, either.

They got to their compartment, sat in the padded seats, and
began to strap in. There were twelve seats, six facing six. They had
been scavenged from a commercial airliner, but the compartment
was so tight that they couldn't recline; the seat backs were smack
against the bulkheads. The safety straps were Air Force issue: not
merely a lap belt but a harness that went over the shoulders as well.
Diminutive Taki looked like a lost little waif in the gray webbing.

The intercom hummed briefly, then, "Mr. Hartunian, could you come up to the flight deck, please?"

Harry's brows shot up. "What the hell for?" he wondered aloud.

"Maybe she wants to give you a flying lesson," Delany wise-cracked.

"Or maybe she's lonely up there," said Rosenberg, with a smirk.

She's got a copilot, a communications officer, and a navigator up there, Harry thought. All men. And all of them a lot younger than me. She's not lonely.

Puzzled, he unlocked his safety harness and went to the forward hatch of the compartment. As he did, he heard the whine of the second of the plane's four turbojet engines start up and quickly turn into a roar. The plane began to vibrate noticeably.

Ducking through the hatch, Harry made his way past the plane's minuscule galley and up the ladder that led to the flight deck. A lanky young black lieutenant was on his feet up there, tall enough that his closely cropped hair nearly brushed the overhead. Harry had never seen him before this morning. He recognized the communications officer, though: a stubby little red-haired captain seated at his board full of dials and screens, headphones clamped to his ears.

The lieutenant introduced himself. "I'm the new navigator, Lieutenant Sharmon. You must be Mr. Hartunian."

"Harry."

Sharmon nodded and put out his hand. "I'm Jon. Without an aitch."

"Jon," Harry said, grasping the lieutenant's proffered hand. The kid's grip was firm, his long fingers wrapped around Harry's hand.

"I'll tell Colonel Christopher you're here."

One by one the plane's engines were growling into life. Harry stood uneasily next to the communications console while Lieutenant Sharmon ducked through the cockpit hatch. Harry caught a glimpse of the control panel, studded with instruments and sensor screens, and the windshield above it. It still looked miserably gray and foggy outside.

Maybe they've canceled the flight, Harry thought. But then he countered, So why's she powering up the engines?

Lieutenant Colonel Christopher came out and forced a smile for him. She was small, petite really, but he could see that she had an adult's body beneath her blue fatigues. Dark hair, bright, intelligent eyes. Really pretty, he realized once again. For a moment he thought she looked familiar, as if he'd seen her somewhere before. But that's impossible, Harry thought. Our paths haven't crossed before this. Still, he couldn't shake the nagging thought that they had.

"Mr. Hartunian," she said without offering to shake hands.

Harry nodded. The colonel looked as grim as death.

"We have a situation on our hands," she said.

"A situation?" Harry asked.

"I just got a top-priority message relayed from Washington. There's been an attack on our orbiting satellites and—"

"An attack?"

"A missile fired from North Korea detonated a nuclear device in geosynchronous orbit several hours ago. Just about every civilian satellite around the world has been knocked out of service."

Harry gaped at her, his heart suddenly pumping wildly. "From North Korea?"

"We've been ordered to proceed to a position over the Sea of Japan and be prepared to shoot down any more missiles that the North Koreans launch." Christopher spoke crisply, with no hesitation, no doubts in her tone.

"But we can't . . . I mean, we're supposed to be testing the laser. We're not ready for a shooting war."

Colonel Christopher said, "You techies are never ready for reality, but ready or not, Mr. Hartunian, those are our orders. Get your people on the mark. Make sure that ray gun of yours works right."

I t had started to rain. Looking out the window of the penthouse suite's sitting room, the Secretary of State saw brittle dry leaves gusting across the pavement far below. The afternoon sky was clouded over, gray and gloomy. Yet she felt excited, eager.

How often had she used this suite over the past few years? she wondered idly. It fit perfectly her need for an informal meeting place, a spot where she could chat quietly in privacy with men or women who preferred to stay safely out of the glare of publicity, a place where she could develop the back-channel contacts of her own, without the State Department bureaucracy's officious meddling. The Jefferson was perfect: downtown, close to the White House, old, elegant, and very discreet.

After leaving the White House that morning she had changed her attire for this meeting: a quietly elegant pantsuit of pearl gray over a tailored white blouse, with a small choker of pink pearls and matching earrings. She turned away from the rain-swept windows, thinking, He'll come. He's got to come.

The phone on the desk buzzed, and she rushed to it before it could ring twice. The face of the young security woman down in the hotel's lobby appeared on the screen. "Mr. Quang is on his way up, Madam Secretary."

The Secretary's pulse quickened. "Good."

In less than a minute the doorbell chimed. The Secretary of State crossed the thickly carpeted sitting room and admitted a portly, blank-faced Chinese. He was wearing a dark business suit, white starched shirt, pale blue necktie—and a tiny red star pin on his lapel.

He bowed slightly as she ushered him into the sitting room. The Secretary of State said, "Mr. Quang, it's good of you to come on such short notice."

His bland expression warmed slightly into a tentative smile. "Madam Secretary, there's no need for formalities," he said in perfect American English. "I understand the gravity of the situation."

Gesturing to one of the comfortable armchairs in front of the dark, unlit fireplace, the Secretary of State said, "We've been unable to establish a reliable communications link with Beijing. Your ambassador seems unable to give us a clear picture of what's going on there."

Quang nodded as he settled into the chair. "I would think there is great turmoil in Beijing at this moment."

"They prefer not to talk to us?"

"They prefer" —he hesitated a heartbeat, searching for a word— "not to commit themselves."

The Secretary of State took the armchair facing Quang's and studied his round, almond-eyed face. How many times have we met like this? she asked herself. How many times have we cut through the red tape and talked clearly and honestly to one another? She had known Quang since she'd first visited Beijing, back when she'd been a law student with political ambitions and he a fast-rising industrial tycoon. She realized that, in truth, she owed much of her advancement to the private, authoritative back-channel link he offered to the highest levels of the Chinese government.

"Have you been able to reach the chairman?" asked the Secretary of State. "Or any of the council members?"

With a modest smile, Quang replied, "As you know, I am merely a businessman. I have no position in the government."

"You are the chairman's brother-in-law."

His smile widened slightly. "A brother-in-law is usually without much influence."

The Secretary leaned slightly toward him, her fists clenched on her lap. "You're the best link I have to the chairman. You've got to help us avert a nuclear war!"

Quang's smile faded. "I will do whatever I can, of course."

"Did the People's Republic of China provide nuclear weapons to North Korea?"

"Of course not."

"Are you certain?"

Quang's eyes shifted slightly, then refocused on the Secretary. "I can tell you this much. Three nuclear warheads were smuggled into the DPRK from Russia last month."

"Last month! And your government didn't inform us!"

"We confirmed the information only two days ago. The council was debating what our response should be when the Koreans set off one of the warheads in orbit."

"We're on the brink of war, for god's sake!"

Shaking his head ever so slightly, Quang replied, "The People's Republic of China has no intention of starting a war with you."

"Nor we with China, but . . ."

Quang raised a stubby finger. "But you wish to strike at the Koreans."

"We've got to do something," the Secretary said. "They have two more missiles. And from what you say, those missiles are armed with nuclear bombs."

"Pyongyang has sent troops to capture the rebels."

"Troops? They should be sending in an air strike to knock out those missiles before the terrorists launch them!"

"They are not terrorists," Quang said flatly. "Do not fall into the trap of painting all your enemies with the same brush. That's how you got into Iraq, remember?"

"What are they then?"

"A faction of the DPRK army, apparently."

"What do they hope to gain by destroying the whole world's satellites?" the Secretary asked.

Quang shrugged his round shoulders. "That we will learn once Pyongyang's troops have captured them."

"And in the meantime they've got two nuclear-armed missiles that can reach Hawaii! Or maybe even San Francisco!"

"Or Beijing," Quang said tightly. "Or Shanghai. Believe me, we are just as concerned about this as you are."

"So why aren't you *doing* something about it?"

"The council is considering several options. We believe the missiles are under the control of a rebel faction of the North Korean army. The government in Pyongyang, such as it is," Quang added with a sardonic sneer, "is seeking to avoid an outright civil war. They want to take the rebels with as little violence as possible."

"They're going to launch those missiles," the Secretary said, her voice flat and hard. "Unless somebody stops them, they're going to launch both those nukes."

"If they attack China we will obliterate them," Quang said flatly. "They know that."

"But if they attack the United States . . ."

Shifting uneasily in the armchair, Quang said, "That would be regrettable. And an American strike on the DPRK would be even more regrettable."

"What do you expect us to do?"

"Think before you act. An American invasion of the Democratic People's Republic of Korea is no more acceptable to China today than it was in 1950. And a strike against the DPRK would force us to retaliate . . . to say nothing of the effect the fallout would have on Japan."

"We wouldn't have to nuke them, necessarily," the Secretary of State said. But her tone was subdued, tentative.

Quang replied, "If you attack North Korea in any way the pressures on my government to protect our Asian neighbor would be overwhelming. It is a matter of face, as well as realpolitik."

The Secretary studied her old friend's unreadable expresson for several moments. Then, "You'd launch a nuclear strike against us?"

Quang stared back at her for a long, silent moment. Then he murmured, "You must realize that there are factions within our council as well. We have our own hard-liners, you must understand."

"But that's just what the terrorists want! Don't you see, they *want* a nuclear Armageddon!"

"As I told you, we do not believe they are terrorists. They do not seek nuclear holocaust."

"Then what *do* they want?"

"Control of the government in Pyongyang. Reunification with South Korea—under their terms. Economic aid. Neutralization of Japan. The removal of American bases and influence in East Asia."

The Secretary sagged back in her chair. It was her turn to be silent now, thinking that what the North Koreans wanted suited the Chinese government perfectly. A stalking horse, she said to herself. Could Beijing be behind this? If we react against North Korea, will the Chinese use it as an excuse for striking back at us?

"They want the impossible," she said at last. "What they're going to get is pulverized."

"Do not overreact, I beg of you."

"If they nuke an American city . . ." The Secretary shook her head. "You saw our reaction to 9/11. And that was only a couple of buildings that were destroyed. If they wipe out Honolulu . . . or San Francisco . . . if they kill the President. . . . For god's sake!"

Quang leaned forward in his chair. The Secretary noticed a thin bead of perspiration trickling down his left cheek.

"Madam Secretary," he said, his tone suddenly stiffly formal, "I agreed to meet with you because I—like you—wish to avert a nuclear confrontation between our two peoples."

The Secretary nodded warily. There was more coming, she knew.

"However," Quang went on, "if the United States attacks the Democratic People's Republic of Korea, my government will be forced to respond."

"So we're supposed to sit still while they nuke a couple of our cities?"

"The rebels will be caught and dealt with. Do not attack North Korea, I beg of you. If you do, China will be forced to respond."

"And the Russians watch us destroy each other."

"This has always been the weakness of the retaliation policy."

"Mutual assured destruction," the Secretary murmured.

"A policy intended to deter nuclear attack. It has worked very well between your nation and ours."

"And the Russians."

"Yes," Quang agreed. "But when fanatics gain nuclear weapons, such a policy becomes useless. Mutual suicide."

With that, Quang got to his feet. The Secretary rose on shaky legs and walked him to the door. They exchanged meaningless words, and he left her alone in the sumptuous suite, leaning against the tightly shut door, wondering if the world was indeed coming to an end.

But then she straightened and headed for the phone. The President's off on a macho trip to San Francisco, she told herself. The Vice President's safely in the National Redoubt, as if saving his worthless hide means anything. I've got to get to the Speaker of the House and Senator Yañez. Somebody's got to take control of this situation. Somebody's got to start acting presidential, and it might as well be me.

Phyllis Mathiessen was more annoyed than worried. Well, no, she really was worried—about the dinner she was planning for tomorrow evening. This was the third supermarket she'd driven to this morning, and none of them had pecans. She needed pecans for the pie.

Feeling nettled as she pushed her grocery cart along the fresh-produce aisle, she couldn't for the life of her understand why a big supermarket chain like Lukkabee's couldn't keep pecans on the blessed shelves. Pecans! It's not like she wanted something exotic. Just plain old pecans.

She saw one of the store's employees staring glumly at a row of empty display cases, where they usually kept the lettuce and cab-bage and carrots. The shelves were bare. The man looked as if he had nothing to do. His kelly green bib overalls were spotless, as if he hadn't lifted a crate or carried a single package all morning.

Phyllis knew the man, at least well enough to smile at him when they passed in the store's aisles. What was his name? She hated to peer at the tag pinned to the chest of his overalls, but she couldn't for the life of her remember—

Giovanni! That was his name. Was it his first name, though, or his last?

"Good morning, Mrs. Mathiessen," he said with a toothy smile. He was short, bald, round of face and body.

"Good morning, Mr. Giovanni," said Phyllis.

"If you're looking for lettuce, this morning's order hasn't come in yet." Giovanni glanced at his wristwatch. "They're awful late today."

"No," she said. "I want some pecans. I'm going to bake a pecan pie."

Giovanni made an elaborate shrug. "They were supposed to come in this morning, with the lettuce and the rest of the produce."

"Will they be in later?"

Another shrug. "Mr. Andrews, he's been on the phone all morning. Called the distributor. Called the trucking company. Called Mr. Lukkabee hisself, got him out of bed."

"What's the matter?" Phyllis asked.

"Everything's all screwed up. Nobody's computers are working. The trucking company says they can't even tell where their trucks are because the GPS ain't working."

Phyllis had the vague notion that GPS had something to do with giving you directions when you were driving. Her husband had been hinting that he'd like one for Christmas.

"So you won't have any pecans?"

"Maybe later today. I dunno."

Phyllis tried to hide her annoyance. After all, it wasn't Giovanni's fault. But she blew her stack half an hour later when she pulled into the gas station and the pumps weren't working. The warning light on her gas gauge was already blinking, and before she could pull out of line she got blocked in by another car behind her. When the impatient old jerk behind her started blasting his horn she jumped out of her car in a fury and told him to behave himself or she would call the police. It took nearly ten minutes to untangle the jam and get on her way home.

She ran out of gas on the way, right in the middle of the high-way. Nervous as a cat, she glided the Cadillac to the shoulder of the road as cars and trucks swooped past her way above the speed limit. Then she couldn't get her husband on her cell phone. Or anybody else. Not even the AAA. The phone seemed to be dead. Phyllis broke into tears when a police car coasted to a stop behind her, its lights blinking red and blue.

She had never had a ticket before in her whole life. And it was starting to snow.

D o you trust him?"

Zuri Coggins finished pouring herself a cup of coffee before she looked up at General Higgins. The general had called for a coffee break, and almost immediately a pair of army tech sergeants had entered the situation room rolling a cart bearing three stainless steel urns, Styrofoam cups, and two trays of buns and pastries. He must have had the sergeants on call outside in the corridor all morning, she thought.

"Trust who?" she asked the general.

His eyes flicking across the room to where Michael Jamil still sat at the foot of the conference table, pecking away at his iPhone, Higgins whispered, "Him. The Arab."

"I believe he's Lebanese," Coggins replied.

"Lebanese, Arab, they're all the same."

General Higgins had removed his tunic and loosened his necktie. His shirt was wrinkled and he looked sweaty. He could stand to lose twenty or thirty pounds, Coggins thought. But despite his physical appearance Higgins wore four stars on his collar and the Joint Chiefs of Staff had appointed him to head this emergency action team.

"He was born here," she added.

Higgins nodded as he picked up a sticky bun. "He's an academic. I don't trust academics. They always think they know everything, but they don't have any real-world experience. Ivory-tower eggheads."

Coggins felt a mild tic of surprise. She hadn't heard the term "egghead" since a graduate class in the history of American politics, nearly ten years earlier.

"Yet he's made an important point, don't you think? If the North Koreans are targeting San Francisco . . ."

Higgins snapped up half the bun in one bite. His mouth full, he still answered, "Scheib thinks that's bullshit, and Scheib knows more about missiles than that Arab kid."

Coggins nodded halfheartedly and stepped away from the general, as much to avoid the spray of crumbs from his mouth as to disengage from what could become an argument. I'm not here to argue, she told herself. I'm here to report to the National Security Advisor on what this team thinks we should be doing.

Can we shoot down their missiles? she wondered. And if we do, would the North Koreans consider it an act of war? Would the Chinese come in?

For several moments she watched Jamil intently hunching over his iPhone. He was the only person still sitting at the table; everyone else was standing in little knots of two or three, either at the front of the conference room, where the coffee cart was, or toward the rear, where the doors led to restrooms out along the corridor.

Abruptly, she went to her own chair and opened her minicomputer. Not much bigger than a paperback book, it still had the power and speed of the best laptops. The Department of Defense's internal data network did not depend entirely on satellite links; it was connected across the continent by hardened landlines. With a few touches of the little machine's keyboard, Coggins pulled up Michael Jamil's unclassified dossier.

Born in Baltimore, she saw. Only son of Lebanese parents who fled their country during the civil war there. They were already living in Baltimore when Israel invaded Lebanon. Graduated magna cum laude from Johns Hopkins in information technology. Hired by DoD, moved up to the Defense Intelligence Agency, appointed to National Intelligence Council last year. A bright young man, Coggins decided. Then she realized that Jamil was only a year younger than she. Well, she thought, I'm a bright young woman.

Clicking the mini closed, she got up from her chair and walked down the table toward Jamil. He was sitting alone at the foot of the table; it seemed as if all the others—military and civilians alike—were shunning him.

He looked up as she sat next to him. He seemed surprised, almost perplexed.

"I have a mini, if you need something more powerful than your phone," Coggins said.

His expression changed. Still surprised, but now pleasantly so.

"I was just going over the figures for the Taepodong-2," he said, almost apologetically. "General Scheib doesn't believe it, but those birds could reach San Francisco, I'm pretty sure."

With a slight smile, Coggins said, " 'Pretty sure' isn't going to impress Scheib. Or General Higgins."

"I guess not," Jamil admitted. His voice was soft, but he was clearly upset. "The thing is, I always thought that military men based their plans on the worst that an enemy can do, not on what they hope the enemy's likely to do."

"That makes sense."

"We ought to recommend that the President stay out of San Francisco."

"We've apprised him of the possibility."

Jamil shook his head. "Not strong enough. It's got to be a recommendation from this emergency committee. Full strength."

"I'm afraid General Higgins doesn't put much faith in your calculations," she said, as gently as she could.

"He's a jackass, then."

Coggins broke into a laugh. "That may be, but he's chairing this group."

Jamil hunched forward in his chair, toward her. "You're inside the White House. Can't you make a recommendation to the National Security Advisor? On your own?"

Her laughter cut off. He was serious. Deadly serious. And he was putting her on the spot.

"I . . . I don't know . . ."

He slumped back again. "You don't believe me either."

"It's not that," she said quickly. "It's just . . . well, if you're wrong, I'd look awfully stupid, wouldn't I?"

Very seriously, Jamil replied, "No, you'd look awfully stupid if the President gets killed in a nuclear attack on San Francisco."

She stared at him. He was intent, totally convinced that she had to stick her neck out and urge the National Security Advisor to get the President to turn back. Not his neck, Coggins told herself. Mine.

"All right," General Higgins bawled from the front of the room, where the snack cart was parked. "We're out of sticky buns. Let's get back to work."

Look! It's starting to snow!"

Charley Ingersoll was passing an eighteen-wheeler when his eight-year-old son, Charley Jr., gave out his delighted squeak. It was getting close to noon, they were hours away from Missoula, and now snow was falling.

"It's only a few flakes," said his wife, Martha, sitting in the right-hand seat of the SUV. Charley Jr. and Little Martha, four, had the second bench to themselves. The rear was piled high with luggage and toys.

"Can we make a snowman?" Little Martha asked.

Cheerily, her mother answered, "If it's deep enough when we get home, dearie."

Snow, Charley thought. Bad enough to be driving all the distance from Grangeville with the two kids yapping every inch of the way. Now they've gotta give me snow to deal with.

He tapped the radio button but got nothing except hissing static. Hadn't been able to raise Sirius Radio or XM all morning. He started to fiddle with the dial, trying to get a local station, but Martha slapped his hand gently.

"You pay attention to your driving, Charley. I'll find us some music."

"Put on one of my CDs!" Charley Jr. piped.

Over her shoulder, Martha said, "Your father wants to get the weather report, dearie. Isn't that right, Charley?"

He nodded vigorously. The snow didn't seem very serious, but out here in the mountains you had to be extra careful. He remembered seeing a sign a few miles back for an RV camp. If the weather turns really bad, Charley thought, we can turn in at one of them.

Charley craned his neck to look at the sky. Some heavy gray clouds out there, but still plenty of blue. Might just be a snow shower. Or if it's a real storm, maybe we'll outrun it. Storms usually come in from the west. We're doing seventy, that's faster than any storm can travel.

He had put the SUV on cruise control once they had hit an area of the highway where there were only a few other cars on the road. Charley didn't mind traffic, although he couldn't use the cruise control when he had to keep hitting the brakes all the time. It's those dratted semis, he complained silently. Specially when it rains, they sploosh up beside you like a dratted tidal wave.

Martha found a local station playing country and western songs. Charley relaxed a little. If there was a bad storm coming they'd be putting out a warning instead of playing their regular music. He decided to wait until the top of the hour, when they played the news and weather. And sports. Martha didn't know it, but he had bet money on the Seahawks.

W e're at cruising altitude." Colonel Christopher's voice came through the intercom speaker in the compartment's overhead.

Harry clicked his safety harness release and the straps slid into their receptacles on the back of his seat. To Rosenberg he said, "Check the tank pressures, Wally."

Rosenberg nodded sullenly and got to his feet.

"Angel," Harry said to Reyes, "I want you to purge the oxygen line."

Reyes gave him a questioning look. "Purge it?"

Standing in the narrow aisle between the facing seats, Harry said, "There was a speck of grease in the oxy line when the rig blew up. I want to make sure the line's absolutely clean."

"That was three years ago, Harry! We haven't had any trouble since."

"Because we've been extra careful," Harry said. "Purge the line, Angie."

With a slight grin, Reyes got out of his chair. The top of his head barely rose above Harry's shoulder. "Okay, *jefe*. I'll purge it." Then he added. "Again."

Nakamura came to her feet, too, even shorter than Reyes. "I'll check out the board."

She had the most critical job, Harry knew. The battle management system had to find the boosting missile and lock the laser onto it. He thought of little Taki as a sharpshooter. But her rifle weighed tons and took up most of the 747's interior volume.

This was supposed to be a test flight, Harry said to himself. We don't have a full crew aboard and we're supposed to shoot down a real missile. A real missile that's carrying a real hydrogen bomb. He wondered if they could do it. Make it work, Anson had told him. But now it's more than the company depending on us. This time it's for real.

As his teammates slowly started for the compartment's hatch, Harry said, "Wait a minute. I've got something to tell you."

They looked at him questioningly.

"The North Koreans set off a nuclear bomb in orbit this morning, and it looks like they've got more missiles ready to fire at us."

"Us?"

"You mean America?"

Delany growled, "Goddam gooks, we should've wiped them out long ago!"

Nodding slowly, Harry said, "We've been ordered to fly to the Sea of Japan and shoot down any missiles the North Koreans launch."

"Shoot down real missiles?" Taki's voice was breathless with surprise.

"That's right," Harry said.

"They can't order us!" Delany snapped, nearly shouting. "We're civilians, for chrissake! They can't—"

"The North Koreans have missiles with nuclear warheads. They're getting set to fire them at American cities. We've got to stop them."

"Now?" Angel Reyes asked. "On this flight?"

"Right."

"How many missiles?" asked Rosenberg.

"Don't know."

"How far do we have to go?"

"As far as it takes," said Harry. "So let's make sure that everything—I mean *everything*—is in perfect condition. We're heading into a real battle engagement."

Delany looked stunned. He sagged back down onto his seat. Rosenberg, for once, didn't have a wisecrack to offer.

"Let's get to work," Harry said.

Taki started for the forward hatch; Monk Delany got to his feet and followed her. Harry and the two other men headed aft. The plane's engines throbbed smoothly; Harry barely felt any vibration as the jumbo jet lumbered through the stratosphere.

The laser bay was crammed with pipes and wiring. Harry insisted on keeping the area as neat as possible, but there were always loops of wire festooned from the overhead, spare parts tucked here and there along the narrow walkway. The clutter was inevitable: Harry remembered the old maxim that if a lab was spic-and-span, it meant no creative work was going on in it.

Rosenberg and Reyes went about their tasks, barely saying a word. It's hit them hard, Harry realized. One minute we're on a routine test flight and the next we're heading into a war. He wondered why he didn't feel excited. Or scared. He felt numb instead. It's too much, he thought. It's just too fucking much.

Slowly Harry walked the length of the laser bay, looking over every pipe, every wire, every weld on the tanks that held the volatile chemicals. Most of the laser itself was hidden behind all the plumbing; only its active lasing cavity was clearly visible and available for immediate adjustment or repair.

He stared at the lasing cavity. Built of thick slabs of solid copper with water-cooling channels drilled through them, that chamber was where the chemical energy of the combined iodine and oxygen was converted into megawatts of infrared energy. Leading into it was another copper section, built like a miniature wind tunnel: that's where the mixed chemicals roared through at supersonic speed, entered the laser cavity and gave up their stored energy, then flowed out to be vented outside the plane.

Harry remembered the first time the Anson scientists had shown a blueprint of the COIL system to a group of visiting Air Force brass. One of the colonels stared at the wind tunnel section and shook his head.

"That's a lousy design for a rocket," he said. "You'll never get much thrust out of it."

The scientists laughed tolerantly and explained that the wind tunnel wasn't designed for thrust. It was intended to feed the iodine and oxygen into the chamber where the lasing action took place.

Now, flying toward the Sea of Japan at more than thirty thousand feet, heading into a possible war, Harry studied the laser assembly with the critical eye of a worried father. It'll work, he told himself. We'll make it work.

But in his mind's eye he saw the rig in the desert explode into white-hot flames, saw Quintana being roasted alive, felt the agony of his ribs cracking as he slammed against the back wall of the control room.

It should've been me, not Pete. I should have been out there. I should have checked the oxy line myself, made sure it was clean.

He shook his head to clear the nightmare vision. Well, Harry said to himself, if she blows today it won't matter where I'm standing. We'll all be dead.

L ieutenant Sharmon unconsciously pressed one long finger against his headphone as the data for their first refueling rendezvous came through. The information was being fed into his navigation computer, but he listened to the beeps and boops of the electronics even while he watched the data rastering across the small screen of his nav console.

They were over the Bering Sea now, just past the miserable rock of Attu, the last island in the Aleutian chain. Nothing but open water for the next zillion miles, Sharmon knew. With the surprising tailwind pushing them along, they'd reach the Japanese islands in five hours, he figured. But first he had to find the Air Force tanker that was heading for a rendezvous with them.

Sharmon was plotting their course by dead reckoning, as well as homing in on the radio signals from as many Air Force bases as he could find with the plane's radio equipment. The satellites were down, but he could triangulate their position from the radio fixes. Would that be good enough to find that one tanker plane in all the broad emptiness of the northern Pacific?

If it's not, we're all dead.

"Coffee?"

Sharmon flinched at the sudden interruption in his increasingly morose thoughts. Captain O'Banion was standing over him with a steaming plastic mug in one hand.

"It's just coffee," said the redheaded communications officer. "I wouldn't poison you, man."

Sharmon tried to grin as he accepted the mug. "Thanks, Captain."

"Brick," O'Banion said amiably, pointing to his rusty red hair as he sat himself at the comm console.

"I'm Jon," Sharmon replied. "Without an aitch."

O'Banion chuckled. "I haven't used my real first name in so long I forget what it is."

He's trying to make me relax, Sharmon figured, as he took a sip of the coffee. It was scalding hot. "Wow!"

"I made it extra strong," said O'Banion. "We're gonna need to stay bright-eyed and bushy-tailed."

"Guess so. You hear anything more about . . ." Sharmon was going to say *about the war,* but he realized that there might not be a war going on. Not yet, leastways.

"All the civilian satellites are off the air. Our milsats are workin', but they're swamped with traffic."

"You hear anything about North Korea?"

O'Banion shook his head. "Not a peep. Except our orders."

Sharmon sipped again at the coffee. It was black and unsweetened. What the hell, he thought. Who needs cream and sugar when they're going into a shooting war?

"WHERE'S THAT TANKER?" Colonel Christopher said into her pin mike.

"Should be out there." Lieutenant Sharmon's voice sounded decidedly shaky in her headphone.

The colonel clicked off the intercom connection. Should be, she echoed. But where the hell *is* it?

She looked out through the windscreen. Nothing in sight but

empty gray ocean. I could break radio silence and call them, Christopher thought, but I don't want to look like some dumbass who can't find her way to the toilet. Besides, it would tell Sharmon that I don't have any confidence in him. Better to wait. Another few minutes, anyway. We ought to maintain silence as much as we can if we're on a war footing. This might not be a war, not yet, but we're sure ready to get into one.

The flight helmet felt heavy on her head; her neck muscles were tensing up. She'd have a headache soon, she knew. As if I don't have enough of a headache already, she thought, flying into a war with a planeload of nerds downstairs.

Glancing at the fuel gauges on her control board, Christopher thought, If we don't find that bird in another fifteen minutes, I'm going to have to call.

She looked across at Kaufman in the right-hand seat. He caught her eye and ostentatiously tapped a stubby finger on the fuel gauge panel.

"I know," Christopher said. "I just hate to undermine the kid."

Kaufman huffed. "His job is to navigate properly, not get us drowned."

"It wouldn't—" A glint of light sparkled against the endless gray of the ocean. "Hey, look!"

And there it was. A big, fat, beautiful KC-45, chock-full of fuel for them.

Colonel Christopher punched the intercom. "Lieutenant, you can stop sweating. We have the tanker in sight. Nice work."

She could hear Sharmon's relieved sigh even through her headphone.

W e've got to warn the President in the strongest terms that he should not land in San Francisco."

Zuri Coggins was surprised to hear herself speak those words, especially since her voice carried none of the doubt that she felt.

General Higgins looked surprised, too. The situation room fell absolutely silent. Coggins could hear the soft murmur coming from the air-conditioning vents up in the ceiling.

After several heartbeats, General Scheib said, "I disagree. Those missiles can't reach San Francisco. They don't have the range or the accuracy."

Coggins looked across the table at the general. "Are you willing to bet the President's life on that?"

"Yes," Scheib snapped, without an instant's hesitation.

"I'm not," said Coggins. Clasping her hands together on the table-top, she tried to be more reasonable. "Look, General, the chances that they can hit San Francisco might be very small, but the conse-quences if they do will be extremely large. The prudent thing to do is to tell the President not to land there."

Scheib started to reply but held himself in check. Clearly he didn't like what she was recommending.

General Higgins said, "Ms. Coggins makes a good point." Then he added, with a grin, "If nothing else, we'll be covering our asses."

A few chuckles rose from around the table.

"The President's not going to like this," Scheib said. "He'll think we're making him look like a coward."

"It's his decision to make," Higgins said firmly. "We can't *force* the man to turn around."

"Turn tail, you mean," Scheib muttered.

Higgins shot him a disapproving look.

"All right," said Scheib. "If we're going to advise the President to stay clear of San Francisco, we should also send a fighter escort to cover ABL-1 as it approaches Korean airspace."

"Fighter escort?" asked one of the civilians.

"That 747 would be a sitting duck for enemy interceptors," Scheib said. "We've got to protect it."

General Higgins nodded. "Send the recommendation to the Air Force chief of staff. With my approval."

"Yes, sir," Scheib said, and he bent over his laptop.

THE NATIONAL SECURITY Advisor raised his hands prayerfully in front of his pursed lips as he stared at the smart screen on his office wall. Zuri Coggins looked so damned solemn, so convinced she was right.

"And that's the recommendation of the full emergency team?" he asked, his voice silky smooth. It was a tone that had terrified Navy officers for many years. Here in the White House, the civilians had been slow to understand its depths, but they figured it out—after a few bloody examples.

"We didn't take a vote," said Coggins. "But General Higgins agrees with me."

"You're not calling from your cell phone, are you?" the Security Advisor asked.

"No, this is a secure videophone center in the Pentagon."

"Good."

"Will you make the recommendation to the President?" she asked.

He hesitated. The President won't like being told he should run away from San Francisco, he knew. Especially if it turns out that the city isn't bombed. Maybe this is all some piece of North Korean gamesmanship to make the President look bad: he backs out of the San Francisco speech and the North Koreans don't launch their missiles. Leaves egg on the President's face.

The Security Advisor sighed heavily. Damned tricky business here. Damned tricky. On the other hand, if it's bombed with The Man in it, then Parkinson becomes President and who knows what that moron will do?

"What does General Scheib have to say about this?"

Coggins' lips pressed into a thin, hard line. At last she answered, "He doesn't believe the North Korean missiles can reach San Francisco. He thinks Honolulu is their likely target."

"I see," said the Security Advisor.

Urgently, Coggins pleaded, "We've only got a half hour or so before he's scheduled to land. You've got to warn him."

The Security Advisor wasn't accustomed to making snap decisions. All his life he'd waited until all the available information was in his hands before putting his reputation on the line.

But he said, "I'll put in another call to Air Force One. You know, he's not going to like this."

"Better fled than dead," Coggins said with a grim smile.

WHEN SHE CAME back into the situation room, the group had again broken into separate little knots of people, except for General Scheib, who sat at his place with a plug in one ear, tapping furiously at his laptop keyboard. And Jamil, who still sat alone at the end of the table. Maybe somebody put glue on his chair, Coggins thought.

General Higgins called to her from the front of the stuffy room. "Well? What happened?"

"He's calling Air Force One and urging the President to turn back."

Higgins nodded. "Okay. That's done. Now we sit and wait."

Slowly, everyone returned to their seats. Turning to General Scheib, Higgins asked, "Did you get the fighter cover you want?"

His face like a thundercloud, Scheib said, "They're bucking the request to SecDef."

"The Secretary of Defense?" Higgins frowned. "He's a civilian."

Coggins didn't know whether to laugh or growl.

General Scheib said, "Nobody wants to take the responsibility."

"Hell, I've already taken the responsibility," said General Higgins. "Did you tell them I approved the request?"

"I did. They're bucking it up the chain of command."

"To a politician," Higgins grumbled. "And he'll just buck it up to the Commander in Chief."

Scheib looked disgusted. "They'd better make the decision pretty damned quick. If the North Koreans send interceptors after ABL-1, that's plane's dead meat."

"You've done as much as you can, Brad. Now it's up to the politicians." Higgins turned to the admiral sitting across from Coggins and asked, "Has Honolulu been alerted?"

Nodding, the admiral replied, "Emergency teams are being notified. We're telling them this is a surprise drill."

"You're not letting them know that they may be attacked?" Coggins asked.

"And start a panic?" the admiral snapped. "More people would be killed in the stampede to get out of the city than if the city really was nuked."

Coggins saw that Jamil slowly shook his head. He knows better, she thought. He knows that if they nuke Honolulu a couple of hundred thousand people will be killed instantly. At least.

Higgins turned the discussion to emergency rescue tactics. Coggins opened her minicomputer and, looking toward Higgins all the time, reopened Jamil's file.

He's a Christian, she saw with a quick flick of her eyes to the tiny screen. His whole family is Christian. That must be why they fled Lebanon and came here. And Higgins thinks he's an Arab. She smiled to herself. She wondered what General Higgins would think if he knew that Zuri Coggins was a Black Muslim.

Linda Suwazi saw her career going down in flames. The baby's due in four months, she groaned inwardly, and this is gonna get me laid off, for sure.

Sitting in front of Linda's desk, Mrs. Markley radiated cold fury. "You are the branch manager, aren't you? Why can't you get the machines fixed?"

Mrs. Markley was the seventh customer to barge into her office in the past half hour, complaining that the ATMs were down. Linda had tried to phone the local service company, but she'd gotten nothing but a busy signal. In desperation she had called corporate headquarters in Houston. No use. The line was so jammed with other calls that all she got was an automated message advising her to call again later.

"I want access to my money!" Mrs. Markley was hissing. "It's bad enough that your machines aren't working, but your tellers *refuse* to cash my Social Security check!"

"Our computers are down," Linda tried to explain. "It's only temporary, I'm sure. If you could come back later . . ."

Mrs. Markley rose grandly to her feet, practically twitching with rage. She reminded Linda of a beady-eyed rat.

"If you can't run your bank properly you should be replaced!"
Mrs. Markley snapped. Then she swept out of Linda's office.

Linda sank back in her swivel chair and fought down the urge to
burst into tears.

Y ou scared, boss?"

Startled, Harry half-turned and saw Delany's big, bearlike form lumbering up the narrow walkway toward him. Harry had slowly worked his way past the lasing cavity and mixing chamber, heading tailward along the tanks that held the liquid oxygen and iodine toward the cramped little monitoring station where Wally Rosenberg sat, checking pressures and tankage levels.

"What are you doing back here?" Harry demanded. Monk's station was up in the nose, at the beam control compartment.

"The optics are all okay," said Delany. "I was just wondering how you guys're feeling. You nervous about this?"

"Nervous? Kind of," Harry admitted. "Aren't you?"

Delany shrugged. "Why should I be nervous? The gooks are about to start World War III and we're in the middle of the action. What's there to be nervous about?"

Harry wanted to laugh, but the best he could do was to crack a thin smile.

"You checked the optics?" he asked Delany.

"Everything's on the tick. No problems."

"Where's Taki?"

"Up at the battle management console, where she should be. Maybe they'll give her an Air Force commission if she nails those gook missiles."

Harry knew that he and the other civilians were manning the laser only because this was supposed to be a test flight. We're only a skeleton crew at best, he thought. When the system's declared operational, Air Force personnel will take over. With more than twice the number of their five-person team, at that.

"Okay," he said. "I'll go up forward and see how she's making out."

Delany gave him that sloppy salute of his. "Aye, aye, skipper."

Harry shook his head. "This isn't the Navy, Monk."

"We ain't the Air Force, either."

The COIL's channel ran through the length of the plane, past the crew compartment and galley, beneath the flight deck and cockpit, and into the bulbous turret that made the plane's nose look like a potato. Taki Nakamura's station was up forward, at the electronics consoles that monitored the plane's sensors and the laser's output beam.

Taki's battle management compartment was directly beneath the flight deck. Harry scanned the row of consoles, most of them dark and unused until they powered up the laser. The plane's slight swaying was more noticeable up here near the nose. Like a ship at sea, Harry thought. This big lunk of an airplane must weigh a hundred tons, but it still pitches up and down a little.

Nakamura was sitting at the main console, her fingers flicking across the keyboard, her eyes focused intently on the display screen.

"Everything okay, Taki?" asked Harry.

She looked up at him, her lean, sculpted face utterly serious. "Everything's in the green, *jefe*."

Harry nodded to her. He remembered that Pete Quintana was the guy they originally called *el jefe*, the boss. Harry inherited the title when Anson put him in charge of the team, after Pete was killed. Angel Reyes had even gotten his wife to stitch the title onto some of Harry's T-shirts and coveralls. Victor Anson had never seen it, thank god. There was only one god in heaven, Anson always said, and one head of Anson Aerospace. Yet Anson had never come out to the desert to see the test rig, never even made his way down to the working section of his own company's laboratory in Pasadena. He stayed in his office. People came to him.

Harry patted Taki's slim shoulder and moved forward, past the battle management compartment and into the nose of the mammoth airplane. Here was the beam control station, Monk Delany's domain, the business end of the COIL, where megawatts of infrared energy fed through the ball-shaped turret in the plane's nose and lanced out toward the target.

The controls for the ranging laser were there, too. Perched in a housing atop the flight deck's hump, the ranger was a smaller carbon dioxide laser that was used like a radar to fix the location of the target and feed that data to the big COIL for the kill. Slaved to the sensors that spotted the missile's hot rocket plume, the smaller laser pinpointed the missile's position and distance. The turret in the plane's nose moved in response to the data from the ranging laser and then, *zap!* the COIL fired and the missile was destroyed.

Harry noticed that the ranging laser's console was not powered up. Idly, he sat at the console and flicked it on. The central screen glowed to life, and the words SYSTEM MALFUNCTION burned themselves onto it.

What the hell? Harry thought. System malfunction?

"What're you doing, Harry?"

He looked up and saw Monk Delany looming over him.

"Something's wrong with the ranger."

Delany leaned over his shoulder and pecked at the console's keyboard. SYSTEM MALFUNCTION glowered at them.

"Shit," said Delany. "You been screwing around with my program?"

"No, I just turned the console on," Harry said.

Mumbling unhappily, Delany nudged Harry out of the seat and

took over the console himself. After several moments he shrugged in frustration.

"Something's wrong," he said.

"No kidding." Harry knew that without the ranging laser to feed targeting information to the COIL, the whole system was useless.

"Lemme fiddle with it," Monk said, still looking at Harry as if it were his fault.

"I'll go check the rig," Harry said.

"You can't check it while we're in the air," Monk growled.

Harry patted his muscular shoulder. "*You* can't, ape-man. You're too big to squeeze in there. But I'm small enough to do it."

"You'll break your stupid ass."

Harry heaved a sigh and said, "It's got to be done, Monk. Otherwise we'll have to turn around and go home."

Monk said nothing, but the look on his face told Harry that he wouldn't mind returning to Elmendorf, not at all.

Harry left Monk sweating and swearing at the ranging laser console and clambered up the ladder to the flight deck. The two Air Force officers looked startled to see him.

"I need to check the laser assembly," Harry said, pointing overhead.

The redheaded captain said, "Colonel Christopher ought to know about this, sir."

Nodding, Harry said, "Let her know, then."

The captain spoke into his pin mike and an instant later Colonel Christopher popped through the hatch from the cockpit.

"What's wrong, Mr. Hartunian?" She looked nettled.

"I've got to check the ranging laser."

"In flight? I thought that unit was sealed off while the plane's pressurized."

"The laser housing is pressurized too," Harry explained. "This won't endanger the plane."

She looked unconvinced. "Is this really necessary, or are you just . . ." She let her voice trail off, but Harry got the implication loud and clear: *Are you nerds just playing around with your techie toys?*

"It's completely necessary," he replied. "Without the ranging laser we can't lock onto a target."

Planting her fists on her hips, Colonel Christopher asked tightly, "Are you telling me that the ranging subsystem is down?"

"That's right. We're trying to find out what's wrong with it and get it fixed."

She stood there before him, her face set in an angry frown. Abruptly she turned to the young lieutenant and commanded, "Jon, you're the tallest guy we've got. Give Mr. Hartunian all the help you can."

Lieutenant Sharmon got up from his console, his close-cropped hair nearly brushing the overhead.

"Thank you, Colonel," Harry said.

"Get it fixed, Mr. Hartunian."

"Harry," he said automatically.

Colonel Christopher looked as if she wanted to breathe fire. "Mr. Hartunian," she repeated.

WITH LIEUTENANT SHARMON'S help, Harry unscrewed the plate that covered the ranging laser's mount.

The tubular housing for the ranging laser was too tight for Harry to do more than stick his head through the opening. The plane's engines sounded louder up here, the vibrations heavier. It felt cold, too. Harry realized that there was nothing between him and the subzero stratosphere out there except a thin sheathing of aluminum.

Teetering on a makeshift ladder that Sharmon had created by stripping one of the crew's relief cots and leaning the metal frame against the bulkhead of the flight deck, Harry wormed one arm up into the shadowy housing and played the beam from his pocket flashlight down the length of the carbon dioxide laser. Everything seemed okay. No loose connections. Seals looked tight.

Turning carefully to inspect the forward end of the laser, Harry froze. The forward lens assembly was gone. Where the fist-sized unit of collimating lenses should have been there was nothing but a gaping emptiness.

Somebody's taken the lens assembly out of the laser, Harry realized. He stared, trembling, at that empty space where the lens assembly should have been. Somebody's taken the lens out of the laser, he repeated to himself. Without the lens assembly the ranging laser can't work, and without the ranging laser, the big COIL can't be aimed properly. The whole system—the whole plane— will be useless.

There's a saboteur on the plane! The thought made Harry's knees weak. But there was no other explanation. That lens assembly didn't remove itself from the ranger; somebody deliberately took it out. Then he remembered the explosion at the test rig, the accident that had killed Pete Quintana and nearly broken his own back. It wasn't an accident, Harry realized. It was deliberate sabotage. By one of my crew.

As Harry stood there, wondering what to do, how to handle this terrible new knowledge, he heard Victor Anson's voice in his mind:

Make it work, Harry. I'm counting on you. We're all counting on you.

HARRY DANIEL HARTUNIAN

Harry Hartunian had never been a fighter. He wasn't a take-charge guy. Instead, he had a quiet, persistent, relentless determination to finish whatever he started. Born and raised in the Boston suburb of Medford, in high school Harry took a lot of ribbing for his flyaway hair and his passive, almost invisible presence in the classroom and outside. The bullies picked on him, of course, but Harry befriended the biggest guy in the school by offering to do his homework in exchange for his protection. The bullying stopped. And his bodyguard even taught Harry a few moves that were down and dirty but effective in an emergency.

He didn't go out for sports—the mindless pressure to win turned him off. In his sophomore year Harry made the chess team, barely, but by the time he graduated he was the best chess player in the school.

Engineering appealed to him; Harry liked the idea of building things and making mechanisms work. He got a partial scholarship to Lehigh University and went into its electrical engineering program. On campus he met Sylvia Goldman, who was in the teacher's college. She was from Media, Pennsylvania. Sylvia was attractive, buxom, with flashing dark eyes. Harry felt flabbergasted that she was interested in him.

For her part, Sylvia saw in Harry a steady, dependable man who could be led rather easily. He had this funny hair that flew every which way at the slightest breeze, but he wasn't that bad-looking and he was doggedly determined to do well in class and get a rock-solid job after graduation. He was quiet, and so shy he wouldn't get fresh with her, so after a few dates she got fresh with him. After nearly a year of dating they moved into a tiny studio apartment together.

Harry married Sylvia in a simple civil ceremony in Bethlehem's city hall. Neither her parents nor his saw fit to attend the wedding. Both families were infuriated by their marriage. Sylvia's mother feared that this *goy* boyfriend of hers had gotten her pregnant; Harry's father asked him why, when there were so many fish in the sea, he wanted to settle so soon for just one of them.

As graduation neared Harry was recruited by a firm in California, Anson Aerospace Corporation. The company was developing lasers and Harry had worked summers in the university's laser lab to make enough money to support himself and his bride.

With their diplomas in their hands, they moved to Pasadena, leaving their disapproving parents thousands of miles behind them. Sylvia got part-time work as a substitute teacher while Harry threw himself into his job as a laser technician.

Anson Aerospace was a happy haven for the young engineer. All his life he had been an oddball, a nerd, a quiet, studious boy who was shy with girls and respectful to adults and preferred reading books to getting involved in teenaged pranks. At Anson, Harry was surrounded by people just like him. Geek heaven. There was a pecking order, of course: scientists were above engineers, even though the engineers all felt that physicists should never be allowed to touch any of the equipment in the lab.

"It's easy to make a laser that's idiot-proof," the head of Anson's safety department told Harry. "Making it Ph.D.-proof is just about impossible. Those guys think they're brilliant, see. They poke into the lab and fiddle with this and twiddle with that until they either give themselves a ten-thousand-volt shock or burn the place down."

Harry knew he was not brilliant. But he worked hard and steadily for long hours and little recognition. Yet he loved it. He loved the technical challenges, the camaraderie that slowly developed among his fellow engineers, the bowling league he helped to organize, even the physicists who unconsciously lorded it over the engineers as if it was their right to look down on the guys who got their hands dirty. Indeed, Harry was not brilliant, but he was dependable. He got the job done, no matter how difficult it was, no matter how long or hard he had to work at it. Quiet and steady as he was, gradually he was recognized by his supervisors, and even by the scientists who ran the lab. To his own surprise, Harry got salary raises almost every year: small ones, but he didn't complain.

Sylvia did. They had two daughters now and a sizable mortgage on their home. She felt Harry wasn't aggressive enough about his salary.

"You should be getting more," she would say. "Gina Sobelski's husband hasn't been with the company half as long as you have and he makes twice as much."

"Sobelski's in the legal department," Harry would counter. "Different pay scale."

Logic did not move Sylvia.

"You're *dull*, Harry. Nobody pays any attention to you. You're a bore."

He didn't argue. He just let her vent and the next morning he went to work, where the only pressure on him was to do his job.

Anson Aerospace landed a juicy contract to build a megawatt-plus chemical laser for the Missile Defense Agency. The whole company was abuzz with the news. Victor Anson himself called a meeting of the entire staff in the company cafeteria to tell them that this program would be the most important contract the firm had ever received.

Harry was surprised when he was picked to be part of the small, select group of engineers who would build the device.

Dr. Jacob Levy was chosen to head the laser group, with Pete Quintana as the chief engineer under him. Monk Delany complained to Harry that Quintana only got the job because he was Hispanic and the company wanted to look good to the affirmative action busybodies.

A couple of the guys began calling Quintana *el jefe*. Harry and the others went along with it. What the hell? Harry thought. He had no problems with a Hispanic being his immediate supervisor. He liked Pete.

Sylvia took the news of Harry's new assignment strangely.

"I suppose that means you'll be working longer hours, doesn't it?" she asked that evening, after their daughters had gone to their rooms to do their homework. Harry could hear the thumping beat of the music they listened to while they were supposed to be studying.

"Yeah, I guess so," he said.

Sylvia grumbled and Harry wondered why she got sore at the fact that he was successful at his work.

"Look, Sylvie, I've got a big responsibility now," he tried to explain. "I know I'm not a genius. I've got to put in long hours and work as hard as I can. These scientists I'm working for are really brilliant; I've got to give it everything I've got just to keep up with them."

Sylvia stared at his earnest face and shook her head.

There were women in the lab, of course: a couple of Caltech grads among the scientific staff; several engineers and technicians. A few of them were even good-looking. The Christmas parties were fun, although Harry always drove straight home afterward. Sylvia would scowl at him the next day as Harry nursed his hangover and thanked whatever gods there be that the Pasadena traffic cops hadn't stopped him on the way home.

Sylvia had given up her teaching career, such as it was, once she became pregnant with Victoria. Then came Denise. Instead of a career in education, Sylvia pursued Causes. Women's rights. Neighborhood beautification. Abused children. Political campaigns. Harry thought of them as hobbyhorses. Sylvia always had some Cause or other to keep her busy, as if raising two daughters wasn't enough of a job. Through her Causes she met people, dragged Harry to meetings and cocktail parties, gave herself a sense of accomplishment.

Harry didn't mind Sylvia's hobbyhorses, as long as they didn't interfere with the increasingly long hours he had to put in at the lab. He settled into middle-class Americana, his wispy hair thinning even more, his kids growing up amazingly fast, his wife slowly becoming more distant. Harry could never understand why Sylvia was resentful that his job absorbed so much of his time and interest, and that he enjoyed it.

"We never go anywhere," she would complain.

"We took the kids to Disney World, didn't we?"

"Last year."

"So?"

"I was thinking about an ocean cruise. Maybe to Hawaii."

Harry scratched his head. "The four of us? Do you know what that would cost?"

"We could leave the girls with the Sobelskis. Just you and me, Harry. On a beautiful ocean liner."

He thought about how much time that would take but knew better than to mention that out loud. Besides, she knew he had amassed lots of unused vacation days.

"We'll see," he said.

Nearly a year later he finally gave in to her drumbeat of hints and accusations. They took a cruise to Hawaii. It wasn't really romantic, just a different setting for the same pair of them. Hawaii actually depressed Harry with its obviously phony façade of tropical splendor and the locals debasing their native culture for tourist dollars.

As their cruise liner left Honolulu for the trip home, Harry stood at the rail and watched the pier gradually slipping away, more and more distant, the gulf of oily, trash-laden water separating the ship from the land slowly, slowly widening. Turning to Sylvia, standing beside him with tears in her eyes, he thought that the same thing was happening to them — they had already drifted apart, and the gulf between them was getting wider every day, every year.

Once they got back to Pasadena, Sylvia threw herself even deeper into neighborhood politics, circulating petitions and phoning city hall over this Cause or that. Harry worked longer and longer hours at the lab. The high-power laser project was moving along smartly. They called it the COIL: chemical oxygen iodine laser. Powerful stuff.

He knew he and Sylvia were becoming strangers to each other, but he didn't know what to do about it. At her insistence they went to a marriage counselor, who recommended they both see a psychologist. Reluctantly, Harry agreed to it, secretly terrified that somebody at the lab might find out.

"You're boringly normal," the psychologist told him.

The marriage counselor recommended they take a romantic ocean cruise. Harry stopped going to her, although Sylvia continued weekly sessions for more than a year. Harry wondered what she found to talk about every week.

The years slid past relentlessly. Jacob Levy was one of the more supercilious physicists on the lab's staff, but he got along pretty well with Harry. Levy knew how to keep his nose out of places where it shouldn't be.

"I'll do the thinking," he often told Harry's team of engineers. "All you have to do is make it work."

They made a good team. With Jake's brains and our hands, Harry thought, we'll make this laser actually work.

Inevitably the COIL program moved into the testing stage, and they had to transport all the hardware out to the Mohave Desert.

Harry sensed Sylvia's eyes boring into his back as he packed his soft-sided travel bag. He turned and, sure enough, his wife was standing in the bedroom doorway, looking distinctly displeased.

"So you'll be gone for a week?" Sylvia asked. She had that accusing stare on her face; her district attorney look, Harry secretly called it. In school she'd been on the student council, combining earnestness and winning smiles to gather votes and move molehills. It had been a long time since he'd seen her smile—except when they were out with other couples. Then Sylvia could be the life of the party. At home, though, she was the district attorney.

"Maybe a little more than a week," he said, feeling almost guilty about it. He brushed a hand through his thinning hair. Maybe I ought to get a crew cut, he thought idly. Save a lot of time trying to keep it looking neat.

"Vickie's birthday is a week from Wednesday," Sylvia said. "You'll be home by then, won't you?"

"Should be."

"Should be? What do you mean, 'should be'? It's your daughter's birthday, for god's sake. Don't you have any feelings for your own daughter? I know you'd rather play around with your buddies than be with me, but you'd better come back in time for her birthday!"

Harry fought down an impulse to throw something at her. Zipping the travel bag, he said tightly, "I'm not playing around out there. It's strictly business, and it's important."

"Important. Sure. More important than me. More important than your daughters. They hardly ever see you! You're out of here at the crack of dawn and you don't come home until after dark. Now you're traipsing out to the desert."

"It's my job, for Chrissakes!" he said, trying to keep his voice down.

"Your job," Sylvia said, dripping acid.

"It's important."

"So important you can't tell me anything about it."

"That's right. The program is classified, military secret."

"Out in the desert."

"Right." Harry glanced at his wristwatch. Monk should be driving up soon.

"Where will you be staying out in the Mohave?"

"The Air Force is putting us up in a motel."

"A motel?"

"That's right." He lifted his bag off the bed and started for the door. Sylvia stood in the doorway like an armed guard.

"What's the name of this motel? The phone number?"

"I don't know yet. I'll keep my cell phone on. You can call me on it if you need to."

Sylvia looked up into his eyes. He saw resentment smoldering in hers, and anger, and plenty of suspicion.

"So you're walking out on me."

"Sylvia, it's only for a goddamned week! Ten days at most."

"Leaving me and the girls to fend for ourselves."

He grasped her shoulder and pushed her back from the doorway, out into the hall. As he reached the stairs he heard the toot of Monk Delany's car horn.

"I've got to go now," Harry said, starting down the carpeted stairs.

Sylvia stayed in the upper hallway, glowering at him. Harry felt enormously relieved to be getting out of the house and away from her.

Over his shoulder he called, "Kiss the girls for me when they get back from school."

"How many girls are you going to kiss out there in that damned motel?" Sylvia yelled after him.

Harry was startled by that. She's worried that I'll shack up with somebody else? The thought had never entered his mind. Actually, it had, now and then. But he'd never acted on it.

He was surprised again when he saw that Monk was driving a mint-new Mustang convertible, fire-engine red.

"Where's the Chrysler?" Harry asked as he tossed his travel bag onto the narrow bench behind the bucket seats.

Monk gave an unhappy snort. "The old gray ghost's transmission crapped out. I've got to use the wife's new car and she's plenty steamed up about it."

Harry slid into the seat and slammed the door shut. As Monk gunned the convertible down the street Harry thought again about Sylvia accusing him of shacking up with some other woman. As if I'd ever do that, he said to himself with some indignation.

T en-*hut!*"

The seven engineers and test technicians turned from their control boards and, grinning, arranged themselves in a ragged line. Several of them gave sloppy salutes.

As he stepped through the steel hatch into the blockhouse, Brigadier General Brad Scheib smiled tightly at them. "I can see none of you geniuses was ever in the military."

Harry felt disappointed. "You're not wearing your star, General."

Scheib wasn't even in uniform. He wore a checkered short-sleeved shirt, open at the neck, and comfortable chino slacks.

"I don't want to look overdressed," he said.

The civilians were all in faded denims and company-issued white T-shirts that read ANSON AEROSPACE across their backs, with the stylized A of the corporation's logo on their chests. Pete Quintana's shirt was emblazoned with EL JEFE sewn just above the logo.

Scheib was accompanied by Jacob Levy, the chief scientist on the laser project. Like General Scheib, Levy wore a sport shirt and slacks, although his shirt was sparkling white and crisply starched, distinctly out of place in the baking desert heat. Levy was the man in charge, working directly with the newly promoted General

Scheib and responsible only to Victor Anson, who owned the company.

"Are you ready to run?" Levy asked Quintana.

Nodding, the engineer replied, "We're going through the final checkout. Be ready to fire up the beast in ten minutes or so."

The control center had been a blockhouse years ago, when the Air Force was testing rocket engines for missiles at this remote desert site. It was unglamorous, strictly utilitarian: bare concrete walls, half a dozen desk-sized consoles with their display screens and keyboards, strip lamps across the steel beams supporting the ceiling, a panel of monitoring gauges fastened to the concrete of the rear wall. The air-conditioning was pitiful: several of the men's shirts were already sweat-stained, and Taki Nakamura's shirt clung to her slim bosom.

"Very well, then," Levy said stiffly as he pulled out a handkerchief and mopped his brow, "let's get down to business and show the general what our COIL can do."

One wall of the concrete building had been punched through and a long window of thick safety glass looked out on the laser itself.

The COIL sat in its own open shed beneath a flimsy roof of corrugated metal supported by four steel beams. Pete Quintana picked up a cordless screwdriver and stepped through the blockhouse's steel door, out into the shed.

"Where are you going, Quintana?" Levy demanded, frowning.

Harry thought maybe Pete went outside because it was cooler there—at least a little breeze was blowing, unlike in here with this crappy air-conditioning.

But Pete answered softly, his voice muffled by the thick glass of the safety window, "Tightening up the mount. Keep the vibration level down."

"You shouldn't be out there when we're counting down," Levy yelled.

"I'll be back inside in a minute. Start the countdown, it's okay."

Levy frowned but turned to Harry and said darkly, "Start the countdown."

Harry glanced at General Scheib, then shrugged. Turning to Delany, he said, "Start the sequence timer, Monk."

The target sat half a mile out on the desert: the sawed-off end of a cargo plane, its fat round fuselage and big tailfin sticking up into the cloudless blue sky. There were several pinpoint holes in the plane's aluminum skin, blackened from the heat of the laser's beam.

General Scheib came up beside Harry and looked out at the laser assembly. "We can't have fussbudgets tinkering when we're flying that dingus. It's got to work without last-second adjustments."

"It will," Harry said tightly.

"Of course it will," Levy added. But the slight lift of his brow told Harry he was not happy.

Harry picked up the intercom microphone. "Hey, Pete, you'd better cut it short and get in here."

Still with his back to the safety window, Quintana hollered, "Yeah, yeah. I'm coming."

"Now," Harry said. "We want to start her up."

"So start her. I just want to check the vibration absorber on the optics platform. I'll be inside before you get her warmed up."

Harry looked at Levy, who frowned but said resignedly, "Get on with it."

Scheib shook his head slightly and thought, These civilians like to play with the equipment. Engineers—they fall in love with the hardware. But they've got to make this beast foolproof, so that tech sergeants can run it without a half dozen geeks tinkering with it all the time.

He heard the whine of the electrical power generator starting up as he peered through the window. Quintana straightened up and planted his hands on his hips, as if admiring the equipment he had helped to build. The COIL looked to Scheib more like a miniature junkyard than a flight-weight laser system. Scheib knew the numbers and understood that these engineers had sized the laser to fit inside the capacious frame of a modified Boeing 747. Barely. But in the eyes of the newly minted general those pressure vessels and pumps and all that piping certainly didn't look like something that could ever get off the ground.

"Congratulations on the star."

Startled, Scheib turned to see Hartunian, one of the engineers, standing beside him.

Scheib was tall and trim, his body honed by a daily regimen of exercise and tennis. His face was lean, too, and handsome: sandy brown hair that was just starting to show some gray at the temples, light brown eyes that crinkled when he smiled. Women found him attractive, even out of uniform, something that his stylish, upscale wife didn't seem to mind in the least. Harry was roundish, almost pudgy, his wispy dark hair terminally unruly. But Scheib thought that Harry was sharper mentally than anyone on the laser team. He was just too self-effacing to push his advantage. Except on the tennis court. Harry beat the general at tennis whenever they played together. Brains over brawn, Scheib thought, although he would never admit it aloud.

"It's about time the Air Force gave you some recognition," Harry went on, his voice low enough that the rest of the people in the blockhouse couldn't hear him.

Almost flustered, Scheib replied, "Thank you, Harry. I didn't know you cared."

Harry grinned at him. "If they passed you up and you got reassigned, we'd have to break in a new blue-suiter."

Scheib nodded, thinking, It always comes down to what's best for numero uno. Well, I've got my star. Now if these clowns can make this contraption work I might even get a second star, eventually.

"Input power ready," called one of the technicians.

Harry turned away from the general and gave Levy a questioning look. "We're ready to power up."

"By all means," Levy said.

"Pete, get the hell in here," Delany thundered.

"On my way," Quintana yelled back.

"Initiate power sequence," Harry said, plucking his sticky shirt away from his chest.

"Initiating power sequence."

"Iodine pressure on the button," one of the technicians called out.

"Electrical power ramping up," another technician said.

"Optical bench ready."

"Atmospheric instability nominal."

"Adaptive optics on."

"Iodine flow in ten seconds."

"Oxygen flow in eight seconds."

"Pressurizing iodine."

"Pressurizing oxy."

Pete Quintana opened the door to the blockhouse. Harry thought that Pete was cutting it awfully close. If anything goes wrong with—

The laser blew up in a spectacular blast that ripped the roof off the test shed. The explosion knocked everyone down; Harry smashed against the back wall of the control room, shattering his ribs against the gauges mounted on the concrete. A jagged piece of metal crashed through the safety window, shattering it into thousands of pellets as a hellish fireball billowed up into the cloudless blue sky. Pain roared through Harry while the heat from the oxygen-fed fire poured through, hot enough to melt the gauges on the back wall.

In the partially open doorway Pete Quintana was enveloped in the flames, screaming, gibbering, flailing in agony. Harry tried to reach out to him, but his own pain was so intense that he blacked out.

Groggily, General Scheib got to all fours, glass pellets crunching beneath his hands and feet. A twisted piece of pipe had embedded itself into the back wall of the blockhouse like a red-hot arrow.

Christ, Scheib thought, if the blast hadn't flattened me that thing would've torn my head off.

Levy and the engineers were all on the floor, knocked flat by the blast. They seemed dazed, in shock, faces and hands burned raw by the heat of the explosion. Hartunian looked unconscious. Scheib got to his feet slowly. The guy who'd been outside lay on the floor of the shed next to the burning, twisted shambles of the laser, a huddled lump of blackened flesh.

Slowly the others got up, coughing, dazed. Somewhere a fire siren was wailing, coming closer. Two of the engineers were helping the woman to her feet. Her face was burned; a trickle of blood ran down her cheek from her scalp. Levy pushed himself up to a sitting position, his shirt and trousers covered with grit. He looked angry, resentful, as if his beautiful machine had somehow betrayed him.

"It shouldn't have done that," Levy muttered through chipped teeth.

Yeah, right, Scheib thought.

Through the shattered window Scheib saw what was left of the COIL: twisted, blackened wreckage, wisps of dirty reddish smoke wafting into the sky. And the body of Pete Quintana, burned red and raw.

Hartunian moaned and opened his eyes. "What the hell happened?" he croaked.

My career just went up in smoke, General Scheib thought. That's what the hell happened.

Harry was sedated and semiconscious while Anson Aerospace medical personnel helicoptered him from the Mohave test site directly to Olympia Medical Center in Pasadena. He went into surgery the next day, then the recovery unit, and finally into a private room paid for by Anson Aerospace. Although Harry didn't know it at first, a pair of Air Police stood guard outside his room. Later they were replaced by private security people hired by Victor Anson himself.

Sometime during that period of half-wakefulness, an officer in Air Force blue entered Harry's room and shoved an official-looking document at him.

"Security agreement," he said, his tone as flat and clipped as an air traffic controller's. "Sign at the bottom line."

"Security?" Harry mumbled, still fuzzy from the sedatives.

"About the accident. It's been classified Secret. You can't say anything about it to anyone who doesn't have a certified need to know." He held the document on a clipboard six inches from Harry's nose and pressed a ballpoint pen into his hand. "Sign it now."

Moving his arm made Harry wince with pain. He scribbled a parody of his signature on the bottom line and the uniformed officer took his clipboard and left Harry to drift back into a drugged sleep.

When Harry awoke fully, on the fifth day after the explosion, he blinked at the almost-luxurious furnishings of the room in which he found himself. Crank-up hospital bed, he saw, but the rest of the room looked like a first-class hotel, rather than a hospital: cool pastel walls, sleek modern furniture, a big flat-screen TV on the wall. The one window looked out on city buildings. Then he realized there was an IV tube in his left arm, and a bank of monitoring instruments softly beeping on the wall above his bed's headboard.

Harry tried to raise himself into a sitting position to see more of the outside surroundings, but his ribs flared with pain. He settled back on the bed and the pain subsided into a dulled ache. They must have me pretty well doped up, he guessed.

The door to his room opened and a nurse stepped in. She was a bit on the chubby side, but she looked cheerful. Smiling.

"We're awake," she said pleasantly.

"Yeah," Harry replied, unhappy with her "we."

"Hungry?"

"No."

"Really?" She came to the bed, peered at the instruments over Harry's head. "You've been getting nothing but intravenous for the past four days."

"How bad was I hurt?"

"A few cracked ribs. Superficial burns on one side of your face. Nothing terribly serious."

She's a professional nurse, Harry thought. Indifferent to the patient's pain.

"The others? How bad—"

She shook her head with a slightly disapproving expression on her dimpled features. "I'll order a breakfast tray for you. See if you can take some nourishment."

Twenty minutes later a Hispanic orderly came in with a tray of breakfast. He cranked Harry's bed up to a sitting position slowly, carefully, obviously aware that the patient's ribs were painful. Harry felt grateful enough to say, "*Gracias.*"

The dark-skinned orderly grinned at him. "Just doin' my job, man."

Harry sipped the orange juice, poked at the rubbery scrambled eggs. Every time he moved his arms his ribs flared up. By the time he'd given up on the breakfast his body felt as if somebody had spent the morning whacking his chest and back with a baseball bat.

A doctor came in briefly, took his pulse, and told him that he'd be fine in a week or so.

"The others," Harry said. "How bad were they hurt? Pete Quintana?"

The doctor pursed his lips. "I don't know about anyone else. The medevac chopper brought you in five days ago. You're my patient. You're recovering well. That's all I know."

It must be bad, Harry surmised. Pete must be dead. Anybody else?

Harry spent the day watching television, banal soap operas, game shows where he knew the answers that stumped the dumbbell contestants, phony courtrooms with idiotic people complaining about one another, psychologists offering advice to young couples and old married folks.

Maybe Sylvia and I ought to go on one of those shows, Harry thought. Then he remembered the marriage counselor they'd seen and the psychologist he'd gone to afterward and how pointless it had all been.

Where is Sylvia? he wondered. Does she even know I'm in the hospital? Did anybody tell her there's been an accident?

Late in the afternoon Monk Delany came into his room. Harry was glad to see the big, shambling engineer, although he thought Monk looked awkward, sheepish, almost embarrassed.

"How ya doing, Harry?"

"It only hurts when I breathe."

"Come on," Delany said. "Seriously."

"Banged-up ribs. I'll be okay."

"Your face is kinda burned. Like you got too much sun."

Harry nodded. The movement sent a twinge of pain along his back.

"You look okay," he said to Delany.

The engineer pulled one of the petite wooden chairs from the wall and sat down beside Harry's bed. The chair looked almost too frail to hold his bulk.

"I got a couple bruises," Delany said. "The blast knocked me down, that's all."

"Pete?"

Delany's face fell. "I told that dumb spic to get his ass inside the blockhouse."

"Is he dead?"

"Yeah."

"Anybody else?"

"Naw, they're all okay. You got it worse than anybody. Except Pete, of course. General Scheib tore out both knees of his pants. Levy got a black eye. A real beaut of a shiner."

Harry knew that Monk was trying to cheer him up. "What caused the explosion? Any idea?"

"Six dozen guys are going over the wreckage, including a gang of blue suits."

"And?"

Delany shrugged. "Looks like it mighta been some grease got into the oxy line."

"We checked that line," Harry said.

"Yeah, I know. But that's what it looks like."

Harry closed his eyes and saw his job going down the drain. Grease in the oxygen line. That shouldn't have happened. Somebody's going to get blamed for it. Me. Maybe all of us. Maybe the whole damned program will get shut down.

"The investigation isn't over," Delany said. "Maybe they'll find something else."

Harry started to shake his head, thought better of it. "What're they going to find? Spies? Foreign agents planted a bomb?"

Delany sat and stared at him in silence for several long moments, his normally cheerful face looking pensive, almost mournful.

At last he got up from the flimsy chair. "Take care of yourself, Harry. I gotta get back out to Mohave, help with the investigation."

"Thanks for coming by, Monk."

"Nothing to it." Delany stopped at the door. "Anything I can get you, Harry? Anything you need?"

"My laptop," Harry answered immediately. "I'll go nuts in here without my laptop to work on."

"You got it, pal."

It wasn't until after Delany had left that Harry wondered when Sylvia would be allowed to visit him. He found that he didn't really care when she came, or if she came at all. And he realized he wasn't surprised by his feeling.

Victor Anson sat behind the gleaming broad desk of his private office and gave the three men sitting anxiously on the other side his coldest, hardest stare.

Anson was totally bald but sported a natty little pencil moustache. He was athletically slim and wore an impeccably tailored Italian silk suit of silvery gray, with an off-white shirt and carefully knotted sky blue tie.

Two of the three men before him were corporate executives in proper business suits and ties; the third was Jake Levy, one of his top physicists, dressed in sloppy, unpressed slacks and a white open-necked short-sleeved sport shirt. Typical scientist, Anson thought: every day is casual Friday for them. At least Levy knew better than to wear denims in his presence, Anson told himself.

Looking closer at the physicist, Anson saw that his left eye was swollen and bruised bluish. The man looked faintly ludicrous; Anson had to suppress a smile.

Anson had made the company what it was and he knew it. Starting with nothing but his father's few millions and a humdrum aircraft-repair operation, Victor Anson had spent his life, his well-known shrewdness, and his single-minded determination to create Anson

Aerospace Corporation and make it into one of the most successful industrial research and development organizations in the world.

Now he glared across his desk at the man whom he'd trusted to make that goddamned laser into a winner. All he had to show for six years of work was a tangled mess of smoking wreckage.

"You realize that SDB has already submitted a formal proposal to the Air Force for their version of a high-power laser?"

Before they could do anything more than nod miserably, Anson went on. "And Vickers has its whole Washington team bending the ears of every major congressional committee chairman, telling them that *they* can take over the laser program. Vickers! They're British, for god's sake!"

Jacob Levy, who'd been born in Liverpool, replied in his studied Oxford accent, "Vickers couldn't possibly handle the task, and everyone knows it."

"Those congressmen don't," Anson snapped. "Those senators don't."

The two men sitting on either side of Levy were James Dykes, the corporation's chief financial officer, and Milton Haas, who headed Anson's Washington office. Dykes was built like a fireplug: thick torso, short limbs, a thick mop of dirty blond hair. Haas was as slim and graceful as a ballerina, with the most beautiful dark eyes Anson had ever seen on a man.

"It's not all that bad, V.R.," said Dykes, his voice rough and throaty, as if he'd been hollering at people all morning. "Our contract isn't up for renewal until—"

"The goddam Air Force can cancel our goddam contract whenever it goddam wants to and you know it, Jimmy!" Anson snarled.

Haas raised a slim finger. "There's no movement in the Pentagon to cancel our contract."

"Not yet."

"We can rebuild the laser in three months," said Levy. "Perhaps less."

"Not until you find out what made it blow up," Anson replied.

"We know what caused the explosion. A speck of grease got en-trained in the oxygen line. Once the oxygen was pressurized it ignited—"

"A speck of grease?" Anson roared. "How in the name of all the devils in hell did a speck of grease get into the oxy line?"

Unconsciously touching his swollen eye, Levy replied with de-liberate calm, "The important thing, Mr. Anson, is to look ahead. I've instituted procedures that will make certain all the feed lines are purged with nitrogen before we power up the laser. That will ensure that the lines are clear."

Anson scowled at him. "One of your technicians screwed up. Fire the bastard."

"I'm not certain—"

"Find out who's responsible and fire him!" Anson insisted. "You don't have to be certain. Pick the likeliest chump and throw him out on his butt. Make an example of him so the others shape up."

"But I can't simply fire someone at random like that."

Anson stared at Levy for several heartbeats. Then, "Well, if you can't—or won't—I'll find somebody who can."

Levy's face went white.

"Find a scapegoat," Anson said, his voice cold and hard. Then he smiled thinly. "It ought to be easy enough for you. You Jews know all about scapegoats, don't you?"

It wasn't until Harry's seventh day in the hospital that Sylvia came to see him. He had the bed cranked up to a sitting position. His ribs ached, but the tight cast they'd put around his trunk made the pain bearable. The head nurse told him that they were weaning him off the painkillers as she changed the plastic bag of his IV drip.

"Don't want to make a druggie out of you," she said cheerfully.

Harry grunted, even though it hurt his ribs.

The nurse left, and before the door closed Sylvia pushed through. Harry felt surprised, then a little guilty. He hadn't asked about his wife, had hardly even thought about her, since waking up in the hospital.

"Hi, Sylvie," he said. It sounded weak to him, as if he were automatically trying to gain her sympathy.

Sylvia stood uncertainly at the doorway. He was surprised to realize how chunky she'd gotten over the years. The curvaceous girl he'd married had evolved into an almost dumpy matron. Like everything else, Harry thought. Everything goes downhill. I should talk, Mr. Bald Flab Guy.

For a moment Harry thought Sylvia was going to turn around

and leave. But she came into the room a few steps, clutching her purse in both hands.

"Are you okay, Harry?"

He tried to smile. "It only hurts when I breathe."

She frowned at him. "Don't try to make a joke out of it. The man on the phone said you were seriously injured."

"Cracked some ribs."

"What happened?"

Harry hesitated, vaguely remembering the secrecy agreement he had signed. "I can't tell you."

She came up to the edge of the bed. "You can't tell your own wife?"

Harry started to shake his head, but the flare of pain made him stop. Instead he merely said, "Air Force stuff. It's all classified."

"Your own wife?" Sylvia demanded. "Do they think I'm a spy or something?"

Harry thought of Ben Franklin's dictum: Three people can keep a secret if two of them are dead. Then he remembered Pete Quintana.

Sylvia stood at the side of the bed. "Leona Rosenberg told me that one of your crew got killed. That Hispanic guy."

"Pete Quintana."

"There was an explosion? Your face looks burned on one side."

"I'll be all right," Harry said. "I should be home in a few days."

She said nothing.

"How're the kids?" he asked.

"Vickie's dating that Vietnamese boy from her class again. I don't trust him."

Harry smiled faintly. "But we can trust Vickie. She's got a good head on her shoulders."

Shaking her head, Sylvia said, "I don't like the way he looks at her."

"He comes into the house, doesn't he? He doesn't just toot the horn and expect her to go running out to him. The kid's got some manners."

"For god's sake, Harry! You'd let your daughter get raped just because you think the boy's polite!"

"Don't start, Sylvie."

"I don't see why Vickie can't date her own kind of boys," she grumbled.

Harry tried to change the subject. "How's Denise?"

"She's fine. Breezing through school. They want her to come out for the orchestra next term."

"That's good."

And suddenly they had nothing more to talk about. Nothing that wouldn't lead to an argument. Sylvia stood by the bed for a few moments more, looking as if she wanted to get away.

"I'll be out of here in a couple of days," Harry said.

She nodded. "Good. Call me if you need anything."

"Yeah."

"I've got to be going now. The kids will be coming home from school."

"Yeah."

"I'll see you tomorrow."

Harry almost said, Don't bother. But he kept the thought to himself.

Harry felt silly in the powered wheelchair, but he had to admit that it was better than trying to walk. Sylvia had come to the hospital and stayed alongside him as he rolled down the hospital corridor, checked out at the admissions counter, and then wheeled himself outside and up to the SUV that Anson Aerospace had provided him for the trip home. The driver and one of the hospital's orderlies helped Harry into the SUV's right-hand seat with a minimum of agony and then stowed his wheelchair in the back.

Once home, Harry realized that the world looks a lot different when you're confined to a wheelchair. The split-level house had only two sets of stairs and they were no more than six steps each, but to Harry they suddenly looked formidable. Carefully, with the SUV's driver grasping his left arm and Sylvia his right, he got up from the chair. Then he stood there with his daughters staring wide-eyed at him while the driver carried the chair down the little flight as easily as if it weighed only a few ounces.

He walked down the steps like an arthritic old man, Sylvia and the driver holding him again, and settled into the chair once more.

"I'll be okay now," he said to the driver. "Thanks."

The guy dipped his chin in acknowledgment, grinned at the

two girls standing there, and left the house. Sylvia stood in front of him, looking him over with a disapproving scowl on her face. Harry nudged the chair's control stick and wheeled past her, down the carpeted hallway.

As he turned into the bedroom, Sylvia said from behind him, "Not there. I set up the guest room for you." Her voice sounded edgy. "The doctor said it'll be better for you."

Harry spun the chair around. Sylvia looked strained, almost frightened. He started to say something to her, but gave it up. Without another word he turned the chair around and rolled it to the guest room.

Sylvia and the girls fussed around him as he got out of the chair on his own and stretched out gratefully on the queen-sized bed of the guest room. His back throbbed and he felt the beginnings of a headache pinching at the back of his neck.

"You have everything you need right here," Sylvia said from the doorway. "If you want anything, just holler."

"You want some juice, Dad?" Denise asked, her eyes full of anxiety.

He made a smile for her. "I'm okay, honey. Thanks anyway."

Vickie said, "We'll be your nurses, Dad. We'll take care of you."

"Thanks," he said, thinking that Sylvia would be happy to let them take care of him. Or anyone else. As long as she didn't have to.

IN TWO DAYS Harry felt almost normal. His doctor came from the hospital to remove the body cast he'd been wrapped in and ordered Harry to make an appointment for an x-ray of his ribs the next week. Denise and Vickie looked in on him before rushing off to school and once again as soon as they got back. The rest of the time Harry spent in bed watching television or pecking at his laptop. Sylvia stayed out of the guest room.

It's just as well, Harry thought. I sleep better alone. She doesn't want me near me anyway.

It was then that he realized his marriage was over. Had been over for years. They'd just been going through the motions, staying together for the kids' sake. This accident broke the bubble.

But where do I go from here? Harry asked himself. How do I tell the girls that I'm leaving them? That their mother wants me to leave them?

W e've got a real problem, Victor."

General Scheib looked more worried than Anson had ever seen him before. The two men were sitting in the corner of Anson's spacious office by the windows that looked out on the parking lot. Scheib was in uniform, although he had loosened up enough to take off his beribboned jacket and toss it on the sofa on the other side of the room. Anson had kept his suit jacket on, his tie precisely knotted at his collar.

It was early evening, the sun was setting, the parking lot was almost empty as a handful of late leavers straggled to their cars and drove home.

Anson had broken out his best scotch and told his secretary she could go home as soon as she set his phone to refer all incoming calls to the answering machine.

As nonchalantly as he could manage, Anson replied, "We've identified the cause of the accident and taken steps to make sure it won't happen again."

"I know," Scheib said, avoiding Anson's eyes. "But there's a ton of pressure coming down on us. The head of the Missile Defense Agency has never believed in the laser; he calls it

'Buck Rogers' fantasy.' That's my boss; that's what I've got to work with."

Anson picked up his glass from the little table between them. He'd poured a generous dollop of scotch for the general; he himself was drinking dry amontillado.

"We've made the laser work. The testing program was only a couple of months behind schedule. So we'll be five or six months behind; that's no big deal."

"The laser blew up, Victor."

"Accidents happen."

Scheib stared at him for several heartbeats. "Do you know what would happen if your laser blew up when it was flying in a 747? You'd have a dozen deaths on your hands. And my career would go down in flames with the plane."

"We'll fix it," Anson said firmly. "We'll make it work."

Shaking his head ever so slightly, Scheib said, "We don't have just the Air Force and the MDA to deal with here, Victor. There's the White House, for god's sake. The President's cut missile defense again. And the committee people in Congress; that's where the funding comes from."

"They're in favor of the airborne laser."

"They *were* in favor. But now . . . even our strongest supporters are wavering."

"But we've proved the concept," Anson insisted, feeling more alarm than he wanted to show. "We've shown that the laser can destroy a target almost instantaneously. We've shown that we can pick up a missile's signature and lock onto it."

"In separate experiments."

"But all we have to do is put them together. Systems integration. Anson Aerospace is good at systems integration."

Scheib took a healthy gulp of his scotch. "There's pressure coming from the top. There's going to be a congressional investigation. We have to show results, Victor, or they'll cancel the whole damned program."

Deciding that it was counterproductive to argue with the man who was pushing for the airborne laser in Washington, Anson cut to the chase. "How much time do we have?"

The general toyed with his glass, then answered, "Four months. That's when the congressional committee will open its investigation of the accident. You've got to have that laser working again in four months. Otherwise they'll cut you off."

"And then we start the integration work? Boeing's on schedule with the plane, I take it."

"Don't worry about Boeing, Victor. Just get that damned laser working again. And give me enough ammunition to show those old farts that you've corrected the problem that caused the explosion."

Anson nodded. Four months, he thought. Four months to make or break the program. Then he corrected himself. No, four months to make or break the company. If this airborne laser program goes down the tubes, Anson Aerospace goes with it. I'm going to have to push Levy and his people hard. And spend a lot on overtime.

Scheib looked bleak. He's under as much strain as I am, Anson thought.

"Well," he said with a forced smile. "At least we've got the weekend coming up. Are you staying here in California or heading right back to Washington?"

The young general tilted his head slightly. "I'd like to stay for the weekend . . ." He let his voice trail off.

Anson leaned back in his chair and said grandly, "Well, why don't you stay at my place up at Big Sur? Beautiful spot. Looks right out on the ocean. I can have the company chopper take you and put you down right on the front lawn."

Smiling, Scheib said, "That'd be great."

"The caretaker won't be there over the weekend. You'll have the place completely to yourself."

Scheib's grin widened. "Maybe I'll bring a friend along with me."

"Do that," Anson said as he got to his feet. "Have a nice restful weekend. Unwind. Enjoy yourself."

The two men shook hands and Scheib left the office. Anson re-filled his glass of sherry and went back to his desk. Maybe he'll bring a friend along, Anson said to himself. He knew perfectly well who the friend was: a certain Major Karen Christopher, USAF, who was normally stationed at some Air Force base in Missouri, but just happened to be in California this week.

Major Christopher was up for promotion to light colonel, ac-cording to the report in Anson's private computer files. She'll make lieutenant colonel, he told himself. But first she'll make the gen-eral. Scheib was a married man, but that hadn't stopped him from becoming quite involved with the good-looking major.

Anson sat at his desk and told himself that he wasn't spying on General Scheib for his own personal gain. It was for the good of the company, for the good of all the men and women who depended on him for their livelihoods. For the good of the nation, when you come right down to it. For the good of the entire free world!

M y God." Sylvia gaped as they got out of their Camry. "It's *huge.*"

Squinting up at the eight-story brick building, Harry said, "It's not all his. He's only got the top two floors."

"Only!" Sylvia said with awe in her voice.

Harry had never been invited to Victor Anson's home before. The invitation had been completely unexpected; it had arrived in the mail two days earlier, on stiff white embossed paper almost as thick as cardboard. RSVP. Sylvia had rushed out in a flurry of shopping. Harry thought she looked pretty good in the light yellow cocktail dress she'd bought; she ought to, after all the time she and the girls had spent fussing over the dress, the shoes, her makeup, her hair.

Harry's hair was slicked down with a gel that Sylvia insisted he use. It made him feel like a pimp, but Sylvia screamed that he couldn't go to Victor Anson's party with his hair blowing every which way, like some nerdy creep. He hated the gel, but he used it.

Now the two of them stood at the front door of the condominium building while a parking valet drove their car down the bricked driveway to the parking lot in back. A doorman in a black uniform was standing by the glass double doors of the entryway. After checking the

invitation Harry handed to him, the doorman led them every step of
the way to the elevator, as if he was afraid Harry would steal one of the
vases that held big bouquets of fresh flowers.

Another guy in a black uniform actually ran the elevator. Harry
began to wonder if this was all security that Anson had hired. All
the guy had to do was press the button marked PH. For penthouse,
Harry figured.

The elevator opened onto a small entryway. Beyond its open door
was a big room already crowded with people, buzzing with conversation, men and women standing and chatting amiably while holding
champagne flutes or heavy cut crystal old-fashioned glasses. The men
were all in suits or at least sports jackets. Harry felt grateful that Sylvia
had insisted he wear his one and only suit, an old tweed that he hadn't
taken out of the closet for years. It smelled faintly of mothballs. He
recognized a few of the senior scientists from the lab. Moving hesi-
tantly into the crowd, he introduced Sylvia to Jake Levy, who was
wearing the kind of dark blue suit that Harry associated with church
services. Levy in turn introduced his own wife, a plump graying
woman who seemed surprisingly older than Levy.

A big picture window swept along the far wall; Harry could see all
the way out to the old Rose Bowl and the hills beyond. It was a beau-
tifully clear day, with brilliant afternoon sunshine streaming down.
Harry nodded to himself, thinking, When Victor Anson throws a
party the smog isn't invited.

Anson himself was standing by the curving staircase that led upstairs, General Scheib beside him in his best blues. A woman in Air
Force uniform was next to Scheib, the gold oak leaves of a major on
her shoulders. She was petite, kind of pretty in a sort of girl-next-
door way, but she looked distinctly uncomfortable.

Sylvia fell into conversation with Mrs. Levy as a young waitress
in a short-skirted black-and-white outfit offered a tray of drinks to
Harry. He took a tulip glass of white wine and handed it to Sylvia,
who accepted it without even looking at him.

"And for you, sir?" the waitress asked.

"Um . . ." Harry thought about the drive home. It wasn't far, but he'd never been up at this end of Pasadena, near the country club, and didn't know the streets very well. He knew the Pasadena police force, though. "I'll have a club soda," he said.

Mrs. Levy excused herself and moved away from Sylvia. For a few moments neither she nor Harry knew quite what they should be doing.

"Where's the other people from your crew?" she asked Harry.

He scanned the crowd. "I don't see them."

"Weren't they invited?"

"Maybe not."

"Didn't you ask them?" Sylvia demanded. "Didn't you tell them you were invited to Mr. Anson's home?"

He shook his head. The thought had never occurred to him.

Sylvia huffed. "Honestly, Harry."

General Scheib came up to him, with the good-looking major hanging a step behind him.

"How're the ribs, Harry?"

"They're fine," Harry fibbed. His back still ached, still twinged when he moved too quickly.

"Good," said the general. "Good." And he moved past Harry and Sylvia without introducing the major, who dutifully followed after him.

The waitress arrived with Harry's club soda in a tall glass tinkling with ice cubes. He began to feel edgy. He didn't really know anybody in this crowd, except for Levy, and Jake was all the way over on the other side of the big room now, by the picture window, deep in conversation with a couple of older men who looked to Harry like bankers or maybe members of Anson's board of directors: white-haired and balding, big in the middle, flabby in the face.

"Mr. Anson's coming this way!" Sylvia hissed urgently.

Harry saw Anson making his way slowly through the crowd, stopping to talk to this one or that for a moment, then moving closer to where he and Sylvia stood. There was something strange about his lean face with its high cheekbones and shaved scalp. His skin looked waxy, slick, like the skin grafts they give to burn victims. Still, he looked stylish in his navy blue blazer and white slacks: pencil-slim, his face taut, his scalp shaved, his moustache trim and elegant.

"Where's his wife?" Sylvia whispered.

Harry shook his head. "I don't know." He wouldn't recognize her anyway; he'd never seen a picture of her.

"She's very big with the opera society," Sylvia said, still whispering as though she were passing on military secrets. "I told you we should get involved in the opera society."

Harry didn't remember that, but he didn't say anything. Anson was chatting amiably with the couple standing next to them, but he was glancing in Harry's direction.

Sure enough, Anson disengaged from the other couple and turned to Harry and Sylvia. "You must be Mrs. Hartunian," he said, making it sound as if it were a compliment.

"Sylvia," Harry said.

"A pleasure." Anson took Sylvia's hand and bowed over it slightly, as if he were going to kiss it. Sylvia's face turned scarlet.

Then Anson said, "Sylvia, do you mind if I borrow your husband for a few minutes? I have something important to discuss with Harry. In private."

"Ce . . . certainly," Sylvia stammered.

"Thank you, Sylvia," said Anson graciously. "I won't keep him long."

Harry felt mystified as Anson gripped him by the elbow and led him through the partygoers, back toward the stairs. The crowd melted away before them. Like Moses parting the Red Sea, Harry thought.

"Can your ribs do the stairs or should we take the elevator?" Anson asked.

"I'm okay," Harry said, stretching the truth. "The stairs are fine."

The staircase curved between walls lined with old, fading photographs. Family, Harry thought. People at the beach, people at formal dinners in tuxedos and evening gowns, a man who looked a lot like Victor Anson shaking hands with President Franklin D. Roosevelt, no less. Some of the pictures seemed to go back to the roaring twenties.

The staircase ended in a single, open, airy solarium. All the walls were tinted windows from floor to ceiling. Harry squinted at the light streaming in despite the tinting; it was almost painful. A big old-fashioned desk of dark mahogany stood on one side of the room, an even bigger, heavy-legged pool table on the other.

"My sanctum sanctorum," Anson said as Harry looked admiringly around the room, his eyes adjusting to the brightness. "I come up here to do my thinking. And my deciding."

Harry couldn't think of anything to say.

A pair of comfortable bottle green–leather wing chairs was in one corner, angled slightly to face each other. A small sherry table stood between them.

Anson gestured to the chairs. "Have a seat, Harry."

Harry eased himself gratefully into the luxurious chair. It creaked a little. Or is that my back? Harry asked himself.

A bottle and two tiny tulip glasses stood on the table.

"Have some sherry?" Anson asked as he sat facing Harry. "It's amontillado, my favorite."

Harry hesitated, then hoisted his club soda as he replied, "I've got to drive home."

Anson nodded. "Smart fellow."

Harry felt uncomfortable. He didn't know what to say, didn't know if it was okay to rest his glass on the inlaid wood of the little table between them.

Anson solved Harry's dilemma by sliding a thick green marble coaster across the table as he asked, "How's the rebuilding work going?"

"We're on schedule, Mr. Anson. A little ahead of schedule, actually."

"Good," said Anson. Leaning forward slightly, his slender hands on his knees, he went on. "This laser project is very important, Harry. Extremely important."

"I know." Harry hesitated, wondering how Anson would react to being questioned, but worked up the courage to say, "Mr. Anson, is it all right if I ask you a question?"

"Certainly," Anson replied grandly. Then, with a sly wink, he added, "I don't guarantee that I'll answer it, though."

Harry forced a perfunctory laugh.

"So what's your question, son?"

Trying not to let his nervousness show in his voice, Harry said, "When . . . when the accident happened and Pete Quintana died, I thought—we all thought, actually—that you'd pick Monk Delany to replace Pete as program engineer."

Anson's face went dour. For several long moments he said nothing while Harry berated himself for going too far.

At last Anson said slowly, "Not Delany. No, Harry, he wouldn't do. Not serious enough. I needed a man who could get the job done. That man is you, Harry, and nobody else."

Swallowing before he could speak again, Harry said, "Thank you, sir. I was . . . well, sort of surprised when you picked me."

With a thin smile, Anson said, "That's one of your good qualities, my boy. You don't have a swelled head."

Harry couldn't think of a thing to say.

Anson went on. "I've talked General Scheib into giving us a go-ahead for flight tests as soon as we prove the rebuilt laser works."

"Flight tests?"

"Yes. That's where the real money is, Harry. Systems integration and then flight tests."

"We'll have to test the COIL on the ground first, make sure we've got all the bugs out."

"Of course," said Anson. "Of course. But I want to stress to you, Harry, how important this program is. I've sunk a lot of the company's money into your COIL. I'm swinging for the fences with this one."

Harry thought, It isn't *my* COIL.

Anson went on. "You see, Harry, I believe in this laser idea. The United States is under threat, you know. A grave threat. It's bad enough that the Russians and the Chinese have whole fleets of ballistic missiles aimed at us—"

"I thought they agreed to retarget their missiles, just like we did," Harry interrupted. "They signed an agreement, didn't they? A treaty?"

Anson waved an impatient hand. "They could target them back on our cities in a matter of hours."

Harry nodded.

"But it's these other people who really threaten us. The Russians and Chinese know that if they try to hit us we'll smash them back to the Stone Age with an overwhelming counterstrike. But what about terrorists? What about the crazies in North Korea and Iran?" A blue vein in Anson's forehead began to throb. "They're fanatics! They're not worried about a counterstrike. All they want is to hurt us as deeply as they can! Blow up an American city! Cripple our economy! Bend us to their will!"

"So the airborne laser—"

"Will be our first line of defense. We've got to be able to stop their missiles as soon as they fire them at us. And they'll be firing them at us, never doubt it."

Harry picked up his glass and took a gulp of soda. "We've got a lot of work to do," he said.

"We do indeed, Harry," Anson said, nodding grimly. "And I'll be perfectly frank with you, son: the company's entire future is riding on that laser. If it fails, if we can't make it work and we lose the contract, Anson Aerospace could go bankrupt."

"The whole company?" Harry felt startled.

"The whole company," Anson confirmed. "I've staked just about everything on this one program."

"Wow."

Anson took a sip of amontillado, then asked, "Do you know why you weren't laid off after the accident?"

Harry's guts clenched. One of the laser team's technicians, Andy McMasters, had been fired. Harry had expected the ax to fall on his neck, but they had booted McMasters instead.

Without waiting for Harry to reply, Anson went on. "Levy suggested we let you go, you know. He wanted to find a scapegoat to blame for the accident."

Harry nodded wordlessly.

"But I knew that the rest of your team looked up to you, Harry. I knew the accident wasn't your fault. I knew we needed you to get the COIL back on track."

"Me?"

Anson nodded wisely. "You."

Dumbfounded, Harry mumbled, "Thank you, sir."

Anson reached out and grasped Harry by the shoulder. "You're important to us, son. Important to me."

"But I'm just an engineer," Harry protested, his back twinging. "Dr. Levy's the one—"

Waving an impatient hand, Anson said, "Levy's a scientist. He's fine in the lab, of course, but what I need now is a man who can make that contraption really work. I don't need equations and theories, I need performance. I need you, Harry. You're my program engineer."

Harry blinked at the man who owned the lab, owned the corporation, owned his future. "I'll do my best, Mr. Anson."

Gripping Harry's shoulder tightly enough to make Harry wince, Anson said earnestly, "I know you will, son. That's why I want you running the test team every step of the way. When the COIL is integrated into that jumbo jet, I want you to run the flight test program. Wherever that plane goes, you go."

Harry felt his jaw drop open. "Me?"

"Make it work, Harry," said Anson. "I'm counting on you. We're all counting on you. The company's ass is on the line."

I've never lost my temper without regretting it, Harry told himself as he tossed his garment bag on the motel room's sagging bed. He cursed himself for being an idiot. You pop off at the wrong time and make a mess of everything.

He unzipped the bag and started pulling his rumpled shirts out of it. The room had a bureau and a wardrobe. One hand filled with the shirts, Harry yanked at the top bureau drawer. It stuck and the shirts spilled out of his hand onto the threadbare carpet.

Harry fought down an urge to kick the shirts all across the room. Instead he sat on the bed and buried his face in his hands.

You and your big mouth, he said to himself. You and your stupid temper. You hold it in and hold it in, and then when you let it go you ruin everything.

When Anson announced that Harry was now head of the laser team, Harry had expected Monk to be disappointed, maybe even angry. Instead Delany looked almost relieved.

"You deserve it, Harry," he'd said. "Anson knows he can trust you."

Harry thought that what Monk was really saying was that Anson knew he could make Harry jump through hoops. So what? Harry said to himself. Angel Reyes started calling Harry *el jefe*; Angel even got his wife to sew the title on some of Harry's T-shirts and coveralls.

Sylvia took the news calmly enough, except to ask, "Does a raise go with it? You're going to be putting even more hours into the job, aren't you? You ought to get a raise."

Harry didn't have the nerve to ask Anson, or even Jake Levy, if he should expect an increase in salary.

For nearly three months after the accident Harry had been working at Anson's test facility out in the Mohave, sweating away feverishly to rebuild the COIL. Victor Anson himself had come out to the desert twice to inspect his team's progress and urge them to move faster.

Harry stayed at the Desert Stars Motel more than he was home, and when he was home Sylvia complained about his being away. He found that he was happy to leave her in Pasadena and dreaded the long drive back home every weekend. His daughters had become strangers to him: teenagers, with lives of their own and friends and school and endless chatter on their cell phones.

The day they fired up the COIL and burned a hole through the target sheet of aluminum half a mile away Harry could hear the relief and triumph in Mr. Anson's voice over the telephone.

"You did it, Harry! I knew I could count on you!"

"We did it, Mr. Anson. The team. We did it together."

"You certainly did. Listen, Harry, give the team a party. Take them to the nearest bar and have a celebration. A blast. On me."

The bar at the Desert Stars Motel wasn't much, but Harry and his team trooped in and took over the place. It was a wild night.

And Harry found himself walking one of the young barmaids back to his room. She was really pretty, he thought, with a warm bright smile and he hadn't had sex with Sylvia since the accident and he'd had more to drink than he should've and she seemed perfectly willing and Harry thought What the hell, why not?

He kept the story from Sylvia for more than a month afterward, tiptoeing around the house when he was home, feeling unable to look her in the eye, ashamed of himself yet happy that a good-looking young woman had willingly gone to bed with him. Harry stayed away from the motel's bar; he didn't want any entanglements. Monk kidded him about the night and told him the kid was asking about him. Red-faced, Harry went to his room and stayed there.

It all came out during an argument with Sylvia, of course. He couldn't even remember how the argument had started, but they were yelling at each other and he blurted out the news that other women found him attractive.

Sylvia stared at him, white-faced with anger. She glanced past Harry toward their daughters' rooms. Both doors were tightly closed. Vickie and Denise had heard plenty of screaming from their parents; they just shut it out of their presence.

"Women find you attractive?" Sylvia asked, the beginnings of a smirk curling her lips. "You? Mr. Dull? Don't make me laugh."

"Yeah, me," Harry snapped. "You've probably forgotten it, but I'm not so dull in bed."

She huffed. "There's nothing to forget, Harry. You're a dud and you always will be."

"Well, you're the only one who thinks so!"

"Are you saying you've gone to bed with other women?"

"Damned right!"

"That's what you've been doing out at that motel? That's why you stay out there more than you're home?"

"I've got more going for me out there than here," Harry snapped.

Sylvia glared at him for a long, long moment. Harry waited for her to burst into tears or start throwing things. Instead she almost smiled as she said, very calmly, "Then you'd better pack your things and get the hell out of here."

"I will," Harry said.

"Now. Tonight."

Harry nodded and walked wordlessly to the guest room, where

he'd been sleeping since the accident. He pulled his garment bag out of the closet and began packing.

Now, sitting on the bed in the seedy Ocean View Motel in Santa Monica, Harry saw that Sylvia had baited a trap and he'd walked right into it. His marriage was over. Sylvia's known it for a long time, he realized. She's always been smarter than me. It's been over for years, he said to himself. Over and done with.

Still, he felt empty, alone. He had nothing left. No marriage, no daughters—they wouldn't even speak to him on the phone. Nothing but work. The job.

They'd start installing the COIL in the plane next week, Harry knew. The flight tests were scheduled to begin before the year's out.

He got up from the bed and began to pick up the shirts that had fallen to the floor. Make the COIL work. Go with the plane wherever it flies.

It was something, at least. Harry had something. A reason to get up in the morning. A job that needed to be done.

APPROACH

Harry stared at the empty space where the ranging laser's optical assembly should have been.

He heard Victor Anson's urgent demand. *Make it work, Harry. I'm counting on you. We're all counting on you. The company's ass is on the line.*

He heard the lanky lieutenant's voice. "You okay up there, Mr. Hartunian?"

"I'm fine," Harry said, adding silently, But we're all in real trouble.

With Lieutenant Sharmon helping him, Harry climbed down from the laser mount and closed its access panel. Then he headed for the beam control station downstairs, Monk Delany's place. The ranging laser is Monk's responsibility, Harry said to himself. And somebody's sabotaged it.

Harry clambered down the ladder, brushed past Taki Nakamura, and ducked through the hatch into the beam control compartment.

Monk Delany looked up at him. "What's the matter, Harry?" Delany had his usual half-quizzical smile on his stubbled face.

"We've got a saboteur on board."

"What're you talking about?"

"The forward lens assembly is missing from the ranging laser, that's what I'm talking about."

Delany's jaw dropped open. "Missing? Whaddaya mean it's missing?"

"It's not there, Monk. That's why the console's reading a malfunction."

"It's gotta be there."

"It's not. I just checked it out."

"Everything was okay last night. I checked it all out." Delany's usual smile was gone now. He looked frightened.

"It's not okay now."

Monk looked up at Harry, his face full of consternation.

"We've got spares. I'll get right on it." He got up from his seat and before Harry could say anything squeezed through the hatch, heading aft.

Harry didn't move. He stood there in the nose of the plane, feeling it rise and fall slowly, majestically, like the big cruise liner he'd been on as it ploughed relentlessly through the sea. But his mind was racing. There's a saboteur among us, he thought. Somebody doesn't want the COIL to work. Somebody on board the plane, somebody who doesn't want to get himself killed. So he disables the ranging laser. Without data on the target's range and position the COIL is useless.

Who did this? Harry asked himself. Can Monk fix it before we get near North Korea? And if he does, what will the saboteur try next?

The place was a madhouse. Sylvia had decided to avoid LAX and take a commuter jet to San Francisco, but the usually quiet airport in Santa Monica was teeming with angry, yelling, ticket-waving customers. One look at the electronic status board showed Sylvia that half the scheduled flights had been canceled. Most of the others were badly delayed.

Her daughters seemed unimpressed by the furor boiling all around them as Sylvia left them in front of the status board to fight her way to the ticket counter.

"Don't move from this spot," Sylvia commanded.

Both girls nodded dutifully.

"And watch my bag!"

"Sure."

As their mother plunged into the crowd, Vickie said, "Must be a lot of people trying to get to San Francisco today."

"Or someplace," Denise agreed.

"The place looks like a zoo."

"This is where they filmed *Casablanca?*" Denise asked her older sister.

The two girls were standing in the midst of the bellowing, surging crowd like a pair of slim palm trees in the middle of a tropical typhoon, Vickie nodded. "The airport scene in the beginning," she said.

A harried-looking, red-faced man lugging a bulging briefcase rushed past the girls and tripped over Vickie's roll-on suitcase. He went sprawling, his briefcase popped open, papers fluttering in all directions.

Vickie and Denise helped to scoop up the papers. The man stuffed them back in his briefcase, his face sweaty and angry, as he muttered something about being late for the last flight to Sacramento. He dashed off, clutching the briefcase under his arm like a football.

"He never said thank you," Denise complained.

"A jerk," said Vickie.

Sylvia came out of the crowd, reached for the handle of her roll-on, and said grimly to her daughters, "Follow me."

They pushed through the fuming, bawling crowd and up a flight of stairs, their roll-ons bumping with each step.

Sylvia pushed through a door marked FLIGHT OPERATIONS DIRECTOR, the two girls at her heels.

It was mercifully quiet inside the office. No one was there except a rake-thin, harried-looking man sitting behind a desk with a phone at his ear and both eyes staring at his desktop computer screen. He was in his shirtsleeves, which were rolled up. His tie was pulled loose from his wrinkled, soggy collar.

"It's a total mess!" he was saying into the phone, his voice high, agitated. "Computers are down, phone lines are jammed, navigation system is kaput—a real mess!"

Sylvia stood before his desk, her two daughters flanking her, and waited patiently until at last the man put the phone down and looked up at her.

Before he could speak a word, Sylvia said sweetly, "Congresswoman McClintock is waiting for us in San Francisco. If we don't get there to be with the President this evening there's going to be a lot of trouble."

"Congresswoman McClintock?"

"We're due to be with the President of the United States this evening at the Cow Palace," Sylvia said in a tone that you could pour over pancakes.

"The President?"

"The President," said Sylvia sweetly. "And Congresswoman McClintock. And the chairman of the Senate Transportation Committee. Among others."

The man groaned, but then said, "Wait right here. I'll see what can be done."

Sylvia gestured for her daughters to take the two wooden chairs in front of the desk. She herself remained standing while the badly stressed director of flight operations picked up his telephone again.

K amchatka Peninsula coming up."

Colonel Christopher heard her navigator's voice in her headphone. The kid sounded more sure of himself since they'd made the rendezvous with the first tanker.

"There it is," Major Kaufman said, pointing to a smudge of gray clouds on the horizon, at about the two o'clock position.

Christopher said into her lip mike, "Jon, we need to stay well away from Russian airspace."

"Workin' on it," the navigator replied. "I'll have a course correction for you in two minutes, Colonel."

"Colonel, we're getting pinged by Kamchatka," said the communications officer. O'Banion's voice sounded worried. "Oh-oh. Message coming in."

"Pipe it to me," she commanded.

A smooth baritone voice said in flawless midwestern American English, "Unidentified aircraft, you are approaching Russian airspace. Please identify yourself."

Christopher thumbed the comm switch on her control yoke and said crisply, "This is U.S. Air Force ABL-1. We intend to remain over international waters."

"We have no information on your flight plan," said Kamchatka, without the slightest trace of anxiety.

The colonel bit her lips momentarily, then replied, "We are on our way to Japanese airspace. We will stay well away from your territory."

Silence for several heartbeats. He's waiting for his superiors to tell him what he should say, Christopher reasoned.

Finally, "U.S. ABL-1, our air defense command has sent a flight of interceptors to accompany you away from Russian airspace. They have no hostile intent."

"Copy," Christopher said curtly. "No hostile intent." Then she clicked off the radio switch and grinned at her copilot. "Bet they've got plenty of cameras on board."

"They'll have air-to-air missiles, too, count on it," Kaufman muttered.

"Of course." She turned the situation over in her mind for a few moments, then said, "We better make a left turn, Obie."

"I guess so."

Lieutenant Sharmon gave them a new heading and the big 747 turned southward twelve degrees. Not enough, though.

"Hey!" Kaufman yipped. "We got company."

Following his pointing finger with her eyes, Christopher saw a trio of swept-wing jet fighters boring in on them from above and ahead.

"Fulcrums," Kaufman said. MiG-29s, the mainstay of the Russian fighter forces.

"No," Christopher said, eyeing the sleek, silvery fighters. "They look too new. More like MiG-35s."

"There's another one," Kaufman said, "comin' up fast."

"That's not a MiG," said Christopher.

"Looks a lot like one of our F-15s."

She nodded, making her flight helmet wobble slightly on her head. "Sukhoi SU-27. Photo recon plane."

Kaufman had an Air Force catalog displayed on the small screen to his right. "Flanker. Supersonic."

"She's not carrying any missiles."

"The other three are."

"That Flanker's a photo plane. Looks like a two-seater."

The three MiGs pulled up alongside ABL-1 on the right, speed brake flaps down to slow them to the 747's lumbering pace.

Kaufman said, "They're keeping themselves between us and Mother Russia."

"Just following orders," said Christopher, "same as us."

At that moment all three MiGs pulled their flaps up and roared ahead of ABL-1. The lead fighter suddenly jinked straight up, then sideways.

"He's viffing," Colonel Christopher said. Then she added for Kaufman's benefit, "Vectoring in flight."

"I know what viffing is," Kaufman replied testily. "Like the Marines' Harriers. They can take off straight up, like a helicopter."

The three MiGs made a tight turn and circled around to take up a station off the 747's left wing tip. Before Christopher could say anything, they zoomed ahead again and turned the other way, then settled into formation again off the right wing.

Christopher laughed. "They're flying rings around us."

"Showing off," Kaufman grumbled.

The Sukhoi pulled up even closer. Christopher could see two helmeted heads inside its elongated canopy.

O'Banion's voice piped up in her earphone. "They're painting us with radar, Colonel."

"I'll bet they are," said Christopher. "And with everything else they've got. They'd x-ray us if they could."

She saw the pilot of the flanker looking over at her as he held the fighter alongside. On an impulse, she waved at him. After a moment he waved back.

"Next thing you know he'll be asking for your phone number," Kaufman muttered.

"That's better than shooting at us."

"Guess so." But Kaufman didn't sound convinced of it.

The snow was getting thicker. Charley Ingersoll nudged the windshield wiper control and the blades smeared freshly fallen flakes across the SUV's windshield.

The weather report on the radio had called for "cloudy and mild" all afternoon, with a chance of snow after sunset. We oughtta be home before sunset, Charley said to himself. Specially if we don't stop for lunch.

Sure enough, Charley Jr. piped from the backseat, "I'm hungry! When are we gonna eat lunch?"

The boy must have mental telepathy, Charley thought.

"Me too!" Little Martha added. She never wanted to be left out of anything her older brother did.

Charley scowled at the thickening snow. The highway was still dry, nothing much had accumulated on the paving, but Charley knew it was only a matter of time before the road became slick and slippery.

"We got anything to feed them?" he asked his wife.

Martha gave him one of her you-always-blame-everything-on-me looks as she said, "No, dear. You said we'd stop for lunch on the way home, remember?"

"Okay, okay."

The gas gauge had dipped well below half, Charley saw.

"Look out for a gas station," he said to Martha. "One with a convenience store. You can get something for the kids to eat while I fill the tank."

They passed a big sign for another RV park up the road. It looked like an old sign, beat-up and weathered. Just as they sped past the entrance to the park, Charley Jr. announced, "I gotta go."

"Me too," said Little Martha.

His wife turned in her seat and said sternly, "Just control yourselves for a few more minutes. Your father's looking for a gas station. You can go there."

The snow was getting heavier. Charley punched the radio on again. Still nothing on the satellite stations. Martha fiddled with the dial until they got the tail end of a local weather report.

". . . cloudy and mild, with a chance of snow this evening," a cheery male voice was saying. "Snow accumulation could be more than a foot in the upper elevations."

"It's snowing now," Martha said, sounding a little nervous.

Charley saw a sign that announced a gas station five miles ahead.

"Five miles, kids," he said. "Just hang in there for another few minutes."

The gas station was nothing much: just a couple of pumps and a little building that looked barely big enough to hold an attendant. A sign saying NO CASH TRANSACTIONS was plastered by the door.

Charley pulled the SUV up to the pumps. Almost before he stopped the kids had the side door slid open and were racing for the side of the building. Martha got out and hurried after them, bundling her coat around herself as she ran through the thick wet flakes of snow that had already covered the parking area with white.

Charley was surprised by how cold it felt. A stinging wind cut through the light jacket he was wearing. His face felt cold, raw. Muttering to himself about weather forecasters, he slid his credit card into the pump's slot. Nothing happened. The screen was blank.

Grumbling now, Charley stomped through the wet snow to the building and pushed its door open. A pimply-faced kid sat huddled in a tatty-looking wool coat. His hair looked as if it hadn't been combed in a week and hadn't been washed in Lord knows how long.

"The pump won't take my card," Charley complained.

"Yeah, I know," the kid said, his voice raspy. "No electricity. We lost power 'bout half an hour ago. Soon's my pop comes to pick me up I'm outta here."

"Don't you have a manual pump?"

"Nope."

"How do I get gas?" Charley demanded.

"Beats me," the kid said.

Where are they now?" General Higgins asked.

"Over the Pacific, approaching Japan," replied General Scheib, pointing to the electronic map on the wall screen. A tiny winking light gave the position of ABL-1, a thin trace of blue line showed its course so far. Scheib wondered if Higgins couldn't see the map clearly; maybe he's nearsighted or something.

Higgins had loosened his tie and hung his blue jacket on the back of his chair. The situation room looked lived-in, plastic coffee cups dotting the oblong conference table, the cart that once held pastries and other snacks now bearing nothing but crumbs and three empty stainless steel urns.

Zuri Coggins had moved from her seat at Higgins' right hand down the table to be next to Michael Jamil, who was still bent over his iPhone. He had connected it wirelessly to the DoD computer that served the situation room and was slaving away over calculations of some sort.

On the wall opposite the big map, screens showed satellite views of North Korea. The two missiles still stood on their launch pads. No sign of the troops that Pyongyang had reportedly sent, but the satellite imagery was spotty, at best.

The admiral seated halfway down the table looked up from his laptop screen. "The Russian planes have turned back," he said, looking relieved. Like Higgins, the admiral had long since taken off his jacket and hung it on the back of his chair.

"They got a damned good look at our plane," Higgins muttered.

General Scheib nodded. He was on his feet, pacing the length of the situation room as if he were doing his daily exercises.

"They can't tell much from the exterior," Scheib said, trying to sound reassuring. But then he added, "Of course, that turret on the nose could be a giveaway. There's been enough publicity about the airborne laser that they'll recognize ABL-1 from that potato nose."

General Higgins shot an angry look at him and Scheib remembered the general's "Possum" nickname. Smart, he berated himself. Real smart.

"Who's flying the plane?" Higgins asked. "I hope we've got a good man at the controls."

Scheib started for his chair and the notebook computer opened on the table in front of it.

"This was supposed to be a test run for them," he said to Higgins. "They weren't expecting this crisis."

"Who the hell was?"

Scheib sat and pecked at his notebook. "Damned security red tape," he muttered, his head bent over the tiny keyboard. "Slows everything down."

Jamil looked up from his calculations. "I think it's imperative that we send a warning to the civil defense operations in Honolulu, Hilo, Anchorage, Juneau—"

"Not San Francisco?" one of the civilians asked.

Jamil looked up the table at General Higgins. Very calmly, he replied, "I seem to be the only one here who's worried about San Francisco."

Higgins made a sound halfway between a grunt and a snort.

Gently, Coggins asked, "You still think it's possible that they've targeted San Francisco?"

"I do. And we ought to be watching what the Chinese are doing. Watching very carefully."

"There doesn't seem to be anything unusual—"

"They've put their missiles on high alert, haven't they?"

"Well, so have we. And the Russians."

"And the Iranians?" Jamil asked.

Coggins studied his coffee-colored face with its fringe of beard as she wondered, What's he after? Why is he pushing us into his disaster scenario? And the answer immediately came back to her: because he believes it. He's scared that we're about to unleash a nuclear holocaust.

To Jamil she murmured, "The Israelis will take care of Iran."

"Before or after Tehran launches its missiles on Israel?"

Coggins hesitated.

"We should at least warn the Israelis of the possibility," Jamil urged with quiet intensity.

"And have those hotheads launch a preemptive strike on Iran? That would start your Sarajevo scenario all by itself, wouldn't it?"

Jamil slumped backing his chair. "Damned if we do, damned if we don't."

General Scheib called from his seat halfway up the table, "Okay, I've got it. The crew for today's flight of ABL-1, civilians and blue suits."

"What kind of experience does the pilot have?" General Higgins asked.

"Let me scroll down to . . ." Scheib's face reddened, then went white.

"Well?" Higgins demanded.

His voice dead flat, Scheib replied, "The pilot is Lieutenant Colonel Karen Christopher—"

"A woman?"

"One of the best pilots in the Air Force," Scheib said without looking up from his miniature computer's screen. "She piloted B-2s in actions over Afghanistan and Iraq. Very experienced, decorated . . ." His voice fell off.

"What's she doing driving a test program plane?" Higgins groused. "A pilot with that much experience and seniority."

Scheib knew, of course. It wasn't printed out on Karen's dossier, but he knew that she'd been stuck in the airborne laser program as punishment for refusing to divulge the name of the married Air Force officer she'd been sleeping with. Her career's been blighted because she was loyal to me, Scheib knew.

And now she's flying right into what could be the start of a nuclear war.

What if she gets killed on this mission? he asked himself. That would solve a lot of problems.

And he hated himself for even thinking of it.

M onk came back through the hatch with both his hands full of black cases that held spare optics components.

"Relax, Harry," he said. "I can get it put together again in an hour, maybe less."

"You can work up there?" Harry asked. "It's a tight space; I barely got into it."

Delany grinned at him. "I know the layout inside out, Harry. All I gotta do is get my arm into the housing."

"You sure of that?"

"If I need to I can get Taki to help me. She's small enough to get in there with no trouble."

Harry nodded but heard himself say, "And how do we test it?"

Monk stared at him.

"You put a new lens assembly in, but how do we know it's aligned right? How do we know it's working the way it should?"

"Jeez, Harry, I'm doin' the best I frickin' can."

"Yeah, I know. But it might not be good enough."

Monk put the boxes gently down on the workbench that ran along one side of the compartment. Turning back to Harry, he asked, "So what do you want to do?"

I want to go home and have a beer and watch the sun go down over the ocean, Harry thought.

"Harry?"

"Get to work," he said. "I've got to talk this over with the pilot. She's in command of this plane."

"If we can't be sure the ranger is okay, we'll hafta turn back, I guess," Monk said softly, almost as if talking to himself.

"We're not turning back," Harry said. "Not unless the woman in charge says so."

"She doesn't know shit about this technology."

"She's in charge. It's her decision, not mine."

Monk looked as if he wanted to argue, but he merely shook his head dumbly.

"You need help with this?" Harry asked him.

"Naw. Another pair of hands would just get in the way."

"Okay," Harry said. "I'm going up to talk it over with the skipper."

Harry ducked out of the optics compartment. Taki was at her battle management console, looking bored. But one glance at Harry's face made her get to her feet.

"What's wrong?" she asked.

"Plenty," said Harry. On an impulse, he said, "Look in on Monk, give him a hand if he needs it. He's got to replace the ranger's optics assembly."

"Replace?" She looked startled. "Why? What's wrong with the—"

"It's missing."

"Missing? How can it be missing?"

Harry thought she looked genuinely surprised, genuinely alarmed. "That's what I'd like to know. You go in and offer Monk your help. Don't leave him alone in there."

Taki's face, normally impassive, was wide-eyed with consternation.

Harry left her and started up the ladder to the flight deck, thinking, If Monk sabotaged the ranger, he probably won't try anything else with Taki watching him. Unless she's in on it, part of the plot. Hell, they could all be in on it. Maybe I'm the only one who isn't.

The two blue-suiters were at their consoles, the lanky black lieutenant and the redheaded captain at the communications console. It seemed quiet up on the flight deck, the big jet engines muted to a distant background drone, the plane's throbbing vibrations barely noticeable.

The redhead gave him a quizzical glance as Harry clambered up from the ladder.

"I've got to talk with the skipper," Harry said.

Without a word to him, the comm officer tapped a key on his console and spoke into his pin mike. Then he looked up at Harry.

"Colonel Christopher will be right with you," he said.

She came out of the cockpit, stretching her slim body as she stepped through the open hatch. Harry thought that sitting for hours on end at the plane's controls must be hell on your body. His back twinged in sympathy for her.

Christopher looked up at him and smiled tiredly. "I was just thinking about taking a little nap." She made it sound like an apology.

Glancing at the two officers at their consoles, Harry said, "Can we go down to the galley?"

The colonel nodded. "A little coffee might do me good."

She gestured him to the ladder, then followed him down. They went past the empty battle management station; Taki was still in the forward section with Monk, Harry saw. The two of them were bent over the workbench, putting together the spare lenses of the optics assembly.

Once in the cramped little galley, Christopher went straight to the coffee urn and poured herself a cup.

"Almost empty," she murmured. "I'll have to get Sharmon to make a fresh batch."

Unable to contain himself any longer, Harry blurted, "Somebody sabotaged the ranging laser."

"What?" Christopher's dark eyes flashed.

"My people are fixing it, but somebody took out the optics from the ranging laser. Deliberately."

She sagged back against the curving bulkhead, as if her legs wouldn't hold her.

"We'll get it fixed," Harry said.

"It couldn't have been any of my guys," said the colonel. "None of them would know how."

Harry agreed with a nod. "It's one of my people. But I don't know who."

"You're sure . . . ?"

"It was deliberate. The lenses were in place when we did our inspection last night. When I checked ten minutes ago they were gone."

"Shit on a shingle," Christopher muttered.

"Somebody in my team doesn't want this mission to go ahead," Harry said.

"You can fix it? We can go on?"

"Yes, I'm pretty sure."

"Pretty sure?"

"I'm not worried about fixing the lens assembly," Harry said. "What worries me is what the guy's going to try next."

"He could blow this plane out of the sky!"

Strangely, Harry felt calm, unafraid. "I don't think so. Whoever did it picked the least damaging way to shut us down. Without the ranging laser the big COIL is useless. And the saboteur is aboard this plane, riding with us. He doesn't want to kill himself, whoever he is."

"You keep saying 'he.' You have a woman on your crew. She's Chinese or something, isn't she?"

"Taki Nakamura," Harry replied. "Born in Phoenix, Arizona. Her family's been in the States since the 1920s. She's as American as you or me."

Christopher digested that information in silence. Then, "You're going to have to keep your eyes wide open, mister."

"I know. But we have another problem."

"Another?"

"We can fix the ranging laser. But we won't know if it's calibrated properly unless we can try it out on a real target."

"Explain."

"It's a low-power laser. We use it like radar, to get a pinpoint fix on the target's distance and velocity. We need a live target to test it on."

Colonel Christopher almost smiled. "That's easy. We're due for another refueling rendezvous in" — she glanced at her wristwatch — "another seventy-three minutes. You can ping the tanker."

"Yeah," Harry said. "That'll work."

"You'll have the laser working by then?"

"We will," Harry said, adding silently, Or I'll jump overboard.

B ut you're supposed to be the intelligence officer!"

"That doesn't mean they tell me diddly-squat. Sir."

Major Hank Wilson held a flimsy sheet of a decoded message from Andrews Air Force Base, back in the States, in one big, hairy fist. He glared down at Captain William Koenig, long, lanky, and as lean as a beanpole. Koenig glared right back at his commanding officer.

Brandishing the flimsy, Major Wilson grumbled, "That tanker's due in fifteen minutes and we don't know why it's here."

"It's out of Chongju, I know that much."

"But why's it landing here? Where's it heading? We don't have anything up there that needs an air-to-air refueling."

"Washington moveth in mysterious ways," Keonig murmured.

College boy, Wilson thought. Give 'em a degree and they think they know everything. But when you need information from them they can't produce anything but crap.

Seeing the anger growing on his superior's face, Koenig said, "We know the tanker's out of Chongju. We know it's on special orders from Andrews, relayed out of the Pentagon."

"We knew that two hours ago," Wilson growled.

"Everything's slowed to a crawl," the captain said. "Our comm-sats are overloaded with traffic. Messages are coming through late."

"But the message from that mother-loving tanker came through loud and clear, didn't it?"

"Yessir. It came directly from the tanker itself, not relayed by a satellite."

"So they have engine trouble."

Koenig nodded. "It's an old bird, a KC-135. Been in service for thirty-some years. I looked up the tail number."

"So it needs to land here and get its engine fixed."

"Or replaced."

"So it's going to be late for its rendezvous with whatever it's supposed to be refueling."

Koening spread his hands in a gesture of helplessness. "Nothing we can do about that."

"But there's a plane out there someplace expecting to rendezvous with that mother-humping tanker and the fucker isn't going to be there!"

"That's the way it looks. Sir."

"We have to tell that plane that its rendezvous is going to be late."

"Yes, sir, we certainly do."

"But we don't know what plane we're talking about! We don't know where the bastard is! How can we communicate with it when we don't know anything about it?"

"I've sent an urgent message back to Andrews, sir. It's in their lap."

Major Wilson's heavy-jowled face looked like a thundercloud. "By the time Washington gets your message and acts on it, that mystery bird could be in the drink."

Captain Koenig said nothing.

"So why don't you find out what plane we're talking about and where the fuck it is?"

"I've queried Andrews, sir. No response, so far."

Wilson restrained himself from jumping over the desk and throttling the captain. It's not his fault, he told himself. Think of your blood pressure. Remember you've got a physical coming up Monday morning. It's not his fault.

But he growled, "You're supposed to be the intelligence officer."

General Scheib's minicomputer chimed with the ding-dong melody of Big Ben. It sounded like a Munchkin version of the London clock's sonorous tones.

Scheib hurried from the newly refilled coffee cart to his chair at the conference table. One of his aides from his office in the Pentagon was on the notebook's miniature screen, a frown of concern etching lines between his brows.

"What's up, Lieutenant?" Scheib asked, his own face tightening worriedly.

"Can we go to scramble, sir?"

Scheib nodded. "Do it."

The computer screen broke into a hash of colored streaks until Scheib tapped the password code on his keyboard.

The lieutenant's worried face took form again. "Message incoming from Misawa, sir. Marked urgent."

Misawa Air Force Base, Scheib knew. In northern Japan.

"Let's see it."

The lean, angular face of a captain replaced Scheib's aide. The man looked more puzzled than concerned.

"We have a KC-135 asking for landing clearance here. They say they're on a refueling mission but have developed engine trouble. Somebody needs to tell the plane they're supposed to be refueling that the rendezvous is going to be late, but we have no information on what plane that might be or where it is."

Scheib sank back in his chair. The timeline hack on the bottom of the screen showed that the message had been sent nearly two hours earlier.

He closed his eyes and suppressed the urge to rip out his aide's intestines. *Two hours to replay an urgent message to me!* Scheib raged inwardly. Then he remembered that the commercial commsats were out and the military satellites were overloaded with traffic. The ABL-1 mission was classified Top Secret, Need to Know. Neither the tanker crew nor the base at Misawa knew what the hell was going on.

He sensed someone standing behind his chair. Turning slightly, he saw that it was Zuri Coggins.

"Is that going to ruin the mission?" she asked.

"Could be," said Scheib.

"What can I do to help?"

"Get me real-time comm links with that tanker, with the base commander at Misawa, and with ABL-1. We're tripping over ourselves with the damned security regs."

She nodded. "I'll call my office."

General Higgins came up, looking bleary-eyed and tired of the situation.

"There goes your laser, Brad," said Higgins. "Looks like we'll have to depend on the Aegis ships and the missile batteries in Alaska."

"I'm not giving up on ABL-1, sir," Scheib said tightly.

DOWN AT THE end of the table Michael Jamil watched the tense little minidrama going on around General Scheib.

Let them play their games, Jamil said to himself. *What's important is to find out who's behind this crisis. Why have they knocked out the satellites? What do they want?*

Again and again Jamil had played out every possible scenario he could think of in his mind. He didn't need computers; he knew the players and their tactics. But none of this made sense. Why knock out the satellites? Why keep those two additional missiles on their pads when they know that regular troops are rushing from Pyongyang to their launching site? It's been more than ten hours since they set off the bomb in orbit; why are they waiting to launch those other two missiles?

Every scenario he ran through his mind ended in the same way: they're going to try to kill the President. They're going to hit San Francisco with half a megaton of hydrogen bombs, but they have to wait until the President's there. There can't be any other explanation for what they're doing. Knock out the satellites to slow our communications links to a crawl, then wait for the President to show up in San Francisco and blow the city off the map. Maybe the explosions will be enough to trigger an earthquake into the bargain.

Jamil looked up at the two generals and the others clustered around Scheib's chair. They look grim, he realized. Something must have gone wrong.

The woman from the National Security office looked up and met his gaze. She detached herself from the crowd around Scheib and walked down the length of the table toward him.

Jamil got to his feet, and before she could say a word he urged, "You've got to get a warning out to San Francisco. You can't let them fire those missiles without warning the Homeland Security people."

Coggins stared at him for a long, silent moment. Then she drew in a breath before replying, "Are you really that sure that San Francisco is the target?"

"Yes!"

She looked away, murmuring, "The city would go apeshit if we told them they're going to be bombed. Mass panic. God knows how many people would be killed in the rush to get away."

"They'll all be killed if we don't warn them," Jamil said. Then he added, "And the President, too."

Coggins shook her head. "I don't know . . . I just don't know."

"Tell your boss, at least," Jamil said. "Let him make the decision. He's the National Security Advisor, isn't he? Let him earn his keep."

She smiled thinly. "When in doubt, buck it upstairs."

The flight operations director put down his phone and made a weak smile for Sylvia, who still stood unmoving before his desk.

"Okay," he said shakily, "I've got a plane to take you to SFO."

"San Francisco?" Sylvia asked.

Nodding, the operations director got up from behind his desk. "It's a private plane. A friend of mine is flying up there on business and he's agreed to take you and your daughters."

"That's wonderful!"

Mopping his brow with a damp handkerchief, the operations director said, "I had to call in a lot of favors for this. I hope you tell Congresswoman McClintock about it."

"I certainly will," said Sylvia.

The operations director glanced at his wristwatch as he said, "You go over to the general aviation terminal. There's a bus outside that'll take you there. Be quick now. He said he'll wait for you, but he wants to take off no later than 4:00 p.m."

Sylvia grabbed the handle of her roll-on. "We'll be there. Tell him we're on our way! And thanks!"

The three women hurried out of the office so fast the operations director didn't have time to pull one of his cards from his wallet and give it to Sylvia so that she could show it to Congresswoman McClintock.

The President looked up from the text of the speech he would give at the Cow Palace as his chief of staff came into the private compartment and sat in the big comfortable chair facing him.

Leaning toward the President, Norman Foster said, "The pilot says we're on the approach to San Francisco."

The President glanced at his wristwatch. "Right on schedule. Good."

"We can still turn around," Foster said.

The President gave him the stare that often froze lesser men. Foster gazed back at his boss without flinching.

"They're still worried about the city being nuked?"

"Took a call direct from your National Security Advisor. The admiral thinks the prudent thing to do would be to turn back."

"I'd look like a damned fool if nothing happens."

"You'd be dead if they nuke the city. Me too."

With an easy smile the President said, "I'm going through with this. I can't afford to look like a coward. I'd never live it down."

Foster clenched his fists on his lap. "The plane could develop engine trouble. We could divert the flight to some other airport. A military base."

The President's smile faded. "You really think they're going to hit San Francisco."

"I think they might try."

"Might."

"If they do—"

"Norm, you've sat in on those intelligence briefings as often as I have. The North Koreans don't have a missile that can reach San Francisco."

"Maybe not."

"Hell, the last time they launched a missile it flopped into the middle of the Pacific. Besides, I've checked the reports," the President went on. "I haven't been sitting back here playing solitaire, Norm. I do my homework. According to the latest intelligence estimates the North Koreans do not have a missile with the range to reach San Francisco. Nor the accuracy. And especially not the reliability."

"And you're willing to pin your life to that?"

The President hesitated for the slightest fraction of a heartbeat, then said firmly, "Yes. I am."

Foster looked around the compartment, gathering his thoughts. Then he said, "There's this guy from the NIC sitting in on the special situation team we put together—"

"In the Pentagon?"

"Right." Foster nodded. "He's insisting that the North Koreans are aiming for San Francisco, specifically because they know you're going to be there tonight."

"He's running counter to the intelligence reports."

"He's got the representative from your National Security Advisor worried enough that she got him to put in another call to us here, warning us."

"One guy from the NIC?" the President asked. "What's his background? What does he know about the missiles the North Koreans have?"

"I don't know. I don't even know his name. But he claims that if they could deliver a nuke into orbit and knock out all the communications satellites, the same kind of missile could hit San Francisco."

The President leaned back in his chair and stroked his chin thoughtfully.

"One guy," he muttered.

Foster nodded.

"What's his background? Where's he from? Could be a Republican who wants to make me look bad."

Foster threw his hands up in the air. "For Chrissakes! We're talking nuclear war here!"

"We are talking," the President said coldly, precisely, "about an unsubstantiated theory by some unknown guy from the National Intelligence Committee."

"Look, there's a lot at stake here. The chances of the gooks nuking San Francisco might be damned small, but the consequences if they do are huge! Enormous!"

"That's what my science adviser says about global warming, for god's sake."

"Tell the pilot to divert to an Air Force base. Tell him to say we've got engine troubles. Tell—"

The pilot's voice broke in from the intercom speaker set into the compartment's overhead. "We are on final approach to San Francisco, sir. Please fasten your seat belt."

The President glanced at the speaker grill, then back at the friend and companion who had guided him to the White House.

"Too late, Norm. We're there."

Harry made his way aft, down the length of the big COIL, through a narrow hatch, and into the plane's rearmost section, where the stainless steel fuel tanks full of liquefied oxygen and iodine stood man-tall and frosted with rime. Rosenberg and Reyes were right behind him. Harry could feel their resentment at his insisting that they check every square centimeter of the tankage all over again.

It took the better part of an hour, but at last Harry was satisfied that the tanks were properly filled, at their correct cryogenic temperatures, and—most important of all—not leaking.

Now the two engineers stood glumly before Harry, both of them waiting for Harry to explain what was behind his sudden insistence on this inspection.

Rosenberg and Reyes couldn't look less alike, Harry thought. Rosenberg had a long, narrow face with teeth that looked a size too big for his jaw and a thick mop of tightly curled russet hair; his body looked soft, potbellied. But his tongue was sharp. Wally always had a quip or a wisecrack at hand. He could be cutting. Angel Reyes was built like Venezuelan shortstop—small, agile, almost a full head shorter than Wally. Dark brown hair cut in bristling spikes, big liquid dark eyes like you see on sentimental paintings of little waifs. Angie was quiet, soft-spoken. At first glance he looked like one of those gardener's guys who runs leaf blowers all day. But Angie had an engineering degree from Florida State University, where he had indeed played four years of varsity baseball for the Seminoles. Shortstop.

It felt chilly and cramped back here near the plane's tail. Harry imagined that's what a morgue would feel like: cold as death. He could see his breath forming little clouds of steam in the air despite the tanks' heavy insulation. At least he didn't smell any leaks.

Rosenberg caught his sniffing. "There's no leaks," he said, his voice resentful. "We've checked from end to end."

"Good," said Harry. But he was thinking, Should I tell them about the missing optics assembly? Should I tell them that we have a saboteur on board? Maybe one of them is the guy. Maybe they already know.

Somehow the steady growl of the 747's engines was louder back here, Harry thought. Just like an airliner: first class is up front; the peasants sit in back.

"Okay," he said to the two men. "I want you to keep your eyes open. We've . . . uh, we've got a problem."

Reyes's dark eyes went wider. Rosenberg looked skeptical.

"What problem?" Wally asked, almost sneering.

"Somebody tried to sabotage the ranging laser."

"What?"

Reyes's mouth dropped open but he said nothing.

"The forward optics assembly's gone missing," Harry explained. "Monk's replacing it from the spares."

"For crap's sake, Harry, that doesn't mean sabotage," Rosenberg snapped. "What's the matter with you? It's not like you to go off the deep end."

Harry studied Rosenberg's face. Wally looks sincere enough, he thought. He's sore at me for thinking it's sabotage.

"Look," he said. "Monk says he checked the ranger last night and it was all right. Now that we're out here over the goddamned Pacific Ocean the forward optics assembly goes missing. Somebody took it out of its setting and hid it. That's sabotage. Somebody's trying to abort this mission. And it's got to be one of us."

"Jesús," Reyes muttered.

Rosenberg, for once, had nothing to say.

Tapping a knuckle on the frosted side of the oxygen tank, Harry said softly, "It wouldn't take much to blow this plane out of the sky. We'd all get killed nice and dead."

"Jesús." This time Reyes crossed himself.

"Watch everything," Harry said. "And everybody."

Reyes nodded. Rosenberg said, "And who's going to watch you, *el jefe*?"

KAREN CHRISTOPHER HEARD O'Banion's voice in her headphone, clipped and businesslike. "Message from Andrews coming through, ma'am."

"Put it through," she commanded.

"It's printing out. No voice."

Colonel Christopher glanced over at Kaufman in the right-hand seat. He'd just come back into the cockpit after flaking out on one of the bunks built into the rear of the flight deck. Still, he looked pouchy-eyed, weary.

"How do you feel, Obie?" she asked.

"I'm okay," he said, clicking the safety harness over his shoulders.

Kaufman hesitated a heartbeat, then asked, "You know the routine for aiming at a missile?"

She nodded. "Point the nose at the rocket exhaust plume. Easy."

He nodded back at her. "Yeah. Easy. In the simulator."

Christopher heard the sarcasm in his tone. She thought about her copilot for a couple of moments, then decided to sweeten his life a little.

"Can you handle it by yourself for a few minutes?" she asked the major.

"Sure!"

Christopher smiled inwardly. That was every copilot's answer whenever he was asked to take the controls. Sure! They want to fly, not watch the boss do the flying.

"Okay," she said, unbuckling her safety harness. "It's all yours."

"Right," said Kaufman.

The colonel slid out of her chair, took off the heavy flight helmet and left it on the seat, then stepped through the cockpit hatch. Lieutenant Sharmon was at his station, a stack of charts on his lap and still another map on his console's main screen.

The lieutenant looked up at Christopher. "Rendezvous in fifty-three minutes," he said.

"Fine," said Christopher. She gave Sharmon a light pat on the shoulder and turned to O'Banion, who was pulling a freshly typed sheet from the printer built into his communications rack. She could see TOP SECRET emblazoned on it in bright red capital letters.

O'Banion passed it to her without reading it.

From Brad again, she saw. Major General B. B. Scheib, Deputy Commander MDA. Skipping past the formalities, she got down to the meat of the message.

1. *Refueling tanker experiencing engine troubles, diverted to Misawa AFB for repair. Refueling rendezvous now scheduled for 1100 hours ZULU.*

Christopher made a swift mental calculation. We've crossed the date line; eleven hundred Zulu time is 9:00 a.m. here.

2. *If refueling rendezvous is further delayed, you have the option of canceling rendezvous and diverting to Misawa AFB and awaiting further orders.*

She stared at the sheet of paper, noticing that it was shaking like a trembling aspen in her hand.

I've got to decide whether we hang out here over the ocean and wait for the tanker to find us or abort the whole mission and land at Misawa.

I've got to decide if we try to stop those damned missiles when they're launched or put down safely in Japan.

Brad's left it to me to decide. He's dropped the hot potato in my damned lap.

Karl Dieter Olbricht hated trees.

It had not always been so. As a youth, growing up on the windswept prairie of Nebraska, he had loved to climb the lone apple tree on the front lawn of his house. But once he started working for the local electric utility as a rugged, handsome blond lineman, he began to acquire a hatred for trees. Not all trees. Only those close enough to electrical power lines to bring the lines down if they were blown over in a storm.

If Olbricht could have his way, every tree within two miles on either side of a power line would be cut down, carted away, its roots dug up or dynamited.

He was standing with his back to the big electronic wall map at the regional headquarters, looking out the windows on the other side of the big command center. Snow was whipping past and the trees out on the parking lot were swaying as their branches loaded up with ice.

The wall map was blank, and had been since the satellites had gone dead. Olbricht had to rely on the already overloaded telephone lines to get some semblance of a picture about the situation over the three-state area. And phone lines were getting knocked out too. Cell phone service was spotty, at best.

The National Weather Service was next to useless, and without satellite data to work with, the regional power combine's own weather forecasters were no better. In short, this storm was going to cause a mess, a frightful, dangerous, perhaps fatal mess.

The president of the regional combine burst into the command center, stamping snow off her boots. She was a large black woman who had yet to prove that she was more than affirmative action window dressing.

"What's the story, Karl?" she called to him as she pulled off her long fur-trimmed coat and flung it on the nearest desk. "Where is everybody?"

Fewer than half the desks were occupied.

"My people are having a hard time getting through the snow," he replied as she came up close enough for him to smell her heavy perfume.

"Tell me 'bout it," she said. "Highway's blocked by a jackknifed semi. I had to detour all around hell and back. Damned near got stuck in a snowdrift coming into the parking lot."

"It's going to be bad," Olbricht said gloomily.

"It's already bad."

He nodded. "We're getting calls from here and there about outages. It's spotty so far, but . . ."

"It's going to cascade, isn't it?"

"Damned right," Olbricht muttered through gritted teeth. "We could see half a million families without power before this is through. More."

The president looked around the half-empty command center, then back at Olbricht. "Okay. Tell me what needs doing. Give me a desk and put me to work."

His respect for her bounded upward several notches. But he still hated trees.

B rad Scheib walked out of the situation room, past the two Air
Police men lounging in the corridor who snapped to attention at the sight of a two-star general, and headed for the men's
room, two dozen paces down the hall.

He had written the order and sent it. Karen should have it in her
hands by now, he thought, unless they're still dicking around with
Need to Know crap. No, the Coggins woman said her office has set
up direct links, Top Priority. If the White House can't get a message
through to Karen nobody can.

In the lavatory he went straight to the nearest sink and started
washing his hands. When he realized what he was doing he laughed
to himself sardonically. How biblical, he thought. Like you can get
rid of your guilt with a little soap and water.

Karen's piloting ABL-1, he said to himself. I'd like to get whatever genius assigned her to that job and stuff his balls up his nose.
Like that's going to help.

She's out there over the North Pacific, heading toward Korea.
Probably over Japan by now or close to it. The tanker's going to be
late, if those guys at Misawa get it off the ground at all. So Karen

has the option of loitering around waiting for the tanker to refuel her or aborting the mission and landing at Misawa.

She's tough, Scheib remembered. Tougher than I am. When the shit hit the fan and the board of inquiry called her in, she didn't say a word about me. Wouldn't tell them a thing. They thought that'd crack her, sticking her with a bus driver's job on a stupid test program.

But now she's in the middle of a real situation. Nuclear war, maybe. It all depends on what she does. What she can do. She won't abort the mission. Not Karen. She'll stooge around over the water until that tanker shows up or she runs so low on fuel she'll have to glide back to Misawa.

Scheib almost laughed as he went from the sink to the urinal. The brass thought they were punishing her, but they've stuck her in the hottest spot any Air Force pilot could be in right now. As he un-zipped his fly, the general thought, She could come out of this a hero. Or dead.

Looking down at his penis as he stood at the urinal, Scheib mut-tered, "See the trouble you've gotten me into?"

AT MISAWA AIR Force Base, Major Hank Wilson glared red-faced and fire-eyed at one of his oldest friends, Major Joe Dugan. Like Wilson, Dugan was squat and burly, built like an old-fashioned fireplug.

"In one hour?" Dugan squawked. "Are you nuts, Hank?"

"In one hour," Wilson said, his voice murderously low. "I want that frickin' tanker out of here within sixty minutes after it lands."

The two men had known each other since their Air Force Acad-emy days. Now they were rushing—sprinting, almost—across the tarmac toward the base maintenance depot.

"Can't be done, Hank," said Dugan, puffing slightly from the unaccustomed exertion. "My guys'll need—"

Wilson stopped suddenly and Dugan trotted several steps before stopping and turning around to face his old friend. The sky above the airfield was turning gray, but the only thundercloud Dugan could see was Wilson's slab-jawed face.

Looking around to make certain that no one was within earshot, Wilson lowered his voice a notch and explained, "Joe, I got a message straight from the frickin' White House. The National Security Advisor signed the order personally. Absolute top priority."

"That don't mean—"

"What it means is that we gotta get that tanker back in the air one hour after it lands. Or quicker. That's what it means."

"But we don't even know what's wrong with its engine!"

"Get another engine on the flight line. Swap it out."

"That's crazy! We can't—"

"The hell you can't. I want a crew ready to swap out the engine soon's that tanker rolls up to the apron."

Dugan looked as if he'd just swallowed a dose of rancid cod liver oil. He glanced up at the sky. "It's gonna rain," he grumbled.

"Clear out a hangar and roll the bird into it."

"Hank, this is crazy and you know it."

"Yeah, yeah. But get it done."

S ylvia tried to keep her terror hidden from the girls. She had never flown in a plane this small. Commercial airliners were so big that she never felt afraid. It was like sitting in a bus, really, especially if she had an aisle seat and didn't look out the windows.

But this flimsy little thing was barely big enough for herself and her daughters. And the pilot. He was a good-looking older man, his short-trimmed hair silvery gray. And he had a sporty little moustache the same attractive color.

Sylvia was sitting in the right-hand seat, her daughters behind her. She couldn't help looking out the windshield at the mountains down below, and the ocean. What if the engines stop? she wondered. We can't land on a mountainside—or in the water. We'll all die!

The pilot kept up a friendly chatter, but she had stopped listening to his words as she sat rigidly and felt every bump and shudder that the plane went through. There's nothing between us and those mountains but empty air! Sylvia realized. She fought down an urge to vomit.

"Oh-oh," said the pilot.

"What's wrong?" Sylvia squeaked.

Tapping the bulbous earphone on the left side of his head, he said over the rumble of the plane's twin jet engines, "Traffic control's ordered us to orbit the field."

"Orbit? In space?"

He laughed. "No, it just means they want us to ride around the airfield for a while."

"How long?"

"Until Air Force One lands."

From behind them, Denise said, "Air Force One? The President's plane?"

"Yep," said the pilot. Pointing past Sylvia's nose, he said, "There she is, right there."

Sylvia saw a huge four-engined plane painted sky blue and white. It looked terribly close, she thought.

"All traffic in and out of SFO is suspended until the President gets out of his plane," the pilot said, as if he hadn't a worry in the world.

Sylvia wondered how long they'd have to stay in the air, waiting. And if they had enough fuel.

Y ou're probably wondering why I called you into this meeting," said Harry. He knew it was weak to the point of inanity, but he couldn't think of any better way to break the ice.

Wally Rosenberg snorted derisively. Taki Nakamura made a polite smile, obviously forced. Monk Delany looked disgusted and Angel Reyes looked worried.

Harry had brought them together in the battle management compartment. Usually manned by six people, it had more seats than any other section of the plane except for the cramped compartment where his team stayed during takeoffs and landings. Now they sat at the row of silent consoles, turned around to face Harry, who stood grimly before them.

"You all know that somebody pulled the optics assembly out of the ranging laser," Harry said.

"It's all fixed now," said Delany. "No problem."

"You replaced the assembly?"

"Yep. No sweat."

Rosenberg asked, "How'd you get that fat ass of yours into that cramped little housing, Monk?"

"All I had to do was get one arm in. The assembly slides in and clicks in place nice and easy. It's designed that way, Wally."

Taki pointed out, "You'll have to check the alignment when the tanker shows up."

"No problem," Delany repeated.

"That's not the point," said Harry. "The point is that one of us deliberately tried to screw up this mission. One of *us*," he emphasized, waving a finger at his four teammates.

"What do you want to do about it, Harry?" Reyes asked, his voice small, soft.

"I want the person who did it to stand up and admit it and swear that he won't do anything else to mess us up."

"He?" Delany asked, turning slightly to look at Nakamura.

"Whoever," Harry said. "I figure that the guy did it before we were told we're going against a real live missile. I don't know why he did it and I don't care. I just want to know that he—or she—won't try anything more."

Dead silence, except for the vibrating drone of the plane's engines.

"No questions asked," Harry promised. "Whatever happened, for whatever reason, it'll be strictly among us. Nobody else has to know."

"You told the pilot, didn't you?" Rosenberg asked, almost accusingly.

Harry nodded. "I had to. But I can always tell her I made a mistake, that the optics assembly was taken out for inspection."

"And that Air Force colonel's gonna believe a cockamamie story like that?" Delany challenged.

"She'll have to, if we all stick together on it."

Silence again. Harry stared at the four of them, wishing he were a mind reader.

"At least tell me there won't be any more of this crap," Harry pleaded. "We're going to a shooting war, for Chrissakes, we don't need somebody trying to screw us up."

They glanced back and forth at each other. Nobody said a word.

Then Rosenberg cleared his throat noisily and said, "Well, I'm not going to mess with anything, Harry."

"Me neither," said Reyes.

"I didn't in the first place," Taki Nakamura said, almost defiantly.

Delany broke into a lazy grin. "Hell, it's dangerous enough up here without trying to louse up the works."

Harry heaved an involuntary sigh. "Okay," he said. "I have your word on it?"

They all nodded.

"Good enough." Harry realized that this was the most he was going to get from them. "But from now on nobody works alone. Understand that? I don't want any one of you out of sight of one of the others."

"Cheez, Harry, that ain't gonna work," Delany complained. "We've each got our own stations and—"

Harry cut him off. "Until we get into a real battle situation, you guys work in pairs. I'm not kidding. I want you to keep an eye on one another."

Reyes nodded solemnly. "Okay, Harry. But who's going to keep an eye on you?"

It took Harry a moment to realize that Reyes was smiling gently. Gruffly, Harry said, "Don't worry about me."

They broke up. Nakamura went with Delany forward to the optics station, Rosenberg and Reyes aft toward the COIL and its fuel tanks.

Harry stood alone in the empty battle management section, thinking that one of his four team members must have sabotaged the laser at the field test out in the Mohave and killed Pete Quintana in doing so.

KAREN CHRISTOPHER WAS stretched out on the bunk in the rear of the flight deck. Her eyes were closed, but she couldn't sleep.

The tanker's delayed. That one thought kept running through her mind. That and an image of the fuel gauges on ABL-1's control panel. We're over Japan now. We could break off this mission and put down at Misawa, nice and easy. Nobody gets hurt and nobody would blame me for aborting the mission.

And the North Koreans launch their missiles.

We could stop them! She knew that as certainly as she knew her heart was beating. If I can get this clunker of an airplane into the proper position we could shoot down those bastards before their rocket engines cut off.

But you need another long drink of fuel to get there, she said to herself. You need that tanker. And if you stooge around over the ocean long enough waiting for it, you could run out of fuel and go down into the ocean.

That'd be a great career move, she thought. Sink a billion-dollar airplane, the only one of its kind. Sink your career in the Air Force with it.

Christopher wondered how much of a career she had to look forward to. She remembered the board of inquiry, the cold, hard faces of the Advocate General's panel of judges.

"You refuse a direct order to name the officer you've been sleeping with?" The crusty old brigadier was smirking at her, seeing dirty pictures in his mind.

"My activities while not on duty are not subject to Air Force jurisdiction, sir," Karen had replied, knowing it was a pathetically weak defense.

"They are subject to United States Air Force jurisdiction when they reflect dishonorably on the service!" the judge had snapped at her.

Karen lapsed into silence. Her USAF-appointed lawyer, a light colonel like herself, had advised her that silence was her best defense.

Not that it did her any good. They couldn't get Brad's name out of her, so they bounced her out of her job with the B-2 squadron and stuck her in a dumbbell assignment driving a cargo plane on milk runs.

But the cargo plane turned out to be ABL-1. Nobody expected the plane to do anything but fly racetrack courses over the open ocean and shoot its laser at simulated targets. Nobody expected the North Koreans to start World War III or ABL-1 to be sent on this mission to stop the war before it started. Nobody expected Lieutenant Colonel Karen Christopher to be placed at the pivotal point of world history.

"Uh, Colonel, ma'am?"

Karen snapped her eyes open. Lieutenant Sharmon was standing over her, looking a little embarrassed.

She pushed herself up to a sitting position. "What is it, Jon?"

"I've got the numbers on how long we can stooge around waiting for the tanker. They don't look good."

Out of the corner of his eye Charley Ingersoll noticed the gas gauge's warning light flicker. The highway was blanketed with snow now; the clouds were low and dark. We ought to be outrunning this dratted storm, Charley fumed to himself, but instead it's just getting worse. He wished he'd put in new wiper blades before starting on this stupid trip; the wipers were smearing his windshield so badly he could hardly see outside.

They'd stopped at two more gas stations, but both of them had no electricity, either, so they couldn't pump gas. We're not going to make it home unless we can fill the ever-loving tank, Charley knew.

The warning light glowed steadily now, a little yellow eye that told Charley he was in real trouble. What to do? What to do? Push on until we run out of gas or pull over and keep the car heated until a snowplow comes by?

Martha was still fiddling with the radio, trying to get a local station.

"Try the cell phone again," Charley said.

His wife shook her head. "It doesn't work. I've tried it a dozen times and it doesn't work."

"Try it again, dammit!"

She looked shocked at his language, but picked the cell phone off the console between their seats and pecked at it.

"Nothing," she said, almost as if she were happy about it.

At least the kids were quiet in the backseat. They'd peed and eaten a couple of granola bars. That ought to keep them satisfied for a while, Charley thought.

"Stay in the middle!" Martha yelped as Charley maneuvered the van around a curve. There was no guardrail and she was on the open side. The snow was so thick now that Charley couldn't see how far a drop it was on her side.

"I'm only doing forty," he growled. He didn't tell her that the road felt slick, slippery in spots.

The radio crackled with the distant voice of a sportscaster reporting that the Seattle Seahawks expected to have perfect football weather for Sunday's game against the San Diego Chargers.

Big fornicating deal, Charley grumbled to himself.

At least a snowplow had been through this stretch of highway, Charley realized. There was less than an inch of snow on the roadway. Good, he thought, leaning a little more heavily on the accelerator. Fifty miles an hour. That's better than—

There was ice under the coating of snow and the van suddenly spun a full circle before Charley could do anything about it. Martha screamed and the kids yelled. The van smacked sideways into a mound of snow on the shoulder of the road, with Charley jamming both his feet on the brake.

Charley could feel his heart hammering beneath his ribs. Martha was sobbing. Glancing over his shoulder Charley saw that both the kids seemed okay. White-faced and wide-eyed, but unhurt. Their seat belts had kept them from being banged around.

"You okay back there?" he asked, surprised at how his voice shook.

"Yessir," said Charley Jr. "I think so."

"Me too," Little Martha echoed.

"How about you?" Charley asked his wife.

"My chest hurts."

"The seat belt must have caught you."

"I think I'm having a heart attack."

"You're not having a heart attack. It's just the seat belt. I bet I'm bruised too."

From the backseat Little Martha piped up. "Can we go outside and make a snowman?"

M ajor Joseph E. Dugan, USAF, had learned one vitally im-
portant thing in his military career: when you need a job
done, and done right the first time, get an experienced noncom to
do it.

He stood in a lightly misting rain in front of the hangar closest
to the flight line and watched befuddled maintenance crews towing
planes out into the drizzle and parking them helter-skelter across
the apron.

Standing beside him was Technical Sergeant Aaron "Scrap Iron"
Clinton, hard-eyed and humorless, his skin as dark as an eggplant,
fists planted on the hips of his rumpled fatigues, an unlit cigar
clamped in his teeth. The "seegar," as Clinton called them, was
Clinton's hallmark. He never smoked them. He chewed them.

When Joe Dugan's old friend and senior major, Hank Wilson,
had commanded him to have the incoming KC-135 refitted with a
replacement engine in one hour or less after its landing, Dugan fell
back on his crucial piece of military wisdom. He sprinted over to
the base maintenance center and hollered for Sergeant Clinton.

"Sergeant," he bellowed, "there's a KC-135 tanker due in here in twenty minutes. It's got to have an engine replaced and be back in the air in one hour."

Sergeant Clinton had been through a lot in his Air Force career. Twice he had been broken down to airman for getting caught with his pants down in married women's bedrooms. Three times he had been offered a chance for a commission—and refused.

"I ain't officer material," he had insisted in his stubborn Arkansas drawl. "I work for a livin'."

Now this white major was demanding the impossible. Clinton saluted and said, around his unlit cigar, "One hour. Yes, sir!"

That was why, as the ailing KC-135 taxied right into the hangar that had been emptied for it, its pilot stared goggle-eyed at the small army of technicians in Air Force fatigues who swarmed around the plane even while its engines were wheezing to a stop.

"Holy shit!" the pilot exclaimed. "It looks like a pit crew from the Indianapolis 500 out there!"

C olonel, I've got the fuel bingo calculated."

Karen Christopher nodded as she sat at the controls of ABL-1. "Plug it into the flight plan, Jon," she said to her navigator.

Sharmon's voice in her headphone sounded reluctant. "I don't have really good numbers for wind velocities, Colonel. With the satellites down and all . . ."

"Give me three estimates," said Colonel Christopher. "Best case, worst case, and the average between them."

"Yes, ma'am."

In a few minutes numbers began to flicker on the control panel's central display screen. Christopher watched them scroll by, then they steadied and held still.

In the right-hand seat, Major Kaufman grunted, glanced at the panel's digital clock, then checked his wristwatch. "Thirty-eight minutes. Then we gotta turn back for Misawa."

"That's the worst case," the colonel said. "If the winds don't buck us too hard we can stretch it another ten, fifteen minutes."

Kaufman said nothing, but the look on his face told Christopher what he thought of stretching their luck. She gave him a faint smile. "Think we should put on our life vests, Obie, just in case?"

"That ain't funny," Kaufman muttered.

Christopher tapped the side of her helmet where the headphone was built in and called, "Brick, anything from Misawa about our tanker?"

O'Banion's voice replied, "Nothing since they reported the bird landed, Colonel."

Kaufman grumbled, "Misawa can't talk to us, so they send the word to Washington and Washington relays the poop to us. Helluva way to run a mission."

"Communications are snarled up," Christopher said. But inwardly she agreed with her copilot. Communications were vital and this Top Secret mission was at the end of a long and very shaky tether.

"Wind velocity's picking up some," Sharmon reported.

With a nod, Colonel Christopher realized that they were facing the navigator's worst-case option. Fuel bingo in twenty-nine minutes, she calculated. Looking out at the swirl of gray clouds covering the ocean below, she thought, If we go down it'll be into a nasty bit of weather. Ditching a plane this size into a cold ocean in the middle of a major storm. Not a good career move.

HARRY WAS SITTING by himself in the cramped little galley beneath the flight deck. There were no windows to see outside, but he sensed that the plane was turning, leaning slightly to the left side as it made a wide, cumbersome turn.

Are we turning back? he wondered. Maybe I should check with Colonel Christopher. If we're going back, then I could make it known to whoever tried to screw up the mission that he can relax, the mission's scrubbed.

As he grasped his lukewarm mug of coffee with both hands Harry asked himself for the thousandth time: Who is it? Which one of them tried to stop this mission? Who took that optics assembly?

He sat in one of the galley's undersized bucket seats and tried to puzzle it all out. Beam control is Monk's job. He knows the most about it; it'd be easiest for him to take out the lens assembly. But he couldn't have gone up there once we took off—the flight crew would have seen him. Whoever it was must've removed the assembly before we took off. And he hid it somewhere on the plane, most likely. Where? Maybe if I can find the lens assembly it'll tell me something about who took it.

But Harry shook his head. Maybe if I could dust it for fingerprints. Not even then, he realized. Monk, Taki, Wally, even Angel had enough time to sneak up to the flight deck last night while we were doing the preflight and take the assembly out of the ranging laser. You don't have to be a rocket scientist to lift the assembly out of its fitting. It's designed to pop in or pop out, just like Monk said.

Why? Harry demanded silently. Why would any one of them want to scrub this mission? Is he a spy, for Chrissakes? With a disgusted shake of his head, Harry reasoned, No, that couldn't be it. None of us knew we were flying into a shooting war when we took off. We all thought it was going to be just another milk run.

Not a spy, then. Not an enemy agent. No James Bond stuff. But then why the hell did he do it?

And did he cause the explosion out on the Mohave? Did he kill Pete?

Harry sat there mulling his thoughts over and over again. Slowly he began to think that he really didn't want to know. One of my people is a saboteur, at least. Maybe a murderer. I don't want to know who it is.

But he realized even so that he had to know. He had to find out. I can't let him try again. He might kill us all, for god's sake. Or her. Maybe it's Taki. Is there something in her background that I don't know about? Something that makes her willing to commit suicide to stop this mission? She's third- or fourth-generation American, but is there some of the kamikaze spirit inside her?

He gulped at his tepid coffee, got to his feet, and went to the tiny stainless steel sink to rinse out the mug. You're going nutso, he said to himself. Absolutely dingbat. Taki's no Japanese spy, for Chrissake.

But somebody removed the lens assembly. One of my people. Somebody who figured that would be the simplest and least dangerous way to abort the mission. Knock out the ranging laser and we're out of business.

Who? Who?

Harry leaned against the sink, his mind spinning. Then he stood up straight and went to the galley's hatch. Instead of standing around asking yourself questions, he reasoned, go out and *do* something. Find the missing lens assembly. Maybe where the guy hid it will tell you who it was.

It wasn't much, but it was all that Harry could think of doing.

Zuri Coggins looked up from her mini's screen and announced, "The President's landed at San Francisco International."

Michael Jamil turned in his chair to face the wall screen that showed CNN, Fox News, and three other news channels. None of them was showing the President's arrival in Air Force One. There must be a crowd at the airport to greet him, Jamil thought, his brows furrowing. That's why he landed at the commercial airport instead of a military base. Why aren't the news nets covering his arrival?

And then it hit him. The satellites are out. No instant news coverage from the West Coast. I'll bet they don't even have coaxial cables anymore to carry TV across the continent.

General Scheib was also bent over his laptop screen. "The tanker's taken off from Misawa," he said. "Should make rendezvous with ABL-1 in about one hour."

General Higgins came down the table and bent over Scheib's shoulder. "Will your plane have enough fuel to make the rendezvous?"

Without looking up at Higgins, Scheib muttered, "That's a decision the pilot has to make."

"THE TANKER'S ON its way! Took off ten minutes ago!" O'Banion called so loudly that Karen Christopher could hear him through the open cockpit hatch even with her helmet on.

"ETA?" Christopher said into her lip mike.

It took several moments before O'Banion replied, more softly, "Sixty-eight minutes."

Major Kaufman leaned toward Christopher. "That's way past our bingo point."

The colonel nodded slowly, her mind racing. "We have enough fuel to wait for the tanker. Once we make rendezvous we can refill our tanks."

Kaufman's face showed what he thought of that. "And what if the goddamned tanker breaks down again? What if it misses the rendezvous? There's a big storm blowing down there. We can't sit here and wait till our tanks run dry!"

"The tanker's on its way," Colonel Christopher said firmly.

"And we're supposed to orbit around here and hope the damned tanker finds us?"

"That's right."

"That's crazy!"

"The tanker will be here before we run dry, Obie. This is no time to panic."

"So when is the time to panic? When we're in the drink, in the middle of a goddamned typhoon?"

A fragment of memory flashed through Colonel Christopher's mind, a legend she had heard while in the academy about a B-17 mission over Germany during World War II. With Nazi fighter planes swarming in on them, the copilot of the Flying Fortress screamed that they had to turn back, get away. The pilot unlimbered his service revolver and threatened to blow the copilot's head off if he didn't shut up and do his job. Karen regretted that she hadn't packed her service pistol on this flight.

"I'll tell you when it's time to panic, Obie," she said coolly. "Now keep your voice down, you're frightening the kids."

Kaufman stared at her, his baggy-eyed face a mixture of anger, fear, and disbelief.

"You're gonna stooge around here until we run out of fuel?" he asked, his voice lower.

"Until the tanker shows up," Christopher corrected. "And then we're going to shoot down any goddamned missile those goddamned gooks launch."

A nd there it was, tucked in behind the spare packs of toilet paper.

Harry had searched the galley and the compartment where he and his team sat during takeoffs and landings, knowing that whoever took the lens assembly wouldn't stash it in such an obvious place but looking in the obvious places first. He worked his way back along the COIL's long, bulky length, sticking his nose into every corner and cranny he saw. Nothing. Rosenberg and Angel Reyes watched him with some bemusement on their faces as Harry sniffed and peeked and ducked under the tanks that held the big laser's fuel.

He started back, intending to check out Taki's station. Somebody could stick the lens assembly inside one of the consoles there, or even between consoles; the assembly wasn't much bigger than the palm of his hand.

The plane seemed to be turning again; Harry felt the sway as the lumbering jet slowly banked right. Again he wondered if he should ask Colonel Christopher what was going down, but again he decided that she probably had her hands full and didn't need anybody pestering her. She had made it painfully clear that she regarded

Harry and his team as a bunch of tech geeks. Well, he mused, that's what we are, really. Besides, I've got my own job to do.

He had to urinate. The lavatory was next to the galley and Harry pushed through the accordion door. On an impulse he bent down and opened the sliding door to the compartment that held the extra toilet paper and paper towels. The boxes looked jumbled, not in a neat stack. Harry pulled a couple of them out and there was the lens assembly.

Harry squatted down and stared at it, his need to urinate forgotten. In his mind he tried to re-create the scene. Whoever yanked the assembly out of the ranging laser must have done it last night, while we were going through the preflight inspection. He knew the rest of us were in the plane and he only had a couple of minutes to hide it. He could carry it down from the flight deck and right through the battle management station, even if Taki was sitting there. She'd be focused on her console with her back to whoever was passing through the area. Besides, the assembly was small enough to hold in your hand, and even if she turned around or glanced over her shoulder she probably wouldn't have noticed it.

Or maybe not, Harry thought. Maybe it was Taki herself.

He carefully restacked the paper goods cartons and started to leave the lavatory. Then his bladder reminded him of why he'd come into the lav in the first place.

THE PRESIDENT STOOD at the forward hatch of Air Force One at the top of the stairs while the band played "Hail to the Chief" and the crowd that had gathered on the tarmac roared its greeting.

It was crisp and cool in San Francisco. Woolly gray clouds were building up along the row of hills that fronted the ocean. The President could not see either the Golden Gate or the Bay Bridge from where he stood, which disappointed him. But the familiar cadence of "Hail to the Chief" always gave him a lift.

He smiled his brightest and waved both arms over his head while a phalanx of secret service agents, most of them in dark

topcoats, filtered through the crowd. His team of security technicians was setting up the portable podium down at the bottom of
the stairs, with the teleprompters and blast-proof screens.

Standing beside him, the President's chief of staff rubbed a
hand over his shaved pate.

"It's always cold in 'Frisco," Norman Foster complained. "Mark
Twain said the coldest winter he'd ever spent was one summer in
San Francisco."

The President laughed and said, "The crowd's nice and warm,
Norm."

Foster agreed with a vigorous nod. "That they are, Mr. President. That they are."

The two men started down the stairs toward the knot of news re-
porters and photographers clustered by the portable podium, Foster
a respectful two steps behind his chief.

It's supposed to start raining in an hour or so, Foster thought.
We'll be at the Cow Palace by then. But he couldn't help thinking
that conditions would get much, much warmer if those two North
Korean missiles reached the city.

ACROSS THE BAY, at the Oakland office of the National Weather
Service, Sam Weathers riffled through the reports that were trickling in to his desk. Reports on paper, most of them radioed or tele-
typed in from weather observation posts from California to Idaho.

Weathers was a compactly built black man of forty-six, his
shoulders wide and his gut still tight, thanks to weekly sessions on
the basketball court at his local YMCA. He wasn't especially tall,
but he was fast and had good hands. He would flash a big toothy
grin whenever he worked the ball around one of those tall, gawky
giraffes and scored another basket.

He wasn't grinning now. His desk was covered with a slowly
growing glacier of papers, none of them bearing good news.

Sam had never intended to be a meteorologist. With his last
name being Weathers, he thought it would be ridiculous to work for

the National Weather Service. Weathers from Weather. He could hear the snickering wherever he went. So he had majored in geophysics in college, then somehow gotten interested in atmospheric physics as a graduate student. By the time he had earned his Ph.D., jobs in atmospheric physics were scarce. So he took a temporary position with the Weather Service in his college town, Berkeley, hoping to transfer to NOAA's atmospheric physics section when the job market loosened up. Twenty-two years later he was still with the Weather Service. Weathers from Weather.

With the satellites down and phone service jammed up the kazoo, Sam had turned to the service's radio system to get reports on the storm that had swept in from the ocean. Even that was hit-and-miss: radio reception was mostly poor because of the storm, and more and more stations were going off the air because of power outages.

Sam had rounded up a couple of kids who knew how to run the computer that fed the big electronic wall map. Even so, the map had large blank spaces in it. The low-pressure center of the storm had moved inland with surprising swiftness and was dumping snow in the higher elevations across the northern Rockies. A surprise autumn storm. There'll be a white Hallowe'en, Sam thought bitterly. And that means trouble.

The last satellite data he'd received had shown the storm's center still out over the Pacific. Then the weather satellites had gone dead and Sam felt blinded, groping in the dark, reverting back to communications systems that hadn't been used, really, since before he'd started in college.

"How's it look, Weather Man?" Sam's boss still had his sense of humor.

Sam looked up from his littered desk and gave him a sour expression. "Major storm. We've got warnings out but a lot of the area is getting hit with blackouts. We got real troubles, Eddie."

The boss shrugged. "Do your best, Weather Man."

"Sure. What else?"

"The President landed at San Francisco International okay. Got in before the rain started."

"Rain?"

"Yeah. Don't you read your own forecasts? It's pouring cats and dogs outside."

The boss walked off toward his office. Sam straightened up and headed for the windows, up the hall from his desk and the wall map.

Sure enough, it was raining out there. Raining hard.

For some reason that has delighted generations of cynics, the United States Department of State is headquartered in a part of the District of Columbia called Foggy Bottom. The Secretary of State's spacious office was on the top floor of the handsome building. The Secretary had come directly to her office after her meeting in the Jefferson Hotel with her Chinese contact, Quang Chuli, still wearing her low-key gray pant suit and pearls. From her desk the Secretary could see across the Potomac River and its busy bridges to the glass-and-steel office towers of Virginia and the row upon row of white crosses lined up in military precision along the rolling green turf of Arlington National Cemetery.

As she sat at her broad, uncluttered desk, however, the Secretary of State was not looking out her windows. She was glaring at the image on her wall-sized display screen of a young brown-skinned upstart with a trim beard tracing his stubborn jawline.

"The Sarajevo scenario?" the Secretary repeated, in the icy, scornful tone that could send senators and White House officials scurrying for cover.

"Yes, ma'am," said Michael Jamil.

General Higgins, whom the Oval Office had put in charge of

this special situation team, was sitting beside Jamil and leaning toward the civilian so he could get his face in the picture that was on her wall screen.

"For what it's worth, Madam Secretary," Higgins said, in a tone that was little short of pompous, "this is Mr. Jamil's personal assessment, not my team's idea."

"Thank you, General," said the Secretary of State, putting on her sincerest smile. Shifting her eyes back to Jamil, she asked, "Is your scenario approved by the National Intelligence Council, young man?"

Jamil felt uncomfortable with General Higgins sitting beside him down at the end of the conference table and the eye of the computer camera staring at him unblinkingly. The others in the situation room were all on their feet, standing over to one side. Zuri Coggins was standing beside General Scheib, who was in front of the satellite image of the North Korean missiles, blocking Jamil's view. But he could see the Secretary of State clearly enough, both on the computer display in front of him and on the wall screen on the other side of the room. No one stood in front of her image. He could see her brittle smile and hear the condescension in her "young man."

"We've run many different scenarios at NIC," he answered tightly. "The Sarajevo possibility is one of them."

"But no one else at NIC has associated that scenario with the present situation," the Secretary said, still smiling. "Only you."

Feeling his insides clenching, Jamil replied, "I'm the only representative of the NIC present at this meeting, Madam Secretary."

"I see," she said.

"It's the scenario that fits the facts best," Jamil insisted. "A rogue attack triggers a full-scale nuclear exchange."

"And you believe that the Chinese are behind this?"

Jamil hesitated. He knew the Secretary of State's reputation. People didn't get to challenge her more than once.

Carefully he answered, "I believe that the Chinese are prepared to profit from it. If we attack North Korea they will respond against us. If we allow the North Koreans to destroy an American city without retaliating, the Chinese will back North Korea's demands. They want to eliminate our influence in Asia and this is the way for them to do it and keep their hands clean."

The Secretary started to reply, but Jamil suddenly added, "We know they've placed their ballistic missile forces on alert. We should try to ascertain if their political leadership has left Beijing and gone to shelters."

The Secretary's eyes flared. "Do you expect me to believe that the Chinese government is ready to have a nuclear exchange with us? That they are willing to start World War III?"

"Yes, ma'am, that's exactly what I expect you to believe."

In her office, the Secretary of State stared hard at this young intelligence analyst. He looks like an Arab, she thought. How can I trust him? He might have all sorts of security clearances, but he could be a plant, a mole who's been working inside our intelligence apparatus for years, waiting for this chance to launch a nuclear jihad.

She took a deep breath to calm herself. Stay cool, she told herself. Every word you say is being recorded for history. You want to come across as concerned, informed, on top of this situation. You want to look presidential. He'll run for reelection next time around, but you're young enough to have a good chance for the nomination four years afterward, especially if you come out of this looking presidential.

She glanced at the data bar running along the bottom of her wall screen as she said carefully, "Mr . . . eh, Jamil, has it occurred to you that I have sources of information that you do not?"

Jamil's lips became a thin, hard line.

"Has it occurred to you," the Secretary went on, "that I have unofficial sources that place me in contact with the highest levels of the government of the People's Republic of China?" Struggling to keep her voice cool, presidential, she went on. "Has it occurred to you that my contacts assure me that China has no wish to attack the United States? Shouldn't you rethink your scenario in the light of those facts?"

Despite the Secretary of State's measured words, Jamil could almost feel her cold fury radiating from the conference room's wall screen. And he felt angry, too—outraged that this woman refused to see the obvious.

"Has it occurred to you, Madam Secretary," he retorted, "that your sources are lying to you? Or at least not telling you the entire truth? Have they told you that China will not under any circumstances launch their missiles against us? Have they offered to stop the North Koreans? Why do you think you haven't been able to speak directly to the Chinese leadership? They're probably in their underground city right now, waiting for the bombs to start falling! While the President's in San Francisco preparing to give a speech!"

For a flash of an instant the Secretary of State looked flustered, but she immediately regained her icy composure. "Thank you for your frank opinion, Mr. Jamil."

The wall screen went blank.

General Higgins pushed his chair away from Jamil and heaved himself to his feet. "You sure know how to make friends in high places, kid," he said. Then he headed back to his place at the head of the table.

Jamil sat there alone. Why don't they understand? he asked himself. It's as if they don't want to understand.

As the others took their seats around the conference table, Zuri Coggins came up to Jamil and placed a hand on his shoulder. "You'd better update your résumé, Michael," she said, shaking her head. "Nobody talks to that woman like that and lives to tell the tale."

Jamil agreed with a morose nod. But as he looked up at Coggins, he saw the wall screen behind her.

"Look!" he said, pointing with a trembling hand. "They've got a bunch of people working around the missiles."

Every eye in the situation room turned to the satellite view of the North Korean site. The two missiles stood on their pads as before, but now teams of men in coveralls were clustered around the base of each missile.

"Final checkout," said General Scheib. "They're starting their countdown. They're going to launch those birds."

W ow!" exclaimed Vickie as she turned completely around, taking in the suite's sitting room with its beautiful draperies and handsome furniture. "Can we afford this?"

Sylvia laughed, delighted that at last *something* had impressed her sixteen-year-old. "It's only for this one night. And besides, the party committee's paying for it."

Denise went to the bedroom door and peeked in. "Twin beds," she noted. "Queens."

Before her younger daughter could ask, Sylvia explained, "You two sleep in there. I'll use the pullout sofa."

Vickie and Denise glanced at each other. Before they could say anything, their mother said, "I don't want you two arguing over who sleeps where. You each get one of the beds, share and share alike."

With a shrug, Denise changed the subject. "When do we eat?"

Their landing at the airport had been delayed because of the President's arrival, and then it had been hell getting a taxi in the drizzling rain. The highway was clogged with slow-moving traffic and now it was dinnertime and their luggage hadn't come up from the lobby yet.

"As soon as the bellman brings our bags we'll grab a quick bite someplace close by and then head out to the Cow Palace."

"If we can get a cab," Vickie said.

Denise went to the desk, where a few glossy magazines were arranged in a fan. "I'll look up a good restaurant."

Denise was always the practical one, Sylvia thought.

A ny word from the tanker?" Colonel Christopher asked.

"Not a peep," O'Banion replied.

Christopher glanced at the fuel gauges, then over at Major Kaufman, sitting as grim as death in the right-hand seat.

"They'll be here, Obie," she said.

"If you say so, Colonel."

She restrained an impulse to whistle at the hostility in Kaufman's voice. Or maybe it's fear, she thought. The major was staring straight ahead at the swirl of dirty gray clouds far below them. The tanker might be having trouble getting through that soup, she thought. Winds must be pretty strong down there. She leaned back in her chair and lifted her helmet partway off. The headache was getting worse. Stress, she knew. Try to relax. Chill out. At least we haven't gotten word that the tanker's *not* on its way to us.

"Take over, Obie," she said, unstrapping her seat harness and getting up from the chair. "I'll be back in five."

Kaufman nodded and mumbled something about a potty break.

Damned creep, Christopher thought. She stepped through the hatch onto the flight deck, where Sharmon and O'Banion sat at their stations. They both looked pretty strained. So different,

Christopher thought. Skinny black kid and chunky redheaded Irishmen. But they're both wearing Air Force blue and that's what matters.

Placing a hand on each of their shoulders, Colonel Christopher said, just loud enough for them to hear her over the drone of the engines, "You heard the major and me hollering at each other."

O'Banion shrugged and Sharmon nodded solemnly.

"That was a difference of opinion between the two of us. It's all straightened out now. And forgotten. Understand?"

Sharmon blinked several times before saying, "Yes, ma'am. Forgotten."

O'Banion broke into a lazy grin. "I gotcha, Colonel. No problemo."

Christopher smiled down at the two of them. "Good. Now where the hell is that tanker?"

HARRY SAW THAT Monk was sitting beside Taki at the battle management station. There were four consoles lining one curving bulkhead of the compartment; in a real battle situation four Air Force blue-suiters would be working battle management, with two backups behind them. For this flight, which started out as a routine test mission, Taki had the station all to herself.

Seeing the two of them talking together, grins on their faces, gave Harry a pang of apprehension. Are they both in on it? Are they working together?

Then he heard Delany finishing one of his stories, "So the highway patrolman sees the guy's too drunk to drive and he asks him, 'Do you realize that your wife fell out of your car three blocks down the street?' And the driver, he's Irish, he says, 'Thanks be to God! I thought I was goin' deaf!'"

Monk hooted at his own joke and Taki laughed politely. Harry had heard the story before, and besides he was in no mood for laughter. But he got a sudden idea.

"Monk, I need to check out the ranging laser with you."

Delany frowned up at him. "Again?"

"Again," said Harry. "When that tanker gets here we've got to test the ranger on it."

Pushing himself up from the bucket seat, Delany grumbled, "Your taking this *el jefe* crap too damned serious, Harry."

"Maybe," Harry agreed. "But let's make certain the laser's ready to ping the tanker."

Once they were in the beam control section, Harry plucked at Delany's sleeve. "Monk, I've got an idea about how to find out who dismantled the lens assembly."

Delany gave him a dubious look.

"If we can find the missing assembly, there's probably finger-prints on it," Harry said. "Once we get back to Elmendorf, we can get the Air Police to check 'em out."

Delany's expression phased from dubious to thoughtful. "Cheez, Harry, my prints are all over that chunk of glass."

Nodding, Harry said, "Yeah, sure. But if there's somebody else's prints on it, too, then that somebody must be the guy who took it!"

"Maybe," Delany said slowly.

"Gotta be," said Harry, convincing himself as he spoke.

Delany shook his head. "You're turning into a friggin' Sherlock Holmes, pal."

Harry accepted it as a compliment, thinking, If Monk took the assembly he knows there's nobody else's prints on it. He'll go back to where he stashed it and wipe it down, clean off any fingerprints on it.

But then he thought, Maybe he was smart enough to wipe it down before he stashed it in the lav. Maybe I'm not a Sherlock Holmes after all.

And he realized that Monk was only one possible culprit out of four. So what do I do now? He wondered.

"MESSAGE FROM THE tanker!" O'Banion sang out.

"Pipe it to me," said Karen Christopher.

"ABL-1, this is your friendly flying gas station. Sorry we're late."

"Better late than never," Colonel Christopher said happily into her lip mike. "Where are you?"

"Three miles behind you and four thousand feet below. We're coming up as fast as we can."

Kaufman twisted around in his chair and did his best to look behind and below the plane.

"Very good," said the colonel. "We're glad to see you. We're running on fumes, just about."

"We'll take care of that. You need anything else, Colonel? Windshield wiped? Oil change? Tires rotated?"

Karen laughed. "Just fill our tanks, thanks." She turned to Kaufman. "Feel better, Obie?"

He gave her a halfhearted grin. "You should've been a test pilot: more guts than brains."

Colonel Christopher nodded. More guts than you've got, butterball, she retorted silently. Then she puffed out a heartfelt sigh of relief.

They're definitely getting ready to launch," said General Scheib, his eyes fixed on the wall screen that showed the latest satellite imagery from North Korea.

Zuri Coggins was speaking hurriedly, urgently, into the hair-thin headset she had attached to her minicomputer. Talking to the White House, Michael Jamil guessed. General Higgins was on his feet, his shirt rumpled, his face pasty.

Jamil wondered if the fatheaded general would send an alert to San Francisco now. The President arrives there and the North Koreans start their missile countdown. That can't be a coincidence. It can't be.

Then he asked himself, How did they know that the President landed? With all the commercial commsats out, there's no worldwide news coverage. And we certainly aren't sending data from our milsats to the DPRK.

They must have one or more satellites of their own watching San Francisco, Jamil concluded. Then he shook his head. The North Koreans didn't have any satellites in space. The bomb they had launched was the first time they've gotten a bird into orbit successfully.

I need access, he realized. Seeing that the Coggins woman had taken off her headset and was watching the satellite imagery along with everybody else, he got out of his chair and went up the table to her.

"May I use your mini for a few minutes?" he asked.

Coggins cast a suspicious look at him, annoyed at being interrupted from her concentration on the wall screen's imagery. The scene looked semi-weird, distorted. The surveillance satellite must be getting close to the local horizon, Jamil figured. It'll be out of the area in a few minutes.

"My computer?" Coggins asked.

"Only for a few minutes. Please."

She hesitated a heartbeat, then gestured to the mini. "Go ahead. It's connected to the Defense Department's information web."

"Fine. Thanks." Jamil slid into the chair next to Coggins and pulled the book-sized computer in front of him.

Coggins got up and stretched. Tense as a tightrope, she said to herself. Why not? You've got a lot to be tense about.

She walked over to the coffee cart. All three urns were empty again. We're drinking too much of it anyway, she thought, even though she wished she had a cup to hold in her hands.

"Coffee's gone again?"

Turning, she saw it was General Higgins glowering at the cart. He waved to his aide and pointed ostentatiously to the stainless steel urns. "I've got to tell him everything," Higgins complained.

Coggins half-whispered, "Do you think they're really targeting the President?"

The general shook his head stubbornly. "Scheib says those missiles don't have the range or accuracy to hit San Francisco. He's our local expert."

"Then it's Honolulu."

"Or Fairbanks. Or Manila. Or Shanghai." Higgins looked back at the screen, muttering, "Our next recon bird won't be over the area for another ten minutes."

She stepped across the room to where General Scheib stood staring at the wall screen while he gnawed his lip.

"How soon before they launch?" Coggins asked.

Scheib cocked his head to one side, thinking. Then he replied, "No more than an hour. Ninety minutes on the outside."

"Can they hit San Francisco?"

"I don't think so."

"But if that's their target, can your people stop them?"

General Scheib looked down at her. He still wore his tunic, ribbons displayed across his chest. Except for a shadow of beard, he looked almost as sharp as he had in the morning, when the group first convened. But he was gnawing his lip.

"Wherever they're aiming for, we've got four Aegis ships in the Pacific and our land-based antimissile batteries in Alaska and California."

"Can they shoot the missiles down?"

He started to shake his head, caught himself. "You have to understand the problem. Once those ballistic missiles' rocket engines burn out, they're on a coasting trajectory to their target."

"So you can track exactly where they're heading," Coggins said.

"Yeah, but they separate the warhead from the body of the missile, release decoys if they're carrying any, even break up the missile's tankage to make a cloud of images, confuse our radar. Our guys have to pick out the warhead from that cloud of crap."

"Can you do it?"

"It's not easy. The best way to discriminate the warhead is when the stuff reenters the atmosphere. Air drag slows down the decoys and fragments; they're lighter than the warhead. Then we can pick out which incoming body is carrying the bomb."

"When it's diving onto the target? How much time do you have to decide which is which?"

Scheib made a sound that could have been a snort. "A minute, if we're lucky."

Coggins felt her eyes widen. "One minute or less? Can you hit the warhead in that time span?"

"We've done it in tests," Scheib said. Then he added, "About half the time."

"Saints and sinners!" Coggins exclaimed. "Half the time?"

"That's why ABL-1's so important," said the general. "If we can hit the missiles with that laser while they're still boosting, while their rockets are burning, before they deploy their warheads and decoys . . ."

Coggins saw the uncertainty on his face. "Does the President know all this?"

"He's been briefed. More than once. I made the presentation myself last year when they were considering the budget for MDA."

He's toast, Coggins thought. If those missiles reach San Francisco the President is toast. Along with half a million other people.

Back at the conference table, Michael Jamil had finally found the information he wanted. He had tried to check through official Defense Department files but found them too slow and cumbersome for his purposes. All DoD's security regulations do is slow down access to the information you need, Jamil complained silently. So he'd turned to the Internet site of *Aviation Week* magazine. He'd heard guys at Langley call it *Aviation Leak* because it often published information that Washington would have preferred to keep away from the public.

And there it was, in last week's issue. The People's Republic of China had launched a quartet of scientific research satellites into polar orbits. Beijing announced that the satellites were part of China's expanding space exploration program.

Space exploration my pimpled ass, Jamil snarled to himself. Those are surveillance satellites. Hardened birds, so they wouldn't be knocked out by the nuke the North Koreans set off. They pass over California every half hour. They're watching San Francisco and feeding the info to the North Koreans, telling them when to launch their missiles so they'll catch the President.

Jamil pushed his chair away from the table and looked for Zuri Coggins in the group clustered before the wall screens.

The Chinese are behind this! He was certain. The North Koreans are fronting for Beijing. We're heading smack into a nuclear war.

Charley Ingersoll had to make a decision. The van was stuck in the god-dratted snowbank on the shoulder of the road. The more he tried to pull out of the snow, the deeper his tires spun into the ruts they were making.

Martha was ashen-faced, barely keeping herself from sobbing. The kids seemed okay, but they were strangely quiet. Scared, Charley thought.

I'm scared too, he realized. Stuck here in the middle of infernal nowhere with the snow coming down harder than ever and the van running out of gas. Stupid phone doesn't work and there hasn't been a snowplow through here for God knows how long.

Lord have mercy! We could freeze to death!

He tried the radio. Nothing but hillbilly music or blaring rock that made him feel as if his eardrums were about to explode. No news. No weather reports.

"It's ten minutes to two, Charley," his wife said, her voice small, frightened. "They'll have news and weather on the hour."

Like that's going to do us any good, Charley thought. But he didn't say anything out loud. He sat and waited. The van was eerily silent. Only the soft purr of the engine and the moaning wind outside. The snow was coming down heavier than ever.

How long will the gas last? Charley asked himself. Once it runs out and the heater goes, we could all freeze to death.

"Can't we go out and make a snowman?" Little Martha asked again.

"No!" Martha snapped. "Stay in here, where it's warm."

For how long? Charley wondered.

"Your headlines on the hour," a man's deep voice intoned over a blare of trumpets. "Surprise blizzard blankets the region with snow! Widespread electric outages reported! Network and cable television still out of service!" He sounded positively happy about it all. "And now the details."

Charley listened in growing impatience as the voice told how television service had been out all day except for local stations. Come on with the weather, Charley prompted silently. Come on!

"A surprise autumn storm has struck the region with more than a foot of snow, and still more on the way." The guy sounded overjoyed about it, Charley thought. "Snowplow crews have been struggling to keep the interstates open, but secondary roads have been officially closed to all but emergency traffic . . ."

"Secondary roads?" Martha asked. "Are we on a secondary road?"

Charley shook his head. "Damned if I know."

Martha glared at his language. Charley was surprised at himself. He glanced back at the kids.

"I'm cold," Little Martha said from the backseat.

"I'll turn up the heat, dear," said Martha. Charley saw that the heater was already on maximum.

Suddenly he heard himself say, "We passed a gas station a couple miles back."

"But they couldn't pump any gas," his wife said.

"Yeah, but I think I saw a tow truck there. They could pull us out of this snowbank and siphon some gas into our tank."

"But we don't have their phone nu—" Martha stopped herself, realizing that their cell phone wasn't working anyway.

"I'll go back and get them," Charley said.

Martha's eyes popped. "Outside? In this blizzard?"

"It's only a couple miles. I can make it."

"Charley, no! Don't!"

But he had made up his mind while he was speaking the words. Anything would be better than sitting here doing nothing. Even freezing out in the snow.

"Charley, please! Don't leave us!"

As he reached for the door handle, Charley said, "I'll be back in an hour or so. With a tow truck." He tried to sound confident. He certainly didn't feel it.

G ot it!" Monk said, grinning.

Leaning over his burly shoulder, Harry saw the return blip from the ranging laser on the readout screen of Delany's console. Numbers rastered down the screen's side. The laser was working fine and pinging the tanker plane with low-power invisible infrared pulses.

Harry grabbed the headset hooked to the console's side and slapped it onto his head. Thumbing the intercom button on the console, he called, "Hartunian to the communications officer."

"Comm here," said O'Banion's voice in the earphone.

"I'm piping our ranging laser's data to you. Please confirm against your radar."

"Will do, Mr. Hartunian."

Monk looked up at Harry, his lopsided grin almost a smirk. "I told you I'd get it working. No sweat."

Harry nodded absently. It was one thing to put the little laser together and make it work. It was another to make it work *right*. Using the tanker plane as a target was a good test, although the plane was practically in their laps and the real test would come when they had to get the range on a missile boosting from a hundred or more miles away. But if their laser results matched the plane's regular radar—

"Mr. Hartunian," said O'Banion.

"Yeah?"

"I'm sending our numbers down to you. They look good to me, sir."

"Okay, okay." Harry felt his hands trembling slightly as the radar numbers began to appear on Monk's screen, alongside the numbers from their ranging laser.

"On the button!" Monk crowed. "Look at that!"

Harry saw that the numbers differed only on the fourth decimal place. Good enough, he thought. Good enough.

"You're right, Monk," he said, forcing a smile. "We're in business."

"Better tell that flygirl skipper, pal."

"I will," Harry said, straightening up. "After I check with Taki."

MONK'S GRIN SHRANK as Harry left him and ducked through the hatch to the battle management station, where Nakamura sat peering intently at one of the four consoles.

Sliding into the chair beside her, Harry said, "Monk got the ranger working."

"I can see that," Taki said, tapping a lacquered fingernail against the console's main screen.

"Is it good enough for you?" he asked.

Nakamura nodded, but Harry saw that her lips were pressed together tightly.

"Problem?"

She looked away from him for a moment, then turned back to the console and its array of screens. "Harry, I can't do this. Not all by myself."

"I know."

As if she hadn't heard him, she went on. "I mean, it's one thing to run a test, just fire the COIL at a spot in the empty air. But now we're going to try to hit real missiles? Come on, there's supposed to be four people at these consoles. I'm only one person. I can't do everything."

"I'll be beside you, Taki. I'll be right here with you. We'll do it together."

Nakamura focused her dark eyes on Harry. He saw doubt in them. And he understood what was going on in her head. It all depends on her, Harry thought. Wally and Angel can fire the COIL. Monk can make the ranging laser work. But it's Taki's responsibility to run the sensors that acquire the infrared signature of the rocket exhaust plume, point the COIL at the target, and get off enough shots to take out the missile before its engines cut off and we lose the infrared signal from the plume.

"Taki," he said softly, "what it takes four blue-suiters to do, the two of us can do."

"You think so?"

"Sure. You'll get an Annie Oakley medal for sharpshooting."

Her brows knit. "Annie Oakley? Who's she?"

The tension broke and Harry laughed. "I'll tell you all about her after this is over."

As he got to his feet, Monk came through the hatch and passed through the compartment. "Kidney break," Delany said.

The lens assembly! Harry thought. He's going to wipe down the lens assembly! He watched Delany duck through the hatch, wondering what he should do.

"I've got to talk to the pilot," he said to Nakamura, and followed Delany out of the compartment.

Instead of going upstairs to the flight deck, though, Harry watched Delany step into the lavatory, then he went into the galley, sat tensely at one of the bucket seats, and kept his eyes on the lav hatch.

Delany came out in less than a minute. He didn't have time to do anything with the lens assembly, Harry thought. Hell, he didn't even take the time to wash his hands!

But Harry entered the lavatory anyway, kneeled down, and opened the cabinet. The cartons of toilet paper were stacked just as he had left them. Taking the top few out, Harry saw the lens assembly still sitting behind them.

As he put the packages back Harry thought that so far he had proven nothing. As a detective he was a total flop.

Message incoming from the Pentagon," O'Banion reported. "I'm running it through decrypt now."

"Let me see it as soon as decrypt's finished," Colonel Christopher said.

"Right."

Lieutenant Sharmon's softer voice sounded in her earphone. "We're approaching North Korean territorial waters, Colonel."

Karen Christopher frowned slightly. They had flown past the storm swirling across the Sea of Japan and were now over open water. Through the windscreen Christopher could see nothing but empty ocean, gray and rippled with waves. No sign of land.

"We're twelve miles off the coast of Korea?"

"No, ma'am," Sharmon replied. "The North Koreans claim territorial rights out to two hundred miles."

"Two hundred? Is that legal?"

"I checked the regs, Colonel. Twelve miles is the international standard for territorial rights, but some countries claim exclusive economic rights out to two hundred. They don't allow fishing boats or stuff like that."

Colonel Christopher puzzled over that for a moment. "Better check with Washington and see what they recommend."

"It'll take awhile; communications are still all fuck . . . er, all snarled up."

The colonel nodded to herself as she thought, We need to get this bird as close to the shoreline as possible. When those gooks pop their missiles we've got to be close enough to nail them right away. Close enough to take more than one pop at them if we have to.

O'Banion came back on the intercom. "Colonel, Mr. Hartunian's asking to talk to you."

"Where is he?"

"Down in the battle management compartment."

She turned to Kaufman. "Obie, take over. Stay on this heading until we're twenty miles off the coast. Holler if I'm not back by then."

Kaufman looked resentful, as usual. But he said, "Twenty miles. Right."

Colonel Christopher nodded at her navigator and communications officer as she went through the flight deck and down the ladder to the tiny niche between the beam control and battle management compartments. Hartunian was standing behind the Asian-American girl, the expression on his face somewhere between grim and determined.

"Any problems, Mr. Hartunian?" the colonel asked, barely loud enough to be heard over the rumble of the plane's engines.

Hartunian gestured toward the galley as he said, "I think we're ready, Colonel."

"You think?" Christopher felt her brows knitting. She had wanted to make her tone light, not accusative. No sense making the nerd get sore at you, she told herself. But her words had come out as challenging, demanding.

Hartunian seemed not to notice as he stepped through the open hatchway and waited for her to enter the galley. Then he closed the hatch behind her, softly, as if he didn't want anyone to hear it shut.

"Well?" Colonel Christopher said.

"The hardware's in operating condition. We tested the ranging laser on the refueling plane and it's working okay."

"Good."

With a shake of his head, Hartunian went on, "But I don't know about the people. We're just a skeleton crew. And one of us tried to sabotage the mission."

"You still don't know who."

"No idea."

Christopher thought it over for all of two seconds. Then she muttered, "Well, let's hope it's not some fanatic who's willing to kill himself." Then she added, "Or herself."

Hartunian said, "I've been thinking about that. Whoever it was tried to screw up the mission in the least dangerous way possible. Knock out the ranging laser and we'd have to abort the test and turn back for home. But now that he knows this mission is for real . . ." His voice trailed off.

Christopher went to the coffee urn and poured herself a mug. "If you're right, that means whoever it was sabotaged your laser when he—or she—thought this flight was only a routine test."

"Right," Hartunian agreed. "Which means that whoever it is wanted to give Anson Aerospace a black eye. He's not an enemy agent, he's just a damned industrial spy, working for one of Anson's competitors."

The colonel stared at Hartunian for a long, silent moment. Then, "You think so?"

The engineer smiled bitterly. "Either that or we're all dead."

A s he spoke earnestly into the telephone, the President hardly glanced at the magnificent view of the Golden Gate Bridge from the penthouse suite's windows. It was raining out there anyway, a steady, gray, cold-looking rain.

Norman Foster sat on the luxurious Louis XIV sofa and ran a hand over his bald pate as he watched his friend and boss chatting away on the phone, charming one moment, intimidating the next. Moscow, Tokyo, NATO headquarters in Belgium: he'd been trying to get world leaders lined up with him despite the maddening slowness of the battered global communications system.

At last the President put the phone down. Before he could get out of his chair, Foster said, "The Air Force wants to send some F-15s to escort ABL-1."

"A fighter escort?" the President. "Why do they want a fighter escort?"

Foster knew that they'd have to change into fresh suits before heading out to the Cow Palace. He glanced at his wristwatch before replying, "The laser plane's a big four-engine 747. If the North Koreans or the Chinese try to intercept it, she'll be a sitting duck."

"This request came from NSA?"

"From the special situation team. They sent it through the Air Force, who passed it up to the Secretary of Defense," Foster said.

"From Lonnie Bakersfield?"

"None other."

"This request came direct from Lonnie himself?" the President asked.

Spreading his hands in a gesture of uncertainty, the President's chief of staff replied, "Nothing's direct just now. Communications are in a mess. SecDef sent this request nearly an hour ago."

"And you just got it?" the President snapped.

"It came to Air Force One and they transferred it to your security team's briefcase."

"God Almighty! How can we manage this crisis when we can't even get telephone calls through?"

Trying to calm his boss, Foster said, "The communications system is working; it's just slower than normal, that's all."

"That's all? You said this request came from that situation team you put together, through the Air Force chain of command, up to the Secretary of Defense, and now to me."

"That's right."

The President glared at his old friend. "Where's that laser plane now?"

"According to the latest report, it's over the Sea of Japan, heading for the coast of North Korea."

"You think the North Koreans might try to shoot it down?"

"Or force it to land in North Korea. It'd make terrific propaganda for them. Not to mention the technology they'll be able to get their hands on."

"We're staring nuclear war in the face and you think they're aiming for propaganda?"

Foster made an exasperated grimace. "Yeah. What the hell do I know."

Standing in the middle of the sumptuously furnished room, the

President scratched at his long jaw once, then decided. "No fighter escort."

Foster could feel his brows hike up.

Waving an extended forefinger like a schoolteacher trying to get a lesson across to a backward pupil, the President said, "You get our fighter jocks into the same airspace as their fighter jocks and you're going to start a war."

"But if they launch those missiles we'll have a war anyway. A nuclear war."

"The laser plane's supposed to shoot the missiles down."

"Suppose the North Koreans shoot down the plane instead?"

"Then they launch the missiles and we go to war. But I don't want to have some fighter jock get us into a war if we can avoid it."

Foster got slowly to his feet. "Mr. President, that just doesn't make any goddamned sense."

"Maybe not to you, Norm. But that's my decision. If there's a way to avert this disaster I'm willing to take it. Now let me see if I can get the British Prime Minister on the phone before we have to head down to the Cow Palace."

General Scheib looked up from his laptop. "No fighter escort," he said, his face dark, grim.

General Higgins stepped over to where Scheib was sitting and stared at the decoded message on Scheib's screen, as if he couldn't believe it unless he saw the words for himself.

"From POTUS," he muttered. With a shake of his head he added, "Can't go any higher in the chain of command than that."

Scheib looked up into Higgins' florid, big-nosed face. "ABL-1 will be a sitting duck if the North Koreans send out fighters."

Zuri Coggins, standing by the newly replenished coffee cart, spoke up. "Maybe they won't. If Pyongyang honestly wants to prevent the rebels from launching those missiles, they won't interfere with our plane."

"How do they know what our plane is?" Scheib snapped. "What if they think it's a strategic bomber, the first part of our counterstrike against them?"

"We'll have to tell them," Coggins said.

"How? Send 'em a frigging telegram?"

Coggins looked stricken, realizing that there was no North Korean ambassador in Washington, no diplomatic relations with the DPRK at all.

"We'll have to go through China," she said. "Get the message to Beijing and have them relay our intentions to Pyongyang."

Scheib gave her a disgusted look. "And by the time that's done ABL-1 will be sinking to the bottom of the Sea of Japan."

"Maybe not," Michael Jamil said.

Scheib glared down the table at him, but asked, "What do you mean?"

Jamil licked his lips before answering. "Whoever's orchestrating this has some pretty good intelligence sources. Maybe they know about ABL-1."

General Higgins plopped into the chair next to Scheib. "You've given the plane a lot of publicity, Brad. I bet there's some gook intel officer who reads *Aviation Week*."

"Or an intelligence officer in Beijing," Jamil said.

Higgins gave him a sour look. "You still think the chinks are behind all this? Dr. Fu Manchu, maybe?"

Jamil's brows knit. "Who's Dr. Fu Manchu?"

The general rolled his eyes toward the ceiling.

But Coggins headed down the table toward the young analyst. "Do you really believe this situation is being orchestrated by Beijing?"

"Yes, I certainly do." Jamil started ticking off points on his fingers. "The North Korean nuclear program hasn't produced anything more than a test device. They don't have nuclear warheads; they had to get them from somewhere else."

"China?" Coggins asked, taking the chair next to Jamil's.

"Or Russia. Second point, Pyongyang's government is in turmoil, but it would be suicide for a group of their army officers to steal those missiles and launch them at the United States."

"They're fanatics," General Higgins snapped. "Orientals. They don't have the same values that we do."

"But they're not fools. They must believe that they have the backing of someone powerful enough to protect them from their own government."

"China," Coggins said again.

Nodding, Jamil went on. "China launched surveillance satellites two days ago. I'm betting that they're hardened against the North Korean nuke and they're in orbit to watch the President's arrival in San Francisco."

Scheib growled, "Not that again! They can't hit San Francisco. We know that for a fact."

Jamil ignored him. "They knocked out our own satellites so we couldn't see their government leaders heading for their underground shelters."

"Our milsats are still working," Higgins objected. "We haven't seen any such movement."

"Have you looked?" Jamil challenged. "Have you ordered the NRO analysts to specifically look for a flow of high-up government vehicles out of Beijing?"

Higgins fell silent.

"The Chinese have wanted Taiwan since 1949," Jamil said. "It's a matter of national pride to them. A matter of face."

"And they're willing to risk nuclear war over it?" Coggins demanded.

With a shake of his head, Jamil retorted, "That's not the question. The question is, are *we* willing to risk nuclear war over it?"

"Aw, that's just nonsense," Higgins insisted.

But Coggins murmured, "I'm not so sure."

"Look," Jamil said, almost pleading for understanding, "The Chinese economy is in the toilet—"

"Whose isn't?" Higgins muttered.

"There's a lot of unrest in China. People got accustomed to a rising economy, rising expectations. Now they're sinking. Getting Taiwan would be a great boost to the government in Beijing."

"And you think Beijing is willing to let a few hundred million of their people die in a nuclear exchange?"

"You still don't get it, General. Are *we* willing to lose a hundred million people or more over Taiwan?"

General Scheib spoke up. "But Taiwan's got nothing to do with this! It's North Korea that's threatening us."

"I know, I understand that. But look at the big picture. North Korea attacks us. We have the option of retaliation or negotiation. If we retaliate, if we hit North Korea, China will come in on their side. They'd have to. They can't sit and do nothing while we attack their next-door neighbor. Remember how they came into the Korean War when it looked like we were going to conquer the north."

Coggins nodded slowly, reluctantly agreeing with his logic.

Jamil continued. "If we let the North Koreans get away with attacking us, killing the President—or maybe just blowing out Honolulu or Fairbanks—then our influence in Asia goes down to zero. So we have the choice of nuclear war with China or allowing China to remake the map of Asia."

Higgins shook his head ponderously. "I just don't believe it."

Coggins said, "They'd reunify Korea, with North Korea in command. China would take over Taiwan. They'd force Japan to get rid of our bases there . . ."

"Chinese hegemony in the Far East," Jamil said. "And we're humiliated worldwide."

The conference room fell absolutely silent. Jamil could hear the faint buzz of the air circulation fans in the ceiling.

General Scheib broke the spell. "Okay. So what do we do if they shoot down ABL-1?"

Harry ran his hand along the smooth, cool metal tubing that ran the length of the COIL bay. The mixture of iodine and oxygen gases would flow down the main tube at supersonic speed when the laser was activated, producing more than a million watts of infrared energy once it raced through the lasing cavity. More than a megawatt, Harry thought. Sounds like a lot, but it's about the explosive equivalent of a lousy hand grenade.

Still, slap a hand grenade against the side of a boosting rocket and you blow it apart. That's what we've got to do, Harry told himself.

Wally Rosenberg sidled up to him with his usual crafty grin.

"*El jefe's* down among the peons, huh?" Rosenberg pronounced the word "pee-ons."

Ignoring Wally's sarcasm, Harry said, "A pinpoint leak anywhere along the tubing could louse up the COIL. Maybe blow up the plane and us in it."

"We ran a nitrogen purge through the system not more'n twenty minutes ago. No leaks."

Angel Reyes came up, looking intent, totally focused on his job. "Don't worry, Harry. Everything back here is okay."

Harry nodded absently. "We've got to make this baby work right. The first time. We won't have the chance to tinker with her and try again."

Reyes straightened up to his full height, barely taller than Harry's chin. "It will work," he said. His voice was soft, but the intensity in his eyes was iron-hard.

Harry looked at the two of them: Reyes standing as if he were facing a firing squad; Rosenberg in his usual slouch, his sly grin fading into something less certain.

"I've got to ask you both," Harry said slowly, "and I swear to you this'll go no further than the three of us: Did one of you pull the lenses out of the ranger?"

Reyes looked surprised, then hurt. Rosenberg gave Harry a disgruntled huff.

"I haven't gone farther forward than the fuckin' galley since we took off, Harry," said Rosenberg. Then he amended, "No, wait, I took a piss in the forward toilet."

"I used the toilet back aft here," Reyes said, clearly insulted at Harry's suggestion.

"I'm sorry, guys," Harry said. "I had to ask. One of us tried to screw up the mission and—"

"It wasn't me," Rosenberg snapped. For once he looked serious.

"Or me," said Reyes.

Harry puffed out a weary sigh. "Then it had to be Monk, or Taki."

Rosenberg's crafty half-grin returned. "What's Tiki-Taki's religion, Harry? She wouldn't be a Muslim, would she?"

IN THE COCKPIT, Colonel Christopher said into her lip microphone, "Brick, where's that message from Washington? Haven't you got it decoded yet?"

"One more minute, Colonel," the communications officer replied. "This one's in a red priority code."

"Jon, how far from the coast are we?"

Sharmon's deeper voice immediately answered, "One hundred and fifty miles, ma'am."

Christopher nodded. Off on the horizon she could see a smear of clouds that must have marked the coastline. Her flight helmet felt as if it weighed a ton. But we're too close now to take a break, she told herself. Got to sit here until we're finished.

She glanced across the console of throttles at Major Kaufman. Obie looks calm enough. He had the sweats when we were waiting for the tanker, but he looks okay now.

"You need a kidney break, Obie?"

He shook his head hard enough to make his helmet wobble.

"Won't have time for it once the shooting starts," she prompted.

Kaufman frowned, then grumbled, "I was okay until you mentioned it." He unstrapped and hauled himself out of the copilot's seat.

Christopher chuckled to herself.

"Got the scoop from Washington, Colonel," O'Banion called.

"Hand it to me."

The redheaded comm officer ducked through the hatch and gave Christopher a flimsy sheet of paper. She read its two lines quickly. "North Korean missile launch imminent. No fighter cover for your mission."

Fighter cover? Christopher was surprised at the idea. She hadn't even thought about having fighter planes escorting her. But it made sense. We'd be a sitting duck if the gooks sent fighters up to intercept us.

"Incoming message," O'Banion said, his voice sounding tense, urgent.

"Pipe it to me."

A calm, reedy voice said in British-inflected English, "Unidentified aircraft, this is Air Defense Command of the Democratic People's Republic of Korea. You have entered DPRK airspace. You will identify yourself and depart DPRK airspace at once. Respond immediately, please."

Taki Nakamura looked up from her main console as Harry stepped through the hatch.

"I've done the dry run sixteen times, Harry," she said before he could get a word out of his mouth. "I'm pretty sure that the two of us can handle the mission."

He sat at the console next to hers, noting that all its screens were alight, displaying data.

"I mean, it's only two missiles, right?" Taki chattered on. "If it was more I'd say we needed a full crew, but for only two of 'em we can handle it. Really, I'm sure we can."

Placing a hand on her arm, Harry felt her trembling slightly. "I know you can, Taki. I don't have any doubt of it. And I'll be right here with you."

Silently, he added, If there's going to be any problems, they'll be here, at battle management. Monk can't do any damage to us unless he hauls out the COIL's entire optics bench or smashes it to pieces, and he's not going to reveal himself by doing that. If he's the one. Wally and Angel know they'd blow up the plane if they mess with the fuel system feed. So Taki's the one who could mess us up, and I'm going to stick right here beside her.

She was saying, "I'll get it done, Harry, I really will. Don't worry about this end of it."

Harry smiled wanly. "Taki, I'm worried about everything. All of it."

She seemed to focus on him for the first time. More softly, she said, "Yeah, I guess you are. Can't say I blame you."

Taking a deep breath, Harry asked, "Um, has Monk come through here in the past hour or so?"

Taki seemed surprised at the change of subject. Her brows nettling, she replied, "I think so. Can't say the time, exactly, but he did come through. Said he had to use the toilet."

Harry nodded. He had checked the lavatory again before entering Taki's station. The lens assembly was still in the closet where he'd found it, apparently undisturbed since the last time he'd looked.

"You still looking for the lens assembly?" Taki asked.

"I'm looking for whoever took it."

"Oh. Sure."

Before he could think about it, Harry blurted, "Taki, was it you?"

Her eyes went so wide he could see white all around the deep brown irises. "Me?" Her screech was an octave and a half higher than before.

Feeling miserable, Harry said, "I had to ask, Taki. I asked the others first. It won't go any further than the five of us. But I've got to know. I don't care why, I just have to know that we'll get through this mission okay."

Clearly seething, Taki hissed, "You think because my great-grandfather fought for the Emperor that I'm a fuckin' kamikaze?"

"No! I . . ." Harry could see the fury in her face. "I don't know what to think. One of us tried to screw up the mission and I've got to find out who."

"It wasn't me."

"I didn't think it was."

"So why'd you ask?"

Shaking his head, Harry answered, "I don't know what else I can do! Christ, Taki, this is awful."

Her shoulders relaxed slightly, but she said, "Don't tell me you're just doing your job, Harry."

"Believe me, Taki, being a detective isn't a job I want."

She almost smiled. "For what it's worth, you're not very good at it."

He almost smiled back. "I know. I know."

COLONEL CHRISTOPHER UNCONSCIOUSLY pressed one hand against her helmet earphone as the smooth male voice repeated, "Unidentified aircraft, this is Air Defense Command of the Democratic People's Republic of Korea. You have entered DPRK airspace. You will identify yourself and depart DPRK airspace at once. Respond immediately, please."

Kaufman, standing at the cockpit hatch, was staring at her. "Well?" he asked. He had heard the message from the speaker on O'Banion's console.

Christopher's mind was racing. Clipped to the control panel in front of her was the message from Washington. Missile launch imminent. No fighter cover.

"Well?" Kaufman said again, more demanding. "What are you going to do?"

"Nothing."

"Nothing?"

"Stay on course. Make no reply to them. Radio silence from here on in."

"They'll shoot us down! The goddamn gooks shot down a civilian airliner a few years ago, didn't they? They'll send out fighters and blast us out of the sky!"

"Go to the toilet, Obie, and get back here as fast as you can. I'm going to need you here."

"You're gonna get us all killed," Kaufman muttered.

Trying to ignore her copilot, Christopher called to O'Banion, "Brick, radio silence. Nothing goes out unless I say so."

The communications officer's voice came through her headphone, "Not even a Mayday when they shoot us down?"

ENGAGEMENT

The Secretary of Defense smiled and rose to his feet as she came in, but stayed behind his broad, gleaming desk.

"Welcome to my humble abode, Madam Secretary," he said, his deep voice grating like a rusty hinge.

"Cut the bullcrap, Lonnie," said the Secretary of State. "We don't have time for it."

She walked across the spacious room and dropped with a sigh into one of the massive leather-upholstered armchairs in front of the desk. With a practiced eye she swept the office, taking in the heavy, dark furniture, the bookcases lined with leather-bound volumes that looked as if they'd never been opened, the wall of photographs of the man with his fellow great and powerful ones, the view from the top-floor windows of the city across the Potomac and the spire of the Washington Monument. It was still raining, but there was a hint of late afternoon sunshine breaking through the gray clouds.

"You came alone?" asked Lionel Bakersfield. "Without your usual entourage?" The Secretary of Defense swiveled his plush high-backed chair slightly to and fro. The Secretary of State thought it betrayed a nervousness in him. Bakersfield was wearing a gray three-piece suit that had been hand-tailored for him, although its jacket hung open and his vest was unbuttoned. Even his old-fashioned rep tie had wormed loose from his collar. Sloppy, thought the Secretary of State. The man's always been a slob, and he'll never be anything but a slob.

A dangerous slob, though. They had campaigned against each other through the primaries and both lost to the current President. Both of them had been senators before joining their onetime rival's administration, and senators always thought of presidents as temporary. The President proposes; the Congress disposes: it was a motto that had warmed many a senator's heart over many, many administrations.

State was still in the pearl gray pant suit and tailored white blouse she had worn earlier. She felt a little grubby, but there had been no time to change.

"Anyone see you coming here?" Defense asked.

She knew he meant news media people. "No. I came in a closed limo. There won't be any headlines about State visiting the Pentagon, I assure you."

Defense made a lopsided smile. "And, if I may ask, exactly *why* have you come from the comforts of Foggy Bottom to grace my office? To what do I owe this honor?"

God! thought State. The world's coming to an end and he still can't get out a single sentence without all his flourishes.

"I want to see a couple of the people on your situation team. That analyst from the NIC and General Scheib."

Defense's shaggy brows rose slightly. "I'll get them up here right away." He pressed a button on his desktop intercom and gave the order. Then, steepling his fingers as he looked back at State, he asked, "Why those two?"

State was surprised by the directness of his question. Then she thought, He's trying to shock me into telling him the truth.

It was her turn to smile now. "I need to be brought up to the minute on this missile crisis."

"Aha."

"Phone links aren't good enough. I need to see the players face-to-face."

"I understand. They'll be here directly."

FIVE LEVELS BELOW the Secretary of Defense's office, General Scheib frowned at the young tech sergeant who had handed him the message.

"The Secretary of Defense wants to see me in his office," Scheib announced to the team. Pointing down the table to Jamil he added, "You too."

Jamil looked shocked. "Me?"

General Higgins grunted. "It doesn't pay to cross the Secretary of State, kid. She's probably got the big brass upstairs boiling a pot of oil for you."

"But we can't go now!" Jamil said. "The North Koreans will be launching those missiles any minute!"

"Nothing you can do about that," Higgins said. "You just follow orders, like the rest of us."

Jamil got to his feet, looking uncertain, fearful. Zuri Coggins went to his side. "I'll go with you," she said.

Scheib snapped, "The call was for him and me. Nobody else."

Eyes blazing, Coggins stood up to the general, even though she was barely the height of his chin. "I represent the National Security Advisor. If there's going to be any boiling in oil, they'll have to do it in front of me."

Scheib actually took a step back from her. Then he shrugged and muttered, "Okay. You explain it to the Secretary, then."

As the three of them followed the tech sergeant toward the door Higgins called after them, "We'll try to keep the gooks from launching until after you get back."

No one laughed. No one even smiled.

Charley had never been so cold and miserable in his whole blessed life. He hadn't gone more than a dozen steps through the wet, fluffy snow before his shoes were soaked and his feet started to hurt like fire. Doggedly he pushed on, heading back down the road toward the gas station he'd remembered seeing.

The wind was in his face and cutting right through his polyester shell jacket. It had a wool lining, but it felt like nothing more than tissue paper. Charley tugged on the zipper. It was already as high as it could go. He mashed his Seattle Seahawks cap as far down on his head as he could, but his ears were exposed and tingling. Turning, he could barely make out the lines of the van stuck on the roadside.

Come on, Charley, he urged himself. Get moving. The more you move, the warmer you'll feel. Get that old heart pumping.

Jamming his bare hands into the jacket's pockets he mushed on, squinting against the snowflakes rushing into his face.

It's only a couple miles, he told himself. I got to get there before the van runs out of gas. Got to get there before Martha and the kids freeze.

They shouldn't have blizzards like this in October, he raged to himself. Those science people claim we're having global warming, for Lord's sake. This don't look like global warming to me!

W e're going to have company!"

Colonel Christopher heard the shrill alarm in Captain O'Banion's voice.

"What is it?" she asked, keeping her voice flat, calm.

"Flash from Andrews. Pyongyang just launched a pair of fighters, vectoring straight at us."

"Fighters?"

"Must be, from their speed."

Fighters, Christopher thought. From North Korea. Info relayed from Andrews.

"How long ago did they send out the warning?"

A pause. Then O'Banion replied, "Time hack says four minutes ago."

At least they've got a direct link with us now, Christopher realized, finally. Now they can watch us get shot down in real time.

She asked O'Banion, "Estimated time to intercept?"

Again a pause. Then, "Ten . . . to twelve minutes."

"Get Mr. Hartunian up here. On the double."

.   .   .

HARRY WAS SITTING beside Taki, helping her check out all the electronic controls for the COIL.

It couldn't have been Taki, he was telling himself. Unless she's a damned good actress. But why would she do it? Why would she try to abort this flight? Why would any of them?

He asked himself again if one of the Air Force crew might have stolen the lens assembly. And again the answer came back negative. They don't know enough about the system to cripple it like that. Besides, if one of them had started tinkering with the laser in its housing up there, the rest of them would have seen him.

Harry realized the gangly black lieutenant had ducked into the compartment, a puzzled frown on his face.

"You guys need to keep the intercom open," he said without preamble. "Our comm man has been trying to get you on the squawk line for the past five minutes. The skipper wants to see you, Mr. Hartunian. And I mean *now*."

Harry pushed himself to his feet as Taki snatched up the headphone from its hook on the console and clamped it over her spiky hair.

Colonel Christopher was standing in the rear of the flight deck, by the mussed-up pair of cots, as Harry clambered up the ladder. The redheaded captain was peering intently at his radar screen. As Lieutenant Sharmon went back to his console, Harry went aft toward the colonel. He realized that she was quite good-looking, even in blue Air Force fatigues. Slim figure, pretty oval face, dark hair cropped short. Sexy, almost. Except that she looked as bleak as death.

"Are you ready for action?" she asked, keeping her voice so low Harry barely heard her over the thrumming of the plane's engines.

He nodded. "All systems are go."

"We're going to be shooting very soon. Within minutes."

"We're ready."

She took a breath, then added, "And we're going to be shot at, most likely."

"What?"

"There's a pair of North Korean interceptors heading toward us."

Harry's mind spun into overdrive. "Look, they won't know if we fire the COIL or not. It's an infrared beam. You can't see it."

Colonel Christopher's brows knit slightly. "That's something . . ." Then she asked, "Could we shoot down a plane?"

"If you can get the COIL's beam on it for a couple of seconds. Heat up the aluminum skin to its ignition point and then the airflow starts the aluminum burning."

"Is that real or some scientist's theory?"

"We've done it on the test range, with fans blowing air across the target."

"At what range?"

Harry had to think back. "Half a mile. But the COIL can hit a target much farther than that. A hundred miles, maybe more."

"So we can defend ourselves, maybe."

"Only if the bad guy's dumb enough to fly in front of us. The output turret up in the nose can only swivel thirty degrees left or right."

Christopher looked disappointed. "They're not that dumb. They'll come up behind us and pop an air-to-air missile at us."

"Jeez." Harry suddenly felt an overwhelming need to urinate.

"Our alternative is to turn around and head for Japan."

"And let them fire their ballistic missiles?"

She nodded grimly. "Nice choice, isn't it?"

Wow, it's big!" said Denise as she, her sister, and her mother followed the crowd streaming from the BART station to the Cow Palace's main entrance. The rain had slowed to a drizzle, but still their hair was wet and plastered on their scalps by the time they got into the huge auditorium.

Once inside the vast, barnlike stadium, Sylvia told her daughters, "They've held national conventions in here, rodeos, basketball games, hockey games, even Roller Derbies."

"Roller Derbies?" Vickie asked, curious despite her practiced teenaged boredom. "What's that?"

Sylvia explained as they climbed the concrete stairs and found their seats. From this high up the platform on which the President would speak looked little bigger than a postage stamp.

"You said we were going to be in the front row," Vickie accused.

"We're not that far away," said Sylvia as they sat down.

"They've set up big TV screens," Denise said, pointing.

"We'll be able to see the President's face very clearly," Sylvia said. "Just like we're sitting next to him, almost."

Vickie muttered, "Big deal." Sylvia pretended not to hear her.

. . .

AS THE LIMOUSINE pulled up at the Cow Palace, the President asked his chief of staff, "What's happening in Korea?"

Norman Foster pulled the phone bud out of his ear. "Looks like they're getting ready to launch those other two birds."

"We can see them?"

"Satellite imagery. From the National Reconnaissance Office."

The Secret Service agent pulled the door open on the President's side of the limo. The motorcade had driven directly into the Cow Palace's underground parking area, which had been cleared for security. No cheering crowds. No band playing "Hail to the Chief." Just a shadowy concrete expanse, chilly, damp.

Before the President could get out of the limo the chief of his Secret Service detail, a tall, lanky man with a weatherbeaten face and a dour expression, ducked his head into the open door and said, "Mr. President, we've got to head back to the airport, sir."

"No, we don't," the President said, smiling pleasantly at the agent's grimly determined face.

"Sir, it's my duty—"

"I make the decisions, Ron. I'm going ahead with my speech."

The black-suited agent looked as if he wanted to argue the point, but he recognized the steel behind the President's smile. "You're the boss, sir."

"That's right, Ron," said the President. As he got out of the limo he asked his chief of staff, "What about that laser plane?"

Sliding across the leather seat, Foster replied, "Approaching the North Korean coast. Should be in position to shoot at the missiles as soon as they're launched."

"If it can get close enough to them," the President muttered.

"Yep," said Foster. "There is that."

The President nodded. Foster slid out of the limo and straightened up slowly. Arthritis, the President knew.

The chief of staff made a small, involuntary groan as he stood up. Then, "The Aegis ships are alerted and ready. So are the ABM bases in Alaska and Vandenberg."

With another nod, the President muttered, "Now we'll see if we've spent the taxpayers' money wisely."

"You bet your life," said Foster, without a trace of a smile.

T hey're going to launch any minute," Harry prodded.

Monk Delany shot a sour glance over his burly shoulder. "I'm ready. I'm ready. Let 'em launch."

Bending over the seated Delany, Harry saw that the ranging laser's screen was clear. Nothing in view.

"Did I hear one of those blue-suiters say we've got fighters coming after us?" Delany had his headphone solidly clamped to one ear. Obviously he'd been tuned in to the intercom chatter.

"That's what they said," Harry replied tightly.

"Are we turnin' back?"

"No."

"But they could shoot us down!"

Harry said, "Or force us to land in North Korea."

"Christ Almighty," Delany muttered.

"You're going to be a hero, Monk. We all are."

"Dead or alive."

Harry tapped Delany's shoulder. "One way or another, Monk. One way or another."

"They got parachutes on this bird?"

Harry forced a laugh. "I'll go look," he said. He left Delany fiddling with the ranging laser's controls and ducked through to Taki's battle management station.

She looked up at him. "We're being chased by a couple of fighters?"

Harry nodded as he slid into the chair next to hers. "That's the news from upstairs."

"This is going to get bad, isn't it?"

"Looks that way. But we don't have any way out of it."

"The pilot could turn us around and head back to Japan," Taki said without taking her eyes off the screens of her console.

"She's not going to do that. They'll be launching those missiles any minute."

"And after that they'll shoot us down."

"Taki, there's nothing we can do about that. We're in this to the brutal end."

The look on her face was really inscrutable, Harry thought. What's she thinking? She doesn't look scared, or sore, or . . . anything.

As Harry slapped a headphone set over his baby-fine hair, Taki said, "You're pretty cool, Harry. Pretty damned cool."

"Me?" He felt totally surprised. "I'm scared halfway to death!"

"Halfway," she said, with a slight curve of her lip. It might have been the beginning of a smile, Harry thought. Or a sneer of disdain.

With a shake of his head to clear his thoughts, Harry turned back to the console in front of him. "We've got business to do."

"Right, chief."

Harry puzzled over the intercom board for a moment, then pressed the key that he hoped connected to Rosenberg, back aft.

"Yo," said Angel Reyes's voice.

"Where's Wally?"

"In the toilet. I think he's throwin' up."

"Great."

"Naw, I'm only kiddin'. He's takin' a leak."

Harry realized that Angie and Wally hadn't heard about the

North Korean interceptors. Good. They've got enough to worry
about just keeping their minds on business.

He asked into his lip mike, "You guys ready back there? Everything up and running?"

Reyes' voice took on a more formal tone. "All systems are go, *el
jefe.*"

"Any problems? Any anomalies?"

"Pressures in the green. Pumps functional. Feed lines purged
and clean. We're ready to rumble, boss."

"Good," said Harry. "Looks like the rumble's about to start."

W ith all due respect, sir, I should be downstairs with the situation team," General Scheib said.

The Secretary of Defense nodded once. With a glance at the Secretary of State, sitting to one side of his wide, gleaming desk, he replied, "We need your honest assessment of the situation."

"And yours," State said, pointed a manicured finger at Michael Jamil, her face a mask of ice.

Scheib was on his feet in front of the desk, his uniform immaculate, his chiseled face clearly showing his displeasure. Jamil stood beside him, Zuri Coggins slightly behind the two men.

"Honest assessment?" the general echoed. "The Koreans are about to launch their two remaining missiles. Our antimissiles systems are on alert. The airborne laser plane is approaching the North Korean coast."

"Are those missiles aimed at San Francisco?"

"No," said Scheib.

"Yes," said Jamil.

With an angry glance at Jamil, General Scheib insisted, "They don't have the range or accuracy to reach San Francisco."

"They do if they've been upgraded by the Chinese," Jamil retorted.

"You're not still accusing the Chinese of this?" the Secretary of State said.

"It's the only scenario that makes sense," Jamil explained. "The DPRK wouldn't dare start this unless they knew the Chinese were backing them up."

"But I've had assurances . . ." State's voice dwindled away as she realized that she had nothing but the unsupported word of an informal back-channel contact.

Jamil took half a step toward her and said earnestly, "Madam Secretary, we know that the North Koreans launched the bomb that knocked out our satellites. That took more thrust and accuracy than their Taepodong-2 missile has. It had to be upgraded. And where'd they get a nuclear warhead? Their own nuclear program isn't that advanced."

Defense was frowning. State looked distracted, as if she was trying to absorb this information and match it with what she'd thought she'd known earlier.

Jamil went on, "Pyongyang wants—needs!—reunification with South Korea. China wants Taiwan. They both want us out of Asia."

Defense put up a beefy hand. "Wait a minute. How does bombing San Francisco and killing the President get them any of those things?"

"Are we willing to have a nuclear war with China?" Jamil demanded. "Are we willing to see half our cities destroyed, maybe more? A hundred million casualties? Over Taiwan and the reunification of North and South Korea?"

"If they kill the President—"

"Even then, sir. The Chinese are betting that we'll back down. And if we don't, if we launch our missiles at China, they're betting they can absorb our attack and come out the winner."

The Secretary of State heard Quang's warning in her mind, *You must realize that there are factions within our council. We have our own hard-liners, you must understand.*

"But we wouldn't attack China," State said, as if trying to convince herself. "We'd attack North Korea."

"And China would retaliate. They'd have to. They couldn't sit back while we destroyed an ally that's right on their border."

"Chongjin," Defense murmured.

State turned toward him with a questioning look.

"The Korean War. China came in when our troops approached the Yalu River, the border between Korea and China." Defense looked suddenly old and frightened, his liver-spotted face gray.

Coggins stepped up beside Jamil. "For what it's worth, I think this scenario makes sense."

"And the President's been apprised of all this?" State asked.

Coggins replied, "I've spoken to my boss, the National Security Advisor, personally. He's contacted the President's chief of staff out in San Francisco."

Impatiently, General Scheib said, "Whatever scenario you want to believe, we've got the airborne laser approaching the North Korean coast and the gooks about to launch their missiles. I ought to be down in the situation room."

"Yes, you should," Defense said. With a wave of one hand he commanded, "Get down to your post. I only hope to God Almighty your people can shoot those damned missiles out of the sky."

Z uri Coggins realized that General Scheib was terribly tense. Despite the cool appearance he was trying to project, she could see that the general was boiling inside. As the elevator stopped at every floor and people got on and off, Scheib nervously jabbed repeatedly at the button for the basement level even before the elevator doors could close.

"Come on, come on," he kept muttering.

Jamil, standing beside her in the back of the elevator cab, half-whispered, "Thanks for backing me up in there."

He looked weary, spent, close to exhaustion.

"I think you've got it right," she told the analyst, also speaking in a near whisper.

"I thought she called me up there to fry my butt," Jamil confessed.

Coggins said, "Speak truth to power."

"And get your head chopped off."

She nearly laughed. "This isn't Iran, Mr. Jamil. We don't hack people's heads off."

His eyes narrowed. "You assume I'm a Muslim, don't you?" Before she could answer, Jamil stated, "My family's been Christian since the Middle Ages. That's one of the reasons my father left Lebanon."

"I see," said Coggins. She debated telling him, then decided it would do no harm. "I *am* a Muslim, you know. My grandfather was a Baptist, but he converted to the Nation of Islam when a prizefighter named Cassius Clay converted and took the name Muhammad Ali."

She thought that if the situation weren't so desperately deadly the stunned look on Jamil's face would have been hilarious.

THE SECRETARY OF Defense leaned back in his plush swivel chair and eyed the Secretary of State closely. She seemed lost in thought, sitting in the big leather armchair, her eyes turned toward the windows but obviously seeing something other than the view out there.

He lied to me, State was thinking. Quang told me China had no intention of attacking the United States, but if what this analyst says is true, then China's actually behind the North Korean attack. Quang lied. After all these years, he lied to me. How long have the Chinese been preparing for this moment?

"Well?" Defense rumbled, tired of the silence. "What do you think you've accomplished?"

State stirred herself out of her private thoughts. She blinked once at the man behind the big ornate desk.

"Do you believe him?"

"Who? That kid?"

"He's a first-rate analyst with the National Intelligence Council. I had my people check him out after we spoke together on the phone earlier today."

"If he's right, we're in deep shit," said Defense. "Whatever we do, we're in for it."

Strangely, State smiled. Defense had seen that smile before. It usually preceded a beheading.

"I read somewhere," State said slowly, "that the Chinese symbol for crisis is a combination of two other symbols: one for danger, the other for opportunity."

"Opportunity?"

"The President has handled this crisis badly, going off to San Francisco to show what a macho strongman he is."

Wondering where she was heading, Defense chose his words carefully. "If that kid is right and San Francisco is nuked . . ."

"Parkinson becomes President."

Defense huffed. "He's a horse's ass."

"Yes, isn't he?"

"I had him bundled off to the National Redoubt this morning, when this missile business came up."

"So he's safe."

Defense nodded and muttered, "Too bad."

"Not at all," State countered. "You wouldn't want the Speaker of the House to be President, would you?"

"God, no!"

"Parkinson can be handled. He can be led."

"By you?"

"By us," State replied, her smile widening. "We can form a sort of committee."

"A triumvirate. Like in ancient Rome, after Julius Caesar's assassination." And he remembered from history that the triumvirate quickly broke apart as Octavian bested the other two and made himself Rome's first emperor, Augustus Caesar.

State nodded absently, her mind already obviously looking ahead. "If the President dies in a nuclear attack on San Francisco—"

"Parkinson wouldn't have the guts to order a counterstrike on North Korea."

"I think you're wrong, Lonnie."

My name's Lionel and she knows it, Defense growled inwardly. But he kept his pique off his face and asked innocently, "Wrong?"

"I think we can get Parkinson to give the attack order while he's right there in the National Redoubt, snug and safe from attack. I think I could convince him."

Defense shook his head. "So we clobber North Korea. And the Chinese clobber us."

"No, Lonnie, you don't understand," State said. "We hit China right away with a preemptive strike. Cripple their missile forces so they can't hurt us too much. *Then* we wipe out North Korea."

Defense stared at her. She was still smiling, as if she were talking about rearranging the flowers on a banquet table.

"The fallout will drift over Japan," he muttered.

The Secretary of State's smile did not diminish by a single millimeter. "Regrettable," she said. "But one of the ancillary benefits will be to remove both China *and* Japan as economic competitors."

Defense realized what her smile reminded him of: a rattlesnake, poised to strike.

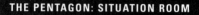

ave they launched?" General Scheib shouted as he burst into the situation room.

General Higgins, sitting at the head of the table, his chair turned so he faced the wall screen, shook his head. "Not yet, Brad." Gesturing to the image on the screen, he went on. "That's the latest imagery. Looks like they're in countdown mode."

Scheib saw that the missiles were standing on their pads, slight wisps of steam issuing from the rime-coated section where the liquid oxygen tanks were.

Sliding into his own chair, he asked, "How old's that picture?"

"Ten minutes," Higgins replied. "We've got a low-altitude bird coming over their horizon in another three minutes. Should give us better resolution."

Scheib tapped at his laptop's keyboard. According to the tracking satellite in geosynchronous orbit, ABL-1 had just made a turn north to parallel the Korean coastline. He squinted at the radar imagery. A pair of tiny dots was also over the Sea of Japan, behind the 747, heading toward it.

Grabbing up the laptop's headset, General Scheib said into its lip mike, "I need a real-time voice link with ABL-1."

A hesitation, then a woman's voice in his earphone replied, "Sir, we need authorization from—"

Without waiting for her to finish, Scheib called down the table, "Possum, I need authorization for a real-time voice link with ABL-1."

Anger flashed in General Higgins' face; he obviously did not like being called Possum.

Without waiting for Higgins to open his mouth, Zuri Coggins leaned over Scheib's shoulder and said crisply, "Authorization code NAS one-one-three, alpha-alpha-omicron."

Scheib heard in his earphone, "Checking . . . authorization verified. Establishing voice link."

Coggins heard Scheib muttering, "Come on, come on."

Still in his chair at the head of the table, General Higgins suddenly realized why Brad Scheib was in such a sweat to have a voice link with ABL-1. He leaned over toward his aide, sitting at his left, and whispered, "Who's piloting that plane?"

"ABL-1, sir?"

With a disgusted look, General Higgins replied, "No, the *Spirit of St. Louis*."

Looking flustered, the aide tapped at his keyboard, then answered, "Lieutenant Colonel Karen Christopher, sir. I have her complete dossier—"

Higgins waved him to silence, thinking, Christopher. The one who clammed up at the Advocate General's hearing. The one who was accused of sleeping with a married general.

One glance at the anxious, intense expression on Scheib's handsome face and Higgins knew whom Christopher had shacked up with.

"FIGHTERS COMING UP fast," O'Banion reported, his voice a notch higher than usual.

Colonel Christopher had ordered her comm officer to activate ABL-1's search radar. No sense trying to stay quiet now, she reasoned. They know we're here. Might as well get a good line on them.

"What's the word from Andrews on the missiles?" she asked into her pin mike.

"Launch is imminent, as of . . . seven minutes ago."

Kaufman muttered from his copilot's seat, "Hope the bastards blow up on the pad."

Christopher nodded. That would solve a lot of problems, she thought.

"Incoming message, Colonel, direct from the Pentagon."

They got a direct satellite link working, Christopher said to herself. That's good. They can hear us get shot down in real time.

"Put it through," she commanded.

"Colonel Christopher, this is Major General Scheib."

Brad! In the middle of all this he's calling me!

"Christopher here," she said, trying to hide the tremor she felt inside.

A heartbeat's delay. Then Scheib's voice said, "Two DPRK interceptors are vectoring toward you."

"I know."

It took half a second for her words to be relayed off the satellite and his response to get back to her.

"You have the option of turning away and exiting North Korean territorial waters."

"We're not over their territorial waters. We're twenty miles off their coast."

Again the delay, longer this time than normal. "I repeat, you have the option of turning around. You may abort your mission if you deem it necessary."

She heard what he was saying. I love you, Karen. I don't want you to be killed. I don't care if it starts World War III—I want you safe.

But then she realized that instead of ordering her to turn tail and leave the mission unfulfilled, he had placed the choice in her hands. Come back to me, that's what he was saying. But the responsibility is yours. The choice between nuclear war or not is yours. I love you, but I don't have the guts to take the blame for what happens next.

Taki looks cool as a cucumber, Harry thought as he sat beside Nakamura and watched her run through the diagnostics on her console. If she's the one who stole the optics assembly she sure doesn't look nervous or scared about it. Harry felt relieved; he hadn't wanted to believe it was Taki. Wally, yeah, maybe, he thought. That wiseass might be up to it. Probably not Angel; he's too straight-arrow. Monk? Why would Monk try to screw up the mission? Why would any of them?

The answer came to him: for money. Whoever it was did it for money. When he thought this was just a test flight he tried to ruin it so that we'd look bad to the Air Force and DoD would cancel Anson's contract and give it to one of our competitors.

Great deduction, Sherlock, Harry said to himself. So which one of them was it? Which one needs money so bad he'd sabotage a flight test? Wally gambles on the football pools. He makes no secret of that. Angel? I don't see Angel getting himself into a hole that way. The kid's worked too hard to get where he is to hand his money over to gamblers. Still, you never know.

Monk? Harry tried to remember if Monk ever took plunges with gamblers. Not that he could recall. Monk wasn't the gambling type.

Hell, even when they were all making bets on who would be named leader of the team, Monk threw in only a couple of bucks. Harry remembered Monk's knowing grin when he put his money down on the pool.

"I'm the favorite," he'd told Harry. "I can't get decent odds."

No, Monk's too smart to get into debt with gamblers.

"Are you with me, Harry?"

It took an effort to snap his attention back to Taki, back to the mission and the reality of an impending nuclear war.

"I'm sorry," he said, flustered. "I was thinking . . ."

Nakamura looked slightly disappointed. "I asked you if you'd double-check the board for me. Looks to me like everything's ready to go, but it'd be better if you double-check."

"Right," Harry said. "Sorry."

The gauges and screens on the consoles showed the status of every segment of the laser's system. Harry ran his eyes across both the console he was sitting at and Taki's, beside him. Everything looked okay. The COIL was pressurized and ready to fire. Ranging laser ready. Electrical power in the green. Computer humming.

"Looks okay to me, Taki," he said. "We're as ready as we'll ever be."

She nodded. The only sign of apprehension on her face was the tightness of her lips. Without a word she unlatched the covers on the amber arming and red firing buttons.

"So who was Annie Oakley?" she asked.

"WHERE ARE THOSE fighters?" Colonel Christopher asked into her pin mike.

O'Banion quickly answered, "Thirty miles behind us, seven o'clock. Closing fast."

"Between us and the coast," Major Kaufman said.

Christopher nodded. "I wonder what their orders are."

"Shoot to kill."

She almost laughed. "Maybe not. Maybe they just want to shoo us out of their territorial waters."

"We're not in their fucking territorial waters," Kaufman grumbled.

She clicked the intercom and called, "Jon, exactly how far off the coast are we?"

"Twenty miles, Colonel, just like you ordered. Uh, actually it's twenty-two, just at this point. We haven't been closer than twenty, though, not once."

"Do you have an accurate navigational fix on all that?"

"Yes, ma'am. I do."

"Pipe it back to Washington. I want our people to know exactly where we are, that we're not in North Korean territorial waters."

"Yes'm," Lieutenant Sharmon replied.

Kaufman gave her a sour look. "So they can drop a wreath in the water where we went down," he muttered.

Charley Ingersoll knew he couldn't get lost, even in this damnable snowstorm. All he had to do was plow straight ahead down the road. The gas station was along the side of the road. His legs flared with pins and needles, his face felt numb, he'd never been so cold in all his life.

But he slogged forward. The snow was almost knee-deep now, and it took a real concentrated effort to pull his freezing feet out of the stuff and take another tottering step forward. He thought about praying, but then he realized that it was the Lord who had put him into this mess. Why? he asked heaven. Why me? No answer. So he staggered on.

Step by step, Charley said to himself. Closer and closer. Somewhere from the back of his mind came the faint memory of some comedy act where a guy says that. Something about Niagara Falls. Step by step. Closer and closer.

At least Martha and the kids are okay. Even if the van runs out of gas it'll stay warm inside for a while. They'll be all right. I'll get to the gas station and they'll come out in the tow truck they've got there and we'll all be okay.

But you've got to get to the gas station first, said a voice in Charley's head.

He blinked against the snowflakes whipping into his face. Can't tell where the road is anymore. Everything's covered with snow. White, white, white everywhere. Maybe this is what heaven's like, he thought: everything is white. Or hell. There were parts of hell that were freezing, he remembered from his Sunday school days, all snow and ice. Then he realized that there were snowbanks on either side of the road, left by the plows that had scraped the highway earlier. Stay in between the snowbanks, Charley, he told himself. Stay in the middle.

He plodded ahead, his legs like a pair of rigid boards that shot pain up along his spine every time he tried to move them. Lord, help me, he pleaded. You put me into this, help me get out of it!

Something coming up the road!

Charley saw a shape up the road ahead, a dark bulk moving through the blinding white, slowly, patiently, soundlessly.

A car? No, too big, more like a truck. Awful slow, but it's coming this way. No noise. Maybe I've gone deaf. Maybe my ears are frozen.

The shape slowly coalesced out of the wind-whipped snow. It's a moose! Charley realized. Or is it an elk? Too big to be a deer. What's a moose doing out here in the middle of the road?

The animal was walking calmly, with great dignity, up the road toward Charley. Strolling along as if this blizzard didn't trouble it in the least.

It's a sign, Charley thought. A sign from God. My deliverance is near.

For a wild instant Charley thought he might jump on the animal's back and ride the rest of the way to the station. But as he staggered toward the beast it stopped in its tracks, snuffled once, then turned and bounded up the snowbank on the right shoulder of the highway and disappeared into the blinding whiteness of the storm.

Charley stood there dumbfounded. It just pranced up that

snowbank like it was nothing, he thought. This blizzard don't bother it at all. And I'm alone again. Alone and cold and scared.

Why'd it run away? he asked himself. I wasn't going to hurt it. What's it doing out here, anyway? Then he realized the reason. Wolves. Where there's moose or elk or whatever that beast was, there's wolves. Charley strained to hear the howl of baying wolves. Nothing but the keening of the wind. They hunt in packs, he knew. They'll come after me.

He sank to his knees. God help me! he screamed silently. God help me.

Major Obadiah Kaufman sat in the copilot's seat looking out at the dark smudge on the horizon that was the coast of North Korea.

Colonel Christopher said, "Keep your eyes peeled for their launch, Obie."

"Right," he said, glancing sideways at her. Sixteen years in the Air Force, he thought, and I'm in the fucking right-hand seat while she gives me dumbass orders. Obie. Like she knows me well enough to call me Obie. How'd she like it if I called her Karen? Or Chrissie? The plane's radar will pick up their fucking launch. She knows that. But she's got to make sure I know she's in charge and I'm just her goddamned stooge.

I graduated fourth in my class at the Academy. Where did she come in? Who the hell put her in here over me? It isn't fair, it's not fair. Hotshot B-2 jockey. She gets herself in hot water screwing some general and they bounce her out of the B-2s and break her down to this test program. This is a fucking demotion for her! But they push me into the right-hand seat so this slut of a colonel can take over my place. I worked hard to get to fly this bird! But they just push me aside and let her have it. The Air Force. Screw you every time.

He heard Colonel Christopher call to O'Banion, "Where are those fighters, Brick?"

"Coming up fast, ma'am. They haven't gone supersonic, but they're pulling in closer."

"Jon, keep us on a course that parallels the coast. I don't want to get any closer."

"Yes, Colonel," Lieutenant Sharmon replied.

Christopher toggled the intercom and said, "Mr. Hartunian, you and your people better strap in. We'll be in action any minute now."

Hartunian's voice answered, "Seat belts. Yeah."

Kaufman spoke up. "You'll have to swing around and point us at the coast when they launch."

"I know, Obie. I just don't want to give those fighters any excuse to open up on us until I have to."

"But you have to be pointing at the missiles when they launch. Point the nose at them and—"

"And let the tech geek's laser system acquire them. I know. I flew the simulator, Obie. I just don't want those fighters to shoot us down before we nail the missiles."

Kaufman stared at her. She looked like a little kid, sitting in the pilot's chair with the safety harness over her shoulders and the big white flight helmet sitting on her head like some ostrich egg.

He knew he shouldn't say it, but Kaufman didn't care anymore. What the hell, he thought, we're going to get our asses shot off anyway.

So he said, "Maybe I should take over now. I've had more experience handling this bird. I can—"

"No."

"But you don't—"

The look on Colonel Christopher's face could have etched solid steel. "Obie, I'm the pilot here. That's that. No further discussion."

He wanted to spit. But instead he shrugged inside his safety harness and said nothing. The plane droned on for a few moments, then Christopher asked mildly, "You ever read *Moby-Dick*, Obie?"

Puzzled, he replied, "Saw the movie, I think."

"You remember where Ahab tells his first mate, 'There's one God in heaven and one captain of the *Pequod*.'"

Kaufman felt his cheeks redden with anger.

"That's the way it's got to be, Obie. I didn't ask for this job, but I've got it. Now let's do what we're here to do."

O'Banion's voice crackled in his earphone, "Message incoming from the gooks, Colonel."

"Let's hear it."

The same calm, reedy voice they had heard before said, "Unidentified aircraft, this is Air Defense Command of the Democratic People's Republic of Korea. You have invaded DPRK airspace. You will follow the two fighter planes we have dispatched and land at their base. If you fail to do so, they have orders to shoot you down. They are armed with air-to-air missiles. You will execute this order now."

Vickie leaned her elbows on her knees and peered down at the platform where the President was supposed to speak.

"How long is it going to be?" she asked no one in particular. "These seats hurt my backside."

Sylvia tried to smile at her elder daughter. "Just be patient. It's not every day you get to see the President of the United States in person."

"With ten zillion other people," Vickie muttered.

"I think it's cool," said Denise, sitting on Sylvia's other side. "Nobody else from my class is here, I bet."

"So what?" said Vickie, with the airy disdain of the senior sibling. "He's a drip, anyway."

"He's the President!" Sylvia snapped, shocked. "Show some respect."

"He said he was going to do a lot for education," Vickie retorted. "I haven't seen any improvements. Have you, Dee?"

Denise thought a moment, then replied, "Well, we got more money for the school orchestra."

"Big deal."

"They were going to have to close it down altogether," Denise pointed out.

"But it wasn't federal money," Vickie countered. "That extra money came from Sacramento."

"Did not."

"Did too."

Sylvia swiveled her head right and left as the sisters argued back and forth, suppressing an urge to grab the two of them by the scruffs of their necks and rap their skulls together.

NORMAN FOSTER APPRAISED his boss with an experienced eye. He's winding himself up tighter, thought the President's chief of staff. He gets high on moments like this. The crowd, the cameras, the band playing and people getting to their feet and cheering: hell, it gives me a thrill; it's positively invigorating for him.

The President was pacing briskly up and down the little bare-walled room where they waited for the ceremonies to begin. Senator Youmans was beside him, scurrying breathlessly to keep up with his long-legged strides. She would introduce the President—after her own speech. The agenda gave her five minutes, but Foster knew she'd stretch that allotment.

His phone buzzed. Four Secret Service agents tensed for a moment, but Foster grinned at them as he pulled the iPhone from his jacket pocket, thankful that the military commsats were still working.

He squinted to read the text message on the tiny screen. "Urgent from Pentagon. Missile launched."

That's it, Foster thought. In half an hour we could all be dead.

ook!" Kaufman pointed at the bright plume of rocket exhaust rising above the horizon.

"That's it!" Karen Christopher shouted.

"Turn into it!"

"Turning."

She banked the big 747 to the left, swinging the plane so that its nose pointed toward the missile plume. Dumb jumbo jet turns like a freight train, Christopher said to herself, slow and ugly.

The colonel flicked a switch on her communications board. "Hartunian, they've launched."

DOWN IN THE battle management compartment Harry heard the urgency in Colonel Christopher's voice. "We've got them on the radar."

His eyes scanned the console. Iodine and oxygen pressurized and ready to flow. All systems in the green.

"Taki?"

Sitting next to Harry, Nakamura's lips were pressed into a thin, bloodless line. "This is it," she muttered as her hands played over her console's keyboard.

"Ranging laser," Harry said.

"Acquisition."

On the screen that displayed the ranging laser's data Harry saw a thin yellow line curving slightly toward the right.

"Locked on!" Nakamura called out.

"Distance?"

"One hundred fourteen miles."

Too far, Harry thought. The COIL's range isn't more than a hundred miles.

"Armed and ready," Taki called.

Harry yelled, "Fire!"

"Firing."

From deep in the plane's innards Harry heard the thundering roar of the laser, like a rocket bellowing: iodine and oxygen racing down the main channel, mixing, streaming through the laser cavity and surrendering more than a million watts of pure energy.

"We're on it," Nakamura said. "We're hitting it."

But is the COIL delivering energy to do the job? Harry wondered. At this range—

The yellow line on Harry's screen abruptly cut off. He blinked at it.

"Did we get it?"

IN THE COCKPIT, Colonel Christopher gaped at the explosion. It was too far away to hear anything, but they could see that the missile's white smoky exhaust plume ended in an orange-red blossom of fire.

"We hit it!" she shouted.

"Sure as hell did!" Kaufman echoed, staring out at the dirty gray cloud expanding out by the horizon.

"Bull's-eye!" Christopher pumped a fist in the air.

Kaufman laughed hoarsely. "Scratch one missile!"

"Where's the other—"

Out of the corner of her eye Christopher saw the flash of a missile's smoky exhaust streak straight into the 747's number two engine. It exploded inside the nacelle, blowing the engine to bits. The plane bucked and slewed so badly the control yoke jerked out of Christopher's hands.

"Jesus Christ!" Kaufman bellowed.

"We've been hit!" Christopher grabbed at the controls, but the 747 was sliding into a shallow dive, bucking like a wild horse, its left inboard engine nacelle shredded and aflame.

"Fire extinguishers, Obie!"

Kaufman, staring goggle-eyed at the flames streaming from where the engine nacelle had been, shuddered for a heartbeat, then slammed the fire extinguisher system's number two button almost hard enough to punch through the control panel.

"Pull her up!" he yelled as he reached for the control yoke in front of him.

"Trying . . ." Christopher panted, pulling with all her strength on the unyielding yoke. The big plane was shaking so hard her helmet was jiggling on her head, nearly slipping over her eyes.

IN THE BATTLE management compartment Harry was almost slammed off his seat. The safety harness cut into his shoulders painfully.

"What the hell was that?" Nakamura yelped.

"We're going down!" he realized.

Rosenberg's voice screamed in his headphone, high-pitched, scared, "What the fuck's happening up there?"

We're dead, Harry replied silently. We're all dead. The plane was jolting and rattling so hard Harry thought it would fall apart any second.

Then Taki pointed a shaking finger at the radar screen. "They've launched the other missile!"

CHRISTOPHER'S MIND WENT strangely calm. One engine out, losing altitude. Altimeter spinning down like it's on steroids. Glancing out her left window she saw that the fire was out. At least there weren't any flames streaming from beneath the wing. She saw ugly gashes in the wing's surface where pieces of the exploded engine had ripped through. A long slick of fuel from a ruptured tank glistened across the shredded wing's top. At least it wasn't on fire.

"Close off that tank," she said to Kaufman. "Shift to the tanks that haven't been punctured."

Automatically, she powered down a little, her right hand easing back slightly on the master throttle. Plane flies okay on three engines, she told herself. We can fly fine on three. Then a sour voice in her head asked, So why'd they put the fourth engine on her?

Automatically, she swiftly scanned the control panel. Pressurization's holding okay, she saw. No shrapnel's penetrated the fuselage. Not the pressurized sections, anyway.

Level off, she told herself. Get her level. The plane was still shaking, rattling, but not as badly as before, responding to the controls now. She shot a quick look at Kaufman. He had both hands locked on his control yoke, knuckles white, face whiter. The 747 was leveling out, the altimeter still winding down, but slower now. Shit, Christopher said to herself, we've only lost a couple thousand feet of altitude.

"Leveling out," Kaufman said, his voice shaky.

"Yeah."

"Colonel, they've launched the other missile!" Hartunian called.

Christopher bit back the reply that leaped into her mind: Listen, buddy, we've got enough to do just staying in the air now. Never mind your goddamned missiles.

Instead, she looked out the windshield and saw the bright plume streaking upward from the distant horizon.

"Point us at it!" Hartunian urged.

"We've been hit," she said, as calmly as she could manage.

As if he hadn't heard her, Hartunian demanded, "Get the nose up and point her toward that plume. Now! We've got less than a minute!"

She looked at Kaufman. "Let's do what the man says, Obie. Get the nose up."

"If we can."

Grimly, Christopher tugged on her control yoke. The lumbering 747 responded slowly, grudgingly. But her nose went up slightly.

"WE'RE BOUNCING IN and out of acquisition," Nakamura shouted.

Harry felt the plane shaking, shuddering, and wondered how long she would hold together. The screens on his consoles were jittering in front of his eyes.

"Get him, Taki," he said, growling. "You've got thirty seconds, maybe less."

"Acquiring," Nakamura said, her voice edging higher. "If they could just hold the plane steady . . ."

Harry saw the yellow line of the missile's trajectory rising toward the top of his screen. In another few seconds the bird would be so high they couldn't get the COIL to point at it.

"Locked on!"

Fire the bastard, Harry urged silently. He heard the rumble from deep in the 747's innards: the COIL was running.

"Missed!" Nakamura snapped. Before Harry could say anything she muttered, "Firing again. Multiple pulses."

The line on Harry's screen reached the top of the display, then winked out.

"Did we get him?"

Nakamura shook her head. "I don't know!"

IN THE COCKPIT, Kaufman yelled, "You're going to stall out!"

Christopher didn't reply. The tech guys needed the nose aimed at the missile and the missile was rising fast. She eased the lumbering 747's nose up, up, hoping they had enough airspeed to avoid a stall. She'll drop like the Rock of Gibraltar if she goes into a stall, Christopher thought. The plane was still vibrating, jouncing along on three engines and a shredded wing. Come on, baby, you can do it. Just hold it for a few seconds. A few seconds more . . .

"Got it!" Kaufman yelped.

Another orange-red blossom of fire bloomed where the missile's exhaust plume had been.

"We hit it!" Christopher agreed. She had a crazy impulse to lean over and plant a kiss on Kaufman's round cheek. Instead she let the control yoke slide forward and the plane's nose eased down.

"We did it," Kaufman said, his voice hollow with wonder. "We shot both the bastards down."

"We sure as hell did!"

Kaufman broke into a major-league grin.

"Let's get this old bus back to Misawa," said Christopher.

"If we can."

Christopher started a right turn, away from the coast.

O'Banion called, "Oh-oh. Colonel, you better listen to this."

"I repeat: American 747," said a steely male voice in her headphone, "do not try to escape. You will follow us to DPRK air base and land there. Or we will shoot you down."

B rad Scheib pressed his hand against the earbud. Karen's voice sounded strained, tense in the tiny speaker. He saw all the others in the room staring at him and knew he couldn't say aloud what he wanted to tell her. *I got you into this mess, Karen. I didn't know you'd be flying the plane, I didn't know you'd be on the hot seat. Don't get yourself killed, honey. Come back to me. Come back.*

"What's happening?" General Higgins demanded, red-faced.

"They got the first missile," Scheib said.

Higgins broke into a happy grin. Zuri Coggins murmured, "Thank God."

Then Scheib heard "Jesus Christ!"

"We've been hit!" Karen's voice.

Scheib felt the blood draining from his face.

"What is it?" Coggins asked. "What's wrong?"

"The interceptor hit them," Scheib said.

"Where?"

"How bad?"

"Shut up!" Scheib snapped.

He heard Karen yell, "Fire extinguishers, Obie!"

"Pull her up!"

"Trying . . ."

Scheib listened, sweat beading his brow, as the others in the situation room clustered around him. Even the academic from NIC got up from his chair and slowly walked up the table toward him.

"Close off that tank," Karen shouted. "Shift to the tanks that haven't been punctured."

Oh my God, Scheib thought. She's going down. They've shot her down.

"Leveling out." A man's voice. Must be the copilot.

Somebody in the room shouted, "Look! They've launched the other missile!"

Scheib looked up at the wall screen. The last of the three missiles was rising up from its pad on a plume of flame.

He heard Karen say, "Let's do what the man says, Obie. Get the nose up."

"If we can."

The satellite image of the North Korean missile launch was grainy, but everyone in the suddenly stuffy, hot situation room could see the missile climbing through a thin layer of cloud, its trajectory beginning to arc slightly, the bright trail of rocket exhaust curving as the missile rose.

"You're going to stall out!" the copilot bawled.

Scheib's guts clutched inside him. They're all staring at me, as if I can make it all right, as if I can do something, say something . . .

Come on, he pleaded with Karen silently. Come on.

"Got it!"

"We hit it!" she said.

"We did it!" The copilot sounded halfway delirious with triumph.

"We sure as hell did!" Karen said, her voice trembling slightly.

The wall screen showed a blossom of orange flame. Everyone cheered. The missile's exhaust track ended in an expanding cloud of dirty gray smoke.

"They did it!" General Higgins crowed. "They shot the bastard down. Both of 'em!"

"Karen!" Scheib called into his lip mike. "Karen, are you okay?"

COLONEL CHRISTOPHER HEARD the tension, the urgency in Brad's voice.

What do I tell him? she asked herself. How much can I say? He must have other people around him. I can't . . . She found that she had to swallow twice before she could reply, her throat was so parched. Stick to business, she decided. Strictly business.

"We have one engine out and serious damage to the left wing," she said, surprised at how shaky her voice sounded. "Plane's buffeting badly. North Korean interceptors have ordered us to land at their base."

No response. Silence. No, Christopher realized. She heard a buzz of voices. They're talking. A lot of people. Somebody laughed! We're flying on three engines and a shredded wing and they're laughing back there in Washington!

O'Banion called, "Colonel, the gooks are telling us to follow them."

"Let's hear it," she said.

"American 747," said the same hard, cool man's voice, "you will follow us to a DPRK air base and land there. You will be interned and treated well. If you do not follow this command we will be forced to shoot you down."

Christopher thought it over for two seconds, then told O'Banion, "Plug me in to him, Captain."

"You're on," O'Banion replied.

"This is ABL-1," she said, working to keep her voice steady. "I read you."

"Turn to a heading of three hundred ten degrees and follow me."

"Turning to three-ten." She eased the control yoke slightly leftward.

"What're you doing?" Kaufman screeched.

"Keep your shorts on, Obie," Colonel Christopher muttered. Silently she said to the North Korean interceptor pilot, Now pull up in front of me, wiseass. Get in front where I can fry you.

S hot 'em down!" Norman Foster exulted.

The President whirled on his chief of staff. "Both of them?"

Foster pressed his cell phone to his ear, a wide grin spreading across his normally dour face. "Both of 'em." He held up two fingers.

Grinning back at him, the President said, "Now *that's* something to tell the audience out there."

Foster's grin evaporated. "Wait a minute," he said into the phone, "let me tell him." Looking at the President, he said, "The North Koreans shot at our plane. Damaged it badly."

"How bad?"

"It's still flying, apparently. But the gooks want them to land in North Korea."

"No!" the President snapped. "They can't have that plane. And they'll use the crew as hostages."

"The alternative is they shoot the plane down and the crew dies."

Biting his lip, the President paced the length of the bare-walled little room before replying, "Get Pyongyang on the horn. Tell them we hold them responsible."

"And they'll say we violated their airspace."

"Call them anyway. We have to be on the correct side of this."

"If you'd allowed a fighter escort—"

"We'd be in a shooting war by now!"

Foster shook his head. "What makes you think we're not?"

IN ABL-1'S COCKPIT, both Colonel Christopher and Major Kaufman were hanging on to the control yokes with both hands. The plane was still vibrating badly and slowly losing altitude. The Sea of Japan looked a rippled gray sheet of steel. But Christopher's attention was on the DPRK MiG-29 that had moved up in front of her, heading for the coast and a landing in North Korea.

"O'Banion, get Hartunian on the intercom for me."

"Yes'm."

"Hartunian here."

"Do you have enough fuel left to shoot down a couple of fighter planes?"

She heard him gasp. Then, "Yeah, I think so, just about, if you can put us in a position to lay the beam on them."

"I've got one of them sitting in front of us now, about eleven o'clock, level."

"Give me a minute . . ."

THE PLANE LURCHED again as Harry turned to Nakamura, sitting at the console beside him. His safety harness cut into his shoulders. I'm going to be black and blue tomorrow, Harry thought. If we're still alive tomorrow.

"You ready to fire again?" he asked Nakamura. His voice sounded unnaturally loud, urgent, in his own ears.

"Another missile?" Taki shouted back.

"Gook fighter plane."

She blinked at Harry once, then said merely, "Let's see if I can get acquisition; we're bouncing around so much . . ." She began to peck at her keyboard.

As he watched her, Harry mumbled, "Sorry about the 'gook,' Taki. I wasn't thinking."

Without taking her eyes from her console's screens, Nakamura said, deadpan, "That's okay. I'm not offended. I'm a nip, not a gook."

"Oh."

"Get your terminology straight, round-eye."

Harry almost started to chuckle.

"Acquisition!" Nakamura called out. "No! Jumped out. The plane's shaking too much, Harry. I can't get a lock on the target."

"You've got to."

"If they could hold us steady for half a minute . . ."

Harry toggled the intercom switch. "Colonel, we've got the fighter in our sights, but we're bouncing around so much we can't get a lock on it."

Without an instant's hesitation, Colonel Christopher's voice replied, "Not much I can do about it, mister."

SITTING TENSELY AT the table in the situation room, General Scheib heard the intercom chatter from ABL-1. His laptop screen was blank, he was getting audio only, but it was enough to make him sweat with anxiety.

Standing in front of the wall screen image of the now-empty North Korean launch site, General Higgins said loudly, "Well, we showed the world that we can shoot down ballistic missiles. We've changed the global strategic picture."

Zuri Coggins shook her head. "Not if they shoot down our plane, General. All we've shown is that we can trade a very expensive air-craft and crew for a couple of cheap missiles."

Scheib glanced at the others, who had drifted toward the wall screen display and stood around General Higgins. Quietly he called up on his laptop screen the command organization of Misawa Air Base.

"He's got to be there," Scheib muttered to himself as he scrolled down the list of names.

And there he was: Mitchell Watson, executive officer of the Thirty-fifth Fighter Wing, headquartered at Misawa.

B rad, are you nuts?"

Brigadier General Mitch Watson stared at the image of his old friend and Academy classmate on the screen of his telephone console.

"I'm deadly serious, Mitch," said Brad Scheib. He certainly looked serious, Watson thought. Absolutely grim.

Watson leaned back in his desk chair. His eye caught the tennis trophy that he and Scheib had won back at the Academy. It was Watson's year to hold the silver-plated cup.

"Let me get this straight," he said, jabbing a lean finger at his old friend's image. "You want me to scramble a flight of F-16s out to North by-damn Korea?"

Nodding tightly, Scheib answered, "There's a 747 out there in trouble. Over the Sea of Japan, near the coast. Your Falcons could mean the difference between life and death for the crew."

"I'm supposed to do this on your authorization."

"I've got a priority code from the National Security Advisor's office."

Trying to read Scheib's taut expression, Watson realized, There's more to this than he's telling me.

"Why in the ever-loving blue-eyed world should I do this? It's crazy!"

"You don't want to know, Mitch."

Watson puffed out a breath. "That bad, huh?"

With another nod, Scheib said, "Just get some fighters out to that plane. Scare the bandits off."

"And to hell with the chain of command, huh?"

"I gave you the priority code. It's my responsibility, Mitch. You're just following orders."

"Yeah," said Watson, wondering if he wasn't flushing his career down the toilet. "Sure."

The MiG-27 was painted a dull brownish gray, same color as the hills up ahead, Colonel Christopher realized. Her 747 was still shaking badly, bouncing around as if it were caught inside a thunderhead.

"We're gonna be crossing their coastline," Major Kaufman said.

"Tell me about it, Obie."

"You want to shoot that guy down?" Kaufman clearly didn't like the idea.

"If we can, Obie. If we can."

"And what does the other one do? He's still on our tail, isn't he?"

Christopher didn't reply to him. Instead, she called down to Hartunian, "Can you lock on or not?"

"If you could keep the plane steadier we could," came the engineer's response.

"Maybe you ought to come up here and try flying this bird," Christopher snapped.

"I wouldn't be any—"

Suddenly the woman tech's voice shrilled, "Lock! We're locked on!"

"Zap the bastard!" Christopher snapped.

Nothing happened. The North Korean MiG flew several hundred yards in front of them just as before.

"What are you guys doing down there?" Christopher demanded.

"We hit him," Hartunian said. "The instruments show we hit him."

Christopher started to shake her head, but Kaufman took one hand off the control yoke and pointed a shaking finger at the MiG. "Look!"

A thin trail of whitish smoke was streaming from a spot on the MiG's fuselage halfway between the cockpit and the jet engine's tailpipe.

"Is that all you can—"

Christopher clamped her mouth shut. The MiG's fuselage was burning. A bright cherry-red circle of flame was growing, spreading. The plane's aluminum skin was on fire.

"It's burning!" Kaufman shouted.

"Took a few seconds to burn off the paint," said Hartunian, almost apologetically.

Colonel Christopher watched as the burning circle spread across the MiG's rear section. The plane yawed violently to the left and suddenly its clear plastic canopy popped off and the pilot ejected, his seat firing up and out while the MiG slid off on one wing and began to spiral toward the sea below. She leaned forward and craned her neck to watch the pilot separate from his seat. A heartbeat later his chute streamed out and billowed. She could see the man's tiny figure hanging beneath the parachute's canopy.

"We got him!" Kaufman exulted.

"Right turn, Obie," Christopher commanded. "We're heading for Misawa."

The lumbering 747 turned slowly while the second MiG flew past them and began to circle the pilot descending into the water in his parachute.

"Let's get our butts out of here," Colonel Christopher said.

Kaufman muttered, "Before the whole gook air force comes after us."

"Colonel, DPRK air command is calling again," O'Banion reported.

Wishing she were flying a B-2 instead of this beat-up hulk of a transport plane, Christopher said, "Put him on."

The man's voice sounded more agitated. "American 747, one of our fighters has suffered a malfunction. Nevertheless you will continue to follow a heading of three hundred ten degrees. Another flight of our planes will escort you to a landing in the DPRK."

Christopher thumbed her radio switch. "This is United States 747 ABL-1. We are leaving North Korean airspace and returning to Japan. Out."

To O'Banion she said, "No more transmissions on their frequency, Captain. Let's get away from here before they send out more fighters."

Kaufman nodded. "Amen to that."

C harley Ingersoll's hands were completely numb. He couldn't feel anything with them. When he tried to wipe the snow off his face it was like a pair of wooden boards scraping against his frozen nose.

With some surprise, he realized that the pain was gone. Numb. Freezing. At least it don't hurt anymore, he realized. God never gives you a trial that's too much for you. He watches over you all the time.

He wondered if God was keeping the wolves away. They must be out there. Wolves. They hunt in packs. Prob'ly go after that moose 'stead of me, he told himself. God won't let me get eaten by wolves.

Without warning, Charley's legs collapsed beneath him. He simply folded up and fell facedown into the snow. No pain. He felt like he was floating. Going to sleep. Somewhere in the back of his mind there was a tendril of fear, a vague memory of Martha and the kids.

God, don't let them die! Charley begged silently. Take me if you gotta, but let Martha and the kids live.

He wanted to hear an answer, but only the biting, moaning

wind came to his ears. And the distant baying of a wolf. Charley fought against falling asleep. You fall asleep and then you freeze to death, he knew. But ultimately he had no more strength in him. He closed his eyes and drifted into the sweet oblivion of sleep.

But just before it all went dark, he thought he heard the snarl of a wolf. Several wolves. Very close to him. He knew he should be alarmed, but it was just too easy to go to sleep.

S o when's he coming out?" Vickie asked, teenaged impatience etched onto her face.

Sylvia frowned at her elder daughter. "He's the President, Victoria. He has a lot of things to do. He'll be out when—"

"Look!" Denise pointed. A portly woman was striding onto the stage. The audience began to applaud.

"That's Senator Youmans," Sylvia told her daughters, feeling relieved that something was happening at last. The chairs were totally uncomfortable.

Senator Youmans basked in the applause for a few moments, then waved both her chubby arms to still the audience.

"Good evening, and welcome to San Francisco, the City by the Bay. This is a momentous occasion for us all . . ."

"Oh, for the love of Pete," Vickie moaned. "She's going to give the same speech she gave at the big rally last week, back home."

THE PRESIDENT LISTENED intently to his chief of staff's cell phone. Foster had laid it on the table between them and clicked on its speaker function.

"Apparently they shot down one of the North Korean intercep-tors," General Higgins was saying. In the phone's minuscule display screen the general's face looked red and bloated, clownish.

"Apparently?" the President snapped. "Did they or didn't they?"

"The MiG caught fire and crashed into the sea, sir," Higgins replied, his voice tinny and small. "Whether it was from ABL-1's laser or just an engine malfunction remains unclear, Mr. President."

The President glanced at Foster, who spread his hands, palms up. "Either way, we win," Foster said.

"So where's ABL-1 now?" the President demanded.

"Over the Sea of Japan, sir, heading for Misawa Air Base."

"Can they send out a search-and-rescue team?"

"If the plane ditches—"

"Now! I want it sent out now. Whether the plane ditches or not."

"Yessir. Of course. I'll get the word to Misawa right away."

"Good. Thank you, General Higgins."

Foster clicked the cell phone closed.

The President stood in silence for a long moment, then said to his chief of staff, "We've done all we should do, Norm. Our skirts are clean."

Foster ran a hand over his shaved head. "But if the North Kore-ans send out more fighters . . ." He let the thought dangle.

"If they shoot down our plane over international waters they're clearly in the wrong. The important thing is that we've gotten rid of the missile threat. I don't want a war breaking out now, there's no need for it."

Foster nodded. "Except for the crew of that 747."

"That's why I ordered the SAR unit, Norm. They'll pick up the crew from the water."

Unless the gooks shoot down the SAR plane, too, Foster thought. But he did not mention his fear aloud.

OUT OF THE corner of her eye Senator Youmans saw the President standing in the wings, waiting to be introduced to the crowd. First I have to talk to them because he's not ready to come out, she grumbled to herself, and now I've got to cut my speech short because he is ready. And antsy, from the looks of him.

She betrayed none of those thoughts on her face. With a dimpled smile, she said into the microphones before her, "So, without further ado, the President of the United States!"

The crowd roared to its feet. The band struck up "California, Here I Come," and the President strode out onto the stage, grinning and waving both his arms.

C olonel, we've cleared North Korean airspace."
Karen Christopher heard the obvious relief in Lieutenant Sharmon's soft voice.

She spoke into her lip mike: "Brick, any more transmissions from their defense command?"

"Just repeating their order for us to head inland and wait for another fighter 'escort,' Colonel."

"Screw that."

Major Kaufman turned toward her and asked, "You think they'll send another batch of fighters after us?"

"Probably." Karen realized that she was tired, emotionally and physically drained. But the plane was flying better; they were barely above twenty thousand feet now, but the buffeting had eased a bit. Still, she wondered how long the bird would hold together.

"Obie, you think you can handle things by yourself for a few minutes?"

Kaufman nodded vigorously.

As she unstrapped her safety harness, Christopher said, "I'll send O'Banion up here, in case you need another pair of hands to work the controls."

The major nodded again, less enthusiastically.

Every muscle in her body seemed to be aching as Colonel Christopher pulled herself out of the seat and took off her heavy, cumbersome flight helmet. Nestling the helmet under one arm, she stepped to the hatch at the rear of the cockpit. Kaufman clutched his control yoke with both hands. The plane was still vibrating, rattling hard enough to make her grab for the rim of the hatch as she went through.

She stepped onto the flight deck and patted Lieutenant Sharmon's shoulder. "How're we doing, Jon?"

"On course for Misawa, Colonel. I've got their radio beam loud and clear."

"Good." Turning to O'Banion, she said, "Brick, go up and sit with Major Kaufman. Don't touch anything unless he tells you to."

O'Banion blinked uncertainly but murmured, "Yes, ma'am" and got up from his seat.

Karen dropped her helmet on one of the bunks, then climbed down the ladder and saw Hartunian and the Japanese-American woman sitting side by side in the battle management compartment.

"Good shooting," she called to them through the open hatch.

Hartunian grinned at her. The woman asked, "What happened to the second fighter?"

"He stayed where his buddy went down. Standard operating procedure. Waiting for an SAR chopper to pick up the man in the water."

Hartunian asked, "Are they sending out more fighters?"

"Maybe," Christopher answered with a weary shrug. "Do you have enough fuel to shoot 'em down?"

He shook his head. "Maybe one or two squirts, not much more. We used up a lot of fuel on that one fighter. Kept bouncing in and out of acquisition."

Colonel Christopher looked at Hartunian, studied his face for the first time. Soft brown eyes, she noticed. He doesn't look like a warrior. Not at all.

But she crooked a finger at him and said, "Come on to the galley with me, Mr. Hartunian."

He looked surprised for a flash of a second, then unstrapped his harness and rose to his feet. The plane bucked slightly and he reached for the console to steady himself.

"We're not out of the woods yet," said Colonel Christopher, with a thin smile.

"I guess not," replied Hartunian shakily.

Once they entered the cramped little galley, Christopher went straight to the coffee urn. There was only half a mugful left, dregs. Still, it was better than nothing. She cradled the mug in both hands.

Turning back to Hartunian, she said, "Now, what about this saboteur?"

The engineer looked surprised. "What about him?"

"We've got to find out who he is and why he tried to scratch this mission, Mr. Hartunian."

"Harry."

Christopher ignored his request for informality as she sipped at her coffee. It was bitter and only lukewarm. And full of grounds. The colonel repeated, "Which one of your people tried to ruin this mission, Mr. Hartunian?"

General Scheib scowled at the blank screen of his laptop. He was getting audio from ABL-1, but no imagery. And now the audio was giving him trouble.

"What do you mean, she's not available?" he grumbled into his lip mike.

A moment's hesitation while his demand was relayed through a military communications satellite orbiting some twenty-two thousand miles above the equator.

Then Captain O'Banion's voice came through the plastic bud that Scheib had jammed in his left ear. "She's not in the cockpit, sir. She's taking a break."

"Did you tell her who's calling?"

"Yes, sir, I did, sir. She said she'll call you back shortly, sir." The young man's voice sounded clearly troubled.

Scheib clenched his teeth together, then growled, "I want her on this frequency right away, mister. Do you understand that?"

"Yes, *sir!*"

From down at the far end of the table, Zuri Coggins watched the grim expression of Scheib's face. More bad news? she wondered. But the general leaned back in his chair, wormed the bud

out of his ear, and simply sat there glaring at his laptop's blank
screen.

General Higgins was at the coffee cart again. Coggins glanced
at her wristwatch and realized with a shock of surprise that it was
after 9:00 p.m. We've been in this room for nearly ten hours, she said
to herself. The President's due to start his speech in San Francisco
right about now.

The speech had been scheduled for the evening news hour, so
that the network and cable TV shows could carry it live. But with all
the commercial commsats off the air there could be no coast-to-coast
TV coverage. Even radio would be spotty. That nuclear blast in orbit
had rattled long-range radio transmission, too. Something about high-
energy electrons in the ionosphere.

Sitting beside her, Michael Jamil had an expression of impending doom on his thinly bearded face.

Trying to cheer him up, Coggins leaned toward him and said,
"Relax, it's all over."

Jamil shook his head. "The missile threat is ended, but this isn't
over. Not yet."

"What do you mean?"

"What's China's next move?" Jamil asked urgently.

"You mean North Korea's next move," said Coggins.

"China," he insisted. "China's behind this. The DPRK didn't
have the resources to do this on their own. Or the nerve. Maybe if
Kim Jong Il was still alive—he was nutty enough to try a stunt like
this. But not now. Pyongyang doesn't have any motivation to start
a nuclear war."

"How can you be sure?" Coggins asked. "History takes weird
turns, you know."

Jamil shook his head. "There's always a motive, no matter how
weird it looks at the time. North Korea doesn't have a motive for
this confrontation. China does."

Coggins saw the intensity, the absolute certainty, in his face. But she heard herself say, "The Secretary of State doesn't agree with you."

Jamil immediately snapped, "Then she's a bigger horse's ass than I thought she was."

Which one of your people tried to ruin this mission, Mr. Hartunian?"

Harry saw that Colonel Christopher was dead earnest.

"I wish I knew," he said.

"Not good enough. One of your nerds tried to screw up this flight. This is my airplane, Mr. Hartunian. I'm responsible for everything that happens in it. I want that guy's head on a platter."

Harry sank into one of the bucket seats on the bulkhead opposite the coffee urn. The plane was still shaking badly, but he'd almost become accustomed to it by now.

"You're taking this kind of personally, aren't you?" he asked the colonel.

"Damned right I am."

He shook his head. "I've tried to figure it out. I know it had to be one of them, but I—"

"It could be you, couldn't it?"

He felt the accusation like an ice pick jabbed into him. "Me?"

The colonel broke into a smile. "No, I don't think it was you," she said, more softly. "Not really."

"It wasn't me," Harry said. Then he heard himself ask, "Could it have been one of your guys?"

Colonel Christopher's smile dissolved. "From what you've told me, whoever it is would have to have some detailed knowledge of your system. My crew doesn't. They're flyboys, not techies."

The intercom speaker in the compartment's ceiling blared, "Colonel Christopher, General Scheib wants to speak with you, ma'am. Right away."

Harry saw the expression on Christopher's face harden. Looking up at the speaker, she said tightly, "All right, put him on the intercom."

A burst of buzzing static, then, "Colonel Christopher? Karen?" The man's voice sounded tight, insistent.

"This is Christopher," the colonel said, her eyes on Harry.

A heartbeat's delay while the signal was relayed to geosynchronous orbit and back. Then, "Are you okay?"

"So far, so good, General."

Again the delay, longer this time. "There's a flight of F-16s coming out to meet you." Harry thought the general's voice sounded lower, as if he didn't want anyone else to hear.

"The DPRK air defense command says they're sending more fighters to us. They want us to land in North Korea."

"According to our tracking data you've left DPRK airspace."

With a nod, she replied, "They claim out to two hundred miles, but my navigator says we're past that."

Silence, except for the hissing of static. At last the general's voice resumed. "As far as we can see they haven't put any more fighters into the air."

"That's good."

"What's your situation, Karen? Can you make it to Misawa?"

"We're going to try."

Harry counted his own pulse silently. Two beats, three.

Then the general asked, "What's your condition?"

"One engine out. Wing damaged. Cabin pressurization holding. So far. Boeing makes tough airplanes, General. You know that."

There was something going on, Harry realized. Something between the two of them that went beyond the words they were speaking. It was like a couple of people talking in code, almost. Harry could see the tension on Colonel Christopher's face, in her strained posture, the way she was gripping her coffee mug in both hands, like it was a life preserver or something.

"Well . . . take care of yourself," the general said. "We're doing everything we can from this end."

"Sure. I know."

A long pause this time. Then, "I'll set up a priority link with Misawa. Call me the minute you touch down."

She closed her eyes as she replied, "If I can, General. I'll call if I can."

The audio link went dead. For a long moment Harry heard nothing but the rumble of ABL-1's engines and the clatter of the plane's buffeting. He realized he had become almost accustomed to the shuddering vibrations.

"You know him?" he asked Colonel Christopher.

She gave him a curious, half-sad smile. "I knew him."

"Knew?"

"Too well," she said. "Not well enough."

Harry felt puzzled but decided the colonel's personal life was not a place he should be poking into.

She sat wearily beside him. "Are you married, Mr. Hartunian?"

"I was. We're separated."

"Going to get divorced?"

Suddenly miserable all over again, Harry waved both hands in the air. "I don't know. My wife wants a divorce. But we've got two daughters. I don't know what it'd do to them."

"Do you still love her?"

Harry thought he should feel uncomfortable talking about his private life with a woman who was practically a stranger to him. Instead, he heard himself admit, "I thought I did at first. But I don't know if we ever really loved each other. Not like in a romance story. We were just kids when we got married."

"And now?"

He shrugged. "Now it's all over, I guess. Has been for years, I was just too dumb to recognize it."

Karen patted his knee. "Welcome to the club, mister. Welcome to the goddamned club."

He saw that her eyes were sad. And really beautiful. Light gray, almost bluish.

Before he could say anything, though, Colonel Christopher straightened up in the seat and said, "Now, how do we go about finding out which one of your people tried to screw up this flight?"

I had a speech prepared for you," said the President into the microphones on the dais before him, "but events have moved so swiftly that I'm going to toss that speech away and speak to you from my heart."

The spotlights were glaring brilliantly on the President. The crowd filling the auditorium was in darkness, but he could sense them out there in the shadows, feel their presence, hear their breathing like one gigantic, expectant animal.

"So tonight we'll forget about the teleprompters and the speech my staff worked so hard to prepare. Tonight I want to tell you about an extraordinary series of events, and about the brave and gallant crew of Air Force and civilian personnel."

He could feel them leaning forward, holding their breath, hanging on his words.

"You know the old joke: I have good news and bad news."

A few laughs scattered through the darkness.

"I'll give you the bad news first," the President said, smiling broadly to reassure his audience. "As you know"—his smile dwindled—"just about all the civilian satellites in orbit were knocked out this morning. It's been a tough day, without satellite phone links, without satellite relays for information systems and commercial television. Why, this speech right here and now isn't being transmitted any farther than Sacramento . . . or so I'm told."

A few more nervous titters out there in the darkness. Good, thought the President.

"And things are going to be tough for a while. It will take weeks, maybe months or even a year or more, before we get full satellite services going again.

"What caused this enormous breakdown? A nuclear bomb exploded in orbit by a dissident element of the North Korean army."

That got them! The audience gave a collective gasp. Rumbles and murmurs swept the shadowed rows of onlookers.

"I say again"—the President raised a slim finger—"that the bomb was set off in orbit by a dissident group of the North Korean army. Not by the government in Pyongyang. The entire civilized world has been attacked by a fanatical group of . . . well, they're fanatics. What else can we call them?"

More grumbling and muttering from the audience. That giant beast out in the shadows was starting to growl.

The President held up both his hands, palms out, and the beast quieted. "The regular North Korean army is rounding up these dissidents. They'll be captured and dealt with by North Korean justice. Which, I may tell you, is a lot tougher and swifter than our own."

He hesitated a moment.

"But before these fanatics could be captured, they launched two more missiles. Toward America. We have every reason to believe those missiles were armed with nuclear warheads."

Now they really stirred. But the President grinned and, raising his voice slightly, told them, "Now the good news. Both those missiles have been shot down. We're not entirely sure where they were aimed at, because they were shot down within a minute or so of being launched. They might have been aimed right here, at San Francisco. They might have been intended to kill me. And you.

"But they were both shot down by an American plane flying over international waters off the coast of Korea. That plane was armed with a high-power laser that destroyed both those missiles within a minute or so after they were launched.

"So, the good news is that we have a missile defense system that works. The North Korean fanatics who launched those missiles are being rounded up and will be swiftly punished."

They broke into applause. The audience rose to its feet like one single organism and cheered long and hard and loud. The President stood before them in the spotlights, smiling his boyish smile, thinking that the next thing he had to explain was that the North Koreans were in no way associated with Islamic terrorists. I don't want this to spill over into a new war in the Middle East, he told himself. We've got to avoid that. By all means.

The rain had stopped. Cool moonlight beamed down out of a silver-clouded sky. The Secretary of State watched the clouds gliding across the moon as she listened to the President's speech on the little plastic radio one of her aides had placed on her desk. His voice sounded scratchy, tinny, streaked with static. Cross-country television had been down since the commercial satellites were knocked out, but radio reception was still serviceable.

Sitting before her were General Higgins, freshly shaved and wearing a new, crisply creased uniform; Zuri Coggins, looking wilted in the same red jacket suit she'd been wearing all day; and that annoying Jamil fellow, with his sliver of a beard and his dark, probing eyes.

Farther back in the room sat a trio of her aides. The Secretary had forbidden them from making a transcript of this impromptu meeting, but she knew that her personal assistant had set up the digital recording system in her desk before she'd gone home for the night. No one else had access to it. *I'll be able to review what we say here but no one else will,* she reassured herself. *If necessary I can erase the record entirely.*

The roar of the crowd sounded in the little radio like surf crashing on a rocky beach.

"They like what he has to say," Zuri Coggins murmured to no one in particular.

The Secretary of State saw that although Coggins' clothes might be wrinkled, the woman herself was still intense, still sharp, her eyes bright, her attention focused on the President's words and the crowd's reaction to them as she sat hunched slightly forward in the big leather chair.

"He hasn't mentioned China," muttered Michael Jamil.

The Secretary of State flared inwardly. There he goes with that China business again!

But she smiled cordially at Jamil and said mildly, "Let's hear the rest of what he has to say before analyzing it."

The President's voice sounded strong, assured. "So I want the people of America—and our allies—to rest assured that we have a missile defense system that *works*. There will be no nuclear Pearl Harbors as long as we have fine, committed men and women in our military and civilian defense establishments."

Thunderous applause. It died slowly.

The President resumed. "And I want the people of the world to know that we have entered a new era, an era where the most terrifying weapons of war are no longer supreme. An era where we can defend ourselves and our allies against surprise attack.

"And finally, I offer this pledge: The United States will work with any nation that is willing to work toward peace with the mutual understanding that we promise to use our missile defenses to shield them as well as ourselves. Against the threat of rogue states or terrorists, we must all stand together to build a world of peace and safety. That is our goal and we will not settle for anything less. Thank you and good night."

The cheering erupted before the President finished his last line and went on and on until at last the Secretary of State reached out and snapped the radio's off switch.

For several moments no one said a word. The cheering from San Francisco seemed to reverberate in the spacious office.

"Well," the Secretary of State said at last. "Any comments?"

Zuri Coggins immediately replied. "He's offering to turn this near disaster into an opportunity for better international cooperation."

"Like Kennedy did after the Cuban missile crisis," said Jamil. "It led straight to the Limited Test Ban Treaty."

General Higgins shook his head. "What he's really saying is that we can shoot down attacking missiles. That changes the whole strategic picture."

"Yes, it does," State said softly, "doesn't it."

She looked past the general to her aides, seated on the other side of the room. They glanced at one another, but none of them offered a word of advice or analysis.

Turning her cobra smile to Jamil, the Secretary of State asked, "Do you still believe that China was behind this?"

Without a heartbeat's hesitation, Jamil replied, "Yes, ma'am, I do. But we'll never know, will we? Those rebel North Korean army officers know they're as good as dead. They won't let themselves be taken alive."

"You think not?"

"I'm certain of it."

"So Pyongyang can tell us the DPRK government had nothing to do with this, and Beijing can sit there and say nothing."

"The real test," Jamil said, "will be how Beijing reacts to the President's initiative."

"Share our missile defense system with them?" State scoffed at the idea.

"Promise to build a system that can protect them against rogue nations or terrorists with missiles."

Coggins shook her head. "The Chinese will want to build their own defenses."

"Good!" Jamil snapped. "Fine. Defensive systems don't threaten anybody."

General Higgins made a sour face. "You don't understand, young man. They'll use their defense system to protect themselves, but they'll still have all their *offensive* missiles. They can attack us and defend themselves against our counterstrike."

"So can we," Coggins said. Then she turned to Jamil. "Right?"

"Right."

The Secretary of State pictured this same debate in the Senate. It's going to come to the Senate, she realized. Sooner or later. The President proposes, but Congress disposes.

Jamil and Higgins were starting to raise their voices, so the Secretary of State said firmly, "We've all put in a long, hard day. Let's go home and get some sleep."

She got to her feet. Everyone else rose and bid her good night. She watched them leave and, once her office was cleared of them all, she picked up her phone and tapped the speed-dial button for the Secretary of Defense. She knew that no matter where Lionel Bakersfield was, her phone system would track him down. Glancing at the digital clock on her desk, she figured that Lonnie was probably working on his third martini by now. Good, she thought. He'll do less talking and more listening.

GENERAL HIGGINS RODE the elevator to his waiting staff car in the basement parking garage of the State Department building without offering a ride to Coggins or Jamil. The two of them got off the elevator at the lobby level and then walked down the building's front steps side by side.

Zuri Coggins looked up and down the rain-slicked street. Not much traffic. No taxicabs.

Jamil pulled his cell phone from his jacket pocket. "I hope they got the towers back online," he said. "I left my car in Langley this morning."

Coggins watched him as he pecked at the phone's keypad. At last he gave up. "Guess not," he said, more resigned than aggravated.

She gestured up the street and said, "Come on, let's walk a bit. We'll probably find a cab on the avenue."

"And if we don't?"

She chuckled at his oh so serious concern. "You like to look at all the aspects of a problem, don't you?"

"Don't you?"

Coggins tilted her head slightly and remembered from his dossier that Jamil was unmarried, just as she was. "Well, maybe as we walk along we'll find a friendly bar. Or a restaurant."

Jamil broke into a smile. "Come to think of it, I'm damned hungry."

"Me too," she said, as she started down the street alongside him.

For a moment Charley thought he was in heaven. He seemed to be floating, as if resting on a blessed cloud. Not a care in the world. Nothing hurt, but he didn't feel numb, not really, more like he was just—floating.

He couldn't see anything except an endless expanse of soft white. Not cottony clumps, like clouds: just flat, plain, eggshell white, kind of restful, really.

I must've died, he realized. There was no terror in the thought. In fact, he would have smiled if he could have. Died and now I'm in heaven. Or on my way, at least. Blissfully peaceful. Not a pain or a worry in the world.

Then he heard a soft beeping sound. Beep beep beep beep . . . Heaven don't beep, Charley thought.

It all came back to him in a rush. The blizzard. Martha and the kids! The snow and the cold. And the wolves.

Charley blinked and it all came into focus. He was lying on his back. Hospital room. Off-white ceiling. Turning his head slightly he saw that the walls were a pastel green. The sound he heard was coming from a bank of medical monitors blinking and beeping at him. There were IV tubes in both his arms.

"We're awake!"

The nurse's boisterous voice made Charley jump.

"Had a good rest?" the nurse asked as she peered at the monitors. She was a chubby Hispanic woman with kinky dark hair.

"Whe . . . wha . . ." Harry couldn't get his voice to work.

"Relax, Mr. Ingersoll. You're still full of Demerol; relax and go back to sleep."

What about Martha? Charley wanted to ask. My kids. But he found he couldn't get the words out. Instead his eyes closed and he drifted back into blessed sleep.

When he woke again there was a blond young man in a white smock standing beside his bed. He had a stethoscope hanging around his neck. Must be a doctor, Charley thought.

"How do you feel?" he asked.

"Where am I?" Charley mumbled.

The doctor grinned at him. "I asked you first. But if you must know, you're in Missoula Community Hospital."

"Missoula? How'd I get to Missoula?"

"Snowplow found you, called the Highway Patrol. They took you here."

"When? How long . . . ?"

"Six hours ago," said the doctor. His cheerful expression sobered. "I'm afraid we had to take four of your toes. You were pretty severely frostbitten. We saved your fingers, though."

"My wife," Charley said. "My kids."

The doctor nodded and patted Charley's covers. "We'll talk about them later. Right now we've got to do some diagnostics on you. You were in pretty bad shape when they brought you in here."

"But Martha. Charley Junior. Little Martha."

"Later," the doctor said. "Later."

N ow, how do we go about finding which one of your people tried to screw up this flight?"

Harry stared at Colonel Christopher. She was deadly serious.

"It had to be one of your people, Mr. Hartunian," she insisted. "You know them a helluva lot better than I do."

Think! Harry demanded silently of himself.

"Well?" Colonel Christopher prodded.

"Whoever it was," Harry said slowly, thinking it out as he spoke, "did it while he thought we were on a routine test flight."

"You already told me that."

"Which means he did it for money. Not to stop us from shooting down the gook missiles. He didn't know we were going against real missiles when he sabotaged the ranging laser. He's not a spy; he's not working for the North Koreans or some other nation."

"He. Why not she?"

Harry shook his head. "I just can't picture Taki doing it. Hell, she almost took my head off when I merely suggested the possibility."

"Maybe she protests too much," Christopher countered. "The best kind of defense is a good offense."

Rubbing with finger and thumb at the ache growing between his eyes, Harry went back to his reasoning. "Whoever it was did it to give Anson Aerospace a black eye. Did it for one of Anson's competitors. Did it for money."

The colonel nodded encouragingly. "Okay. So which of your nerds has come into some extra money lately?"

Closing his eyes, Harry thought aloud, "Wally likes to bet on the football pools, but he's just penny-ante. Small-time."

"The Hispanic kid?" Christopher prompted.

"Angel? He's strictly a straight arrow. Four kids, nice wife."

"Mortgage? Debts? College tuitions? With four kids—"

Harry cut her off. "They're all in elementary school, and Angel's working on them to get baseball scholarships by the time they're ready for college."

"Still . . ."

"It's not Angel."

"That leaves the big guy."

"Monk."

"Has he come into some extra money recently?"

Harry leaned back tiredly in the bucket seat. The plane was still shuddering, but the shaking didn't seem to be getting worse.

"Are we going to make it to Japan?" he asked.

Colonel Christopher smiled tightly. "If I have to get out and push."

Harry smiled weakly.

"Now what about this Monk guy? Has he been flashing some extra money around lately? Bought a new house maybe?"

Shaking his head, Harry replied, "Hell, Monk's been living in the same dinky bungalow since I've known him. Hasn't bought a new car in years, drives a beat-up old Chrysler . . ."

His voice tailed off. Harry remembered that Monk's wife had bought herself a Mustang convertible. Fire-engine red. Or had Monk bought it for her? Madelaine worked for Anson, Harry recalled, in the human resources department.

"What is it, Mr. Hartunian?" Colonel Christopher prodded.

He blinked at her. "It's probably nothing." He pushed himself up from the seat. "Let me talk to Monk."

Christopher got to her feet beside him. "It's him?"

"I don't know. Probably not. Let me talk to him before we go jumping to conclusions."

She studied his face for an intense moment, then nodded. "Okay. You do that. I've got a plane to fly."

AS SHE STEPPED back into the cockpit, Karen Christopher saw that Captain O'Banion's shirt was dark with perspiration as he sat in the left-hand seat. Even though his hands were in his lap, they were balled tightly into fists. Kaufman was doing the flying, she saw, and the communications officer was clearly afraid to touch the controls.

O'Banion looked relieved as Colonel Christopher leaned between the two seats.

"How's it going, Obie?" she asked pleasantly.

"She's flying straight and level," said the copilot, glancing up at her. "Buffeting a lot, but she's holding together."

"Good. Captain, you can go back to your comm station. Thanks for keeping the major company."

O'Banion pushed himself out of the chair. "You're entirely welcome, ma'am."

"How'd you like sitting up here?" Christopher asked as she slipped by him and into the seat. It felt warm, hot almost.

"Makes me think of W. C. Fields," O'Banion replied.

"The old comedian? How come?"

"He said he wanted on his tombstone, 'All things considered, I'd rather be in Philadelphia.'"

Christopher laughed. "You don't want to be a pilot?"

"No, ma'am. You can keep the job. I'll stick to communications."

O'Banion ducked through the hatch.

As Colonel Christopher strapped in, she said to Kaufman, "No competition from him."

Kaufman grunted. Christopher could see that he was reluctant to turn control of the plane back to her.

Looking through the windshield, the colonel saw that they were back over the gray swirling storm that they had passed on the way to the Korean coast.

"Hope we don't have to put down in that mess," she said lightly.

Kaufman gave her a sour look. "Misawa reports it's starting to rain there. We'll be landing in the storm, looks like."

Christopher shrugged. "Not much we can do about that—unless you want to head back to Elmendorf."

Kaufman said nothing, but the expression on his face could have curdled milk.

M onk Delany was asleep when Harry stepped through the hatch to the beam control compartment. He was sitting in front of his main console, head lolling on his shoulder as the plane bounced and staggered through the air. Up here in the 747's nose, the constant rise and fall of the plane was more noticeable than farther aft. The noise of the engines wasn't as bad, but the shaking and shuddering caused by the damaged wing seemed more intense up here.

"Monk," he called. "Hey, Monk. Wake up."

Delany stirred and grumbled to himself. His eyes fluttered, then opened fully.

"Harry," he said blearily. "Musta dozed off."

"Yeah." Harry sat in the chair next to the big engineer. "Monk, when we get back to Elmendorf, the Air Force police are going to dust that optics assembly for fingerprints."

Delany shrugged. "My prints'll be all over it. Hell, you know that, Harry."

"Yeah. Your prints and nobody else's."

"So whoever took it wore gloves."

"They'll search the plane. And each one of us. They won't find any gloves."

Delany's face clouded over. "What're you telling me, Harry?"

"You took the lens assembly out of the ranger, Monk. Last night. You wormed your big ape arm into the housing and popped it out, nice and neat. Just the way you popped the replacement set into it."

Glaring at Harry, Delany looked as if he wanted to answer but thought better of it.

"It was you, Monk," Harry said quietly. "I know it was you."

The big man's eyes narrowed. For an instant Harry thought Delany was going to get violent. But then he put on his lopsided smile and said, "What the hell, Harry?"

"You're not denying it?"

"I didn't do any damage. We shot down the gook missiles, didn't we? We're all heroes."

"Yeah. All of us—except Pete Quintana."

Delany look startled. "What's he got to do with this?"

"How'd the grease get into the oxygen line, Monk?"

"Now wait a minute!"

"You put it there," Harry insisted. "You knew what would happen when the line was pressurized. You killed Pete."

"Dumb spic shouldn't've been out there. He shoulda come into the control room with the rest of us."

"You let him get killed."

"I warned him!" Delany shouted. "I told the dumb sonofabitch to get inside! You heard me!"

"You didn't tell him the COIL was going to explode. You didn't tell me to stop the test."

"Tell you fuck! Who the hell are you? Chief of the test team! Why you, big shit? It shoulda been me!"

Harry felt the fury radiating from the big man. "I know," he said softly. "I told you so when Anson picked me."

"Anson! Big fucking asshole! You know why he picked you?

Because he can push you around. He calls the tune and you do the dance."

"And Pete burns to death."

Delany jumped up out of his seat, making Harry twitch with surprise and sudden fear. Monk's a big guy, Harry thought, remembering the way the big guys at school had always run roughshod over him. He'd learned to talk his way out of most trouble, but there were always gorillas who took special pleasure in beating up smaller guys who got As in class.

"So Pete's dead," Delany roared. "Whattaya want me to do about it? *I* didn't kill him! Damned brownnosing spic had to show Levy and Scheib how good he was, how fucking *concerned* he was about getting every fucking detail just right! So he killed himself. I didn't do it!"

Slowly, Harry rose to his feet. He barely reached to Monk's nose.

"I know you didn't intend to kill him," Harry said, trying to placate Monk.

"Fucking right I didn't!" Looming over Harry, Delany growled, "And you're not going to say a word about this, buddy. Not to anybody. Understand?"

Before he could think of anything else to say, Harry heard himself reply, "Monk, I can't keep this quiet. The colonel knows about the ranging laser."

"So what? That's all been fixed. No damage done."

"We've got to know why you did it. Who paid you to do it."

Delany slammed a big fist against the main console, making Harry flinch backward a step. "Dammit, Harry, you don't hafta know anything! Not a damned thing! You got that?"

"Yes I do, Monk. But the Air Force will want to know. Mr. Anson will want to know. Pete's widow, too."

"Harry, I'm warning you! Drop it!"

"I wish I could, Monk."

"But I can't."

Whirling, Harry saw Colonel Christopher standing in the compartment's hatch. Monk stared at her, frozen, his mouth open, his hands balled into fists.

"From what Harry tells me, you'll be charged with negligent homicide, I imagine," the colonel said, her voice tight, her face hard and unforgiving.

"Now wait—" Harry began. He never got any further,

Delany gave out a strangled roar and grabbed Harry with one big hand, punched him squarely in the face with the other. Harry's head snapped back. His nose spurted blood. He tried to push himself away, but Monk kept punching him.

Colonel Christopher sprang at Delany, kicked him in the knee, and chopped at the side of his bull neck. Monk dropped Harry and turned on her, but she ducked under his wild swing and deftly rammed a fist into his chest. A smaller man would have gone down, but Delany just grunted and reached for her.

Through a world of pain Harry saw the colonel jabbing at Monk's eyes. Staggering to his feet, he punched with all his might at Monk's side. Kidney punch, strictly illegal in boxing but the best defense Harry knew when being beaten up by a bigger guy.

Monk yowled and twisted backward. Colonel Christopher chopped with the side of her hand at Delany's throat and the big man went down, gasping and floundering on the deck of the narrow compartment.

As Harry sank to his knees he saw another Air Force officer stepping through the hatch, the redheaded captain. No need, he thought. No need for reinforcements. He saw Colonel Christopher standing over Monk's prostrate body like an Amazon warrior, her eyes blazing, every line of her face and body daring Monk to try to get up again.

It was a three-story row house on O Street, narrow but deep. Like all the houses on that block it had a flight of concrete steps leading up to the front door, a basement garage, and a lushly flowering garden in back tended by a small army of brown-skinned immigrant workers. Its exterior differed from its neighbors only by the startling abstract mural that the lady of the house had lovingly painted—to the clucking disapproval of some of her neighbors.

Bradley Scheib's den was on the top floor, insulated from the guest bedroom suite by soundproofed walls. General Scheib was sitting in his oversized recliner chair, a tumbler of single-malt scotch, neat, on the walnut table beside him, his private telephone held to his ear. The phone's landline tapped directly into the Department of Defense's shielded line that ran beneath the District of Columbia's streets, connecting the White House and the Capitol building with the Pentagon, across the Potomac.

The only light in the room came from the computer screen on the desk, over in the corner. Brad Scheib sat in the shadows, bone-tired, emotionally spent, feeling ragged. He had torn off his uniform the moment he'd arrived home from the Pentagon and put on a comfortable old sweatshirt and baggy gym pants. He'd nodded

hello to his wife and bounded up the stairs to his sanctum sanctorum.

"I gave you the priority code," he growled into the phone.
"What more authorization do you need?"

"Sorry, sir," came the voice of the harried operator in the Pentagon. "Circuits have been overloaded all day."

"I don't care! Get me through to that plane! That's an order!"

"Yes, sir. I'm trying, sir."

The door swung open, spilling light from the hallway into the
darkened room. Scheib's wife stood framed in the doorway, wearing a floor-length flowered silk robe: lean, curvaceous, a tribute to
relentless exercise and cosmetic surgery.

Angrily, he said, "Do I have to put a lock on my door? You know
this is private territory. You can't—"

"I'm not going to steal any military secrets from you, Brad," answered Carlotta Harriman Scheib coolly. "I'm quite sure your call
is personal. Isn't it?"

Cupping one hand over the phone's receiver, Scheib said,
"Whatever it is, it's none of your business."

"Calling your little slut of a colonel?" Carla asked, smiling
coldly. "Do you make her stand at attention for you? No, I imagine
it's you who stands at attention when you're with her, isn't it?"

"You've done enough damage to her career," Scheib snapped,
nearly snarling.

"So what? There are plenty of other women panting after you. I
could set you up with a couple of the dewy-eyed twits you met at
my birthday party. They'd love to flop into bed with you."

"Carla, this is Air Force business."

"Of course it is."

"For god's sake, we nearly went to war today!"

"So now you're a hero."

"No, but *she* is."

Carlotta's face contracted into a puzzled frown.

Suddenly understanding the reality of it, Scheib grinned

maliciously as he told his wife, "That's right, she's a hero now. Thanks to you, she was in the right spot at the right time to shoot down a pair of ballistic missiles that were launched at us. What do you think of that?"

She started to reply, but hesitated, then snapped her mouth shut, spun around, and disappeared down the hall, leaving the door open. Scheib could hear the clop-clop of her high-heeled slippers going down the stairs.

He put the phone down next to his scotch and swiftly went to the door, closed it firmly, then returned to his recliner.

"Well?" he demanded.

"I'm still trying, sir."

"WHERE'D YOU LEARN to fight like that?" Harry asked. His voice sounded funny to him because his nose was stuffed with cotton batting.

They were in the galley. Lieutenant Sharmon was leaning over Harry, dabbing a pad soaked in rubbing alcohol over the bloodstains on his face. The plane lurched and the first-aid kit sitting on the next seat slid to the deck with a clatter. Harry barely missed getting the pad shoved into his eye.

"Sorry," the lieutenant said.

Colonel Christopher stood behind Sharmon, watching the first-aid work closely.

"Four older brothers," she answered Harry's question. "And self-defense classes at the Academy."

"You're a terror," Harry said.

"That wasn't a love tap you hit Delany with," Christopher replied, grinning.

"Kidney punch. Learned that at good old Medford High."

"Must've been a great school."

Harry chuckled despite the pain from his nose. "We had a pretty good football team. But winning the game wasn't as important as winning the fight after the game."

Lieutenant Sharmon stooped to pick up the first-aid kit. "For what it's worth," he said, inspecting his handiwork, "I don't think your nose is broken. You're gonna have a pair of beautiful shiners, though."

"Thanks." Harry sighed.

Colonel Christopher shook her head slightly, then said, "I'd better get back to the cockpit. Weather's getting thicker. Jon, you'll have to get back, too."

"Yes, ma'am," said the lieutenant, shutting the first-aid kit's lid with a click.

Harry asked, "Where'd you put Monk?"

"Locked him in the forward lav," said the colonel. "Your people helped drag him in there."

"What's going to happen to him?"

She shrugged. "That's up to the AG's people, I suppose. And your own corporate execs. From what you said, he killed somebody?"

"That was an accident." But Harry knew it was more than that. "I mean, he didn't intend to kill Pete. He just—"

The plane lurched again, much worse. Sharmon staggered against the bulkhead, Colonel Christopher grabbed at him for support.

"I'd better get to the cockpit," Christopher said. Silently she added, Before Obie wets himself.

O'Banion had both hands on the control yoke as he tried to help Major Kaufman keep ABL-1 flying steadily. Christopher could see the dark, swirling clouds of the storm below them, smothering the view from horizon to horizon.

"Thank you, Captain," she said to O'Banion. As the captain got up gratefully and she slid into the pilot's seat, Christopher said to Kaufman, "Sorry to be away so long, Obie. We had a bit of a ruckus downstairs."

"Hasn't been a tea party up here," Kaufman muttered.

The plane was buffeting worse than ever as it plowed ahead on its three remaining engines. Colonel Christopher put on her heavy flight helmet and plugged in her communications line.

"Jon, I need an ETA for Misawa," she said into her lip mike.

"Lieutenant Sharmon's still downstairs, ma'am," O'Banion's voice replied in her earphone.

"Get him up here," she commanded.

"We got a shi . . . a big load of messages piled up, Colonel," O'Banion said. "Including a top priority from Washington. General Scheib."

"Give me that one first."

Some stranger's voice, a woman, asked, "Colonel Christopher?"

"Right."

"General Scheib, I have Colonel Christopher for you."

"Karen?" Brad's voice.

"General," she replied.

IN HIS DARKENED den, Brad Scheib heard the stiffness in Karen's voice. She's not alone, he understood. She's in the cockpit of that plane with the rest of the goddamned crew tapped in.

"Are you all right?" he asked.

"We're approaching Misawa." Karen's voice sounded cool, totally under control. "One engine out, wing damaged, but we're maintaining altitude and airspeed."

"You'll make it to Misawa? Met reports there's a storm over the area."

A hesitation. Then she answered, "We'll make it, General."

"Good."

Silence, except for hissing static. What can I say? Scheib asked himself. What can I tell her with the rest of her crew listening in? Even if she tells them to stay off the line there's no guarantee that they won't eavesdrop. Hell, half the Pentagon could be listening to us. And it'll all get recorded, too.

"I . . . I'm glad you're okay."

Again a long silence. She's thinking of what she can say, what she should say, Scheib told himself. Helluva way for us to talk. For all I know this is the last time we'll ever talk to each other. Helluva way for it all to end.

At last Karen's voice said tightly, "I'm fine, General."

"That's good," he said, feeling inane. Suddenly he couldn't control himself any longer. He blurted, "Karen, I'm sorry it had to end this way."

"I am too."

"If things had been different . . ."

"Brad, it's over and done with. You made that perfectly clear."

Feeling utterly miserable, Scheib said, "I wish it could be different."

"But it's not, General. It couldn't have ended any other way."

He nodded in the darkness of his room. She's right, he knew. It couldn't have ended any other way.

IN THE COCKPIT of ABL-1, Karen Christopher heard the sorrow in Brad's voice. And she realized that he felt sorry for himself. Not for her. Not for the mess she'd made of her career. For himself.

And she understood. He'll never have the strength to leave his wife. His career is more important to him than I ever was. I made him happy for a while, but that's all over now. It was doomed from the start.

"You still there?" He sounded like a lost little boy.

When she tried to nod, the damned helmet wobbled on her head. "I've got to sign off now, General. The weather's closing in."

Silence for several heartbeats. Then, "Good-bye, Karen."

"Good-bye, General."

And the connection went dead.

Karen looked over at Kaufman, who was studiously staring straight ahead. Looking out, she saw that the weather was indeed closing in.

"Colonel?" Sharmon's voice.

"Go ahead, Jon."

"ETA to Misawa, one hour seventeen minutes."

"Better get their weather report. Looks like we'll be in for a shaggy ride."

The Bakersfield residence was not pretentious, except for the wrought-iron fence that surrounded the lot and the armored Humvee parked in the driveway, occupied by at least three heavily armed Secret Service guards at all times.

The Secretary of Defense was in bed, his fleshy face ashen, his corpulent body soaked with perspiration. His physician, a close friend since Lionel Bakersfield had first arrived in the capital as a newly elected senator, stood over him with a severe expression on his lean, nearly gaunt face.

"I could've been Vice President, you know," said Bakersfield as he lay propped up on a mound of pillows in the king-sized bed. "One heartbeat away from the White House."

The physician, rake-thin, white-haired, shook his head and replied, "Another day like this one and you'll be one heartbeat away from your own funeral."

The Secretary of Defense tried to chuckle at his old friend's dismal attitude. "You've always been a sourpuss."

"Lon, you can't take so much stress," the doctor warned. "I think you ought to retire."

Bakersfield snorted at the idea.

"You're killing yourself."

"Bullshit! I'm just a little tired. It's been a long day."

"You can't put in days like this without hurting yourself. That old ticker of yours is going to explode if you're not more careful."

"Another year," said the Secretary of Defense. "After next year's elections. If the President gets reelected I can retire with dignity. If not, I'll be asked to leave anyway."

The doctor shook his head again, his face a bony mask of disapproval.

The phone on the bedside table buzzed.

As the Secretary of Defense reached for it, his doctor snapped, "No!"

Bakersfield hesitated, his fingers inches from the phone. "It's probably important. Only a half dozen key people have access to this line."

"No more stress!" the doctor insisted. "You've had enough for today."

The Secretary of Defense made a weak grin. "Just one more. It could be important."

He picked up the phone's receiver while the doctor gave a disgusted sigh and started for the bedroom door.

The phone's minuscule screen showed a prim-looking young woman. "Mr. Secretary," she said, "I have the Secretary of State on the line for you."

"Put her on," said Bakersfield. With his free hand he waved good-bye to the doctor, who shook his head with frustration and left the room, closing the door behind him with a bang.

"Lonnie," said the Secretary of State, smiling her news-conference smile. "Celebrating our victory?"

Defense realized that the phone's miniature camera showed little more than his sweaty face.

"Should we celebrate?" he asked.

"I suppose so," State replied. "We shot down the Korean missiles. They didn't bomb San Francisco."

"And the President looks like a brave young hero."

State's smile faltered a bit. "I suppose he does."

"What do you hear from the DPRK government?" Defense asked.

A small crease furrowing her brow, State answered, "Pyongyang says its troops have taken the site where the missiles were launched. Most of the rebel officers have been killed—or committed suicide instead of allowing themselves to be captured."

"So there's nobody left to question."

"Probably not."

The meds his doctor had given him were beginning to take effect, Bakersfield realized. He felt relaxed, no pain. Almost giddy, in fact.

"So we won't find out why they tried to attack us," he said, feeling nearly relieved about it.

"Oh, I think we'll find out, sooner or later, one way or the other," said the Secretary of State.

Backdoor channels, Defense thought. She puts a lot of faith in her personal contacts in China, he knew.

To her blandly smiling face, he said, "It was good of you to call me and bring me up to date."

If she caught the sarcasm in his tone she gave no visible inkling of it. "Actually, Lonnie, the reason I called is about how we should react to the President's position. He's bound to get a big bounce out of this in the polls."

Bakersfield shook his head wearily. "That's for you to worry about, my dear. I'm not interested in the White House anymore."

"Not interested? How . . . ?"

The Secretary of Defense enjoyed the play of emotions flickering across the Secretary of State's face: surprise, satisfaction, anticipation—all replaced by a hard-eyed calculation.

"He's going to be reelected and neither you nor I will oppose him," he said.

"Yes, but four years after that . . ."

"I'll be too old for it. It's all yours, my dear."

"I can count on your support, then?"

Bakersfield thought that in politics five years is an eternity. How can you commit yourself to anything so far in the unguessable future?

"Of course," he said, knowing the obligation was unenforceable. "But don't you have more immediate problems to worry about?"

She blinked at him, her thoughts obviously two election campaigns down the road.

"More immediate problems?"

"I don't think the Chinese will be happy with our shoot-down of those missiles. Do you?"

"Self-defense," the Secretary of State immediately replied. "We have a right to defend ourselves."

Defense nodded, picturing the speech she would give at the United Nations. A good platform for her, he thought.

"I suppose you're right," he conceded.

"Of course I am." She smiled as she said it, but it was clear that she meant it with all her heart.

Defense said, "Well, you have a lot of work ahead of you."

"So do you," State countered.

"Yes, I know. Get a good night's sleep, my dear. Big day tomorrow."

And he clicked off the phone connection, carefully replaced the receiver on the console, rolled over, and swiftly fell asleep.

The President was jubilant as he spoke to his wife

"They loved it," he said, a big boyish grin splashed across his face. "I told them we shot down those missiles and they loved it!"

The First Lady smiled back at her husband from the screen set into the bulkhead of the plane's compartment. "Of course they loved it. You showed them that you're strong, and at the same time you prevented a war from breaking out."

The President sobered. "The threat isn't over yet."

"It's not?"

Glancing at his chief of staff, sitting out of range of the First Lady's vision, the President said, "We're not entirely out of the woods yet. We've got to find out who was behind this attack, why they did it, and what they're after."

She bit her lip, as she always did when she was unsure of herself. "But you said they got the soldiers who launched the missiles."

"Yes, but we've got to determine what was behind this business. They weren't acting on their own, you can bet on that."

"Oh." Then she brightened. "But you proved to the whole world that we can shoot down any missiles that they fire at us. That's important, isn't it?"

Norman Foster rolled his eyes to the heavens as the President replied, "We showed we can shoot down two missiles, honey. Russia's got more than a thousand and China's not far behind that."

The First Lady said, "I thought the real problem was unstable countries like North Korea or Iran. And terrorists."

"That's the first problem, true enough. But there's a lot more to worry about, as well."

Still smiling, she said, "Well, you'll handle it. You always do. I'm really proud of you, and I know everybody else in the country is, too."

"Even the Republicans?"

Laughing, she replied, "Even the Republicans. Most of them, anyway."

They chatted for a few moments more and the President insisted that the First Lady stay in the White House instead of driving out to Andrews Air Force Base to meet his plane when it landed.

"It'll be nearly dawn when we touch down. You stay with the kids. I'll sleep on the plane, don't worry."

"I miss you, baby," she said.

"Me too. See you in a few hours, though."

"Oh!" The First Lady's eyes went wide with a new thought. "Listen. You ought to invite the crew of that plane to the White House."

The President scratched at his chin. "Good idea. There's civilians in the crew, you know. As well as Air Force people."

"Even better. Congratulate them personally."

"Right. Good image." Smiling at his wife, the President said, "Smart idea, honey."

She beamed back at him. "Good night, Mr. President. I'll be waiting for you."

"Good night, Mrs. First Lady. I'll be coming to you."

Foster put his head down and stared at the deck.

Once the screen went blank, the President turned to his chief of staff. "Sorry if we embarrassed you, Norm."

Looking up at his chief, Foster put on a smile. "Nothing to it, boss."

The President started to get out of his seat, but Foster put out a restraining hand.

"It's late," the President said. "I need my beauty sleep. There'll be plenty of news media at Andrews when we land."

"I just want to ask you to think about where we go from here."

"Where we go?"

Foster rubbed at his eyes for a moment, then said, "What you were talking about with your wife. We've got to find out who was behind this attack and what they're after."

Arching a brow at his chief of staff, the President countered, "I would think our first order of business is to get our satellites working again. If we can't fix 'em, we'll have to replace them."

"That goes without saying."

"I just said it."

Foster was obviously not in a joking mood. "Those gook soldiers didn't pull this stunt for the hell of it. Somebody was behind them. Somebody big."

"The government in Pyongyang? Are they that crazy?"

"The situation team came up with the possibility that China's behind it all. That's what this analyst from the NIC has put together as a scenario—"

"China?"

"The NSA representative on the team agrees with him."

"China," the President mused. "But why would they do it? Why would they risk a nuclear confrontation?"

"That's what we've got to find out," Foster said.

Suddenly breaking into a substantial yawn, the President said, "That's what we've got the intelligence agencies for. And the State Department. Now, I'm sleepy. Let's pack it in."

But Foster pressed. "You want to hand this problem to the Secretary of State?"

"And the intel people."

"It'll put her smack in the middle of the spotlight, you know."

At last the President understood his chief of staff's reluctance. "So she gets the spotlight. Don't sweat it, Norm. I've got the reelection sewed up after this. I'm the president who showed the world we can defend ourselves against missile attack! I'm the president who saved us from a nuclear war! The Republicans don't have anybody who can come close to beating me."

"But you'll be giving her a big boost, you know."

"What of it? She can't challenge me next year. And four years after that she's welcome to run for the top. That's what she's been after all along, right?"

"Right."

"So let her have it. After I've finished my second term." He yawned again. "Now I'm going to bed. G'night, Norm."

The two men rose to their feet. "Good night, Mr. President," said Norman Foster.

C hrist, I'm pissing blood!"

Harry heard Monk's frightened roar as he sat strapped tightly into his seat in the narrow compartment. Taki Nakamura, facing him, looked startled.

The plane was bouncing, jinking as they bit into the storm clouds. The thumping made Harry's swollen nose hurt.

"We'll have a doctor waiting for you when we land, Monk," Harry shouted, feeling embarrassed, almost ashamed.

"What the hell did you do to him?" Wally Rosenberg asked.

"Kidney punch," Harry mumbled.

"He break your nose?" Angel Reyes asked.

Harry started to shake his head but winced with pain. "No. I don't think so."

"Your eyes are swelling up," Nakamura said, her face etched with concern.

"Yeah," said Harry.

Rosenberg chuckled softly. "You're gonna look great for the photographers, Harry. Two black eyes." He laughed mockingly.

The plane lurched so badly all four of them clutched their seat arms.

I'll look great for the photographers, Harry thought. If we land okay. If we don't go into the drink and drown.

"GOT MISAWA'S BEAM," O'Banion reported.

Colonel Christopher answered, "Great! Pipe it to me."

She heard the thin, scratchy tone of the airfield's radio location beam. We can ride in on it, Karen thought. Even if the weather's zero-zero at the field, we can home in on the beam.

"Getting nasty," Kaufman said, his voice high, nervous.

"Yeah."

They were in the storm now, bouncing and lurching in the turbulence of the thick black clouds. Lightning flashed every few seconds. Hold together, baby, Karen crooned silently to the plane. Just a little bit longer. Hold together and we'll get home. Just a little bit longer.

"What's the ceiling at Misawa, Jon?" she asked into her lip mike.

"Checking," Lieutenant Sharmon answered. Then, "Eight hundred and lowering. Raining hard."

"Obie, get Misawa traffic control and tell them to clear a runway for us."

"Already did that, Colonel."

"Good." We'll make it, she told herself. But we've only got one shot at it. With the condition this bird is in, we won't be able to go around and try a second approach if we goof the first one. I've got to make it on the first approach. Got to.

C harley Ingersoll knew it was bad news when three doctors came into his room with a clerical-collared minister accompanying them. They all looked like they were going to a funeral.

"Martha?" Charley asked before any of them could open their mouths. "My kids?"

"They're fine," said the oldest of the doctors.

"Really?"

"Really. They're right here in this hospital, being treated for exposure. But they'll be released later today and they'll come to see you."

Charley was sitting up in bed. One of the IV drips had been removed from his arm, but the other one was still connected. Charley had tried to figure out which of his toes they'd taken off, but he couldn't tell by wiggling and the bedclothes covered both his bandaged feet.

Suddenly all the breath seemed to gush out of Charley, as if he'd been holding it in for a year. He felt light-headed, like he was drunk or high or something.

"You saved their lives, Mr. Ingersoll," said one of younger doctors. He didn't look happy about it, though.

"They're okay," Charley said, his voice shaking. "That's the important thing."

"The same snowplow that found you picked up your family a little farther up the road," said the older doctor. "You were semi-delirious, but you kept telling the driver that your family was stuck in a snowbank."

"You saved them," the other younger doctor said, almost in a whisper.

"Then everything's okay," Charley said, hoping it was true.

"Well," said the older doctor, "*almost* everything is okay."

"Whattaya mean?"

Looking very unhappy, the doctor explained, "We did some routine tests on the blood samples you gave us—"

"Gave you?" Charley snapped. "I didn't give you no blood samples."

"You were unconscious when you were brought in. We took blood samples as a matter of course. Strictly routine."

"So?"

Glancing at his two younger colleagues, the doctor said, "The routine screening we did indicates that you have . . . uh, cancer."

"Cancer?" Charley yelped. "Me?"

"Prostate cancer."

Charley sat there gaping at them.

"It's apparently in the early stage," said one of the younger medics. "It's definitely treatable."

Charley had heard about prostate cancer. They cut it out of you and then you can't control your bladder or even get an erection anymore.

The other younger doctor produced a thick sheaf of papers. "These are forms you'll have to sign."

"Sign?" Charley echoed.

"For the tests and therapy. Maybe surgery." He put the wad of papers on the nightstand by Charley's bed.

The older doctor put on a phony smile. "Well, in an hour or so your wife and children will visit you."

Then he turned and headed for the door, trailed by the two younger docs.

Charley stared at the minister, who reminded him a little of the pictures he had seen of Jesus: a little bit of a beard, sad, sorrowful eyes. And he remembered when he'd been freezing out in the snow that he'd asked God to save Martha and the kids even if it meant taking him.

"Reverend," Charley asked, feeling lost and bewildered, "why does God give with one hand and take away with the other?"

The minister shook his head. "The Lord moves in mysterious ways, Mr. Ingersoll. But it's all for the best, believe me. Trust in the Lord."

"Yeah," Charley said. "Sure."

The penthouse suite was brightly lit, as if a gala party was to take place there, but the only two people in the spacious sitting room were the Secretary of State and Quang Chuli.

The Chinese businessman appeared to be perfectly at ease as he sat in the plushly upholstered armchair watching the Secretary of State at the bar, pouring herself a glass of wine. It was close to midnight, but he seemed as fresh as ever, wearing the same dark suit he always wore. Does he have a closet full of them? the Secretary of State wondered. It can't be the same suit.

For her part, State had changed into comfortable peach-colored slacks and a white silk blouse that hung over her hips. She had a long-stemmed glass of California chardonnay in one hand. Quang had politely refused a drink.

"I thought we would toast to avoiding a war," she said as she settled herself onto the little sofa that faced her visitor.

"I congratulate you," said Quang equably. "You came through the crisis very well."

"Have we? Do you mean that the crisis is over?"

Quang dipped his chin slightly. "The hard-liners in Beijing are in disgrace. You have proven that you are capable of defending against missile attack."

"Only two missiles," said State. "We couldn't stop a full-scale attack by the People's Republic."

"Not yet."

State blinked at that, her mind rapidly deciding, He thinks we're going to increase our missile defenses! He thinks we're going to build them up so we can stop a Chinese attack. Or a Russian one.

Carefully, she asked, "Do you mean that this was all a test? Nothing more than a test?"

Quang sighed. "Ah, if only the world were that simple, Madam Secretary. Unfortunately, it is not."

State had no reply. She studied her visitor's face, trying to fathom what was behind his bland smile, his enigmatic words. It was like trying to get hard data out of the Sphinx.

Sensing her uncertainty, Quang said, "As I have tried to explain to you in the past, the government in Beijing is not monolithic. Far from it. It is a coalition that includes moderates, hard-liners, and even a few farsighted statesmen."

"Like your brother-in-law," she murmured.

"The chairman is indeed a farsighted statesman. But he must balance the various forces and attitudes that are present in the Central Committee."

Slowly, State said, "I think I'm beginning to understand."

Leaning forward slightly, toward her, Quang said, "Today you demonstrated that missile defense is possible. Yes, it was only two missiles, but you proved that they could be stopped. Today could mark a turning point in the global strategic picture."

The Secretary of State noticed the slight but definite emphasis Quang put on the word "could."

Trying to hide her exasperation, she asked as sweetly as she was able, "Just what do you mean?"

"Let me be frank, then."

"By all means. We're alone here. There are no recording devices." That was a lie, but an understandable one, she thought. No one would see the transcript of this conversation but herself and her closest aides.

Raising a stumpy index finger, Quang said, "The Democratic People's Republic of Korea is a rogue nation, we both agree."

State nodded.

"There are other such rogues in the world. Iran, for one."

She nodded again.

"The world must be protected against such rogues."

"And against terrorists," State added.

"Agreed. Terrorists armed with long-range missiles could plunge the world into nuclear war."

"Which neither of us wants."

Now Quang nodded. Vigorously.

Reaching for her chardonnay, State asked, "So what do you propose?"

"The United States is in a position to . . . suggest, that is the proper word, I believe . . . suggest an international conference on the subject of missile defense."

She felt her brows knitting.

Quang went on. "At such a conference the leading governments of the world could come to an agreement that any unauthorized rocket launch anywhere in the world will be shot down by missile defense forces."

"Unauthorized rocket launch?" State asked. "What do you mean?"

"It is very simple, Madam Secretary. An international commission would be established to send inspectors to examine the payloads of all rocket launches."

"Like the International Atomic Energy Agency."

"Just so. But with this difference. Any rocket launch that has not been inspected and approved will be shot down."

State leaned back against the pillows of the sofa. "But that would mean . . . we'd have to make our missile defenses available to this international commission."

"Perhaps. At the very least you would have to pledge that you will act on the commission's recommendations."

She put her wineglass down on the coffee table between them before replying. "I don't know if we could ever get that through Congress."

"You must! Recognize that now, this very day, Beijing and Moscow and others are moving to create their own missile defense technology. The United States could lead the way by offering to share such technology—under international control."

State shook her head. "Congress would never go for that."

With a shrug, Quang said, "Then there will be a new arms race in missile defenses. Far better for the U.S.A. to take the lead on this issue, to show the world how to move away from the threat of missile attack."

"That's a very tall order, Mr. Quang."

"It is the way to end the threat of rogue nations and terrorists using long-range missiles. It is the way to a new stability in the international political situation."

"Beijing would agree to this?"

"I believe so. What is more important, my brother-in-law believes so."

The Secretary of State picked up her wineglass again and twirled it in her fingers, her thoughts swirling with the wine. She remembered that the first Limited Nuclear Test Ban Treaty came directly out of the confrontation of the Cuban missile crisis. Maybe we can pull something good, something worthwhile, out of this.

To Quang she said, "I'll talk to the President about this. I'll suggest he call your chairman."

"If you like, I could suggest to my brother-in-law that he call your President."

"That would be very good. Very good indeed." And she thought, If I can set up a global missile defense agreement I'd be a shoo-in for the nomination five years from now.

L eft main gear is no-go," said Major Kaufman.

Colonel Christopher saw the red light glaring on the control board. It wasn't the only one, but it seemed bigger, hotter than all the others.

"Must've been shot up when that missile hit number two engine," Kaufman added.

Christopher nodded, wondering what else was damaged by that missile hit. Deep inside the swirling storm, the plane was shaking badly, shuddering like a palsied old man.

"Jon," she called into her mike, "how far from the field are we?"

"Eighty-two miles, Colonel."

"Brick, get me the tower."

A moment's silence, then, "Tower on freak four, ma'am."

"Misawa tower here. Report your—"

"ABL-1," she interrupted. "We're on final. One engine out and left main gear won't deploy."

Karen could hear voices chattering in the background. She remembered the old story about a pilot telling the control tower that his engine was dead and his controls weren't responding. "What should I do?" the panicked flier asked. And the control tower calmly responded, "Repeat after me: 'The Lord is my shepherd . . .'"

At last, the voice from the control tower replied coolly, "Abort your final approach and orbit the field until you've burned off your fuel."

"Can't do it!" Christopher snapped. "We're damaged. I don't know how long this bird'll hold together. I'm going to dump our fuel."

"Negative. Environmental regulations forbid—"

"Screw the environmental regs! We're shot up and bouncing around up here like a kid on a trampoline. I'm dumping our fuel and coming in!"

Colonel Christopher clicked off the connection with Misawa and turned to Kaufman. "Open 'em up, Obie."

With a grim smile, Kaufman reached for the fuel tank controls. "What about the stuff for the laser? They got anything left in their tanks?"

HARRY HAD DECIDED to let Monk out of the lavatory. The big engineer, his face somewhere between surly and sheepish, sat in the bucket seat next to Wally Rosenberg.

"Strap in good," Harry said tightly. "It's going to be a rough landing."

"Like it ain't rough already," Delany muttered.

It was getting even rougher, Harry thought. It was difficult to click his safety harness shut, the plane was stuttering around so badly.

"Hartunian!" The overhead intercom speaker cracked like a rifle shot. "Blow out the fuel in your tanks. Pronto!" Colonel Christopher's voice.

Harry stared at the speaker grill above him. Then he turned to Wally Rosenberg. "You heard the lady," he said, unclicking his harness. "Let's get it done."

Rosenberg reluctantly got to his feet.

"I'll go, *jefe*," said Angel Reyes, fumbling with his harness.

"Stay here," Harry said. "Wally and I can do it."

The plane lurched so badly that Harry jolted into little Taki Nakamura's lap. Rosenberg banged against the bulkhead.

"Oof!" said Takamura. "Watch it."

"Sorry," Harry mumbled. Getting to his feet, he grabbed for Rosenberg's arm. "C'mon, Wally. Pronto, the lady said."

Rubbing his shoulder, Rosenberg grumbled, "Of all the gin joints in all the towns—"

"Never mind the wisecracks," Harry said. "Let's get the job done."

"FUEL'S ALL DUMPED, Colonel." Hartunian's voice sounded over the intercom.

"Get back in your seat and strap in tight," said Colonel Christopher. "We're going in. It's going to be rough."

"Yes, ma'am."

Karen Christopher was as scared as she'd ever been in her life, but once again she felt an icy calm engulfing her. It was as if she were somewhere else, somewhere in an ethereal world, watching this slim woman who looked just like her wrestling with the controls of the massive jumbo jet.

ABL-1 was shaking badly now. From somewhere in the plane's innards something was banging, like a wild beast trying to get out of its cage. Hold together, baby, Karen cooed silently to the huge airplane. Just a few more minutes. I know you're hurt, but just hang together for a little bit longer. Just a little bit—

As they broke through the bottom of the clouds she could see the runway lights strung out straight and beautiful like a guiding arrow leading her to safety, glistening wet with rain.

"The runway!" Kaufman shouted.

We're on the nose, Karen saw. Got to thank Jon for getting us through the soup and lined up exactly right. Now comes the tough part, the real test. She remembered the old adage: Flying is the second most exciting thing a person can do. Landing is the first.

"Full flaps," Kaufman said. "Speed on the button."

Nothing in the fuel tanks but fumes, she knew. If we break up on the runway we won't burst into flames. Not a big fire, anyway. Maybe some, but not so much we won't be able to get out. We'll be okay if I can get her on the ground without tearing her apart.

Gently, gently, Karen eased the big plane onto the runway, kissing the concrete with the right main gear so smoothly that for an instant she wasn't certain the wheels had actually touched the ground. Out of the corner of her eye she saw a long line of fire trucks standing by along the edge of the runway. And two ambulances. They don't expect to pull many of us out, she thought.

Bring the nose down, she told herself. Kaufman was babbling something, but she paid no attention to her copilot. The plane was rolling along the runway now on its nose and right main gear. Losing speed. No thrust reversing, Karen told herself. Not enough fuel left for that.

She pressed on the brakes and the plane slowed with a screeching, squalling shriek. And the battered left wing dipped toward the ground.

"Hang on!"

The wingtip caught the concrete and the outboard engine nacelle smashed into the ground in the next instant. Christopher felt herself lurch painfully against her harness straps, her head thrown forward and then snapped back against the seat back with a thump. The plane was grinding against the concrete, slewing to the left, tilted at a crazy angle. The cockpit was shaking, bouncing, slamming her sideways, back and forth with a roaring, tearing, groaning noise like a monster truck being smashed and squashed by car crushers.

And then it stopped. The cockpit filled with gritty, dusty fumes as Christopher sat there, totally wiped out, too weak to lift her arms.

But only for a moment. "Hartunian!" she yelled at the intercom microphone. "You okay?"

"No broken bones . . . I think."

"You and your people go out the forward hatch with us."

"Yes, ma'am!" came the heartfelt reply.

Kaufman was already getting out of his chair. Karen heard the wail of sirens approaching.

Kaufman reached over and helped her to her feet. "Helluva landing, lady. Helluva landing."

"Thanks," she said, feeling weak in her knees. "Now let's get out of here before something blows up."

S o you've never been married?" asked Zuri Coggins.

Sitting across the narrow table from her, Michael Jamil shook his head as he swallowed a mouthful of well-done hamburger, loaded with ketchup.

"No," he said at last, reaching for a paper napkin from the dispenser at the end of the table, where it abutted the wall. "My parents picked out a wife for me when I was in undergrad school, but by the time I graduated she had gone off to school herself and she met a guy there and married him instead."

Coggins watched him dab self-consciously at his lips. The diner was almost empty this late at night; only one other couple in the booths, and one policeman sitting at the counter, munching a doughnut.

"No serious relationships since then?" she probed.

He smiled self-deprecatingly. "I didn't have a serious relationship then, Zuri. You didn't go to bed with your fiancée. Not in my neighborhood. Wasn't done."

"But since . . . ?"

He started to look uncomfortable. But he replied, "I've had a few girlfriends. Nothing serious." He hesitated, then went on. "I haven't met anybody I could get serious about."

Zuri nodded understandingly. "Same here. Men seem to get scared of a woman who has an IQ higher than theirs."

His smile came back. "So what's your IQ?"

"One forty-two," she answered immediately. "Yours?"

"Not that high."

"How high?"

The smile widened. It was a good smile, she thought. Warm. Jamil said, "One thirty-eight."

She leaned back on the thinly padded bench and said, "Well, that's within the statistical margin of error. We're practically on the same level."

"Yeah."

She felt herself smiling back at him. "Do I scare you?"

"You? No. Why should I be scared of you?"

"Because I'm as smart as you are."

"That's good, isn't it?"

"Because I might be your boss."

"Huh?"

Zuri hadn't really thought about it until the words popped out of her mouth.

"How'd you like to work in the National Security Advisor's office? With me?"

Jamil's face clearly showed surprise. And a good deal of uncertainty.

She continued. "I mean, the Secretary of State is pissed with you. She's got a mean hatchet, you know. You could use a new job."

He said slowly, "But if there's a change in the White House next November . . ."

"There won't be. We'll have five years together."

"You mean it?" Jamil asked.

"I sure do."

He nodded. "You're certain? I mean, you're not just doing this because . . ." His voice trailed off.

"I'm not doing it because I feel sorry for you, or because of anything except I think you're damned smart and I need somebody in my office who's as smart as I am."

"Oh. I thought you were doing it because you like me."

"That too," she admitted.

Minutes later they left the diner. The streets were still wet from the earlier rain. Hardly any traffic. No taxicabs in sight.

"It's after midnight," Jamil muttered. "And my car's over in Langley."

Zuri Coggins slipped her arm in his. "That's okay. My apartment's within walking distance. You can stay the night at my place."

He nodded thoughtfully, then disengaged his arm and moved around her to be on the curbside of the street. "A gentleman always walks on the curbside," he said, quite seriously.

"Sure," she retorted. "The muggers always hide in the doorways."

They both laughed and started down the street into the new day.

I t was pouring rain as they jumped, one by one, down the inflated chute that extended from ABL-1's forward hatch to the puddled concrete of the runway.

This isn't going to be good for my back, Harry thought as he waited behind Monk Delany and the others of his team. Three of the Air Force crew had already slid down the chute; Wally Rosenberg was next.

"Off I go into the wild blue yonder," Rosenberg wisecracked. He jumped from the lip of the hatch, hit the chute with his rump, and slid down into the waiting arms of a team of Air Force noncoms.

Harry saw a quartet of Air Police down there in white helmets and sidearms. Waiting for Monk, he figured.

"Will you be okay?"

It was Colonel Christopher, waiting last in line.

"I can do it," Harry said.

"I heard you had a bad back," said the colonel.

"Who told you that?"

In the shadows of the hatchway he could see a smile light her face. "I have my sources," she said.

Taki Nakamura squealed as she jumped. Monk was next, big and lumbering. Now Harry stood at the lip of the hatch.

"Don't make a big jump," the colonel advised. "Make it easy on yourself."

Unconsciously, Harry closed his eyes as he jumped. He felt his heels hit the inflated chute, then his rump. He expected a flare of pain but he felt only a tweak. He slid to the bottom on the rain-slicked chute and was grabbed by the Air Force noncoms, who helped him to his feet.

Squinting in the pelting rain, Harry saw that the Air Police were walking Monk off to a waiting Humvee. Turning, he watched Colonel Christopher slide down the chute. She got to her feet almost unaided.

"Nothing to it," she said to Harry, grinning.

She's really pretty, Harry thought. Kind of tiny, like a pixie. Really pretty.

The colonel turned to look back at the wreckage of ABL-1. Harry stepped up beside her, already soaked by the cold rain.

The plane was resting on its belly, slightly tilted. The left wing had ripped off and was resting several hundred yards down the runway, flames flickering from its root, where it had torn off from the fuselage. The pouring rain was pelting the fire, keeping it down as a dozen or so firefighters sprayed the whole wing with fire retardant.

ABL-1's fuselage looked to Harry like a stranded whale, resting on one side, its right wing angled defiantly against the thick gray clouds scudding above.

"We can salvage the COIL," Harry said.

The colonel looked up at him. "They'll build a new plane. More than one."

"Damned right."

"Your back okay?"

"Yeah. Fine."

She gripped his arm lightly. "It's been a helluva day. There's an interrogation team waiting to debrief us."

Harry thought about Monk and nodded.

One of the noncoms came up to them and pointed to an un-marked minivan standing a dozen yards away. Taki, Angel, and Wally Rosenberg were getting into it, together with the Air Force crew members. "Your transportation, ma'am," she said to the colo-nel.

Karen Christopher tugged at Harry's arm. "Come on, buddy, our chariot awaits."

He let her guide him toward the minivan.

"After the debriefing's finished," said Karen Christopher, "I'm taking you to the officers' club and buying you a drink, Harry."

He felt pleased. Very pleased. And flattered that this good-looking and very competent woman liked him. I'll have to go through with the divorce, he said to himself. I've got to get on with my life and let Sylvia get on with hers.

With a final glance over his shoulder at what was left of ABL-1, Harry ducked into the minivan, ready to face whatever was waiting for him in the future.

In his penthouse aerie, Victor Anson stared at the blank screen of his telephone. They're down, he repeated to himself. They made it to Japan and they're all safe.

He nodded once and then commanded the phone's voice-recognition system to call Gaetano Bartoni, in New York. It took some time to get a connection through; Anson got up from his desk and poured himself a glass of amontillado.

"Christ, Victor, it's past midnight here!" Bartoni's usually cultured tone was buried by burning indignation.

Sliding into his desk chair, Anson made a tight smile for the banker's image on his phone screen. "Sorry, Guy, but this can't wait."

Bartoni had spent much of his adult life training himself to be polished and soft-spoken. His banking fortune may have started on street corners in Brooklyn, but for years now he had made his headquarters in midtown Manhattan. Cosmetic surgery had given him a reasonably straight nose and a smooth, tight face. His thick gray hair was always perfectly coiffed. But now, roused from his bed after midnight, his Brooklyn origins glared through his careful façade.

"All the friggin' satellites are off the air, Wall Street's in a panic, the President claims some gooks tried to nuke us, and you can't wait until a decent hour to call me?"

"How are you fixed for investment capital?" Anson asked, knowing that it would cut through Bartoni's ruffled emotions.

"Huh? Investment capital?"

"Our ABL-1 plane crash-landed in Japan less than an hour ago." Before Bartoni could react, Anson went on. "*After* successfully shooting down a pair of North Korean missiles."

Bartoni's expression went from anger to surprise to curiosity. "So that's what the President was talkin' about in 'Frisco?"

"It was indeed. Anson Aerospace's Airborne Laser system defended this country against a nuclear missile attack."

Bartoni muttered, "Jeez."

Anson continued. "The government is going to want to replace the crashed plane. And build new ones."

"And you need investment capital for that," said Bartoni.

With a shake of his head, Anson corrected, "No, the Missile Defense Agency will give us a contract for that, no problem."

"Then what . . . ?"

"Satellites!" Anson chirped. "There's going to be an immense demand to replace all the satellites that have been knocked out. Now's the time to invest in building satellites—and rocket boosters to launch them."

"That's already a crowded market, isn't it?"

"Not now, Guy. The market's suddenly wide open. It's going to be raining soup! Let's start getting as many buckets for ourselves as we can!"